CC

CU00735142

Chapter 1

When the sun rises behind it, Moor Cliff is a rusty blade whose handle is lost to the sea and whose point is buried in the hill that slopes to the valley. When the afternoon sun hits the curve, the cliff becomes a sheltering arm. From here westwards the land flattens to the estuary and its abandoned furniture of spent industry. Eastwards, the grass and the fields rise stately to the moors.

The cliff thus divides two regions, the practical and the picturesque. The industrial coast drags its failings to the banks of Weir and Tyne. The coastal paths along the cliff rise and wind over the eroding clay steeps through coves and villages to the old whaling town; sea and the rocky shore on one side, moor on the other. The westward has its gasping ports and industries. The eastward has the ruined abbeys of the Celtic and the Catholic faiths.

But these northern shores are changeable. They are the twilight shores. On an autumn evening Moor Cliff glowers deep red. In bright daylight its crisp wrinkles, from which the kitty-wakes complain, are made indistinct as the sea-fret comes. On a bank holiday afternoon, when the sand turns the sky upside down, it is a stage curtain to the crowded dramas of dogs and children at play, but to the solitary walker its crags and little caves emanate silence. The visitors around the pier, cheerful and unaware, seem far away. But these charms hide its threats. People picnic on the cliff edge unaware that a few years ago the depression which offers them a view of the sea over the gorse was a look-out post erected by Romans in the days of Julius Caesar, now gone to the weathers. Self-satisfied walkers might not know its nic-name is Suicide Cliff. At low tide the cliff temps someone to investigate the rock pools and the smoothed stones under its frown, or to bucket the whelks. Then the wind comes. With grim humour, the tide returns. The sound of helicopter blades announces someone surprised by incoming waves.

Even the sea cannot make up its mind. It owns no colour. It is a war of winds and clouds and water and sunlight. A wild sky froths it dirty white. Winter cloud shows it battleship grey, dull as the submarines on its shallow bed. At high tide in summer, it flops and splashes like a lover against the stone. And under a southern wind a flat calm gleams electric blue, and the white horses spread over the sand like lace. At evening the broad sweep of the bay shows a warm glint in the west and cools the cliff with silver in the east.

And then, when night starts, and the sea seems lit from beneath, and the sky makes its imperceptible gradations from pale blue to black, and the lights of the ships appear, Moor Cliff is a sleeping giant that nothing can disturb.

To this dreamscape between decrepitudes, where rests the comfortable town of Saltscar, a young woman from London arrives: Lillian Miranda Delph.

Chapter 2

She had all the advantages except a mother a girl could want: a home in South Kensington, good grades, a good nature and good taste, friends with few issues, an allowance, no eating disorders, blond hair (straight), toned thighs and, now she was over William, a life free of sexual tension. Then her father went bankrupt and was arrested for fraud.

She rose in her running outfit to overhear a war with The Trophy. Not all her father's girlfriends had been rubbish, but the Trophy had rarely gone well.

The Trophy was saying, 'You do what you want and pass on the risk.'

'I'm not asking much,' Daddy answered.

'I think it's much!'

Lillian stepped lightly down the stairs.

'I'm the one with the hit,' Daddy complained.

'I'm not playing ball on this one!'

'I'm thinking of Lily.'

'Oh, yes! Let's protect Lily!'

There were few problems so great that a run could not reduce them to manageable size. She had chosen white shorts, white top, dark grey baseball cap (without an insignia, thank you) and the pink trainers - the amazing pink trainers - and grey cotton socks: for grey and pink were classic. She took the bus to Piccadilly to run back through the parks. The other way risked sitting sweaty on public transport, which was inconsiderate and wrong. She found a seat next to a black lady with a boy on her lap, which was cute, and filed off at the stop near St. James's church. She marched to Eros and cut to the Mall, trotting down the steps, and jogged for fifty yards along the path of past potentates towards Buck House, then slipped onto the grass. Three Asian guys turned. One shouted, 'Yo.' as the awesome pink trainers flashed past. She raised an arm in acknowledgement. At the Corner she stretched, waiting for a change in the lights, then led the way over the road into Hyde Park. She was focused. She pumped arms, her stride lengthened: she overtook joggers, bounced past a strolling couple, a little slim dart gliding over green, all the way to the café at the Paddington exit where she swerved left to make full pace at the Albert Memorial. Her bright ankles flashed past the Gothic indulgence of the widow-Queen's gloom. She whooshed with bouncing thighs and bursting knees south to the exit. Her calves felt the burn; her chest was forced. Smoothly, with control, she slowed. She sucked in, she blew out, and she came to an amble. She swung her arms along Exhibition Road: she warmed down, kicking up her heels, and so came to a stop, safe in South Ken, and she stretched. She pushed her hands through her hair at the door and gave a last heave of her chest.

He was alone in the kitchen. He sat on a stool at the island.

'Madelaine's gone,' he said.

'Oh.'

'I think it's for good.'

'Oh, dear.'

'There's something you must know,' he started. He did not look up. 'We may need to change our lifestyles a little.'

'That's all right, Daddy,' she said. 'It'll work out.'

'Of course it will, Sweetheart. I'm in a fluid situation, but I'm very employable.'

'I took five seconds off the run.'

'Splendid. We'll be coming up roses.'

'Goody gumdrops,' she answered. That usually made him smile.

It did, but without joy. 'I've a lot of calls to make today. Can you sort yourself out?'

She showered: shampoo, conditioner, gel. She waited fully three minutes before she washed off the conditioner. She was a slim little thing, bare and innocent, in a room all white. The water was warm like a hug.

Lilian was not a curious girl. She worked on a need-to-know basis. The world that adults had made was often annoying, but essentially benign. If you followed instructions and only made a fuss in urgent cases, it placed most of what you wanted into your hands. She knew her father was stressed, more than when the auditor had grilled him about his work with Carling and Daughter, so she did what good girls do. She cancelled her cinema trip and tidied her room and the kitchen and bought sushi out of her own allowance. When he came down from his office, he looked at the effect as though working out what was different, then saw the sushi and hugged her. The hug was longer than usual.

'You're very good,' he said.

'Thank you, Daddy. You may drink.'

He laughed. 'That's my Lillian,' he said.

The following day, however, was more confusing.

The Trophy returned. She stepped through the front door as Lillian came down for breakfast with a face set for battle. She was ripping the wrapping off a cigarette packet.

'Don't be prim,' she said.

'I'm just going out, actually.'

'Good idea. It could get messy.'

Her father appeared from the kitchen. He held a mug of coffee. He had not used the stove pot, so it was Nescafé, which he only took in a rush. But he was not rushed.

'Madelaine and I need to talk,' he said.

She had a latte, a croissant, and a banana for the potassium in Fait Maison and sent texts and looked at job-search. She window-shopped for an hour, then decided rather crossly that that was time enough. There was no sound when she opened the door: they turned to her wearily, with an air more of acceptance than resolution. 'Ok, Sweetheart?' Daddy asked. 'Did you see anyone?'

'I made arrangements.'

The Trophy slung her bag over her shoulder. 'I'll let you two have quality time together,' she said. She pronounced 'quality time' as though it hurt her gums.

Daddy waited for the door to close, then looked at his daughter.

'I've just made a brave decision,' he said. 'It was hard, but right. For you, Randa.'

'Thank you, Daddy.'

He was contemplative. 'The things we do for those we love! Do you remember Aunt Jenny?'

'Aunt Jenny? I don't think so.'

'Your biological mother's cousin. She lives in the north.'

'My mother's ...?' Her mother was The Unspoken.

'She 'mailed me. She's in London. She'd like to meet you.' 'She's not part of our circle.'

'Well, there it is.'

'How very odd.'

'Yes. The 'mail came out of the blue, and then I had a voicemail. She's very keen.'

'Whatever for?'

'Sentimental reasons, I expect. You stayed up there once.'

'I remember.' He cocked his head and raised his eyes. 'Vaguely,' she added.

'She's realised you're eighteen. Perhaps you should go. It might be amusing.'

'I wouldn't know what to say to her.'

'You could just show her how well you've turned out. But if you don't want to ...'

Lillian was perplexed. She knew she had relations in a sea-side town far away, but they were from the other side. Sometimes she wished she could be ten years old again; she had felt the lack of a mother when boys first took an interest in her, though the girlfriend of the day, Julia, had been a help. Her father had been intimidated by the changes in her body from twelve to sixteen, and she had therefore felt it best to keep the sexual side of life on hold until she lived alone. It was not a problem. But Aunt Jenny? She could just recall a woman with a son by a beach, who moved unpredictably in different directions at once, and a dog. She could picture the dog: grey and furry. A fun dog. She could trust no other image of this Aunt Jenny.

'I'd have to change my schedule,' she objected.

'Perhaps tomorrow then. Or the next day. Randa, I've got to make some calls.'

She had an idea just as she fastened the laces of the pink trainers. She knocked on daddy's study and went in.

He looked round from the screen with concern. 'This Aunt Jenny,' she said.

'Yes?' His voice was strained with impatience.

'I don't know why she's suddenly taken an interest. I'll go if you want me to, but I don't want to make any sort of commitment. I've got my plans.'

'To be honest, Randa, I think the idea just popped into her head. It's no big deal, but she did sound keen.'

'She still knows my mother, doesn't she?'

He took off his glasses and rubbed the sides of his face. This was his stress signal. He had two empty coffee mugs on the desk. That was a bad sign. 'To be honest, I'm going to be up to my neck in it now. I guess this woman will be in London for a time. I wouldn't mind you having some other adult company. Keep you out of mischief.'

This last was a joke. It wasn't a very good one, but just now Lillian had to please him. 'I'll go then,' she said. 'Or is she coming here?'

'Good lord, no. I've enough to think about. Meet her at the V&A. That's your territory. It'll give you the advantage. I don't believe she has an agenda,' he shouted after her.

Lillian had first to meet her friend who was called Chloe. Chloe's mother was a Malaysian woman from a high-born Christian family and her father was someone important in the police. Lillian's father was particularly nice to him when they met at school events though they never socialised. Chloe's lush black hair and rich skin, toned like a polished violin, made some people think she was Italian, and she stood out like a proud individualist among the blond schoolmates. She was sporty like Lillian, and happy, though she talked too much about sex. This was probably because her parents were controlling. Chloe said her father behaved too often like a policeman at home. Her mother was from a minority group, which made her anxious. The atmosphere in Chloe's house was therefore rather like school. Frank, Chloe's father, had told Edward, hers, that Lillian kept Chloe on the straight and narrow. Edward told Frank that Chloe made Lillian feel brave.

They met at Oxford Circus tube. Chloe suggested lattes and cake at Liberty's.

'I'm not into cake these days,' Lillian said. 'Especially if we're meeting the crew.'

'You're such a fitness bitch,' said Chloe.

'It's better than being a fat bitch,' Lillian replied.

'Fat is gross. That's hardly your problem.'

'Hardly. I'm worried about my dad,' she said, then realised that was an odd thing to say.

'My god, what's he done?'

'He's broken up with The Trophy. Or she's broken up with him.'

'You don't like The Trophy.'

'No, but something new has happened.'

'Dad says he has issues with the Fraud Squad.'

'What?' They were on the corner of Piccadilly, two mates among many hanging out on the Circus and too engaged with each other to notice the pedestrians.

Chloe shrugged. 'It's just work gossip,' she said. 'You know what my dad's like.'

'Fraud? What even is that? We're not that kind of person.'

'Don't be so serious.' Chloe took her arm and marched her to the crossing.

'You don't perhaps think that sometimes your dad is judgmental?' Lillian suggested.

'With balls on!'

Lillian suggested they went to a film that evening, only the two of them, like in the times before clubs, but Chloe was off to the boyfriend. His parents were liberal and would have let them sleep together, but they insisted Chloe had to have her parents' permission and Chloe didn't think it was wise to risk another lie. 'It won't be long before I can do what I want.' Chloe said. She was going straight to university. Lillian didn't think the dispersal of friends around the country was such a good thing, particularly for the disappointing intimacies of sex.

They strode into Soho to meet what remained of the crew. The Department of Coffee and Social affairs off Carnaby was the place of choice: Chloe liked the name and Lillian liked the cool grey exterior and the clean lines inside. Few more charming or more enviable had hogged seats around the deep grey tables like the upper sixth the back seat of the coach. The buzz of Soho flicked by at the end of the alley, but the crew sat in satisfaction at the almost secret location so near to Liberty's, a place for Those In The Know. There was Annabelle who was famous for cheek to her teachers, and Nia, who had a Welsh ancestor and was good at gymkhanas, and quiet Maria who was good in a crisis and Annabelle's new friend. The new friend was Swedish and a model in Stockholm and was going to drama school, which was impressive. Her name was Karin.

'Who's coming to see me in France?' Chloe asked.

'I've just been to my auntie's in Italy,' Nia said. 'They've got the best house ever and their own vineyard.'

'That's so cool,' Annabelle said.

'Can you party there?' Chloe wanted to know.

'The last time we went into Florence. It was amazing.'

15

'There's nowhere better than London,' Maria said. 'There's this company that does trips to remote islands and you can swim with dolphins. I'd quite like that.'

'I'd love that,' Lillian said.

'We should go.'

'Really? After my intern –'

'That is a beautiful thing,' Karin announced. She had listened to them all with an aloof smile. 'I am thinking that I would go around Sweden in a yacht because it does not have a large footprint.'

'Karin knows Greta Thunberg,' Annabelle said.

'Oh, wow,' Nia said. 'Is she actually weird?'

'I don't really know her.' Karin looked modest. She was not, Lillian thought, especially beautiful, but perhaps what mattered was how you held yourself. She was certainly self-assured. 'My father, he is directing films and he was knowing Greta's mother. She is opera singer. Greta has stopped her from singing abroad because of the footprint.'

'Harsh,' Chloe said.

'It is why I will not go to Los Angeles,' Karin said. 'My father he said I have chance to go for the Oscars, but I said the Oscars can wait.'

'That's ever so grown-up,' Lillian said.

On cue, Chloe gave Lillian a look. The look said, Karin is a pretentious sod. Chloe was easy to be with because she kept everything simple. She had often made friends that Lillian didn't particularly like, and too often she disappeared at a weekend when they were supposed to go shopping, but she always came back and said she'd never really liked that crowd very much. Lillian accepted that. Chloe was less forgiving about people Lillian met.

'I woke up this morning, and realised I'll never have to go back to school,' Annabelle said.

'I know,' said Nia. 'Imagine watching schoolkids go back and us not with them.'

'That'll be strange,' said Lillian.

'No, it won't,' Maria contradicted her softly. 'We were at school for too long.'

'But you were really good at it,' said Lillian, surprised.

'Oh, my god!' said Annabelle. 'Angelo's on!'

Of Angelo, there was much to discuss. That he was beautiful was indisputable. That he was an actor who waited tables was proved by a nifty google. But a black guy of Italian descent? Really? Whose mother was an astrophysicist?

'Morning, ladies. What can I give you?'

There was much flicking of hair and crossing of legs. Chloe pushed herself forward and opened her mouth and considered. Don't say it, Lillian silently urged. 'Cappa-chin-o,' Chloe said. Lillian ordered a single expresso; yes, with water.

Angelo paused mid-order. 'Someone has a very nice perfume,' he said.

'I don't do perfume,' said Karin. 'It's not eco.'

'That will be Lillian,' said Annabelle.

'It's only Armani. It's quite subtle.'

Angelo cocked his head and flicked a finger at her and finished the order. They watched him glide between the tables to the bar.

'So, would *anyone* kick Angelo out of bed?' Chloe asked.

Karin looked lofty. Maria smirked. Lillian was silent. Annabelle smiled. Nia raised her eyes, but no-one raised their hands. They all laughed.

The gabble bubbled like champagne. Nia talked about her eccentric auntie in Italy, who had promised to take her riding in the hills, and there was a valley where horse people met and you could gallop. Lillian said she'd tried horse-riding once. It was tragic because her dad had insisted that she worked to pay for it, so she mucked out the stables which was disgusting, then when she tried she was petrified. 'I was like – aaaargh,' she said. Karin liked all animals, even snakes. Yes, but no-one likes spiders. Maria liked spiders. They ate flies. Flies were sickening. Angelo came with the drinks, and they were attentive.

'Have you any acting jobs on?' Annabelle asked.

'I've two auditions next week. Wish me luck.'

They wished him luck. Nia said it would be cool if he was famous one day. They'd watch him and remember he served them all lattes.

'I wouldn't like to be too famous,' said Karin. 'Then you couldn't have a nice time with friends like this.'

They briefly discussed the advantages and problems of fame.

Lillian's phone sounded. 'I have to take this,' she said in the voice detectives use in the dramas and took it to one side. Chloe was watching her.

Lillian got rid of Aunt Jenny as soon as she could. 'Can I text you?' she asked. 'I'm with people now.'

'I know you're both very busy. But I'd so like to touch base. Do you still use that expression? If you give me the time and place, I'll make my way there.'

'The V&A,' said Lillian. 'Do you know it?"

'I love the V&A. Of course, I've only been twice. Where exactly shall I see you? It's quite big.'

'I'll text you, Aunt Jenny. Can you wait an hour?'

'I'll wait for you as long as you need. There's lots to see here,' Aunt Jenny answered, though she did not specify where 'here' was. She seemed a contented old bird, but scatty.

Lillian's return paused her friends' chatter. They looked at her with neutral faces. She guessed Chloe had said something about her. 'That's done. It was nothing,' she said.

There was a plan to shop at TK Maxx, but Annabelle said she and Karin were going skating, oh my god, how quirky was that? Chloe had arrangements with David – she was so loved up - and Nia was to have afternoon tea with her mum. Maria looked questioningly at Lillian, but Lillian was musing on her father and Aunt Jenny and what Chloe had said. She would be, she had to admit, a bit miffed if Chloe had mentioned fraud to the crew. The girls made tentative plans for the weekend. Maria nudged Lillian.

'You're very quiet.'

'It's because I'm content,' Lillian answered. Maria was boring, but she was very considerate. That was why Lillian liked her.

Lillian said it was her turn to pay. Annabelle said she was a star, but the machine refused her card. She tried it three times. Angelo was looking on, which made it more embarrassing. She had only five pounds and some change in her purse.

Bags were over shoulders when she reported back. 'It's so annoying!' she complained. 'I know there's money in there because I've hardly spent anything.'

'Have you wiped your card?' Maria asked.

'I tried three times. God, I hope I've got my bus pass.'

'It'll work next time,' Chloe said. 'I shouldn't fuss.'

They chipped in with bits and bobs of silver and copper, and Lillian, embarrassed, counted it coin by coin. They'd already done the cheek-kissing and hugs when she joined them on the pavement. Chloe reserved one for Lillian and scampered west to Piccadilly; Annabelle and Karin were moving east to Leicester Square. Nia was gone as into the ether. Lillian found herself on the street with Maria. Maria smiled as she watched Chloe disappear and announced, 'I don't suppose we'll all be friends much longer.'

Lillian was shocked. 'Why ever not?'

'We'll go different ways,' Maria said.

Maria had always been a bit too serious. They parted on Regent Street with an intention to do something sometime,

Without card or cash Lillian felt vulnerable. She would die if she was caught bankrupt on a bus. She approached the barrier at Piccadilly Tube: she swiped: nothing. She stood baffled and confused like a lost tourist while London pushed past her. Daddy, The Trophy, the lady and now the card. This was a difficult day. She was tempted to call Aunt

Jenny off, to find an excuse, but that would be rude, and the rest of the day stretched out pointlessly in front of her and, to be honest, the lady's arrival intrigued her. She had best get it over with. It was not a long walk by Lillian's standards: west past Fortnum and Mason's and the grey eminence of The Royal Academy, then past Harrods and through the parks at the corner, the crossing point on her standard run, then the right fork past The Billionaire's Club and on to The Rembrandt and, hey presto, there you were. She hoisted her bag with a sigh and strode out.

She realised in the foyer that she had no clear idea what Aunt Jenny looked like. She attended to WhatsApp and sent her a text to say she'd arrived, and when she looked up a lady was smiling with recognition at her. It was odd to be smiled at. The lady had curly dry hair, almost an Afro, but it was blonde like her own. Her loose frock was pinned with an old maiden brooch, an odd combination, and instead of a belt she wore a rope that hung with a tassel the colour of her hair and she had a leather bag that was on a long strap. Lillian had never shared a space with anyone quite so eccentric.

'Lillian Miranda,' the lady said.

'Yes?'

'I'm your Auntie Jenny. Jennifer Goodman.'

She said it as though this explained everything. 'Of course, I'm not your real auntie,' the lady confessed. 'I'm your mother's cousin. Do you remember Ferdy?'

'Ferdy?'

'Once, you were close. Gus is dead, of course. That's to be expected. It's been a long time. A lot has changed, but not as much as everywhere else. Lillian, you're beautiful!'

This was an exaggeration. It should not have sounded surprising though, true or not. The lady waited.

'Thank you. You look very well too, Aunt Jenny,' Lillian ventured.

'I can see you struggling,' the lady said. 'That's me. I do gabble on. You must stop me. What about the beach? You loved the beach.'

'The beach at …?' Lillian ventured.

'Lillian Delph,' the lady repeated. She turned her name into a sigh. 'Lillian Miranda Delph.' She uttered it with such admiration and pleasure that Lillian, though confused, was flattered.

'I'm sorry,' she said. 'I really don't remember anything much.'

'I've waited so long. We never really forgot you. Why don't we have a coffee?' She suggested this as though it was the morning's bold notion. 'I'm sure there's a café.' She looked around. 'We can catch up and then I'll leave you alone. It's over ten years.'

'The café's in the other building,' Lillian said.

'What are we waiting for?' the woman asked.

It was hard to resist this without looking frightened or rude, so Lillian led the way through the grand hall over its polished floor that made you feel grown up, where the exhibits told her the world was rich and varied and strange, but still under control. This time they were simply big because she was embarrassed. She considered flight, but then people would look at her and the lady would complain to her daddy, and she wouldn't know what to say. She might brush her off. I'm sorry, I honestly don't know who you are and I'm really busy at the moment. Bye.

On the other hand, Aunt Jenny was easy to impress. The old dear was glancing at the entrances to passing rooms, turning round to take them in, in wonder.

'You know your way around here,' she said.

'It's quite local,' Lillian answered.

'Of course! Oh, Lillian, how wonderful.'

They stepped out to the courtyard where children babbled and splashed around the fountain, screaming as they felt the cold. The smart tourists lounged on the chairs. Lillian was touched with pride. Then the lady said, 'How's your father?'

'Why?' Lillian asked.

'He's done a tremendous job with you. Where do we go?'

'Over here.'

She took her to the café, the long white gallery with the passionless Canovas, not the crowded Morris rooms, dim and too rich, and waited for a table.

'So, how is he?' the lady asked again.

'Oh, fine, fine,' Lillian said. 'He's changing jobs.'

'Ah, right, I see.'

'We're hopeful on a good deal.'

The lady nodded as though that was to be expected. She appeared to consider it. 'There's a place,' she said.

'We order first,' Lillian explained.

'Oh, yes. Like Costa.'

Lillian suddenly remembered she had no money and a faulty card. She was considering how to deal with this when, with fairy-godmother timing, Aunt Jenny said, 'Don't worry. I'll pay.'

'Oh, thank you, said Lillian.

The lady took cash from a grubby purse that seemed to be made of cork. Lillian carried the tray. The table had gone once they were served, but Lillian noticed a couple leaving and they waited for their table, despite the finished cups and the milk jug. The lady looked around again. Lillian surmised it was her first visit.

'Are you staying with a friend?' she asked.

'I'm with Dorothy. You won't remember Dorothy. She had a daughter in Clapham. It's very exciting. Otherwise, you and your father are my only contact, and I don't want to impose. We're here for Frieda.'

'Oh?'

'Kahlo. A great feminist icon. At the Tate.'

Oh, yes.'

'So you don't think about Saltscar?'

'Where?'

The lady swallowed and waved her hands in apology. 'Why would you? It wasn't an easy time when you were there, but I remember it with great fondness. This is very good coffee, by the way. Perhaps a little too hot. You can scold coffee, you know. Yes, I can still see your skinny little legs flashing along the beach - 'along the margin of the salt-sea strand' - as Ferdinand says. You were very concerned about getting your knickers wet because people would think you'd had an accident, but then he dumped you in a pool and that was that. We did laugh. Your mother was there. It's such a shame how she lost her roots, but it's a global world, isn't it?'

'We don't really communicate,' Lillian said, blinking at the barrage. 'She's in Australia. With Jeremy.'

'No, she's in Scotland,' Aunt Jenny said. 'Who's Jeremy?'

'I thought he was her partner?'

'I've never heard of a Jeremy. So far as I know your mother had no attachments at the time. There is a Malcolm, but it's not clear what the relationship is.'

'I wouldn't know.' Her tone said, as politely as feasible, Don't talk about my mother.

Aunt Jenny regarded her. It was an appraising stare such as a housemistress delivers when you give a reason to bunk off Economics. Lillian wasn't sure she liked it. Then she looked around to clear the subject away, and simply said, 'But you're doing well otherwise?'

Lillian saw her way clear. 'Very well. My A-levels were good and I've got a place at Oxford Brooks. It's a course on retail management. My teachers said I should do History or History of Art, but I think these days it's better to do something practical to be competitive, and dad's completely on board.'

'Retail management?' Aunt Jenny queried. 'Shops?'

'And ... retail. I've got a GAP year set up next January for the experience. I'm going to Paris where there's an internship in a fashion shop. It was set up by my Gap advisor. The scary thing is my French, but at the end I'll be fluent, which is nice. Everyone says it's cool. I'm very excited about it!' She smiled as she leaned for the cup. There were plenty of Parents' Days and practice interviews behind that smile, but when she put the cup down and looked to see the impression she had made, the lady was wiping her eye. It was a real tear.

'Dear me. What an idiot,' Aunt Jenny remarked. 'I had a picture of you and Ferdy together.'

'Ferdy?'

'Your cousin once-removed.'

Lillian had never heard of such a thing.

'Oh. Is he well?'

'He's the gentlest soul behind the bluster that ever walked on a beach by day, and that's a worry,' she answered. 'You seemed such soul-mates, though of course you were barely more than a toddler. Anna-Marie on the other hand is steaming ahead.'

'She's ...?'

'Your other cousin once-removed. She's there to help with the family business, but she'll go soon, unfortunately. We've promised.'

'I see.' Lillian had no idea what she was talking about.

'One day when you're less busy you must come and see us all again. Ferdy will be touched. And there's the new dogs; Mary, Joseph and Jesus. The Holy Family.'

Lillian valued clear intentions. This was why she had never minded the classroom, regardless of the boring stretches, the pointless knowledge, and the annoying teachers. At least you knew the point of a lesson. Life was like running: you started at one place, ended at the end and worked out how well you'd done against the competition. So long as the focus and preparation were good, the outcomes were happy. Aunt Jenny, leaning forward with a cup in her hand as though she'd forgotten it, puffed by general enthusiasm and in clothes with mixed signals, seemed encouraging Lillian off course, though why and when and to what end was mysterious.

'It sounds lovely,' she said.

'I can see I unsettle you,' Aunt Jenny said. 'Don't mind me. I'm from the north. We do tend to over-familiarity.'

'I wish I remembered more. I'm not being rude.'

'Lillian!' Aunt Jenny was so earnest she had to put her cup down. The coffee trembled, but did not spill. 'You were the sweetest, happiest, politest, laughingest – well, that's not a word – the loveliest little creature, and that despite the Issues. And look at you now! A real princess.'

Lillian giggled and put her hand to her mouth. 'At school, that's what we called the girls who were spoiled and awful.'

'I mean,' Aunt Jenny started, and cast around. 'I mean, in the destiny sense. You were the most precious little girl and I can see you are made for greatness. You have an aura. It shows in your poise.' She suddenly flapped away this nonsense with an arm. 'Anyway, that's in the future. But for now, you're holding up all right?'

'Holding up?'

'With this – this change of job.'

'Oh, yes, absolutely!' Lillian was offended. She would not show it. 'It's a fluid situation, but that's business. 'Feast and famine' Daddy says.'

'He sounded a little anxious on the phone. Of course, I hardly know him so it's probably just his way. Do you see his family often?'

'His family?'

'His parents.'

It was difficult to know if Aunt Jenny was nosy, or just over-friendly, but she was certainly right when she said she was familiar. Lillian had not visited her father's parents since grandpa had slapped her on the side of the head and grandma had taken her husband's side. They lived on a residential estate near Maidenhead which her father said was a dump, and which showed their lack of ambition. He visited a couple of times a year, at Christmas and on his mother's birthday, but they were never invited to London.

'Daddy has a difficult relationship with his parents,' Lillian said. 'We don't talk about them.'

'Then I won't ask,' said Aunt Jenny sweetly.

'I think that's best.'

Lillian heard her own tone. Aunt Jenny had made her sound like a snob. 'Thank you for asking, though,' she followed up. Aunt Jenny, however, was distracted. She was looking around, turning in her seat. Was she on the spectrum? Did she have ADD? Some adults did. She turned back and said directly, 'Where's the toilet here? They must have one.' Lillian pointed the way. 'Do excuse me, Lillian,' Aunt Jenny said.

Lillian made sure she had finished her coffee before Aunt Jenny returned. She took her mobile to text her father, but the thought of him made her anxious, and that raised the problem with her card. She sat, disconsolate like a betrayed lover, and did not hear Aunt Jenny's return.

'I must say, this is a splendid place. Even the loos are top notch. That's probably not an expression you use.'

Lillian put on her bright face. It was time to bring this to an end and go home. 'And how are things in Saltscar. Is ... How is Mr Goodman?'

'Your Uncle Jimmy – also once removed, of course - died three years ago. Two days after Gus. The two deaths weren't related in any way, though it seemed symbolic at the time.'

'Oh. I'm sorry.'

'I wouldn't expect you to remember him. He was a lovely man. Ferdinand was hardest hit. But life moves on. Do you work in London?'

'No. that is, not yet. I'll get something to help pay for Paris.'

'You have no commitments then?'

That was a strange question. That question had a plan behind it. Lillian saw an elderly couple looking for a table and took her chance. 'There's a couple over there need a seat,' she said. 'Perhaps we should give them our table.'

Aunt Jenny looked round, saw whom she meant, and smiled. 'Lillian, you're so considerate. There's a lot said against your generation, but personally I've found today's young people a reprimand to us all. Here's what we'll do. You take my number, and if you ever need to get in touch, you have it. I'm not a text-pest. Do you know that expression? Anne-Marie used it once. I like the assonance. Then we'll go. You have your schedule and I have Freida.'

Lillian didn't know how to frame a refusal, and because she could always block her later, made no objection. Aunt Jenny waved to the couple to indicate they were leaving. Lillian stood. Aunt Jenny moved her phone to and from her face and squinted, then read the numbers too loudly. Lillian put them into Contacts in a few seconds under 'Jenny'.

'Try it. Let's see if it works.'

Lillian obediently tapped on the number. Aunt Jenny's phone rang.

'Bingo! That's one of Frank's expressions. He wasn't around when you were with us.'

'You didn't finish your coffee,' Lillian said in apology.

'I've had quite sufficient. Oh, look here.' She peered into the Morris rooms. 'That must be William Morris. We could have gone in them, but I suppose you prefer this. More modern.'

'I do rather.'

Lillian offered her hand at reception. 'It was lovely to meet you,' she said. The lady ignored the hand and hugged her. Lillian accepted the hug.

'You are so beautiful!' the lady said.

'Thank you.'

'Now listen.' Aunt Jenny stared into Lillian's face. She was standing too close. Lillian glanced to the doors and into the inviting street, but she was patient. 'If ever you need it, there's a home for you in Saltscar. We have the same house. We've even got the bed you had. Gus used to jump on it every morning before you got up. Throughout life's ups and downs, and there are always downs, you know you've somewhere to go.'

Lillian suddenly got Aunt Jenny. She had severe leave-the-nest syndrome. Her children had left home, and her husband was dead.

'Thank you. And give my best to Birdy. Say I remember him.'

'Ferdy. He loved you. I think he still does. One day, when you're ready, you'll wake up in that same little bed to the cry of the seagulls over Moor Cliff.'

Lillian suppressed a gasp. She felt a stir in her stomach, as though in reaction to a memory without the memory itself. She heard a gull's primitive complaint and saw a flash of sun over a dark cliff and felt the shift of a whispering sea.

'Give my best to your father,' the lady added. 'Edward, isn't it?'

'Yes. It is, actually.'

'The wealthy guardian. That's what the name means. I can tell that you're close. But if you ever need someone to talk to, you know you can telephone me. Goodbye, Lillian Miranda Delph.'

Jenifer Goodman was swallowed in the milling visitors and disappeared like a mirage, and Lillian breathed out with relief. How weird was that.

There was still the annoyance of the card. Her daddy would sort it, so she rushed home. He was at the desk-top in the office where she hardly ever entered, but this was an emergency. He did not have an absolute injunction on entering the office. The girls of such fathers assumed it was because their dad watched porn or had mistresses, but Edward, thank god, was not like that. She knocked and said, 'Daddy, something's happened,' and went in. As soon as she saw him she recognised a change. Her father was the Nordic type, with blonde hair like herself and cheekbones, a man with a bounce in his step and flashing

31

eyes, who made her friends giggle. They often thought him fit. Lillian was not sure what she thought about this, but she took it as a compliment to herself. This time, however, the slowness of his turn and his distracted air made him look like other dads, so stifled with their own concerns they regarded anyone under twenty as a different kind.

She made her tone light. 'Something really annoying's happened,' she started. 'It's not an issue. I don't think it is. But the ATM refused my debit card! I've not spent a lot so there's money in there, and I gave the card a rub, but it still didn't work.' Her father looked at her with parted mouth. She reassured him. 'I suppose the machine's out of order, and they haven't put a sign up yet. I can try-'

'Fuck!' he interrupted. It was like a dog's yelp and entirely out of character. 'Sorry, Sweetheart,' he said, for either the swearing or the inconvenience. 'Don't worry, I'll sort it. It's to do with this business thing.' He paused, only for thought, so she waited. He gave her an earnest stare. Then he sprang to the moment. 'Right. I'll bite the bullet. It's time to talk to Mr Harris.' Mr Harris was the family lawyer. He leaned forward and lowered his voice. 'You know, Lillian, we may need to sell this place.'

'Oh.'

'It's a temporary downsize.' He was struck by the new thought. 'Have you no cash?'

'It doesn't matter. I'll go to the bank tomorrow.'

'Oh, Lillian, why are you so good?' This was an odd thing to say. 'It would be easier if only you were a little bad sometimes!' Lillian couldn't quite agree to this. The streets of the bad were unruly and stressful. She had no time to respond, however, because her father jumped up.

'Wait there,' he said and left. She heard him bang a drawer in his bedroom, then he stepped back and stuck out two twenties and a ten. 'That will tidy you for a couple of days.'

'Thank you.'

'Thank Madeleine,' he answered and laughed. It wasn't a happy laugh.

'It's Madeleine's?'

'See it as a tax-free rebate on an overinvestment,' he said, chuckling. Lillian had never seen him so manic. 'She left it, bless her. She was in too much hurry to ditch the ship to think about it, but she was always careless with cash.' He saw his daughter's face. 'Just take it, Lillian. Everything she has she got from me. She can spare us a fifty.'

'She won't want it back, I suppose?'

'Don't you worry about Madeleine,' he said. 'Madeleine comes up roses whatever - I wouldn't be surprised if her husband doesn't take her back.'

Lillian was startled. She'd never known that Madeleine was married.

'She was nice to me sometimes,' she said.

'Everyone's nice to everyone sometimes,' he answered. 'Did you see this Aunt Jenny?' he suddenly asked.

'I've just come from her.'

'And?'

'She's very ... eccentric.'

'But friendly?'

'To a fault!'

'That was my impression too. Terror Attack From Friendly Northerner. Personal Space Invaded.' He smiled at his own joke then stared out at the window, lost to her. Lillian searched for an encouraging comment. She had considered asking if he knew her mother was in Scotland, not in Australia, but his sudden gravity made any observation by Aunt Jenny beside the point. The precise location of The Unmentioned was a not a practical issue anyway. Her father gazed a few moments at the solid rooftops of South Kensington, dark grey slate roofs, with the mounting pale grey clouds behind them, and suddenly announced, 'Sometimes I really don't like London.'

Lillian was shocked. 'But London's the best place in the world,' she said.

'Sure. A given. But the mortgages, Lillian, the mortgages.' He contemplated the mortgages.

She recalled him with a notion. 'I suppose,' she said, 'if Madelaine's not coming back, it makes sense to downsize anyway.'

Her father nodded with some of his old certainty. 'That's just the right attitude,' he said. He roused himself and picked up his phone. 'Right. Mr Harris. Can you give me an hour or so, Sweetie?'

'I'll go for a run.'

'Good. Keep the fifty in your room. Things will be sorted tomorrow. Believe me.'

She started well. When she passed through the gates she was ready for a full circuit, but after the first clump of trees she slowed. She was breathing too rapidly. She had not found the inner calm. She slowed to a fast walk, to compose herself, but, looking round, she was struck by the emptiness. The thing about the parks was that, except for St. James's, they were quiet. That was one of the wonders of London. You could be on the agitated street with the cars growling past, avenues of dark brown brick or canyons of stately stone, then slip into a park, however small, and suddenly you were into the calm of countryside, the surprise of colour, or to a more sedate past, like settling into yourself. At this moment, however, Hyde Park was a spreading comfortless green across which a few small figures walked to no apparent purpose, and she felt the wind in her hair like a warning. What was wrong with her? She was worried about her father. She was seriously worried. She needed a plan. She thought. She struck on the answer, practical and fun. She would get him to run with her, as they used to do before she got faster than him.

Perhaps the meeting with the lawyer had sorted everything. The house was silent as she climbed the stairs. She had expected his voice on the phone, or the low jazz he played while working to creep from his study. 'Daddy?' she called. She heard a stifled gasp from his room and paused on the landing. 'Daddy?' she repeated and got a soft moan in reply. She listened outside his door. She never went into his bedroom. His bedroom, where he and the Trophy sometimes made noise in a weekend morning, was excluded even from her imagination. But when she turned away there was a gasp and a bang of a fist on the wall, so she knocked, and peeped through the door.

He was moaning on the bed. He did not respond to her call, and he shook. She blinked at him. She could not think what to say. She called him again. This time he looked at her and waved his hands, but it was not clear if he was waving her away or beckoning so she stood where she was. 'Are you all right, Daddy?' she asked, which sounded stupid even to her, but what else could she say? She had an urge to walk out of the house, and down the street, and then come back to see if things were normal, like rebooting a computer, but then her father suddenly said, 'I'll kill them!' and added, more ominously, 'But then I'd have to kill us.' He looked at her. 'Oh, Lilly, I'm sorry. I'm so sorry,' he concluded, and turned from her.

This must be a panic attack. Perhaps it was a heart attack. Her father gave a loud breath, a wheeze like the end of hope and something clicked in Lillian's mind. She dashed downstairs and telephoned for an ambulance.

The operator was clear and calm and made her feel grown-up. Her voice cracked once, when she said about the killing, but the operator told her to hold it together. She was no use to her father if she broke up. Lillian did the breathing. 'That's a good girl,' the operator said. He told her to make sure the doors were unlocked and if she was frightened to go outside.

'If I go outside, I won't know what's happening.'

'The ambulance will be here shortly. I'm with you until then.'

It seemed to happen in slow motion. She suggested a glass of water, but the advisor said not: there was a chance her father might vomit. She watched him. He was making an effort. Then there were voices downstairs. Lillian ran down for the ambulance people, but, in fact, it was the police, a man and a woman. In confusion she put down the phone on the hall table. The ambulance voice sounded beneath it, then stopped. The man ran upstairs. The woman wanted to ask a few questions.

Lillian did not understand why the police were there and not the paramedics. Someone had seriously messed up, but she led the policewoman into the sitting room, nevertheless. 'Try and stay calm,' the policewoman said. She was a plump woman, a little too fat for her uniform, but she had a kind face. 'My colleague is trained. Shall I make you a hot drink?'

Lillian did not want a hot drink.

The policewoman was Mandy. She wanted to know if her father had been like this before. Was this the first time he'd mentioned killing? Lillian's cheeks burned. She was stupid to have mentioned it. Of course it was the first time! But Mandy's phone sounded. Lillian watched her face turn serious. This was horrible. Mandy thrust her phone back in her top pocket and said, 'Your father has difficulties at work. Has he said anything about that?'

'Why are you here?' Lillian asked. 'I didn't call.'

'The ambulance service informed us. Just to be on the safe side. It's a precaution.' She'd put her kind face back on. 'We have to check you're safe, but I can tell you're a capable young lady.'

'Thank you.'

'Your father hasn't said anything about these work difficulties, has he?'

Lillian shook her head. 'He's in a fluid situation, that's all. This kind of thing is common for people in his line. He expects it to be sorted very soon.'

'This isn't the first time?'

'He once got very cross with a Russian investor who pulled out of a deal, so we had to cancel a holiday. I was only little then, though. We were doing very well.'

'I see.' Mandy looked serious again and scribbled in her notebook.

Lillian didn't believe Mandy saw at all. 'My debit card's blocked,' she said. 'That's a new thing.'

The paramedics arrived. There was a little thin one who greeted them cheerfully and a silent bulky one. Lillian jumped up and started to explain that her father couldn't talk, he was having a seizure, but Mandy simply said, 'Upstairs.' There were jolly greetings on the stairs as the paramedics, going up, met the policeman, coming down, then Mandy asked, 'How 'blocked'?'

'Like, not working.'

That seemed to impress Mandy because she said to the policeman, 'Looks like something serious going on.' The policeman sat without being invited and faced Lillian with his hands between his thighs in an over familiar way and looked round. 'Nice place,' he said. He did not say it as a compliment.

'Assets frozen,' Mandy said. 'You want to check?'

'Remind me of the name.'

'Edward Delph,' Lillian said. 'You can sort out my debit card?'

'Not exactly, miss, not us.'

Lillian did not like this policeman. She was glad he went into the corridor with his phone. Mandy said this was very upsetting, but she must try not to worry. Her father would get the very best treatment. 'Do you have anyone to stay for a few days. Your mother? Stepmother?'

'My mother's in Australia. No, Scotland. She's somewhere.' Mandy visibly blinked at this, and Lillian wished she could just order them out, like a prefect when the Years 9s are too loud in the corridor. But she did not.

She explained. 'At the moment he's single, but I've loads of friends.'

'Grandparents?'

'We're not really in touch.'

'No other relations?'

'Why?' Lillian asked in alarm.

Mandy was sympathetic again. 'It's very stressful for you. I don't like to think of you alone.'

'I have lots of friends, like I said.'

'That's good.'

The thin paramedic appeared. 'Miss Delph? It doesn't seem too awful. Definitely not a heart-attack or a stroke, so you can relax, but we're taking him in for observation.' Then her father appeared: he was with the bulky one. The thin one moved aside so her father could come in while the bulk stayed in the doorway. They stood as on stage for the touching scene between father and daughter.

'Daddy,' said Lillian.

'Hello there, Sweetheart. I'm going in for a few silly tests. Can you pack me a bag?'

'Of course, Daddy. Will you need the cologne?'

'Good point. Why not?' I'm not sure what the hospital policy is on razors, but include it anyway.'

'What's your blood-pressure?'

'A hundred and forty-four over eighty-eight,' the thin paramedic butted in.

'That's high!'

'In the circumstances, not,' the paramedic reassured her.

Her father cast a cold eye on the police. 'You're not upsetting my daughter, I hope.'

'No, sir,' the man answered. 'We're finished here. Thank you very much for your cooperation.'

Mandy rose. 'Thank you, Lillian. You're coping wonderfully.'

Martin and Lillian hugged. He would be at the Chelsea and Westminster, and said he expected to be out and fighting again in a day, but when the ambulance doors closed Lillian felt more alone than she ever remembered. She remained a practical girl, however, and there was no time to brood. It was important to do this well. She chose the Armani bag and made sure the toiletries were wrapped in kitchen paper in case the shampoo leaked as it was wont when laid on its side. It was funny to handle his underpants, but she folded them too, and once the bag was tight she placed the photograph of the two of them on her twelfth birthday face down on top and zipped. That was the only touch of sentiment. The bag was orderly and neutral: it did not exude any of her father's personality, any sense of haste or of crisis. He was going away to rest. That was all. She was so practical, so orderly and so sure that all would work out in a matter of days that she did not text nor telephone anyone, though in theory that's what friends were for.

The Chelsea and Westminster was a flat-sided building with rows of identical windows like a factory and an awning above the ground floor, supported by square metal pillars that were all frame, like garden furniture. It was not a comforting building, but it wasn't spooky like some of the Victorian brick ones. Lillian had to wait five minutes at reception. There was a lot of drifting and shuffling around on the ground floor, an air of helpless waiting she did not like. It was the NHS, but you'd have thought there'd be a greater sense of urgency.

He looked exhausted, and tense: the storm had blown out leaving a desolate terrain. He sat in bed in hospital pyjamas, unfetching in pale blue and white, and no collar, so she was glad she'd remembered the cologne. She put her bag on the floor and took out *The Times* and sat on a chair on the other side. The room was tiny, but at least he was not sharing like the other poor creatures she'd seen from the corridors. 'Daddy, what happened?' she asked.

'I'm at a low ebb, I have to admit,' he replied. He fingered *The Times*, then dropped it on the table with a sigh, as though the things of the world were too difficult to deal with right now. 'But the thing about ebbs, Lilly, is that they become whatever the opposite of an ebb is. The tide comes in. The tide goes out. It really wasn't my fault. I had to think of you.'

'I love you, Daddy.'

'I know you do.'

He took a breath like an actor preparing for his entrance. 'We've just got to buckle down. Hang in there, Lilly.'

'I'm hanging, Daddy. Have they given you lunch?' She assumed terrible things about NHS food.

'Lunch -' her father started. 'Lunch ... I don't care about lunch, Randa.'

'Can I do anything? I could get you some things.'

Her father scrutinised her. He was calculating. Then he gave up. 'There's just one thing you need to know, Randa,' he said. 'The directors at the firm were all bastards. Criminal. I'm the victim here. I didn't know … It's so unfair!'

He sank back. The unfairness of the market was, according to her economics teacher, and all that her father had previously implied, a contradiction in terms. The people and forces that had laid her father low were too vague and grand for inquiry, so she kept the conversation local.

'I forgot to tell you. I had a text from Aunt Jenny.'

'Auntie Jenny?'

'That cousin on the other side of the family. You asked me to meet her.'

'Of course! Jennifer Goodman. You told me. What about her?'

'She just said it was nice to meet me.'

'Aunt Jenny,' he mused.

A nurse stood at the door with a glass of water and blood pressure equipment. She was a homely lady whose uniform gleamed with cleanliness. 'Mr Delph - your pill.' She smiled at Lilly and gave her father glass and pill and waited for him to take one.

'Thank you, Monica.'

'We'll see how you are later and give you another at seven if need be. Hello. Are you Mr Delph's daughter?'

'Yes. Lillian.'

'Would you like a coffee, Lillian?'

'Yes - I mean, no.' She had little faith in NHS coffee.

'How did Jake get on, Monica?' Edward asked as she attached the band to his arm.

'Well enough. He can go into the sixth form.'

'Jake's had his first day at work, Lillian.'

'Oh.'

'Are you relieved, Monica?'

'Jake always does his best. He's not particularly bright. But he's a good worker.' Lillian watched the band tighten.

'Industry is more important than talent,' Edward advised. 'He mustn't let people exploit him, though.'

'The things you say, Mr Delph!'

'What do you think of my daughter, Monica? Isn't she a jewel?'

'Daddy!' It was encouraging though slightly annoying that he seemed to revive more for an attractive lady than for her, but that was her daddy.

'She looks like a proper young lady,' Monica acknowledged, her eyes on the monitor. 'One more, Mr Delph.'

'Call me Edward.'

'What's the blood-pressure?' Lillian asked.

'One moment. A hundred and forty over seventy-nine. A little high, but it's not a worry. Now I'll leave you to have a nice chat. Are you expecting any other visitors today, Mr Delph?'

'Not unless you're coming again, Monica.'

'I'll be around. My shift doesn't finish until nine.'

'She's excellent,' he said when she'd left. 'That's one good thing to come from all this. I appreciate the work these small people do much better. Good people – non-judgemental. That must mean that deep down I'm not a bad person.'

'Who said you were?'

'Madelaine wasn't too impressed.'

Lillian turned down her mouth. 'The Trophy doesn't matter any longer,' she said.

'The Trophy! Is that what you called her?' Lillian clapped her hand to her mouth. 'That's as much a comment on me as her, but good on you, Lillian. Were all your step-mothers awful?'

'They weren't actually step-mothers.'

'Step-partners then.'

'I quite liked Julia. Julia was nice. She used to play with me, and she did actually look after me when I was sick. Sophia was fun, but a bit scary. She offered me a cigarette once when I was stressed about an exam. I didn't take it, Daddy, and I didn't tell you. But The Trophy was the worst.'

Edward laughed. Lillian laughed too. It was like the old days between them.

'I'm afraid you got that one right. What were you saying, Sweetheart? Australia-Emily's cousin.'

'Oh, yes. She sent me a text. Also, she invited me up there. As if.'

'Aunt Jenny.' He considered the name. 'Was she acceptable?'

'She wasn't a chav, if that's what you mean.'

'She's certainly not that. She invited you to visit them?'

'Yes!' Lillian laughed.

'Actually, that might not be such a silly idea. For a few days. Get you out of the way. Keep up with your friends on Facebook.' Lillian giggled. Her father frowned back. 'Why's that funny?'

'Facebook! That's so your generation.'

'Or Scype or Zoom, or whatever.' He sighed heavily and brushed back his hair like someone who had just survived a battle. 'I worry about you, Lillian. Now, what about money? The current account will be open soon. Mr Harris will see to that, at least. They can't close that for long.'

'But it will be sorted by then.'

'Yes. Yes. I'm sure it will.' He closed his eyes. He looked tired.

'I could get a job,' she said. 'Don't worry about me, Daddy. If I get lonely, I'll stay with Chloe.'

'No!'

He was abrupt. 'A slightly unpleasant thing, Lilly. I bumped into Frank and he was rude about my circumstances. A bit of a snob, Frank. At heart, he's only a policeman. It's best we keep all this stuff between ourselves. Sorry, Randa.' His weak smile showed he still loved her. 'You can have a holiday with Chloe when this is all over. When I'm not at such a low ebb.'

'That's all right. She's all loved up, anyway.'

'I owe a lot of money, but Mr Harris is a whizz on bankruptcy law. I'm unemployed. Unemployed! Me! Bastards.' He closed his eyes again. 'Aunt Jenny,' he mused. 'I went there once with your mother before we married.

Her family were awful. They had this massive house on a hill. I think it was on a hill. You stayed one summer when I was out of the country. There's a boy, a big gentle creature, not very quick.'

'That's Ferdinand. They have a dog called Jesus!'

'Are they religious?'

'I don't know. I don't think so.'

'I suppose if they were they'd consider it blasphemous to name a dog 'Jesus''

'It doesn't matter. I won't see her again.'

Her father looked wistful. 'You have no-one but me,' he said. 'It makes me wonder...'

'Are you thinking of grandad and grandma?' she asked.

'No!' he exclaimed again. He was suddenly an angry man. He sat up. The top button on his hospital trousers was unfastened. Lillian saw the bones at the base of his neck. He had lost weight. How had she not noticed earlier? 'That's another terrible thing. If they knew that ... that I was at such a low ebb, they'd be glad! They say, Told you so. They always resented that I was a clever one, with real aspirations. Their purpose in life is to lower our self-esteem. Don't even think it!'

She shrank from his glare. He saw it, and lay back, then patted the bed. She sat on it. He put his arm round her shoulders. 'That isn't me, Randa,' he said. 'It's the illness speaking.'

'I know, Daddy.'

He released her and sunk back. 'You're such a good girl,' he said. 'I'll sort it, Lillian. I'll sort it.'

She sat by his bed. He fell asleep.

There was no relief for Lillian Miranda.

Madelaine had let herself in. She was picking her clothes from the wardrobe. Lillian peered through the door, unnoticed. Madelaine was quick, folding and pushing the clothes into her case on the bed like a fugitive. She pulled her fingers through her hair and saw Lillian.

'Dear God! How long have you been there?'

'Sorry. I just came in. I didn't know-'

'You know now.'

One of the many annoying things about Madelaine was that she said things that sounded like they made sense, but they didn't.

'Been to the hospital? How is he?'

'He's bearing up well,' Lillian said.

'And you?'

'Fine. I'm concerned about him, of course.'

'Course you are.'

'But I've no doubt soon we'll be coming up roses.'

Madelaine laughed. 'Pass me that dress over the chair.'

Lillian passed the dress. Madelaine folded it deftly and plumped it in the case. 'So where are you going? I'm off to my sisters'.'

'I'm staying here, of course.'

Madelaine fixed her with cold eyes. Lillian wanted her gone, but she hated confrontation. 'Shall I help you?' she suggested.

'If you like.' That was another irritation. She didn't give you credit. 'You know he's selling this house?'

'He may have to. I know that. We've talked about it.'

'May have to?' The Trophy responded in angry disbelief. Lillian recognised that tone. When she'd moved in The Trophy had been quite sweet. She'd picked Lillian up after parties and asked her how it had gone. She was never shocked when Lillian said what some of her friends had done. 'Any weed?' she'd ask casually. She was supportive in tough-girl mode when the thing with William ended. In the last months, when the financial troubles began, however, she'd got exasperated.

'You have to wise up, kid.'

How could her father ever have thought The Trophy was a viable partner?

'The house will be on the market in days,' The Trophy announced. 'It will sell like that!' She snapped her fingers.

Lillian did not believe it. She said nothing. 'If it doesn't, he'll rent it out,' The Trophy continued. 'Come downstairs. We'll have a last coffee together.'

Lillian arranged the coffee grinder, beans, cups, milk jug and the thin hygge beakers in a neat row on the counter. She needed to take care with this. These things were important. She made sure not to overfill the kettle because she'd heard on the radio that too much water in a kettle was a massive eco-issue, but then The Trophy joined her and said, 'Oh, for god's sake, Lilly, don't bother will all that now. There's Nescafé in the cupboard!'

'I like making it,' said Lillian.

'Please yourself. I'm sorry you heard about the house from me. Ed rather hoped it could all be sorted without you having to worry about it.'

Lillian hated it when she called her father Ed. The buzz of the grinder made conversation impossible, then The Trophy said, 'You shouldn't blame him, Lilly. He's more an idiot than a bastard.'

'I wouldn't dream of blaming him for anything,' Lillian answered.

'Well, I do. I wasn't quite the trophy, you think. Yes, I know what you call me. I warned him, you know. All through those ventures that went tits up, I told him it wasn't worth the risk. Then this last thing. That was the straw. You really want to know why I left him?'

'You've every right to put your side,' Lilly said.

'Stop the passive-aggressive crap, Lilly. We're beyond that. I told him if he took this last risk that was it, if there were problems, and he said he had to do it for your future. You or me, really. He chose you.'

'I see.' She didn't, as a matter of fact. The cafetière was filled. She would normally let it brew, but this time she pushed. Coffee spurted out.

'Oh, god, I hate that!'

'Don't make such a fuss.' The Trophy wet a cloth and wiped the surface and tossed the cloth into the sink without rinsing it. 'You needn't look so glum,' she concluded. 'You're not the one he dumped.'

That The Trophy considered her daddy could dump her showed how ridiculous she was.

'Well,' said Lilly, 'I'm sure whatever happens we'll manage till Paris and then we'll have a bright outlook. Daddy has contacts.'

'He's got those alright.' The Trophy took her coffee. 'Get to college as soon as you can, Lilly,' she advised. 'Ed's got talent and he doesn't want to screw anyone up, but the bad times are getting bigger than the good ones. On the graph it's a downward zigzag. Though you can't deny, he's amusing company.' She smiled wryly at the adoption of Edwards's terminology and went with her beaker upstairs.

Good riddance, Lillian thought. Then the Trophy came back down.

'I have to tell you this. If ever you're in the witness stand, tell the truth. Whatever anyone might want you to say, *tell the fucking truth*! It's your duty to yourself as much as anything else. That's my final motherly warning. Tell Edward I won't block his calls.' Finally, she left. She was hysterical. That was the word.

Lillian was at the Chelsea and Westminster that evening. There were disturbing words in her head, sentences and phrases that circled like birds, and broke away, and left her unsettled, but when she stepped into his room and she saw her father sitting on a chair by the bed next to a man in a grey suit with a plump face, a smug face, with very blonde hair, standing beside her, she was wrong-footed.

'Oh,' she said.

'Lillian! You're back already!'

'I wanted to see you. Hello,' she said to the stranger.

'Lilly, this is Mr Shevchenko. Mr Shevchenko is being very helpful.'

'Hello, Lillian. This is distressing, but there's no danger for your father. We'll all get through this.' Mr Shevchenko offered Lilly a moist hand. 'You're as fragrant as the flower of your name,' he said. 'My favourite flower. Symbol of purity.'

Lillian took his hand, ignored the waffle, and looked at her father. 'Madelaine said the house is already up for sale.'

'Madelaine? She came back?'

'She came for her things. It's not true is it, Daddy?'

Mr Shevchenko interrupted. 'Should I give you a minute?' he asked.

'Thank you, Ivan.'

Mr Shevchenko left on soft feet.

'I didn't know,' Lillian said. 'I felt like an idiot.'

'It's not so simple as that. It's fluid, Lillian.'

'But what about my stuff? Where will we live?'

'Sit down, Sweetie.' Lillian sat on the bed. Only the pain in her father's eyes stopped her from creasing her face. He sat next to her. 'These temporary difficulties – I can't cope with them just now. I feel so bad about it, Randa. When I get out of here – I'm making progress – I may need to go away for a few days, to meet some people and have a rest. When I do, it's possible to deal with the liquidity problem, in the short-term at least, by renting the house. That's one option. Do you see?'

'But where would I live?'

'Exactly! That's what I'm working on.'

Lillian bowed her head and sighed much of her anger into Chelsea. She was deflated like an old balloon.

'Why didn't you tell me?' she asked.

'I'm not myself, Lilly. I wanted to organise it without having to worry you.'

Lillian trusted her father, no daughter a parent more, but even she knew this was not entirely satisfactory. When she saw the misery in his dropped mouth, the unfamiliar tone of defeat, however, she could not bring herself to remonstrate further.

'I suppose,' she said, 'we could simply downsize – get a little flat in a suburb.'

'In due course. There is another option.'

'I come with you?'

'Lillian!' He clenched his hands and he crunched up his face. His words were squeezed out as though they hurt him, each one. 'It's business. These new people – it isn't suitable, Randa.'

Lillian looked at her father in wonder. Who were these mysterious people that determined what she did in the next weeks, or even for life?'

'I'll be all right, Daddy,' she said. 'We're the Delphs. I can stay in the house until it's rented and then stay with someone – with Chloe – not her, with Maria – and I'll get a job.'

'I want you to be with people who are invested, Lillian,' he said.

'I don't know what you mean.'

'What about the Goodmans?'

'The Goodmans?'

'Aunt Jenny seems a very nice person.'

'The Goodmans?'

'They'd welcome you. Of how many others can that be said?'

'You want me to stay with strangers?'

'Only for a couple of weeks. Three weeks tops.'

It was hard to know if he had lost his senses under the pressure or knew things of which she had better be innocent. She would calm him.

'Don't be silly, Daddy,' she answered lightly. 'They live in the north.'

'Not in all of it.'

Lillian had been to Oxford twice, and three times to Stansted. She knew what urban decline was. They had done the industrial revolution in Geography, or History, whatever, and she'd watched *Happy Valley* with Sarah Lancashire because a teacher had said it was excellent, so she was not entirely ignorant of the north, and what she knew was not encouraging. It was like Slough, but without the ethnic diversity.

'But they're all poor.' It was a long way from London. 'They'll feed me take-aways. I'll get fat.' She laughed. It was not a happy laugh.

'They're not all poor,' Edward countered. 'Your mother's family were loaded.'

Lillian frowned. 'You're serious?'

'It's a trip to the sea-side.'

Lillian bounced off the bed and strode to the window. 'I can't believe this is happening.'

'Oh, Lillian. Lillian, I'm sorry.'

Lillian heard again the croak in his voice, an animal sound. 'Don't cry, Daddy!'

'Forgive me.'

A nurse appeared at the door. 'Is everything all right?' she asked.

'Yes. Yes, sorry. Is Monica around?'

'She's on her break. I can ask her to look in when she's back.'

'That would be lovely.' The nurse gave Lillian an appraising glance. Edward waited on her exit. 'Lillian, please, come here.' She stood over him. He took both her hands. 'I've done a silly thing, Randa. But the last thing I want is for you to be inconvenienced. I need to know you're strong, and you're all right. Then I'll get better.' .

The strangeness of it all gave Lillian a thick head. 'I'll think about it,' she said. 'But I want to stay in London.'

'I know you do, Randa. But perhaps the best way to get that long-term is to leave for a while.'

Her voice was weary. 'What about my card?' she asked.

'Oh, yes, that. God, I almost forgot. There's money in that drawer by the bed. That will tidy you until it's sorted.'

'Cash?'

'Yes, Lilly, cash. It's old fashioned, but it works.'

There was something humiliating about taking notes from a drawer. It was like the pocket money she was given as a child. 'Is it there?' her father asked.

'A hundred pounds.'

'Some people have to live on that for a week,' Daddy said. He stood. 'Give me a hug.'

They had a nice hug. He was in pyjamas, and he had not shaved, but he still smelt like her father.

'I have to talk to Mr Shevchenko,' he said. 'Then I must try and sleep.'

'I'll come in the morning, Daddy.'

'That's my girl. I hate you to see me like this. I just want you safe.'

'Oh, Daddy!'

'We'll sort it. Are you eating?'

'I'm starving. I didn't have lunch.'

'I think there's some rib-eye in the fridge.'

'Goody gumdrops,' she said without enthusiasm.

She had her bag on her shoulder and her hand on the door, but she had to show him she was strong. 'Daddy, I don't know what's happening, but I'll do what it takes to get things normal again. Don't worry about me. I can put up with things. I can live in a little room. I did at school. And I can cook. And I can organise things. But I'm going to do Paris. I really want to do Paris. I'll die if I can't do Paris.' It was one of the longest speeches of her life.

He looked her in the face. 'You will do Paris,' he said.

The nurse who had come in gave her another look as she marched out, but Lillian did not care. She was sad, but no longer angry, and when she heard her name called, she did not start or frown, but accepted her sound of her name in this strange place as in keeping with the unreal temper of the time. Mr Shevchenko stood above her.

'I'm sorry we meet in such circumstances,' he said. 'I don't think Edward has mentioned me, has he?'

'No.'

'There was never any need. How are you bearing up?' Lillian thought it was impertinent of him to enquire, but she was getting beyond insult. 'We're doing all we can to get him back on his feet.'

''We'?'

'His recent associates. Would you accept something from me?' He held out notes. 'This is an unstructured loan. Pay back what you can in your own time.'

Lillian looked at him with an open mouth.

'Why?'

'There's a bit of re-structuring to do, business-wise, but you come first, Lillian. You are your father's top priority. I want you to think well of me.'

'Who are you?' she asked.

'I'm in real estate,' he answered. 'Do you need this?'

Lillian actually did, but she wasn't going to let this stranger into any secrets between her daddy and her.

'I don't think I should,' she said.

If Mr Shevchenko was offended, he didn't show it. He nodded gravely.

'I understand,' he said. 'But take it. You can give it back if you're still ashamed in the morning.' Lillian took it in wonder. 'May I wish you the best?' He offered his hand for the second time. His grip was firmer this time. She watched him until the lift doors closed. He was as smooth as cream, but there was something about him that made Lillian think he'd be happiest if she was thrown onto landfill and burned.

The next blow was not the most important, but it was perhaps the most cruel.

Maria telephoned. Lillian was finishing the rib-eye and wiped her fingers on the paper towel before picking up. It felt grown-up to cook for herself at home. And she had done something for the first time. She had opened one of daddy's wines. The process of cooking and the food and the merlot, the solid proportions of the house and its familiar things, had reassured her. This, surely, could not pass away.

'Maria!' she said, almost cheerful.

'My god, Lillian. Is it true?'

'What?'

'Are you all right?'

'Yes.' Had the world gone mad?

'You're dad's in hospital?'

'It's not serious. How did you know?'

'Chloe.' She said the name like a bullet shot. 'She's telling everyone.'

'Is she concerned?'

'Have you spoken to her?'

'Not since this morning. Oh.' She remembered her father's injunction.

'She says we should be careful of you.'

'Sorry?'

'She's such a bitch. I always thought she was bad for you.'

'But what's she said?'

The sentence was sobering. 'Your dad's involved with the mafia.' Lillian was speechless.

'What?' She sat open-mouthed. 'What the fuck!' Lillian did not swear. She was shocked at herself. 'Why would she do that?'

'She likes the drama of it. Are you sure you're all right?'

'You don't believe it!'

'I never really believe anything Chloe says.'

'What do the others say?'

'I don't think they take it seriously. Annabelle got in touch with me and agreed Chloe had crossed the line, but she sort of thought it was a joke. I think it's so harsh to say something like that when your dad's not well.'

Daddy was right. The Tengku-Watkins had turned nasty.

'My god.'

Chloe was prone to exaggeration. Everyone knew that. That was why they treated her tales as entertainment value. The veracity was a secondary issue. This was different. This was more than catty. This was worse than rude. This was malice.

'Didn't anyone stand up for me?'

Maria did not reply straight away. That was discouraging. 'Maria?'

'You know what they're like.' Lillian wasn't sure she did. 'I think it brightens up their safe tiny lives.'

Lillian knew little of the evils of the world. But she knew the dangers of young ladies like her. She had seen enough backs turned on the unwanted, and she suspected the worst. They had seen her card fail. Her father wasn't at work. Chloe had reported her father's words about

Edward and fraud before slipping her Judas arm through hers. She was out of the set.

'I don't believe it,' she said.

'I shalln't have anything more to do with them,' Maria said.

'Thank you, Maria.'

'Why don't we meet up?'

'What? Oh, yes, Come over.'

'I can't tonight. Baby-sitting. Tomorrow?'

They would meet in the morning on Clapham Common where Maria walked her dog.

Lillian slumped in her chair. What would she do, with whom could she go to the cinema, if her friends had turned? What had she ever done to any of them? The unfairness burned her cheeks. She poured more wine and paced the room, glass in hand, alone.

There was something she might try. She took her father's laptop from the study, but she did not have the password. Perhaps it was written down somewhere. She rummaged through his drawers. This was the naughtiest thing she'd ever done in the house. She took a few gulps for courage. Twenty minutes later she realised she was drunk, and nothing was achieved. The office could be tidied in the morning. She darted into her bedroom, a place of comfort, and flicked through Contacts. In desperation she considered calling William, but he would be out with his friends, or a new girlfriend and he wasn't much use at moral support, and, looking through the list, there were no others, except a teacher perhaps, who might say the right thing, but how could she telephone a teacher with a husband and children and say that daddy was in trouble?

Lillian was popular because she didn't do demands. She swigged once more. She clumped downstairs. Daddy under pressure sometimes had a snifter. Daddy would knock back the snifter and thump the glass down and do an exaggerated sigh of pleasure. She would have a snifter. The whiskey was at the back of the drinks' cabinet, and she knocked over a bottle of something to get it, but, never mind, in the morning, all done in the morning, in the morning the world would reboot. She leaned against the fridge and knocked it back, then coughed, spluttered, was almost sick, put her hands on the island, did deep breaths, then was sick. The kitchen sink could not be left for morning, but when it was rinsed she staggered upstairs. She lay prone on her back helpless to stop her world's dissolution and fell asleep.

She had a hangover like death. She did not remember getting undressed. She crouched on the loo with her hands over the back of her head and swore she would never drink again. She wobbled downstairs in her dressing-gown and took Pellegrino from the fridge, but the top was too tight. She rammed it back and drank a tumbler of tap water. She burped. She drank again. She groaned, took a third glass, and hoisted herself back to bed.

There was blissful sunshine when she woke. The linen duvet, pastel pink, almost mauve, gleamed like a rose in Eden. The time on her watch roused her. 10:30 and Daddy not visited. Then she recalled Maria. She had to rearrange Maria. She made Nescafé. She was lowering her standards, but these were not normal times. She would not, however, compromise on making her bed. Science showed that successful people are the ones who make beds, though she wasn't sure if it counted with duvets. Whatever. Lillia made her bed. She made her bed first thing every morning.

The malice against her father was outrageous. She knew this as she tidied the kitchen. One day's clues meant nothing. She had only seen him with respectable men. He had made money, and he had travelled, but he had never gone to Russia, and he had only worked for viable clients. No rumour had ever wafted among their set, nor tainted the school corridors. Her face hardened as she thought of Chloe and her betrayal.

She would go and tell him he was right. Chloe's family were vulgar, and gossips.

The phone beeped. It was not a normal beep. She stared at the screen in confusion. She had one unread message which was from the company that said the service was disabled, which made no sense, so she phoned again and got the same weird beep, so now she knew something was wrong.

She had no mobile.

And if she had no mobile -

She dashed upstairs to her computer as though it was a poorly child. She went through the menu. She re-booted. She checked the leads and, lacking all connectivity, she panicked. She did the yoga breathing, but though it helped a little, it offered no practical end. On whom could she call? Then the landline sounded.

The listened with dread. They did not use the landline. They'd stopped using the landline to avoid cold callers when she went into Year 10. She had not even known that it worked. Why would it sound the moment her mobile was dead? She looked at it in the hall from the top of the stairs as though an evil spirit inhabited it. It stopped. She crept by it surreptitiously and took a bowl from the cupboard. Then it sounded again.

This was beyond weird.

There was only one thing to do. The Chelsea and Westminster was just the same this Saturday morning as yesterday, but illness knew no timetable. She scampered out of the lift to her father's room, but the nurse who'd come in yesterday turned to her.

'You've come for your father?' she asked.

'Yes. Yes, how is he?'

'He's sleeping.'

'I have to talk to him.'

'I'll tell him when he wakes up.'

'But I want to talk to him now!' Lillian insisted.

'I'm afraid...' the nurse started, and to finish splayed out her hand as though introducing an unexpected guest. A policeman rose from a chair outside her father's room. 'No visitors just now, miss,' the policeman said.

'But I need to know something.'

'Would you like to speak to a doctor?' the nurse asked.

'No. I want to talk to my daddy!'

Her wail cut into the solid routine of the ward. Reception looked at her. A man with a trolley looked back. The nurse, however, was unmoved.

'We've taken your father off medication to see how he fares and it's very important he gets rest and isn't upset. The sooner he's back to his old self, the sooner he can help you.'

Lillian realised she was being told off. Her mouth opened. Then it closed. She stood, in her fabulous pink trainers and the shirt with the hoodie; another spoiled Chelsea teenager making a fuss.

'If you're really in difficulty I can give you the Social Services number.'

'Social Services?'

'They can step in if you need help. How old are you?'

'Eighteen.'

'Ah. You could try. I can find someone for you to talk to.'

'No. It's just that I've no connectivity.'

'I see,' the nurse said coldly. It was so unfair her father was not in a private ward where they'd understand the importance of such a thing. 'He might wake up soon. We can let you know if you wish to wait.'

'No, I've just said – I'm sorry. I'll come back.'

It was beyond ridiculous. She checked the time as she turned north out of the doors. She should now be meeting Maria. Maria was the only one who had been in the least sympathetic, and now she was waiting with her dog on Clapham Common, and Lillian not there. She could imagine the conversation. 'I was to meet her, but she's not turned up and I can't get in touch with her, and there's no message or anything. There's definitely something going on.' Who else was there? She thought of William again, but that was a minefield best walked round, and given a good birth to boot. Lillian was alone in the world.

She felt the quiet of her home upon her. The computer still did not respond. The password wobbled like an idiot. She crept down the stairs and put her hand on the landline receiver as though it were the handle of a cupboard behind which a ghost might lurk. Return Call was 9. She pressed 9.

'Thank goodness,' Aunt Jenny said. 'I've had such a to do! I can't get in touch you or your father. I'm sure it's my end. I don't have much luck with technology. He telephoned me last night. He's in hospital.'

Lillian knew he was in hospital.

'He wanted me to check you were all right, but unfortunately I'm heading back up north. I'm on the train. There, I said it. Listen, he asked –'

'How did you get this number?'

'That was very lucky. I asked your mother, and she got back and said to try this one, and it worked. When you didn't answer, I thought it wouldn't. But it did. Has your father spoken to you today?'

Lillian had never considered that Aunt Jenny would have her mother's number. But they were cousins, so why not, and that was not important now.

'He's asleep. You see, the thing is, I've no connectivity and then there's no card. I don't want to trouble you. I've got about a hundred and thirty pounds.' Her voice broke. She hated that her voice broke.

'Lillian, calm down,' Aunt Jenny said. 'We won't let anything bad happen. Now, tell me the whole thing.'

So Lillian Miranda Delph, hearing kind words when she most had need of kindness, told a stranger called Jennifer Goodman whom she'd met for only the second time in the Victoria and Albert Museum yesterday that her father was in hospital and in trouble and they had no money and she was all alone in the world as in a dark wood like Gretel, though she omitted the actual comparison. Jennifer Goodman had a solution.

'You must come and stay with us for a few days.'

'I couldn't possibly go up there.'

'Lillian, that's what your father wants.'

'Are you sure?'

'That why he rang me. He said, 'If it's necessary, please would you take care of Lillian for a few days until I'm back on my feet?' That was the very expression. Now it is necessary. He says he'll know then that you're safe.'

Lillian was surprised at her own response. At the bottom of her anger, and stress, and her lashed pride, was relief, The relief was not a cathartic experience. It lay like a sea fret creeping up the stark sides of a cliff, fragile, ephemeral, but the most arresting feature in view. Her faith was tested, but not broken. If she followed instructions, however tiresome, things would work out.

'Oh, all right.' She could not force the resentment and defeat from her voice, but that wasn't important now. 'How do I do that?'

It was a ticket from King's Cross and a packed bag. The rest was in the hands of others. She surrendered. She had no options.

That was how Lillian Miranda Delph of South Kensington, eighteen, ended up in the north at the seaside.

Chapter 3

Past Gordon's Crag where eagles perched, through mist along the blasted heath where sheep stood like ancient things, a man walked solitary with an assertive chin and a propulsive swing of his arms. He wore a long black coat and a black hat with a brim and his beard was wet from the damp air, though he took the stone path with its muck patches, its turns, its spaces, and its drops, and he turned at the forks, with the confidence of one who knew its barren indifference as a black cab driver knows Knightsbridge. He ploughed out of the gloom, a bursting spectre, over Dark Ridge in view of the white-wreathed Redberry Topping into the view of a couple huddled in cagoules by the wall at the descent to the mount, and he did not slow, but called, 'You going up Topping?'

Their faces were white moons in their tight black hoods.

'Take the broad path left,' he advised. 'Slip on the steep one yonder and you'll break your leg,' he explained with relish.

He took the short path through the field where six cows lay under the shelter of the single oak in a circle, happily burping methane into the ozone. He gave them a salute in benediction, for a beast brought from cool pasture to this grim place needed all the help it could get. His stride neither slowed nor gathered pace on the well-laid path down through Gorborough Woods where the big ferns and mosses hid behind every hue of green the little strange things that thrived in their dank world. He nodded to a party climbing the slope with conscientious straight backs, a party of regular modest trekkers out for health and good humour, and strode on without altering his gait, and approached the shed surrounded by trees at the end of the path; a large shed, with large windows, and thick wooden tables outside, green like the leaves, a shelter in a child's story from which a woodsman might dash to save the innocent from wolves.

He burst in. Unstained wood tables and chairs; a cooler with soft drinks; a long counter in the gloom. He stood in silhouette against the doorway and heard a clatter of cups locked into a dishwasher, then saw as the gloom cleared a slim woman turn and regard him. She wiped the counter while he took a seat at the table, draping his canvas bag over the back of the chair and dropped his hat on the table with a swagger. He thrust his hands in his black coat and sat back with proprietorial stillness.

'You want anything?' the thin woman asked.

'Tea,' he answered. 'Yorkshire tea. Strong Yorkshire tea, two bags, and milk, full fat, hot water on the side and, by God, I want it soon. It's an insult to summer out there on the moors and I need an appropriate bevvy.'

'Yes, Mr Heathcliffe. Two pounds twenty.'

'How much!'

'You heard.'

'Don't I get a discount?'

'No, you don't get a bloody discount.'

He sighed. Then he looked round the room with exaggerated care, shielding his eyes. 'Busy today then?'

The waitress turned to prepare his tea. 'I thought Jesus was with you,' she said.

'Jesus? On the moors? Think flocks of sheep.'

'Oh, yes.' She poured boiled water into the pot. 'Would you like anything with this? A scone? Carrot cake? We have some soup if you prefer the healthy option.'

'Your scones are rocks, your carrot cake stinks and your soup is the brew of the devil,' he answered.

'I'll take that as a 'no'.' She brought tea, milk and mug over on a tray. 'Move your hat,' she said. He moved his hat. She placed the tray down with a bob. 'Enjoy,' she finished.

He thought about this. 'Is that in the subjunctive or the imperative sense?'

'I don't know what that means.'

He poured milk in the mug. 'I shall do my best in either case.'

'I don't suppose you checked your texts?'

'Texts! On the moor? The moor is a wild and a lonely place. There ain't no reception out on the moor!'

'You forgot it, then.'

'I was de-toxifying modernity.'

She brought over the water in a stainless-steel pot and sat opposite him.

'She wants to talk about something.'

He was serious. 'The Thing of Darkness is moving out?'

She shook her head. 'No. The Thing of Darkness wants Yorkshire puddings. Can you get some? As you're *not working* today.'

'He can get his own Yorkshires.'

'He's doing a sunset on the cliffs.'

'What's that to the purpose?'

'You know what he's like!'

'A sunset.' The man looked pointedly out of the window at the rolling grey clouds beyond the trees.

'There you go,' she said. 'She's excited about something.'

'Mother? It's probably the caravan site.'

'The what?'

'New counsel proposals. On the hill beyond the Gardens. She was quite aerated about it.'

'No. I think she's found another one.'

He raised his eyes again.

'Someone she met in London. Our cousin once-removed.'

He poured the tea and clasped the mug in both hands, then blew out his cheeks. 'Oh, mother, what have you done?' he exclaimed. 'Is this long-lost kin likely to -?'

'No idea.'

'I expect we'll find out tonight.'

'Anyway, you're warned,' she said and returned to the counter as the door opened. 'And Dave wants to talk to you.'

'He wants your freedom.' The waitress was blank. She did not deny it. She did not affirm it. 'He is your advocate such as Ariel never had. This new case – it couldn't be Emily's daughter, could it?'

'How would I know?'

'Well, whoever it is,' he concluded at length, 'Jesus will love them. Note the plural for non-gender singular.'

'Yes. Jesus loves everyone. You're being particularly Saltscar today.'

The two cagoules entered in a flurry of unzipping, rucksack dropping, and the liberation of hair from hoods. The man approached the counter as the woman rummaged through her bag.

'Could we have two lattes, please.'

'Of course.'

'You decided not to try the Topping then?'

They had not noticed black coat at the table by the window. 'Not today,' the man answered. He did not have a local accent. 'The weather's closing in,' he explained and turned pointedly back to the counter.

'Wise choice. The moor's an unforgiving place when the gloom settles in. You on holiday?'

Neither visitor looked eager to answer so the waitress said, 'Four pounds twenty.'

'Four twenty!' Black coat was outraged. 'That's hardly more than my tea.'

'You had two bags.' The waitress spoke softly to the gentleman. 'Ignore him. He's a prat. Take a seat and I'll bring it over.'

The man in the black coat finished his tea in silence. The visitors spoke in murmurs. There was a sense of calm and remoteness and gloom, and when the waitress brought over the lattes the man stood and said, 'I recommend the carrot cake.'

'Thank you,' the woman answered. 'Actually, we're regulars.'

The waitress giggled. Black coat nodded and hoisted his own bag on his shoulder, rammed down his hat and walked past them with a nod and finished, 'Enjoy your coffee anyway.'

'Is that in the subjunctive or imperative sense?' the waitress called after him.

'Either. Or both.' He closed the door and was gone.

The waitress noticed bemusement on the faces of the guests. 'Sorry. My stupid brother,' she exclaimed. It came out with more venom than she'd meant.

The stupid brother thumped homeward towards his mother's news. It was raining again, a rattle among the leaves and the blackening path. He passed the wooden badger and went through the gate with the acorn, then he stepped over the little bridge and up the hill to the housing estate and along to the town centre where he stood disconsolate for a bus. Gosborough with its wide street for the market stalls had that effect on him. This was The North. In the south and the midlands market towns had squares where the denizens loitered and made civil discourse, but in North Yorkshire they presented a single wide street up which the wind ranted like a Calvinist in case anyone was tempted to regard the full stalls more in terms of pleasure than business. He pressed himself tight against the window on the bus like a homeless child in a warm shop entrance, but as it came into Saltscar the sun blasted through like a song from God or at least a Bach chorale so he took an early stop to walk for the millionth time through the town he loved not wisely but too well and even turned onto High Prom to once more make his ancient shout of discovery, the cry of fishermen through the ages.

The sun had brought out the people like the speech of birds after rain, and the white horses laughed onto the sand.

Thalassa!

A man awaited in the Italian Garden. It was a long oval cut out of the wooded west side of the valley, fringed with shrubs and benches that looked onto the formal layout in the centre. He had long scorned these Victorian grandiosities, ghosts of fake gentility, just as he felt when he heard the drone from the bandstand on summer Sundays. As a young man beset by practical affairs, he better understood this dream of reason. Nevertheless, his eyes were upward where a cavalry of cloud with plumes of dove-feather drove from the west over the trees into the blue.

'David,' he greeted his new acquaintance. 'Am I late?'

'Not by much.' David pointed at coat's head. 'Loving the hat,' he said.

He removed said hat and regarded the brim. 'It's made from the pelt of a kangaroo. They cull them so I don't feel guilty.'

'That is so Saltscar!'

'I was in full moor-mode recently.' He took possession of a bench. 'I entertained my sister at her lonely vigil at the Walking Centre café.'

'How was she?'

'You don't know?'

'Don't be defensive.'

Ferdy, the black coat, sighed and sat next to his old mucker and his sister's aspirant lover, on the bench. He lodged the cap of contention on his knees.

'I'm looking for jobs in London,' Dave said.

'Good for you.'

'I want Anne-Marie to come with me.'

'I see. This is an ambush?'

'No. Anne-Marie hasn't said Yes. She hasn't said No.'

The ramifications of Dave's ambition were obvious to both. 'I'm not surprised,' Ferdy said. 'Why London?'

'Opportunities, Ferdy.' He flickered with irritation. 'You know why London, Ferdy!'

'The shop's a family decision, Dave,' he protested.

'Anne-Marie isn't family?'

Ferdinand threw out his arms. 'She's a quarter of it.'

'Who happens to be right.'

Ferdinand sighed again. 'It's only until I'm up and running,' he said. 'Less than a year. I'll be here forever, at least until mum isn't around. I just need enough to keep me here.'

'You can't ask it of her, Ferdy.'

'Of course not. So this is a warning, not an ambush?'

'It's more the frank and honest discussion between old friends.'

'Yes, and thus it is. I had a glorious childhood,' he announced. It would rain again. Water had already arrowed the estuary and soon the innocent would scamper from the sands into the refuge of arcade and café. 'There was the beach every evening, and books in the house, and dad's stories that entranced us, and a sister who taught me to study, and a mother who produced food like magic each day, and school friends were plenty, and I barely remember a frightening or envious word. It took me a while to realise why I was so unsettled everywhere else. It's not only the sea. I know she's leaving, Dave. One day you two will be a complete unit. I have to stay here.'

'You won't if you throw all your money away.'

'I'll find someone to help me.'

'Good luck with that!'

Ferdinand had no resentment, but he had gloom. 'Anne-Marie would find it a doddle. But she hates the place.'

'You know that's not true. She just doesn't see a future here!'

The dog was called. There were three splashes and a crash of undergrowth and an encouraging command. Children's cries rose like spray from the play area near the beach. The valley was a safe and a gentle place.

'I know I'm not a shop-keeper,' Ferdinand admitted, 'but I'll give it a go.'

Ferdinand was a stout and hairy man. David was more slender and more smooth. He looked younger and sounded senior. 'There's nothing definite,' Dave said.

Ferdy sighed, then blew out his cheeks. and laughed. 'Anne-Marie says there's two clientele: the day visitors and the north Yorkshire commuters. She says I'll fall between the two of them.'

David's silence was an implied sympathy with the views of Anne-Marie. Ferdy knew that, and he stood. David looked at him with his legs stretched and his hands in his pockets.

'If in a year it's losing money, I shall tell mother to sell,' Ferdy answered. 'Anne-Marie will get her share, work on it or not.'

Dave finally looked fondly on his old mate. 'You're too noble for business, Ferdy,' he said.

'No, just a bit rubbish. Any road, the shop is actually mum's. Come on, let's walk.'

The two dropped down to the stream that ran along the tracks of the miniature railway to the sea. Their past alliance, their shared dreams and plans, their discovery of what they might be, seemed to Ferdinand to be tangled in the branches, lodged on the puckered holly leaves, rendered in the chuckles of the stream, so when they arrived on the broader valley floor it was like stepping from a dangerous enchantment to the everyday world of balance sheets and stock and timetables. Dogs on the green sprang for no reason over the grass, chased each other, crouched, jumped up and spun, came panting back to their owners. They gambolled in the land of magic. David glanced across.

'The simple pleasures of the poor,' he said

They were stopped by Margery and her fat labradors. The hounds, like their owner, were ancient and slow of limb. Dave remembered Margery. It was not certain Marjorie remembered Dave. She made her enquiries about the family.

'And Frank? Is he still...?'

'He is indeed,' Ferdy said.

'I do so admire what your mother has done.'

Ferdy spread out his arms. 'Family,' he said. 'Thicker than water.'

'The Robinson's were telling me.'

'Give them my regards.'

Margery turned slowly away and then, with a thought, turned only a little less slowly back. 'Oh yes, I meant to say, Chomski has given a new lecture - at the University of South Carolina of all places. He is still maintaining the innateness of language, and that his linguistic theories have no logical connection to his democratic anarchism, which I find rather irritating, though it's remarkable how he continues. He must be in his eighties.'

'Age cannot wither him,' said Ferdy. 'Nor custom stale his infinite variety.'

'I wouldn't have thought,' Dave butted in, 'infinite variety is in Chomski's make-up. He is remarkable for consistency of thought.'

'That's my view,' said Margery. 'But I must be getting on. The dogs are booked in for grooming.'

'How will she get up the hill?' Dave asked as Margery and hounds waddled away.

'She leaves her motorised scooter at the Garden Café.'

'Why is a woman of her age and circumstance worrying about Chomski?'

'What should she worry about?'

'Her dogs. They're obese.'

'Chomski doesn't make them obeser.'

'You really are the Saltscar Warden. It's remarkable to think she was once our mentor. She sent me on a false trail, from which it took me a year to return.' They stepped towards the big sky over the sea.

'Thalassa,' Ferdinand said for the second time.

'It's aggravating that all think Saltscar's so wonderful.'

'You thought so once.'

'Then I grew up.'

The cloud had not yet conquered Moor Cliff. Its fields, the last yellows of summer, glistened like a banner on a fort. Under the rumble of the cars, the sea shushed its disquiet. Ferdy waved at the Thai waitress who smiled back at the café by the road. He made her laugh.

He saw the tumbling clouds charge at the rusty blade of Moor Cliff. But it's all about love, he thought. Nothing without love.

'I only ask, you don't keep pressing my sister with financial sense,' he said. 'She can do that herself. Yours is an affair of the heart.'

'So is yours.'

'And so is hers.'

They wound up the bank and crossed the wide road past the Marlborough Hotel with its Disney turrets and gleaming pale brick and along Milton Street to the cell. Dave stared at the long sign above the lintel in old-fashioned script: Prosper-oh. The whitewash on the windows was still not cleared, but through them he saw a long bar along a side wall, stools against it, and behind an array of empty shelves. Packed stock was stacked against the opposite wall.

'The edifice of contention,' Ferdinand said. 'This cell's my court. Here I have few attendants. Shall we go in?'

'The rain is due. Let's get back.'

Ferdy saw the thickening cloud. Dave was beginning to weary him. His mind tugged away like a lost kite.

'I'm working on getting our-up-and-coming poet to make it her writing centre. I'll have comfortable chairs, and workshops, and exhibitions, and other marvels of such kidney.'

David sighed in sympathy for his old schoolmate. 'That's your USP?'

'Unappreciated Special Person?'

'You know what it means.'

The rain came. It spattered at them like a rebuke. Now the two old friends were silent. 'Just in time.' Dave resumed, regarding the rain. 'I have to go. I'll be soaked.'

'Indeed not!' Ferdy barked in triumph. 'Look here.' He darted into the shop, unlocking it deftly, disappeared in the gloom and returned with two umbrellas. He opened one to display a print of Starry Night. 'If these do not make my fortune,' he said, 'then the defecation of bears will be non-arboreal.'

'This is your stock? Up-market kitsch?'

'Just because they are popular doesn't mean they are bad.'

Dave took it and laughed. 'A loan or a gift or a transaction?'

'As you like,' Ferdy said.

'You know what your business partner will say?'

'I do. Are you staying at the house?'

'I'm taking Anne-Marie to the Hall, then going back. I believe you have a family conference?'

'We do indeed.'

'I'll see her after. Give Jesus a pat from me.'

'He will enjoy that.'

He opened the other umbrella, unabashed. The moist-lipped face of Girl With An Ear Ring rose like a spirit. 'When you see one of these in London you will eat your words.'

He opened the door to a clattering of paws; mother, father, son. The comfort of dog after a difficult day! He rubbed and patted as needed and sent them off to their diverse beds in the recesses of the house and climbed the stairs. His swagger had gone. He knocked with a flat hand on the door at the end of the long landing and entered though no invitation had been offered. A man crouched over a keyboard; the blind was down; the glow of the screen outlined his indistinct form. He did not look up.

'Have you heard from mum?'

The computer man still did not look up. 'Spoke this morning.'

'And?'

'Hold on.' He made an adjustment. 'Bingo!' he whispered and finally turned. He was not a handsome man. Nor was he hideous. The computer light etched a thin face that was

79

grooved, but brilliant-eyed, an image of the proud and beleaguered, a figure locked away among the rubble of his own things; a column of books in the corner, canvasses piled between bed and window, clothes crumpled on the duvet and unpacked cardboard boxes making problematic the journey from door to computer.

'Yup. She's met someone.'

'Any ideas?'

'Some spoiled little bitch from London I gather.' He chuckled.

'Right.' This was resigned. 'I'll take the dogs. I'll get some Yorkshires on the way back.'

'Good man.'

He returned after a few steps along the landing. 'I thought you were on the cliffs today?'

'In this weather!'

'Good point. 'I'm in the Cell later if you wish to bring down some prints.'

'As you like.'

He left The Dark Knight to his arcane art and trundled down the steps and called the dogs. Let me have men about me that are fat, he prayed. The dogs twisted round his ankles as he dispatched the leads from the hooks by the door. Unless she's a tough one, he mused, the monsters up here will wreck mum's latest stray, should that be the plan. The uncomplicated dogs pulled him into the dampened air. 'On, bacons,' he trumpeted and stepped out.

The family conference did not last long. Jennifer Goodman ruled them all with absent-minded benevolence. It was her house. Anne-Marie had virtually left, the Thing of Darkness was practically a dependent and Ferdy was compliant. 'She's your cousin once-removed,' Jennifer announced. 'Emily's child.'

'Ah!' Ferdy sighed in modest triumph. Anne-Marie looked grave.

'Her father's in hospital and in serious trouble. She needs some of our wholesome air.'

Frank grunted as he rolled a cigarette. Anne-Marie sat on the sofa arm. She looked ready to leave. Ferdy leaned over and tickled Joseph's stomach.

'Metaphorical or actual?' he asked.

'It is an interregnum,' Jennifer said.

'I remember her,' Ferdy mused. 'She was a charming child.'

'I think I do,' Anne-Marie added. 'Skinny little kid. Posh. Helpless.'

'Champion,' grunted The Thing of Darkness and licked his paper.

'We need to nurse her through it until she goes to college.'

Anne-Marie raised a hand. 'No, mum. We need to give her somewhere to stay until her dad's on his feet and sorts out their own place. Let's keep it practical. And if she expects me to do her washing, I'll slap her.'

'Is she sexy?' Frank asked.

'Don't be misogynist, Frank,' Jennifer reproved.

'Don't be a dick,' added Anne-Marie.

'Just considering the photo-opportunities,' Frank explained.

'She liked Gus.' Ferdy said. 'That bodes well.'

'And everyone loves Jesus,' his mother answered. 'Jesus loves everyone. Mary and Joseph will probably ignore her. She liked Gus, yes, though that was over ten years ago. The father seems to have had his assets frozen so he's doubtless part of an international crime-syndicate. It is rather exciting.'

'Jesus!' said Anne-Marie. It brought the pad of paws along the hallway. 'So she has no money! We're supporting her!'

'The liquidity problem is temporary. They call it 'liquidity' for some reason. It means money. We can at least afford to feed her.'

'She has no friends in London?' Ferdy asked.

'Bugger off, Jesus,' Anne-Marie said as he poked his head round the door. He padded in and curled up next to Joseph.

'You know what Londoners are like,' Jenny retorted.

They knew what Londoners were like. Into the silence that followed Jennifer expounded on the plight of the innocent, the sea-air and its virtues, the minor expense and the duties of family and the feasible help that Lillian Miranda could offer. Ferdinand pondered. She had met her. She was sharp and beautiful and very polite. His mother was appeasing, not persuading, because her mind was made up, though she asked Frank what he felt: ('It's your house,' he answered) and then Anne-Marie: ('Against, but it's too late, mum, isn't it?') and finally Ferdy, who sighed.

'It is an honour that I dreamed not of.'

Anne-Marie raised her hand again. 'And Emily?' she asked. There was silence. Aunt Jenny held her mouth open in thought, but her daughter prompted. 'Well? Does she know?'

'It was unavoidable.' Jennifer said. 'I had to ask her for their house number.'

'Does *she* know that?'

'She thought Emily was in Australia.'

'No, then.'

'She wasn't wrong,' said Ferdy.

'Mum?' Anne-Marie asked, as a warning. 'What are you playing at?'

'No-one's playing anything, Anne-Marie. There's no 'game' in that nefarious sense. Not in the least. Of course, if Lillian were to ask about her, then obviously I'd give honest answers, and we don't need to excuse ourselves if, one day, you know ... But there's no plan.'

'We ought to set a time-limit, 'appen,' said Frank.

'If Emily wants her, Emily can keep her, surely?' Anne-Marie insisted. 'Obvious.'

'Anne-Marie, you're being rebarbative,' her mother admonished.

'I don't know what 'rebarbative' means.'

Ferdy interrupted. "It seems to me it's just what Saltscar needs,' he said. 'A skinny posh metropolitan elitist whose life is in ruins. Perhaps she'll transform our little world like Rosalind the Forest of Arden. Or perhaps she'll rave. Perhaps we'll have to chase after her along the cliff path so she doesn't become an Incident. There are many Gothic possibilities.'

'Shit,' said Anne-Marie.

'She's a sensible down-to-earth girl. I could tell,' said Jenny.

'That will be dramatic, won't it, Jesus? A liberal elitist Goth?'

Jesus wagged his tail once.

Jenny noted that. 'She can have Ferdy's room,' she said. 'Though we'll have to keep the dogs out. Anne-Marie can share with me. Or she could have your room, Anne-Marie-'

Anne-Marie stood. 'No way,' she said. 'She can share my home for a while, but she's not having my bed! She can have the air-bed and be grateful.'

'No need,' said Ferdy. 'I rather like the air bed. It's romantic.'

'That's settled then,' said Jenny. 'And I'm sure she won't rave. She's a suppresser. Like her mother.'

He left the holiday crowd with their games and their screams and their fish and chips and strode, dogless but with purpose, over the burn which splayed into the sea towards the rocky fringes where Moor Cliff ended the yellow curve of the bay. It was a cool and bright evening that brought out the red of the cliff and turned the sea electric. Kitty-Wakes flickered and glided over the unbreaking waves. Ferdinand Goodman found himself a seat of a rock with edges smooth as sea-glass. He drank in the rhythm of the plop of waves and took a long fill and sky and sea and felt at home.

Lillian Wottayoucalled.

He remembered her. There was no face or gesture, no ring of voice. There was nothing he could place, but there was a feeling: comfort, touched with gravity. What is it that makes one child choose another as a friend? She had sought him out that long summer ago: his was the hand she'd grasped on a busy Low Prom. He had carried her over the pools and washed her grazed knee. That he knew. He had told her stories at night, she whom he could not visualise except as a blur of yellow hair. She had made him know what it was to be trusted, so welcome whatever the reason Wottayoucalled.

She stood on Darlington station with a sense of desolation beyond words. She had queued so long in a dingy café with the silly name Pumpkin she'd given up. The station was no more than a long tunnel with a platform and tracks on each side, which encouraged one to think the town was no place in which to stay and was, in fact, designed solely for leaving, or for passing-through, an anti-town in all but name. It wouldn't surprise her if it wasn't the oldest train station in England, in the world, maybe. She put on her headphones and drew the hood up, though the evening was balmy, and she dragged the wheelie to where her train was due and stared down the line with a concentrated vacancy that discouraged discourse. When a youth offered to help with her wheelie she shrank; her refusal was barely audible. She hoisted it onto the rack in one great heave and pressed herself against the side and folded her arms and sank into the headphones

But the sights within and without confirmed her fears. The sullen passengers were not more sullen, the giggling teenagers not more crass, the spreading men were not more expansive than on the South-East Network, and she could not say there was more obesity, but the absence of style looked absolute. The train, which was hardly a train, more a bus on tracks, jogged past grim rooftops in tight rows, then by straggling industrial plant and stopped at stations with only one sign. After Middlesborough it staggered past a metal landscape of giant tubing, iron cranes as black as despair, mysterious domes like alien beehives, roads that went nowhere, and trundled under filthy brick bridges. She was a reluctant heroine in an apocalyptic computer game. Then it arrived at a name she recognised from Aunt Jenny's text: Rebburn. After the platform there was a white gate that stopped the cars. She'd never seen such a thing before. Cheap houses, identical: one had a flag of St George with This Flag With Pride written on it so it was deep Brexit around here. There were more houses that looked forgotten, some with boards where the windows should be. She remembered from lessons on the Industrial Revolution that there were towns in the north where all the homes had toilets outside. How horrible was that.

Her father was out in two weeks, tops.

The landscape changed. They slid past open fields towards a long low wooded hill and to her left, though it should have been on the right because she was surely going north, she caught an opal flash of sea. Then the engine noise changed, and the recorded voice said they were arriving at Saltscar where this train terminated, and passengers were reminded to take all their belongings. Allotments; more cheap housing, a white fence with pleasant streets off it, a platform, a Sainsbury in pale stone, gilded in the evening light, and so it stopped.

The lady was there to greet her. A hairy man in a yellow t-shirt stood next to her. Behind them was an iron entrance hung with flower-baskets. Beyond that, the station front stood in the same straw brick as the supermarket. It faced a little roundabout with a miniature clock-tower in the middle. A wide road with bus shelters rose gently to the sky on her right. It was dignified and modest and there was a café with plastic tables outside where old people were sitting, a place quite at ease, it seemed, with its own insignificance, and Lillian, approaching her hosts, felt immediately that this was a town in which she would be safely and torturously bored.

'Lillian!' Aunt Jenny beamed. 'Welcome back to Saltscar. The family is dying to meet you.'

Lillian forced a smile. 'Thank you,' she said.

'Ferdy will take your bag. This is your cousin, once-removed.'

The hairy man did not greet her or even offer a hand. He seemed transfixed. Perhaps he was an imbecile.

'I can manage. Thank you.'

'We are literally only a minute away.'

'That's very ... convenient.'

The hairy man took her wheelie. 'Now spurs the lated traveller,' he said.

Aunt Jenny and Lillian ignored this cryptic remark. They left the entrance and turned by the white fence. The wheelie rumbled behind them. 'So,' Aunt Jenny said with force, 'you made it.'

'Yes, I made it.' Lillian Miranda Delph had arrived. She was not happy about it.

She was not the kind of girl who was trafficked, but it would start, had she been, with a person like him. She stood in the hallway with the woman and hairy man behind and three dogs sniffing her legs, while the man leant on her an appraising stare. Her belly shrunk at the fact-absorbing survey of the cold eyes, with the mean thin smile, and his unnatural stillness. His black jacket and combat trousers suggested someone more familiar with throwing things and people around than with proper work in an office. Aunt Jenny was hanging her cotton scarf and telling her not to mind the dogs and did not heed the male gaze upon them until she turned and said, 'This is Lillian, Frank. Here she is.'

'I can't see with the light behind her.'

'Then come down and shake her hand.'

'In due course,' he said, and sloped upstairs.

'Don't mind Frank,' Aunt Jenny said. 'He has Issues. Get down, Jesus.'

The smaller of the three dogs had his front paws on Lillian's hip. He obeyed, but wagged his tail at her. When his tail wagged his bum wagged as well, though not so fast. The darker trotted off and the biggest sat and awaited events with ears cocked.

'Good boy, Joseph,' said Aunt Jenny. 'Come into the sitting room, Lillian, and we'll sort you out.'

The sitting room was unsettling as well. It was not clear where you sat in it. An armchair opposite the window had a book and an empty box on it. A tan sofa by the wall housed Jesus and a pile of cushions like egg yolks and furled knitting. A chair with wooden arms in the bay window looked ready to splinter. There was a side table tucked in a corner behind a standard lamp with an abstract wooden sculpture in front of a vase of sunflowers. One of the two buttery curtains in the bay was closed. There were two lamps on the floor and coats on the sofa arm. The television in the corner was tastelessly large. Lillian had never seen such a disorganised space in her life, unless it was the boy's schoolbag she had once picked up by mistake.

Aunt Jenny threw the knitting and some of the cushions onto the soft toys on the coffee table and sat next to Jesus. Lillian looked around. 'Just throw those things on the floor,' Aunt Jenny said gesturing to a corner chair. Lillian sat upright with the box and the book on her lap. Ferdinand's feet sounded on the stairs.

'It's a very relaxing place, Saltscar,' Aunt Jenny started. 'Do you surf? Of course, the first thing is to sort your phone and your cards. Ask Anne-Marie. She knows about algorithms. I'm more on the artistic side, like Frank and Ferdy. Anne-Marie is sometimes here and sometimes in Newcastle, but Ferdinand is as immovable as the cliff so there you are. Mainly, he's working in our shop. I do work but not on Wednesdays. Frank's mostly in his room or on the beach and the cliffs. He photographs, you see. Well, you must take us as you find us.'

This was a northern expression. It meant they would not excuse their limitations. Lillian thought, what choice do I have, but said, 'Of course.'

'You are family, Lillian. Do you have any food allergies?'

'I don't like it too spicy, that's all.'

'We'll go gentle on the chili. There is one thing. We don't have alcohol in the house. Because of Frank.'

Aunt Jenny said this softly, as though in confidence.

'I don't drink much, anyway. Not at all really,' Lillian answered.

'And are you a night owl or a morning lark?'

'I'm not sure.'

'You can be either of them here. Your room's rather small, but when Anne-Marie leaves you can have hers. You get the sunset from her window.'

Lillian did not mind about the small room.

'And if you want to cry, my darling, you carry on. We're not frightened of emotions.'

The hairy man padded in. 'Your bag's on the bed,' he told Lillian. 'It's rather a small room and it has a draught because the window doesn't close, but it's still summer.'

He settled in the frail chair in the bay. He was too big for it.

'We do get wind here, but you won't be cold, don't worry,' Aunt Jenny said.

'If she does, we can always put another dog on the bed.'

'Ferdinand!' Aunt Jenny remonstrated. She threw a soft toy at him. It sailed over his head and billowed a curtain. 'That was a joke,' she explained. 'We are a funny house -'

'Stop talking, mum.' Ferdinand leaned forward. 'Harvey Nichols or Harrods?' he asked.

This was surprising. 'Harvey Nichols,' she answered.

'We don't have either in Saltscar. Arsenal or Chelsea?'

'I don't follow football, I'm afraid.'

'Good. Saltscar lost eleven-nil to Rebburn last year. What you need to know is to use the upstairs shower. The bottom one's blocked. The kitchen is your own. We have instant and a cafetiere. Or are you tea?'

'I don't mind, really.'

'Myself, I'm tea. But you'll work it out. You have the freedom of the house. Doesn't she, Jesus?' Jesus thumped his tail three times in agreement. 'If you need to ring your dad there's a landline in the hall.'

'Oh, thank you.'

Ferdinand nodded and sat back, done.

'Perhaps you wish to sort your things out?' Aunt Jenny suggested. 'Then Ferdy can show you round. The light is stunning on the cliff.'

A young woman appeared in the doorway. She had Frank's thin mouth, and his frame. She pointed rudely at Lillian.

'This is Lillian?' she asked.

'Whom else?' Ferdy asked.

'Hello, Lillian. You'll need these.' She threw a jingling object that landed on the box.

'This is Anne-Marie,' Aunt Jenny said.

'Her father had a mole upon his brow,' Ferdy added. 'And so had mine.'

'Ferdinand, stop it. If you want to know where things are, Lillian, ask me.' Abruptly as she had arrived, she left.

'You'll love Anne-Marie,' Aunt Jenny said.

But the sullen man in black now hung in the doorway. He had a camera with a massive lens slung over his shoulder. 'Lemon light,' he said, and left too.

He was followed immediately by the biggest dog. Jesus cocked his ears. The big dog nosed the cushion on the coffee table. He nuzzled it onto the floor and took the tiny yellow teddy bear in his maw and padded out. Jesus dropped off the sofa and trotted after.

'You'll get used to the Holy Family,' Ferdinand said. 'They're all mad, but their bites are much worse than their barks, and they rarely bark.'

For the moment Lillian did not care about the Holy Family or their madness or their bites or their barks for she had the keys that Anne-Marie had tossed to her clamped in her moist fist. This must mean she could come and go as she pleased so if anyone was inappropriate, she could leave and no-one could stop her and she could come back without asking permission, which was a kind of freedom, at least.

Lillian's first impression of Saltscar was yellow and then sky. Evening light continued to gild the station. Ferdinand had led her down the street and along the white fence and now she looked at the two arches onto a yard where a northern version of bustle was going on. 'That's the entrance to the old station,' Ferdinand told her. 'It's from the days where Saltscar had pomp. Our supermarket is on the old site of the shunting sheds. This is where third class alighted. The tracks ran on into the courtyard of the Marlborough Hotel so the rich people could avoid standing on a platform with the polloi.' He turned to the arches through which a man walked to the square, whistling. 'Whistling Joe,' he told her. Lillian ignored him. She looked up the street from the station, past the little roundabout with its miniature clock tower, and noted the nondescript shops and the tops of trees on the broad avenue beyond the brow; beyond, sky. To her right the train line disappeared into a wood, and on the other side, to her confusion, the street ended in a view of a hill, with fields. The fields gleamed the vicious yellow of rapeseed. She felt she had been dropped onto a village on top of a hill with no connection to anywhere else.

She pointed through the arches. 'What's that way?' she asked.

'That way is more wonders,' Ferdinand said. 'We'll walk round.'

He led towards the fields which cut across the street like a giant billboard. He pointed out the charity shop ('From the dead to the old'), the clothes shop ('Very North Yorkshire') the shop that sold crystals and Indian clothes ('A whiff of Whitby') and the dog-friendly café ('The Holy Family's victualler of choice'). He was weird. At the end of the street a broad road curved away past tall stone apartments. On the far side a little stone building was cradled by trees. 'Come,' he said, 'you'll see,' and crossed over. They stopped by the railings of the building, and then she understood. A wooded valley fell below them. On the other side of the valley the cliff shouldered its way into the sea. It was a real cliff and beyond it, the real fields, and above it the sky, and at its base, the sea, and between the sea and the wall of the cliff was a beach, an unruffled scarf, saffron in the evening. This was not a quaint town surrounded by the enduring institutions of finance, culture and power, but an intrusion on moor and rock and sand and sea. She felt small.

There was a breeze on her cheek.

He drew her along the curve of the road sunwards: it dropped at an alarming slope down to the bay, but he led her across it, keeping to the high town. They curved past more large stone apartments and a sliver of a formal garden and looked out over the water. 'High Prom,' he said.

She gazed over the railings at the pier below, a thin grey arrow that pointed to the infinite. The sand gleamed on either side. A queue waited at a red and cream shed besides them, and she saw with a blink it was one of those outside lifts you got sometimes on the lower ski slopes. She watched the cabins cross and the top one clamp with a hiss to the shed.

'The only hydraulic funicular left,' Ferdinand said. 'The Pride of Saltscar.'

She was grateful she'd been born in a city that had not crushed her expectations.

'It's lovely,' she said.

'And there -' pointing away from the cliff - 'seven miles of sandy bay, beyond which the poor people live.'

He was *so* weird.

'It's pretty.'

'The bay's tame. It's at the cliff with its moat of rocks that the monsters begin. Don't go there. The beach is shallow, and the tide is quick. We call it Suicide Cliff.'

She stared at him with wide eyes.

'Be sombre when you hear of an Incident.'

'Of course.'

'Come on.'

He led her up a street of bay windows towards the square with the supermarket. 'That's the basic layout,' he said. 'There is more stuff. There's the Valley Gardens, the sweetest decay in the north and as good a symbol of western decline you'll find this side of the Tees. There's the Yoga and Meditation centre where mum works and a community theatre and a gym and once a month a farmer's market, and there's a little chapel that was for lost sailors that is closed but which I intend to open one day, and there's lots of dogs. Saltscar is very doggy. Just ask Jesus.'

'A gym?'

'But then, there is this.'

He turned left towards the fields on top of the cliff for the second time, but stopped by two large windows with smears of white-wash on them next to a bustling café. He held out an arm.

'Mum's shop,' he said. 'And mine.'

He was trying to impress her with his fancy talk of wonders and dangers. She looked up at a sign. 'Prosper-oh,' she pronounced aloud. She squinted at the window. 'I can't tell what it sells,' she said.

'Come in.' He unlocked the door. The window was plate glass, and normal, but the door was a thick wooden door with many panes of frosted glass, like the doors in period films that come on at Christmas.

There was little except size to give a clue to the family's state. It was certainly big. The main room had a long counter and led into an opening to another whose end was sunk in gloom, and there was a stair to another level. It was exposed brick. Some of the bricks were new, but most were dark and old and gave the impression that the place had been long abandoned or recently renovated. The ceiling had a light without a shade on it, and there were ropes in horizontal lines on the walls, which was sinister. There were stacked boxes and a frame with cards stuffed in them and stacked pictures. It did not smell damp, but it did smell musty, a papery smell. The stacked pictures seemed to have a lot of sky in them, as far as she could tell. The cards were the only bright note.

'This cell's my smithy,' Ferdinand said, which didn't help.

95

'What kind of shop is it?'

'A shop of dreams. When open it will play sounds and sweet airs that give delight and hurt not.'

Lillian frowned. 'Computer games?'

Ferdinand smiled. 'Not computers. It's for curiosities, and things of beauty, and most of all the town. It's the smithy in which I shall forge the sleeping soul of the shore.'

He was actually scary. 'I see,' she said.

'Art stuff. Frank's photographs. Souvenirs,' he said more plainly.

'Oh. Right.'

'Perhaps picture-framing. I have the skills.'

A comment was called for. 'It's very ... sensible.' He looked askance at this. 'I mean, every sea-side place has a shop that sells the views and stuff.' He looked back in silence. He really was quite dim. 'You could do tea-towels with the pier on them, for example,' she suggested. 'It's only an idea.'

'And a very good idea too.'

Lillian felt patronised. Why was he showing her this? She stared into the other room to disguise her offense. She was only being nice. As far as she was concerned, he could sell second-hand soap or yesterday's newspapers or pet hedgehogs, it was nothing to her.

Perhaps he sensed that. 'Shall we move on? You need to settle in at the house.' He smiled, and shuffled on his soles, as though he sensed he'd made a mistake.

But his name was called. A man like a mast with arms and legs that flapped like sails strode towards them. He had blue jeans and a white t-shirt and a flat cap. He was smiling. He showed his hand which Ferdinand took.

'You're back,' Ferdinand remarked.

'Aye, I'm back,' the straight man confirmed.

'Back long?'

'Not long.'

'This is my cousin, Lillian.'

The man looked down from the clouds. 'Yer said nowt about a cousin,' he objected.

'She's once removed,' said Ronnie.

'Wheer from?'

Cousinhood.'

'Aye, right. Pleased to meet you, Lillian. I'm Curly,' the straight man said. 'She's a grand looking lass.'

'You're a grand looking man, Curly.'

Curly thought about this. 'Touché,' he conceded. 'And what brings you to Saltscar, Lillian?'

'Such wind as blows young girls about the world,' Ferdinand answered for her, 'to seek their fortunes further than at home, where small experience grows.'

'Is that right? Fancy a coffee?'

'Where?' Ronnie asked.

The mast-like man jolted a thumb at the café next door. 'Grubby's. The kippers are in.'

'Will you fit?'

'I'll squeeze.'

'Lillian?' Ferdinand asked.

Lillian did not want a coffee, especially with a sexist beanpole and a hairy round cousin however removed in a place called Grubby's. 'Of course,' she said.

Grubby's was a surprise. It was a café-deli, a fragment of Soho dropped into the wilderness with little pine tables on a pine floor. They sat in a corner by the window. Lillian pushed back to disentangle her feet from Curly's which went on forever. A waitress snapped towards them. She had short black skirt and fishnet tights, which bordered the inappropriate.

'Maccyarter, love,' Curly said. 'And a kipper.'

She waitress smiled at Lillian. 'Americano, please. Black.'

'Ferdy?' the waitress asked.

'Give me to drink mandragora.'

'We're out. Tea?'

'Russian Caravan. Redolent of orient spice and mystic charm.' He was firm.

'You can have Yorkshire. You'll have to come to the counter for the kipper.'

'That's telling yer.'

'I'll get your kipper,' Ferdinand said.

To leave her with the skyscraper eccentric did not seem kind to Lillian, particularly after the formalities when Curly began to pronounce on the place in which she was for the moment marooned. 'Don't be put off by the name,' he said. He sat back with his hands flat on the table. The peak of his cap arrowed her. 'There's nothing 'scar' about Saltscar, though some think it refers to the cliff. 'Scar' is Old Norse: 'hill'. The Hill of Salt. This is Cleveland, from Old

Norse, Cleve - cliff. The Land of Cliffs. Then there's Lofthus, from Old Norse again, hus - house, and 'Loft' like 'low'. Low House. Rebburn was originally 'Redburn' but that's hard to say. Anglo-Saxon 'burn' as in 'stream' and red in as red. We pronounce it 'Rebbun' which softens the last syllable to make it iambic. We like to think we're Vikings, but we're just as much Anglo-Saxon, as in 'Easington'; 'ton - town; 'ing' - sons of, or 'descendants' in these PC times; no-one knows who Ease was. Ease is obscure.' Lillian was horrified. No wonder northerners had no money if all they thought of was names. She'd had teachers like Curly, socially inadequate bachelors who banged on about Geography and thought there was something wrong with you because you didn't care and only wanted a grade after which you never needed to think about alluvial silt or anti-peristalsis ever again. She did her best to smile.

'Where're you from?'

'London.'

'Ah, now that's a minefield. Ameliorated Latin, basically. Whereabouts?'

'South Kensington.'

'There you are!' Curly slapped the table. 'The South Town of the Descendants of Ken. But who was Ken?'

Who cared? She had a sudden longing to be back at the Coffee Warehouse, with its cool grey shell and clean lines and the bright chatter all around, flicking her hair at Angelo. She was saved by the return of Ferdinand and the waitress. He passed over the papered kipper.

'I started a new poem,' Curly said, once they were settled.

'Go on,' Ferdinand encouraged him.

Curly put on a poetry voice.

'These are the crepuscular shores.

The sands are the light of evening, paused:

The chameleon waters elude us

And the winds blow through us.

Somewhere, out there, a ship's bell hammers at the ooze.'

Curly looked apologetic. 'I was looking for the false rhymes, like.'

Ferdinand sipped. 'That's it?'

'It's far as I've got.'

Ferdinand considered. 'Needs work,' he concluded.

Lillian noted the customers. They were old. There was no-one there to appreciate her. She longed for her mobile and wondered what she had seen to put on Instagram or her Twitter to get a few likes. The funicular might just about cut it. Ferdinand and Curly talked of things she knew nothing about and people she'd never heard of, but they showed no wish to include her in the conversation. She would normally find that rude. When they left, Curly, who had paid, shook her hand while still talking to Ferdinand and sailed away from where he had come with a purposeful stride at odds with the casual meeting.

'Sorry about that,' Ferdinand said. 'He's a bit of a bore, Curly, but he does much good.'

'He seems very nice.'

Ferdinand squinted at her. 'Your hair – with the light behind. Golden. Like a halo. Just an observation.'

They returned in comfortable silence, which was smashed by Aunt Jenny when Lillian stood in the hall. 'And how did you find Saltscar?' she asked.

'It's very ... cosy,' Lillian answered.

'Where are the dogs?' Ferdinand enquired.

'Down the Grove with Anne-Marie and Dave. Join me in the kitchen, Lillian.' The kitchen was a nightmare of piled plates and pans and earthenware pots, though the oven was gas and Aunt Jenny seemed to know where everything was. 'You find us rather in transition at the moment,' Aunt Jenny told her, 'but everyone clears off tomorrow morning when we can have a nice long chat. Did you ever get to see Freida?'

'No, actually –'

'You have a lot to get used to. You haven't been here in over a decade, but you can open your heart to us whenever you like.' Lillian thought this idea rather alarming. 'Do you eat couscous?'

'I've had it a few times.'

'Good. I love the colour. Like the yellow sand of story books. We have an interesting dinner philosophy here. We eat separately.'

'Oh.'

'It stops arguments. Also, I like to concentrate. Lemon chicken, is that all right? We preserve our own lemons. Don't worry, they're unwaxed. We're good, aren't we, Lillian?'

'Yes, auntie, we're good.'

'Yes, we are. And I'm so glad about Ferdinand.'

Lillian's heart lifted. Had he got a job elsewhere? Her face was a question.

'He still loves you,' Aunt Jenny said. 'I knew as soon as he saw you. He'll look after you. Do you mind coriander?'

Lillian did not mind. She did not know what alarmed her most: Ferdinand's love or Aunt Jenny's pleasure in it.

When she heard how loud Aunt Jenny had the television, Lillian crept to the landline. She had asked for hangers on which she'd arranged four outfits to the back of her door and had organised her stuff well enough in the three-door cabinet at the side of the bed, which made her feel better. Now for Daddy.

'I can't say exactly how long yet,' he told her. 'It's still very fluid.' There was a weariness in his voice that was like nothing she'd heard before.

'I can stay by myself in the house.'

'There are short-term tenants in. They're associates of Mr Shevchenko. Very good rates for us. That means you'll soon have your mobile sorted, and even perhaps an allowance.'

'I could get a job and a bed-sit.'

She heard him sigh. It was not fair that he should be impatient with her, but he was ill so she forgave him. 'There are very few short-term tenancies on bed-sits at the moment. You'd have to give up Paris. You're best out of it here.'

'But they're so weird,' she hissed. 'I have to do *something*.'

'It's weird everywhere just now. A few weeks and then you can get back to civilisation. See?'

'I could help look after you.'

'No, Sweetheart. Don't be so good. Let me tidy things up here.'

'But where will you stay when you're out of hospital?'

'Mr Shevchenko will be able to give me a room. I'm in no position to refuse at the moment. I thought I might start again out of London. What do you think of Leamington Spa?'

'I've never heard of it.'

'What about Norwich?'

'Norwich? Daddy, are you mad?'

'Sometimes I think I probably am.'

'Oh, Daddy!'

'I will bounce back. I still have contacts.'

'What about my stuff?'

'Boxed, I think.'

'Keep my wardrobe collection wherever you are,' she instructed him, 'and I'll get some more when I visit.'

'It isn't rough around there, is it?'

'The poor people live on the other side of the bay.'

'Don't go there, Randa.'

'Of course not, Daddy.'

'Love you, Sweetheart.'

'Love you, Daddy.'

The stood against the wall with the phone tight in her grip. She couldn't scream or stamp her feet because she was in someone else's house.

She had at least the oblivion of sleep until a sniff in her ear woke her. It took her a few seconds to recollect where she was and then a flash to register the sniff.

'No,' she exclaimed in a whispered howl, and turned on her lamp. It hurt her eyes. Jesus whined at the side of the bed.

'Oh, God!'

Even the dogs up here did not recognise your personal space. The people had set a bad example. How had Jesus got in? It was intolerable! She pulled him to the door, and hissed at him to go, but he jumped on the bed.

'No, get down.'

She stood behind the part opened door. There was a lit standard lamp on the landing. Who did that? 'Jesus! Jesus!' she whispered, waving an arm to indicate his way of egress. Jesus put his head to one side with his ear cocked. She tried to drag him off the bed, but she heard paws on the stairs, so she shut the door on Mary and Joseph at which Jesus jumped down and sniffed at the crack. Mary or Joseph scratched at the door on the other side. She crouched to put her hand on Jesus's bottom and opened the door a little to force him out again, but instead Mary and Joseph, all muscular curiosity and love, forced their way in. All three dogs circled and wagged their tails and jumped on the bed. She regarded them in despair.

'Oh, all right then!'

She dug out her pyjamas, shoved them on grumpily, turned off the lamp and forced herself under a heaving canine rearrangement and wrapped the duvet tight round her ears. One dog pinned down her feet with its stomach. The other curled against her with its head over her hip.

Jesus - it was definitely Jesus - snuggled round her back with his nose under her pillow. She tried to think of nice things, but the picture of herself in the Versace she'd admired last year in the V&A, the laughter with friends, her belting the hell out of the opposition, slim as she was, on the lacrosse field, soon faded. In its place, she saw and heard the lazy flop of waves on sand, a supple watery breath underlying the faint wheeze of Jesus's snores; thus, in the warmth and mouldy smell of the Holy Family, racing in her mind over the lacy tug of breakers, she fell asleep.

When she woke the dogs had gone. She tried to interpret the sounds of the house. A toilet flushed, and she heard a soft tread she took for Ferdinand, which was confirmed at a jingle of leads, and his call, 'Howay, canines,' which was followed by eager pattering and a wheeze as one of them stretched.

'On, bacons,' he commanded, and the door shut.

He was beyond weird.

Shortly, the bathroom door opened, then closed and a faster tread on the steps announced Anne-Marie. She disappeared into the silence of the walls, then her steps resumed in the hall and the door clipped shut a second time. Lillian waited. Stillness and quiet, and gloom on the landing and stairs. Was that a clatter in the kitchen? She dressed, fumbled in her bag for make-up, but picked only her toothbrush and paste and glanced along the landing. Frank's door was shut. He was downstairs or out or concocting in silence whatever spells his darkness required. She latched the bathroom door. She swilled and swilled, but did not floss. The landing was quiet with the heavy silence of a forgotten place, so she put back her things, combed, dressed and darted downstairs.

Aunt Jenny was sat at the table in a baggy blue dressing-gown in a mess of toast, butter and marmalade. There were sunflowers on the dining table, a heavy gold and brown that drooped as though sorry for the location in a clashing yellow vase. Aunt Jenny sucked her fingers with relish. She beamed.

'You are beautiful!'

'I haven't done my face yet.'

'Nevertheless. You'll turn all the heads of Saltscar - but don't fall in love. You're vulnerable. Breakfast?'

Lillian demurred. 'I don't want to be a trouble.'

'Don't be silly.' Aunt Jenny scrubbed her fingers with kitchen towel which she left on the counter. 'I think you had night-visitors.'

'Oh, yes.'

'They were taking advantage. I gave them a good telling-off. Coffee or tea?'

'Coffee would be lovely.'

'We have Guatemalan Elephant. I'll make a cafetière. Then I have something to show you.'

The sitting-room curtains were only partly opened, and made a a warm, yellow gloom on the jumble inside. Lillian felt she was in a child's story, a princess hiding in the wreckage of a boat on a faraway island, though the coffee Aunt Jenny gave her as she plumped beside her on the tan sofa was delicious. She watched as Lillian sipped.

'That's really good!' she said.

'It's expensive, but coffee does matter. Look at this.'

Aunt Jenny retrieved an old-fashioned photograph album from under a cushion. She lay it before them on the coffee table like a relic on an altar. She turned pages and Lillian leaned forward.

'There you are,' Aunt Jenny said. 'There was digital then, but I do like my print-outs.'

'It's rather dark.'

'You're right.' Aunt Jenny opened the final curtain. Light exploded in. Lillian blinked.

'Have you seen?' Aunt Jenny asked.

'What?'

Aunt Jenny sat softly and touched a print. 'This one.' Lillian squinted at a child in a one-piece swimsuit. The swimsuit was yellow and cream with puckered rims round the chest. It was very old-fashioned. The child was pale and blond with skinny arms. She squatted flat-footed on the sand and frowned up at the viewer as though unsure who was taking the photograph or why.

'That's you,' Aunt Jenny said. 'Look at this one.'

The girl was laughing or grinning with a boy with a plump stomach in trunks beside her. The boy was bigger and solemn. Behind them a woman gazed with folded arms in quarter profile beyond the camera, calm and softly defiant. Lillian made out the end of the pier. The beach beyond it was empty. Behind the pier was the cliff.

'Who's the lady?' she asked.

'You don't remember at all?'

Lillian felt Aunt Jenny's eyes on her face. She did not know what to say.

'Perhaps you remember this one.'

Lillian looked at herself squinting, quizzical, by a fence before a field, wheat-gold and endless. The woman was crouched behind her with her head to one side and her fingers on Lillian's shoulders. There was a glimpse of sea beyond the field, deep blue against the wheat.

'What about this?'

The same skinny blonde girl was standing in front of a white house with the boy next to her. The boy was grinning. She recognised a younger Aunt Jenny behind them. The lady stood next to her on one side, and a woman in a broad-brimmed hat was laughing on the other.

'That was your house then,' Aunt Jenny said. 'Our house, I should say. The Ellesker farmhouse. It's owned now by the lady in the hat, and a great friend of ours. You'll meet her shortly. There's a lot of history in that house.'

'It's all a blank,' Lillian said. 'I know I came here once, but I can't seem to place ... The lady from the other photograph – she's a friend as well?' She offered back the photograph from a limp hand.

Aunt Jenny nodded. 'That's my cousin, Emily.' She lay the photograph on the table with sudden reverence instead of putting it back in the album.

'Oh,' said Lillian, then realised. 'Oh!' she exclaimed, as though ambushed.

'She was here for the summer, like you. You were very young,' Aunt Jenny conceded. 'And it's a beautiful day. Now, I want to take you where I work. You can meet Jean and Dorothy. Dorothy is the lady with the hat. They're sympa. That's a French term. I know it's a strain meeting new people, but it's better than being alone in a strange place. Do you mind?'

Lillian searched for an excuse, but failing to find one, complied. Nevertheless, she touched the photograph with the tips of her fingers.

'May I go for a run first?' she asked. She felt she could run a very long way. She could run all the way to London if someone told her in which direction to start.

She ran the beach. It was flat, and the sand was mostly firm, and she was soon out of the holiday crowd and their children and their dogs. She gathered pace when it opened up and had to jump the clear water streaming from the grassy dunes to protect the wonderful pink trainers. She should have brought a spare pair. She quelled her annoyance and pressed on. A golden labrador dropped its ball in the foam and galloped after her, and circled her, and jumped up, and ran around her, barking. Its owner called in vain.

'Oh, go away!' she said.

She was plagued with dogs.

He left as abruptly as he had come, and she powered on until her chest was heaving. A church spire appeared over the bank. She slowed, then walked with her hands on her hips and looked back. The pier was tiny. There was a film of sea-spray over it, insistently brilliant, and beyond it, Moor Cliff stopped the beach like a castle wall at the end of a lonely track. A gull glided, alone, over the blue. The sun burst from the feathery hulks of cumulus and brightened the sand into a uniform straw sash. It was rather lovely, but she felt so alone, she needed to do the breathing all over again. Calmer, she jogged back, and kept a steady pace until she delved into the noise of the holiday makers. She kept by the clear route at the sea's fringe and sprinted under the iron legs of the pier and slowed. She gave up her face to the breeze, panting. She watched the surfers paddle out. They did not seem part of the place in their sleek strength and their settled purpose. She walked to the sea's edge. Actually, with the gabble of people and birds around her, it was a relief to be alone. Then she walked to the other side of the pier and squinted up. This was not quite the place. She strolled, glancing up, in a figure of eight, and though she could not be sure, she stopped.

It was very near here, she told herself. I was here, and my mother was there.

How did that happen? It made the town yet more strange, as though she was being dragged through a wormhole to an alternative world.

There was a long queue of people in bright t-shirts for the fish and chips, which she skirted. She looked up the steps to high prom. She had counted them on the way down. One hundred and sixty-seven, but she set off, and she breathed and she pumped, high-kneed and furious. People on the way down stepped to one side. A black couple hugged their little ones and flashed smiles which she acknowledged with a nod. She arrived with burning thighs at the top where the funicular was wheezing to stillness.

'By, 'ell, lass. That's showing us,' the man in charge said. He had a uniform like a bus conductor in by gone days.

It certainly is, she thought, but managed not to say it.

There was a murmur and muted applause from those waiting to descend by mechanical means. Lillian blushed.

'Thank you,' she said, and jogged away along the high prom. These people were simpletons.

The days' barrage was not yet ended on Lillian Delph.

Aunt Jenny took her to the Mindfulness Centre. It was a red brick building with a porch in the centre and two wings and was depressing like an old hospital building. 'Once the primary school,' Aunt Jenny said. They entered from the back door through the car park into a corridor a cheap carpet and cream walls with notices on them that made Lillian think of a waiting room in a run-down clinic. She glimpsed a shop that sold accessories, though the accessories all looked the same, and was ushered through the next door to a shock. The shock was India. The chairs were striped in primary and secondary colours. The chair backs had tin bells on them. The round tables had garish tablecloths that hung in points. An elephant with a blue and gold covering, and gilded tusks was painted on a saffron wall. At one of these tables two women raised faces of recognition.

'So this is she!' one of them said, standing, and gazing at Lillian.

She was monstrous at first glance. She had a fully grooved face, but wore bright red lipstick. Not only that, but she had striped coloured socks, a red skirt to the knee, a green jumper, a yellow jacket and a vermilion beret. She jumped up like a crackerjack and exploded self-satisfaction into Lillian's face. She was as gaudy as the room and probably lived in it. The other woman, stockier and still, was less alterative, but nevertheless had long greying hair elaborately tied. Didn't they know they were old? Aunt Janny suddenly appeared more normal.

'This is her,' Aunt Jenny confirmed. 'This is Dorothy,' she introduced the colourful woman, 'and Jean,' nodding to the other.

'We're your auntie's naughty friends,' Dorothy said. She twinkled. 'You won't remember, but I once taught you to sing The Drunken Sailor. We went up and down the funicular three times and entertained the passengers. Jenny got quite cross with me.' She laughed.

'Dorothy is my oldest friend in Saltscar,' Aunt Jenny explained.

'Though I don't live there.'

'You are a Saltscarian, nevertheless.'

'Where is your house?' Lillian asked.

Dorothy and Aunt Jenny glanced at each other. Dorothy, granted permission from Jenny's look, said, 'I live in the house where your mother grew up. Whitby way.'

'Shall we order?' Jean asked. Jean had a North American accent.

'It's vegan here, Lillian,' Dorothy said. 'It does make the coffee a problem. Do you mind vegan food?'

'I do like to eat healthy food.'

'Jenny has the best food in Saltscar,' Dorothy said.

'Get on with you!' Jenny said, pleased.

'She can do amazing things with bacon.'

'Don't be nonsensical, Dorothy!'

'What's that about the station?' Jean asked.

'Bacon!' Dorothy shouted at her.

'Hearing aid, Jean,' Aunt Jenny said.

'Oh, yes.' Jean fiddled in her ears, then looked at them with relief. 'They weren't turned on.'

'I'll go to the counter. Orders?' asked Dorothy.

Lillian would have a single espresso. Jean leaned over. She spoke surprisingly softly for a deaf woman. 'I knew your mother in Australia,' she said. 'We shared such magical experiences. I came here ten years ago.'

Her mother, again! She smiled. 'You're from America?' she asked.

'We don't need to talk about that now,' Aunt Jenny said.

The ladies were in serious debate about the Autumn Programme. Slots were available, and options broad. Lillian had not expected this. She was not sure, apart from ugliness and shouting like in a soap opera and excessive rudeness, what she had feared. It had never crossed her mind –why would it – that she was coming to her mother's home. Her mother was beside the point. Wherever she was and whatever troubles she faced, it was her daddy who was in crisis, and her daddy that Lillian bothered about. To refer to her mother at all was rude. They could talk about her mother to their heart's content when she herself was not with them. And now they were talking about things she knew nothing of, which was rude as well. They should ask about her life in London, and at least pretend to be impressed, not behave as though she was only there to join them. It's because she was in a financial transition and so had no status. Aunt Jenny was friendly, but she had no idea, no idea at all.

'Tribe Tattva Dance are available,' Aunt Jenny was saying. 'Is that cultural appropriation?'

'The Tattva tribe aren't here to object,' Dorothy said. 'What's the harm?'

'I'll see what Ferdinand thinks,' Aunt Jenny said.

Jean leaned forward. She was a stolid woman. She spoke as though caressing her words. 'I went to look at the rock paintings with an aboriginal guide,' she said. 'They're forty thousand years old. They're fantastic. It was a humbling experience, really.'

'We're very arty in Saltscar,' Dorothy told Lillian. 'Are you arty yourself?'

'I don't mind. I did Theatre Studies at AS. I'm more into the design part.'

'Oh, but that's fantastic,' Jean breathed at her.

'I'm more on the sporty side.'

'Lillian runs like the wind,' Aunt Jenny remarked.

'She could do the Scramble.'

'What's the Scramble?'

'It's coming up soon,' Jean said, unhelpfully. 'It's one of your wonderful English eccentricities.'

It's a race,' Aunt Jenny reminded informed her. 'It used to be a fun thing, but it's got a little too serious now.'

'You're American?' Lillian asked. She wanted to know why and American was in this place. It didn't seem probable.

'Yes, but the Pacific coast,' Jean answered.

'Jean says, 'aloominum.' We say 'aluminium',' Dorothy said pointlessly, returning.

'Why are you here – in Saltscar?'

'It's my home,' Jean said. 'It's quite wonderful – and no guns.'

An absence of guns was a modest compliment, but now a pair of younger women turned and the taller of them stepped forth with a clarion call. 'Hey, you guys! We're doing the Scramble, women's section! Don't diss the Scramble!'

The ladies turned to them. Wrinkled age faced youth in yoga pants. 'You're looking fantastic,' Dorothy told them, though the compliment could only apply to the taller one as the other was a little stout for serious running. The women absorbed the compliment as taken.

'Hi, Jenny,' the shorter one said. 'Is your Ferdy coming to do my granny today?'

'I think it's tomorrow, Shelley. He's doing Mrs Metcalfe this afternoon.'

'I'll tell her,' Shelley said. 'It makes her day when Ferdy does her.'

The taller looked at Lillian. 'I thought you were Anne-Marie,' she said.

Lillian smiled back.

'This is Lillian,' Aunt Jenny announced rather grandly. 'She's my niece once removed. This is Chardonnay, Lillian.'

'Moved where?' Shelley asked.

'This is Shelley, Lillian. It's complicated.'

'Are you here on holiday?' Chardonnay asked.

'More of a family reunion,' Aunt Jenny corrected. 'Lillian runs.'

'Join us!' Shelley said. 'We're in training for the Scramble.'

'We're going to win,' said Chardonnay.

'Not this year perhaps, Char,' Shelley corrected.

'Isn't Jane Brown competing?'

'Thank you,' said Lillian. Their accents grated on her ear.

'I must get back to exercise,' said Dorothy. 'I was very good last year. It did wonders for my sex life.'

'With whom?' Jean asked.

'Mike was still vigorous then,' she answered.

Lillian looked at Dorothy and felt a little sick.

'Dotty!' Chardonnay exclaimed. 'You make me blush!'

It was not their difference from the adults she'd known that unsettled Lillian. Every weekend she had left the safe conformity of her boarding school to the London medley; its exhilarating crash of races, languages, of new and old squeezed together like strangers on the tube, of staid parks, immensely private houses and of flashing Piccadilly. But in London everything got on with its own affair like a marble in a pinball machine and did not barge into one's agenda with such laughing recklessness as these provincials. London ran on a happy natural segregation based on age, beauty and wealth so Lillian had never needed to relate to anyone with a worse complexion than her own. She was beginning to understand that Saltscar was more like a family in which the farting uncle, the vulgar auntie, the loud cousin, and the brother with acne claimed as much right to your space as your friends. Aunt Jenny mercifully recognised that Lillian was lost, so she said, at the end of Dorothy's account of someone's new sculptures, 'We have to go. We need to sort out Lillian's room before Anne-Marie comes back, or she'll get into one of her states.'

Dorothy and Jean glanced up with faces that showed familiarity with Anne-Marie's states.

'House,' Dorothy said. 'While summer lasts. We can sip cocktails at the French windows and think ourselves in a Raoul Dufy.'

'You're so original, Dorothy.'

Aunt Jenny sailed down the corridor. A man wobbled in front of her, with the dull eyes of someone with learning difficulties, to whom Aunt Jenny said, 'Hello, Stevie,' in a voice like a bell. Stevie muttered something and gave a lopsided grin.

'That's right, Stevie. Look in here, Lillian.' She gestured into the shop. 'Very nice shop. All from cork for eco reasons.'

'Like your purse.'

Aunt Jenny was impressed again. 'That's very well observed,' she said. They stepped into the car park where a cleansing breeze lifted Lillian's hair.

Aunt Jenny gazed at a dull grey sky. 'Lovely day,' she said with a flourish. 'The wind's dropped. I hope that wasn't too excessive for you. They're a bit much at first. Jean lives alone though there's a husband somewhere in the past. You have to get used to Dorothy. Dorothy is an inspiration. She's seen me through many bad times. And you saw Stevie. Stevie has Issues as well. There are many people come to Saltscar with Issues because it is a healing place. Elsewhere, they are picked on.'

Lillian had a question. 'Your friend lives in my mother's old house. That's a coincidence, right?'

'No, darling. Mike, her husband, bought it for her when the Elleskers, your grandparents, were forced to sell. Once, your mother and Dorothy were like sisters.'

'I see.'

'That's when they were little, both tomboys, but they had different outlooks when they grew up. Now it's a friendship of opposites. Isn't human nature amazing? If you do yoga, Lillian, this is the place and it has meditation. The idea, you see, was that your mother would still have access to her old home, but it backfired at the time. Now it's a blessing.'

If ever Lillian bumped into Dorothy she'd pretend not to see her and walk very quickly in the opposite direction.

Lillian got organized. She put folded underclothes in the mini-cabinet and hung three outfits on the door hangers and placed a stool from the kitchen in the corner, and finally connected her tablet to the Goodman's wi-fi. She was sitting on the stool pondering whether access to her online community would make her happier or more miserable when Anne-Marie opened the door and stood in the frame like an exclamation mark.

'Can we talk?'

'Of course.'

Anne-Marie plopped on the bed. 'Bit small this room, I'm afraid.'

'Oh, no,' Lillian protested. 'In London rooms this size –'

'It's normally Ferdy's. Ferdy takes mine when I'm gone. He's on the air bed in the spare room. Never mind. The thing is, have you any idea how long you'll be here?'

'I'm sure my father will sort things out as soon as he can –'

'What exactly has happened to your father?'

What, indeed? Anne-Marie's scrutiny triggered the morning of the break-down; her father moaning in bed, the smug police, the over cheerful paramedics, and her panic at being alone and with nothing. 'He has some business difficulties,' she ventured. Anne-Marie continued to watch her as though about to pounce. 'His world is one of feast and famine. That's how it goes. It's a stressful time, but he's-'

Anne-Marie held up a palm. 'He's bankrupt, yes?'

'Oh,' said Lillian. 'I don't *think* so.'

Anne-Marie now took the pressure off by looking at the ground. Her voice was softer, though it remained on the harsh side of acceptable. 'I want to talk to you as one adult to another. This is how it is. Understand it. Mum wants to help because she's loving. She's become big on the Elleskers since dad died. It's a coping thing. Ferdy will go ahead and do his best because he's kind and Frank won't care because he's Frank, but they're all pretty hopeless. If you think they can sort you out –'

'Oh, no! No, I don't expect-'

Anne-Marie held up her palm for a second time. 'Do you know why your father's assets are frozen?'

'I'm sorry?'

'Your debit card is defunct.' A canine snout poked through the door. It gazed on the scene with melancholy eyes. 'Bugger off, Jesus,' Anne-Marie told him. Jesus, improbably, buggered off.

'For the moment,' Lillian managed.

Anne-Marie leaned forward and dropped her hands between her legs. She spoke with gravity. 'I've a suggestion. I can wangle you a job where I do holiday work. It's only for a couple of weeks, perhaps a month, but it'll give you pocket money until your card is sorted. It's easy enough.'

She paused. Lillian thought she might add, 'Even for you,' but she didn't. Lillian did not like Anne-Marie. She did not like her at all. Anne-Marie thought herself smart, but put her in with Lillian's friends on the King's Road and she'd be invisible. 'It doesn't pay much, but it's only a week's notice and better than nothing. Part-time. Well?'

Lillian wanted to speak. She even opened her mouth, but no words came out. She looked at the door in the hope Jesus might return and save her, but Jesus had gone.

'Think about it. I need to know by tomorrow. I'll help you register as self-employed.'

'Of course. Yes.'

'Yes, you'll take it, or yes, you'll think?'

'I'll consider it seriously,' Lillian answered.

'And what about your mother? She's out of the question, is she?' Anne-Marie watched her carefully.

'My mother and I have a difficult relationship.'

'You and your mother don't seem to have a relationship at all.'

That was brutal. 'No, actually, we don't. I don't want one.'

'You don't? Right. Interesting. That's important. What about friends? You have friends?'

'I have a lot of friends,' Lillian said with pride.

'They haven't exactly rallied round, have they?'

Anne-Marie was the nastiest person Lillian had ever met. She saw Lillian's shock, at least.

'Sorry to be blunt,' she conceded, 'but it's better to learn the facts from me than from bitter experience. Also, keep your hands off Ferdinand. He's smitten already. I can see by your face the idea revolts you. That's good. Don't worry, he not a predator, quite the opposite. Nice jeans,' she added, glancing at where they hung. 'TK Maxx?'

'No. No, actually-'

'Of course not. Before I forget.' She pulled out a capsule from her pocket and handed it over. It was plastic and fitted Lillian's palm. Lillian did not know what it was. 'I've put ten pounds on it,' Anne Marie explained. 'For emergencies.'

'What is it?'

'My old pay-as-you-go phone.'

To Lillian, technology started at iPhone5. Before that, it was a landfill site of cannon balls, gas lighting, analogue televisions, spitfires, The Great Age Of Sail, wind-up clocks. 'How does it work?' she asked.

'Flip it open. Type in the number. Press 'phone' icon.'

'Oh.'

Anne-Marie rose. The interview, it appeared, was over. She touched the sleeve of Lillian's linen jacket, after Chanel.

'Nice jacket,' she said. 'Think about that job. It will do you good.'

'Oh, yes. Absolutely.'

Anne-Marie turned and stood in the doorframe again. This time she was less like an exclamation mark and more like speech-marks, hanging there to make a point. 'We can't afford you, Lillian,' she said with weary finality. 'You can't afford you. I like you by the way.'

'I like you,' Lillian replied.

Anne Marie's smile was forgiving. 'No, you don't. But you will.' She left.

Lillian turned back to the tablet. Frank's step on the stairs, heavy with menace thundered close, then he closed his door with a soft curse. He was scary. She considered Instagram again: with her father's downfall, the north, her mother's photograph, Curly's names, Frank, and now Anne-Marie's bluntness she was overwhelmed and could not for the moment face the great times and amazing things she knew her friends were enjoying, so she let out a great sob, and at the sob Jesus suddenly prodded open the door. She put the tablet on the cabinet.

'Hello, Jesus,' she said.

Jesus came forward and wedged himself between her legs, his head on her thighs, and she stroked his neck. She would get back to London if she had to camp out by the Serpentine.

Chapter 4

All cemeteries are remote even in the centre of town, viewed from the tops of buses. They are, after all, for long-term residents. But those lifted above shores are particularly lonely; the empty sea and the sky sound out the long voyages and the unreturned. Waves leave no memorial, and some of the plots belong to those whose companions can never share their space. Ferdinand's father was commemorated among their number, for though he had not been lost at sea its presence had been a draw upon his soul. The church had a spire as well as a tower; in fact, it had only a spire and a tower, for the nave was long gone to ruin. That combination gave Ferdinand the sense of a little place locked to the infinities of elsewhere; the tower pressed upon the earth in which the dead lay, while the spire pointed to the undefined to which the good aspire.

He felt rather than thought this as he stood before the spot, marked by a solitary shrub, where some of his father was scattered. He placed the birthday iris under the leaves.

Fear no more the heat o' the sun,

Nor the furious winter rages.

Thou thy wordly task hast done;

Home art gone, and ta'en thy wages.

He sucked in the air. He saw under the hazy sun the big-hulled whalers, rowing boat with long oars aloft the decks, and felt the village praying in the church, and younger wives and sweethearts shielding their eyes to sea. He was sad.

Jesus was licking his parts between his tolerant parents. Ferdinand heaved past them, and they sprang to their paws and followed him down the links over the pebbles onto the packed sand. He turned east. Moor Cliff stood in haze before them. The Holy Family were addressed by an assortment of dogs, all of them ignorant of death, that bounded over the democratic shore, but Ferdinand's followers kept their plodding pace as relentless as tides in his wake. They cut through children running in circles, other dog walkers, the elderly out for exercise, the four of them, like pilgrims. When the pier was clear to view, he leashed them. Jesus looked back at cantering horses with regret, but even impulsive Jesus obeyed the tug.

He knew from the dog's scamper from the door he was not alone, and then he heard his sister's impatience. She was cross at the dishwasher. The bottom drawer would not close.

'Why,' she asked her brother, 'are things so difficult?'

'Let me try.'

He lined up the recalcitrant tray. Gently, he pushed. The tray slid and stopped with a dropping clunk, a mechanical sigh.

'It just needed a bit of love,' he said.

'It just needed to do what it was told. Feel better?'

'Duty done.'

'Daddy's boy,' she said and went into the dining room where a pile of ironing awaited.

He followed. 'I do not have from you that show of love that I was wont to have,' he said.

'Oh, stop it', she answered. 'Have you seen this?'

She pointed at the ironing. 'What am I looking at?' he asked.

'Where are Lillian's clothes?'

His expression showed ignorance of the whereabouts of Lillian's clothes.

'She taken her own and ironed them. If you look on her bed, you'll find them in a neat little pile.'

'Ah.'

'So why didn't she do the lot of them while she was at it?'

'She was remiss. But it's better than leaving them for us to do.'

'You're as bad as mum,' she answered and left him.

He took up three dog bowls which brought the Holy Family to their paws. He swilled the bowls, wrestled out cans from the cupboard under the sink and filled them. The dogs regarded him with cocked ears and Jesus whined in a minor key. He put down two, for Mary and Joseph, then added a dollop extra for the younger Jesus, who was looking at his parents with outrage and at Ferdinand with interest.

'The first shall be last, Jesus,' he said. 'And the last shall be first. This is something you seem unable to learn.'

Jesus ate without regard for appearance. Joseph sniffed at Mary's food and joined her. Mary, untroubled, ate on, then sidled over to Joseph's and took his. Ferdinand mused on the etiquette of canine dining, that easy tolerance of each's foibles. It was not so with human families. He heard action upstairs, ascended, and knocked on his sister's door.

'Does Her Ladyship require anything?' he asked.

'She requires you to fuck off.'

'Very good, M'Lady.'

He awaited her in the sitting-room. She returned tidily coiffured in a fresh blouse and her work bag. 'So? Are you concerned?'

'I am.'

'And?'

'It's difficult.'

Anne-Marie flopped in the chair opposite him with exaggerated despair. 'This bloody family,' she said.

'We can't just throw her back.'

'Actually, we can. It's just that mum won't. 'Poor Emily's child'. Poor Emily's child will be the straw that pushes us over the edge. Did I say that right?'

'The drift is clear.'

'It's not just us. I'm not being mean. I'll keep my promise to you, but I'm not taking her on as well.'

'It may be that she'll go back very soon.'

'Or she might not! He's gone bust and there's a fraud thing. What if he goes to prison?'

'That seems unlikely.'

'Yes, but it happens.'

Ferdinand conceded in his face the immensity of this. 'All right. You ask me then for a strategy? I can't give you one. The child doesn't know what she is. Or who she is. She understands the world no better than Jesus. She has no idea what's going to happen to her, and I doubt she has the resources to deal with it when it comes. Boom! However she copes, whatever we do, ultimately it will have to come from within her. We can be kind to her - though with regard to Frank that might be a transformation beyond the powers of reason, magic or God's grace - and we can give her a safe space, sort of, but beyond that, I don't know. '

'She'll be here for ever.'

'Or until she goes to Paris.'

'She'll never go! She has no money.'

'She thinks she has.'

'Mum's spoken to her father. There's a buyer for their house. Who knows what'll be left when the mortgage and the debts are paid? He wouldn't admit it openly, but that seems the case. Someone has to explain to the child the truth of her situation.'

Ferdinand looked at his feet. If dad were alive, it would be easier. Jim Goodman had not been a great provider, had been, indeed, a dreamer like Ferdinand himself, but a tenacious dreamer, a dreamer who could take a waif like Lillian aside and tell her the unwelcome truth with the plodding calm that reassured the most troubled, even while pointing out the enemy in the woods. But there was no dad.

'I don't know, Anne-Marie!' he protested. 'Perhaps I'll take her to Whitby. She might think better of the place after that.'

'Whitby's a dump.'

'Off-season, it has character. But, yes, she's too good for Whitby.'

'She's too good for us. She's too good for herself. That's the problem.'

'We'll talk to mum,' he said. 'But what if it all works out: father in the clear and Lillian returned? Should we destroy her innocence just *in case*. If she must stay, why make her hate the place?'

'She hates it anyway. She's entirely unsuited to life in Saltscar.' Anne-Marie rose and slung her bag over her shoulder. She held the strap as though it might try to escape. 'Perhaps we should make her hate it more. Leave her alone with Frank for an hour.'

'Frank likes her.'

'What?'

'He says she has spirit.' He shrugged. He didn't understand it either. 'But let me ask, are you angry at us, or at Lillian?'

'Both. And at mum.' His face expressed enquiry. 'Ferdinand, for someone who places such stock on the intellect, you can be very stupid. She's invited her here for Emily!' Her eyes burned at him a second, then she turned away. '

'That's interesting.'

'No, it's not. Lillian made it clear she wants no relationship with her mother. Mum is a kind of bully, you know. It's' inverted, but it's there.'

'Emily has suffered a grave injustice.'

'That's as maybe. But the child's eighteen. She's technically adult. It's her initiative or no-one's!'

'I must think on this.'

'And your papers are in a mess. I'll sort them, but it'll take me an afternoon. Then I'll do that research. But if you're serious, Ferdy, you've got to learn it. Oh, and there's this.' She took an umbrella from the urn in the hall. She proffered it to him. 'You won't make money if you give the stock away,' she said. 'That's a rule you can follow.'

'Not even to Dave?'

'Not even to *me*.'

She was gone. He was left with the contented dogs, to whom the world was simple, and with the problem of Lillian Delph. Anne-Marie wanted out. She really did.

Lillian was so intent on the rhythm she did not see the water. The beach was puffy pale sand at the bank where the tide never reached, then a spongy band the colour of brioche, and then, by the sea, a broad belt of post-card yellow, along which she pelted. But in this good bit, oddly, there were new rivulets of water determined to die in the sea, and it was through one of these that Lillian found herself before she knew it. She yelped, in annoyance, and felt an idiot before the elderly couple walking a dog, so ran on bit before plopping on the sand to pull off the trainers and shake off the excess. The beautiful pink trainers! They were wet with salt water! She had to take Anne-Marie's phone out of her back pocket, and as she sat cross-legged, she noticed her thighs. They were bulking up nicely, which was a good thing. If she could not control her life, she could at least take charge of her body, and then it mattered far less what these northerners thought. But what about her wet socks?

She had to try twice before she got through. The second time she was made to answer security questions, and then she was forced to wait for a doctor. Lillian felt the ten pounds leaking away. The doctor was brisk, however. 'He's off suicide watch,' he said. 'He's doing fine. There's nothing medically unsound. He's simply taking time adjusting to his circumstances, so he'll be discharged shortly. He's agreed to stay with Mr Shevchenko. We think that's a good idea.'

'Mr Shevchenko? I don't understand.'

'I'm afraid I can't say any more about that. I'll hand you over to reception and they'll put you through.'

He sounded tired. His voice in the first and subsequent calls had brought brisk north London to mind; its sharp definitions and its hard intent. Now it was from another time.

'Randa, my girl. Where are you? I'm so glad to hear from you. Are you well, Sweetheart?'

'I'm on the beach.'

'Is it nice?'

'I suppose so. What's with Mr Shevchenko?'

'It's a good thing, Randa. Mr Shevchenko continues to take an interest in me. He's been a bit of a star.'

'I want to come home, Daddy.'

.'I know, Sweetie, I know.'

'I want to come home soon.'

'You see, Randa, it isn't possible until I've cleared this up and got going again.'

'I could help you.' Her father sighed. She took it as a sign of sympathy. 'Why can't I just do that?' she asked him. 'We'll manage, Daddy -'

'Lillian, listen to me.' He only called her Lillian when there was something important to say. 'You will be fine. You must believe that. Whatever happens to me, you will be fine. Do you know how you can help me? Really help me?'

'How, Daddy?'

'You can look after yourself. Try and make the best of things up there, Sweetheart. Just for a while.'

'But, Daddy.'

'Sweetheart, I'm ill. I'm getting better, but I'm ill. I need to know you're safe so I can - so I can concentrate on *myself*. I haven't had much chance to concentrate on myself, but now I must for a time. You are safe there, aren't you, Randa?'

Her father used to show her off at Events. The last was an art exhibition where the clients said they thought she must be a model. She thought of the city where the world roared by at the end of the drive, for her room with its clean lines and built-in wardrobe and for the babble of her friends in a queue at a restaurant, for people who understood make-up and clothes, and for places where stuff was always happening. She'd give up this whole beach for an hour with friends in Battersea Park and a stroll round Sloane Square.

'Oh, I'm *safe*,'

'Aunt Jenny does sounds nice.'

'She's so absent-minded. She has old friends who talk funny. And Anne-Marie is even more horrible than before. She's rude. Ferdinand is weird. And I don't like Frank. They don't, they're not –' It was difficult to express why these people were so exasperating. 'They treat me like I'm not from anywhere!' she attempted. 'And I work in a café and I'm the best worker and no-one notices.'

'Randa, Sweetie, they just don't know about things. That doesn't mean they're not kind. How's your diet?'

'There's no good restaurants – well, there's one that's ok - but Aunt Jenny cooks.'

'When we're sorted, Randa, we'll eat at the Savoy every week.'

'Oh, Daddy.'

'Be strong, Randa. For me.'

'All right, daddy.'

'You're the reason for everything, Sweetie.'

'I know, Daddy.'

'That's my girl.'

The conversation was resolved, but she felt cheated, and her feet were wet. It was so unfair! There was nothing she could do about the socks. She knew from the bitterest experience that to run sockless in wet trainers meant blisters.

When she trotted back, before she got up to speed and started the breathing, she realised she hadn't asked why Mr Shevchenko was butting in. Why did Daddy interest him in particular? But she didn't care about Mr Shevchenko. If her father was staying with him, Mr Shevchenko must be on their side so that was that.

She had slowed to a walk on the road by the supermarket when she heard her name called. Ferdinand was standing in the doorway of the shop.

'I saw you going past,' he said.

'I've been for a run.'

'Would you mind coming in? I'd like a word.'

'I'm all sweaty.'

'That doesn't matter.'

The shop was not very different from the first time she'd entered. If anything, it was more of a mess. There was a hangar with cotton clothes, Indian style, and a globe on a stand, and a range of postcards and stationery on free plastic frames. Lillian wondered if he'd taken stuff from the shop in Mindfulness Central. The walls were still marked with parallel lines of string and against them additional canvases were stacked, some showing their backs and others glimpses of Saltscar pier. Most of all there were boxes and planks of wood, five rows deep against the far wall. 'It's coming on,' Ferdinand said.

'I can see that.'

'Come and look further.'

On the second story there were metal animals under bubble-wrap, and lamps in strong colours, and more string on the walls and more stacked canvases, and even more boxes, and three folded round tables with round tops in distressed yellow, like broken yolks, and what looked like a scarecrow turned to a wall. The boxes had multiplied like rabbits. Lillian obediently wandered round and wished he would get to the point.

'It's so big,' she said.

'Such is the Saltscar character. The houses look little on the outside, but they keep going and going inside, like the Tardis.'

'It's a wonderful space,' she said.

The scarecrow suddenly spoke. It was a lady scarecrow with a low rasping voice, out of a dream, a voice of someone very much pleased with herself. 'Is this Lillian?' she asked.

'The very same,' said Ferdinand. 'Lillian Miranda Delph! This is Fiona, Lillian; graffiti artist and general star of the Mindfulness Centre. Fiona May.'

'Hello,' Lillian said and forced a smile. The scarecrow was indeed a woman with flying hair and baggy shirt and trousers who held a spray can. She had been lettering a board on the wall.

She looked down on Lillian with almond eyes and smiled in condescension. 'Miranda and Ferdinand – perfect.'

'She's a blood relation,' Ferdinand pointed out, 'and she's beautiful and I'm not and I'm fat to boot.'

'Platonically,' the scarecrow-lady purred and returned to her board. 'You're not exactly *fat*,' she finished.

This conversation made no sense to Lillian, which was not unusual in Saltscar. She suspected something belittling in it, however, so to seem assured she said, 'So this is what you sell?' and realised as soon as the words dripped out that that was a stupid thing to say. She looked around to hide the pale flush on her cheeks.

'In due course. What do you think?'

'It's difficult to say. It's not all unwrapped. But it's ... different.'

'Different is good.'

'But?' asked Fiona May without turning round.

Lillian wanted to say something intelligent, and then go. 'It's a wonderful space,' she tried, and realised she'd already said that. 'It's hard because it hasn't got an identity yet.'

'It's liminal,' Fiona May suggested.

Oh, do shut up, Lillian thought. I don't know what 'liminal' means. Perhaps Ferdinand saw the sting of annoyance on her face because he said, 'You're right, unfair question, let's go back down,' and led down the steps. Lillian had probably offended him, but he'd asked, and she'd given, and, anyway, whatever his difficulties were, they were nothing compared to hers. She was not here to consider the Goodman family's retail circumstances.

Ferdinand sat on a box. 'That's interesting. A little surprising.' He nodded. Then he made a swerve. 'You must be worried about your father,' he said.

'Yes. But he's very strong.'

'Have you wondered about ours?'

She felt there was a judgment in the question, and because she didn't want to appear uncaring, she said, 'No. I didn't want to intrude -'

'He died three years ago. It was hard.'

'Oh. I'm sorry.'

This was his ... But you don't want to hear this now.'

'A family business – that's best.' She was glad to have a positive comment, because now he might let her go. 'Marx and Spencer. Fortnum and Mason.'

'Goodman and Goodman. It's also part of Frank's rejuvenation. It gives him a gallery space.'

'Right, I see. The pictures are his?'

'Many of them. Not all the family are on board – but don't bother about that. Does this sort of thing interest you?'

'Retail's my thing.'

'I want to open before the season ends. If you're bored and find opening a shop interesting, you could pop in and help.'

'I see. Yes, of course, but - I can't commit because I could be going home any time.'

'I'd value your expertise.'

'Oh.' It was the only acknowledgment she'd had so far of her metropolitan status. Retail presentation really was, after all, her thing, for there were few shops in London of any prestige at which she had not looked with a discerning eye. Aged ten on her first visit for afternoon tea at The Savoy she had understood with the force of epiphany the centrality, the utter and absolute imperative, of good lighting. While an indifferent display could be a little helped by well-placed lamps, nothing, however brilliant, could recover from a dim or a glaring overhead light. 'I'm not sure I'm such an expert,' she said modestly. 'I'm quite good at arranging things.'

'For now, it's mainly lifting and carrying.'

'I can lift and carry.'

'I suspect, Lillian Miranda, your lifting is beyond scope of ordinary lifters.'

'Well, I'd be happy to repay your kindness. But of course, it's quite impossible just at the moment -'

'You're a good person, Lillian.'

'Oh. Thank you.'

Lillian saw the softness of the eyes that surveyed her and heard the tenderness in the voice and hoped to God that he was not actually falling in love with her as Aunt Jenny had hinted.

'You're a good person too,' she said.

He threw out his arms. 'That, then, is established. There's one more thing.'

Lillian feared he was about to declare himself.

'Uncle Frank.'

'Uncle Frank?'

'Yes, Frank. Mum's brother. That Thing of Darkness. Frank.' That he smiled as he said this only made the description the more chilling.

'He's taken a fancy to you.'

Lillian shuddered inside. The comfort was that it was obviously untrue.

'That's not usual. Frank doesn't like many people. Not even himself. When he takes a fancy to someone, he insults them. It's a Yorkshire thing. The south is full of smiling villains who keep the word of promise to our ears and break it to our hope. Up here it's the other way round. You need to understand this.'

'I'll keep it in mind.'

'Good.' Ferdinand shifted on his box. Lillian swallowed. 'This might be a lot to ask,' he continued, 'but ...'

'What? What is it?'

'Could you ask to see his photographs?'

Lillian opened her mouth, then closed it. 'Why?' she managed.

'He needs encouragement. He won't take it from us. I don't suppose you've heard of Hiroshige, the *Thirty-Six Views of Mount Fuji*?'

Lillian had not. Her Art History course had been resolutely Euro-centric. Ferdinand read the ignorance in her face. 'Let Frank explain it,' he said. 'It will bore you to madness, but it might make him happy. Could you do that?'

'You could put some southern charm and insincerity to use,' Fiona May's voice floated down. Lillian gasped at the insult.

'Fiona!' Ferdinand remonstrated, but Lillian laughed.

'I suppose so. Yes.' Anything to get out of here. She shouldn't care, but it felt unnecessary. She knew, she had suspected it all along, these people thought she was silly. They probably said so behind her back. She felt moisture in her eyes and forced a smile.

He slapped his thighs. It signalled conclusion. He held out his hand. 'Let's be friends' he said.

'Of course.' She shook his hand wetly, softly. She hoped he did not see her lip tremble. 'I've got to shower,' she said. 'Perhaps I'll come round later.'

'That I would like.'

Ferdinand watched her down the street, a stiff, determined little person, eager to please, but wracked with tension. Fiona's question floated down. 'Why do you want her to take an interest in Frank?'

'She needs to feel valued,' he said.

Which, in this instant, she certainly did not. She would not acknowledge Curly who raised his hand to her as he turned into the supermarket square. She drove with swinging arms and smarting eyes along the white railway fence. Whistling Joe was in full whistle by the arches, warbling in a major key as though no-one had any trouble in the world. Ferdinand meant well, she was ok with Ferdinand, but it was oh so awful that she was stuck among people who not only refused to acknowledge where she was from, but who thought her slight and foolish, and did not, could not, guess what she had lost. That southern insincerity! Yes, they all thought she was stupid, which only showed what ridiculous bumpkins they were.

She did deep breaths in the hall. She needed a plan: Jesus pawed her while Mary and Joseph scrutinized her, as though they wanted to know the plan too. She had nothing.

'All right, Jesus,' she said and gave him a pat.

Footsteps on the landing: Frank's footsteps were heavier than anyone's. He slouched against the wall. And if you say the wrong thing! she thought, taut like a string on a racquet. 'You're back then,' he observed.

She wanted to say, Yes, unfortunately; or, No, I'm cruising Bond Street, can't you see? But instead, she agreed she was back. 'Mek us a coffee then, lass, while you're at it,' Frank answered and turned to his room.

It was outrageous. It was inappropriate on so many levels. She plumped on the living room sofa regardless of clutter and put her face in her hands. Jesus padded after and whined at her. She ignored him, but he jumped beside her, insistent with love, and pawed her arm. 'What is it?' she asked. He stretched and made a sound between a whine and a yawn, at which Mary and Joseph trotted in and settled on the rug to regard her.

'Not now, Jesus, I can't be bothered.'

Jesus dropped his head on her lap with a grunt. She put a hand on his neck and dropped her head and saw her trainers, the so cool trainers. Salt patches, like a mould, had already invaded the vamp and the cap, and that would get worse. She felt very very sad for her trainers. Her trainers did not deserve what was happening to them. She put her face in her hands again and she cried.

Frank's footsteps down the stairs: she composed herself into a tight face. He went down the corridor. Then he came back. He regarded her in bewilderment.

'What's wrong with thee?' he asked.

She shook her head in bitterness. Jesus, in solidarity with her misery, did not move. 'It's not right,' she muttered. 'I'm not a servant.'

Frank scratched his head. 'I only asked for a coffee.'

'It isn't the coffee,' she answered.

Frank's confusion turned to curiosity. 'Are you one of them snowflakes?' he asked.

'No. I'm not a snowflake!' she burst out at him.

'Then what…?'

'It's not *appropriate*!' she said.

Frank gave up. 'If you can't make the coffees then I'll have to,' he concluded, and left.

And now she had been rude to the people who put a roof over her head, so they wouldn't accept her anymore, and her daddy didn't even have a roof of their own, so what happens now? Everything was rubbish. He had let her down. Her only option was to go to London anyway and sort stuff out. If her life was to be taken away from her, she wanted to be there when it happened.

She did not acknowledge Frank until he said, 'Here y'are, lass,' and laid the cup on the table at her knees. He swayed from side to side. She looked up. He looked down. He had the face of one who has known pain, and who knows it in others.

'Thank you,' she answered.

'I'm in my room if you want owt,' he said. He might be embarrassed. He might be tender. Who knew with these people?

The coffee was terrible – instant with full fat milk – but she drank it anyway, pushed off Jesus's head, and rose. She drifted to the kitchen to put the mug in the dishwasher, the dogs watching her from the corridor, then went to shower. The dogs dispersed like dismissed courtiers. She sighed under the sound of the gush. The water was comfort, even though she was almost out of L'Occitaine and had no immediate means of replacing it. As she bathed in the warm flush her angry misery turned to emptiness and then to cold resolution. She stepped out as clean as waking Eve. She dried her hair sitting on the edge of her diminished bed with the travel hairdryer and gazed through the window like an abandoned princess.

She would go to London whether Daddy agreed or not.

She knocked on Frank's door. He rustled inside like a roused animal in its lair.

'Aye.'

The door stuck. 'Hang on,' Frank shouted. She heard him move the obstacle and went in. The blind was down. The space was lit by a computer screen that filled the room with an unhealthy yellow glow. He faced her on the swivel chair while she took in the clutter. How did he sleep with all that stuff on his bed?

'It's not very tidy,' Frank admitted.

'It certainly isn't,' she agreed.

'I'll have to sort it one of these days.'

'I'm good at sorting,' she said.

'I bet you are. Want to start?'

'No. Why would I? '

'Course not. So what is it?'

'Can I see your photographs?' She asked. 'Ferdy says they're really good.'

This cell's my court, Ferdinand reminded himself, as Frank burst in. Here I have few attendants, and subjects none abroad.

'Bloody hell!' Frank said.

Ferdinand paused with arms extended to a shelf, hands full. He showed neither alarm nor joy. He shuffled the box of soaps, bright as candy, to safety and waited.

'I've been talking to Lillian.'

Ferdinand took his hammer and string to the toolbox. He was grave. 'You were nice to her?' he asked.

'Course I was. She was upset about summat, but she soon got over that. Didn't say why. I made her a coffee and left her to it and, bugger me, she comes into my room minutes later and asks about my work. I told her about *The 36 Views*.'

'She was upset?'

'Aye. The thing is, I told her about the Hiroshige and Mount Fuji, the sacred mountain - and then I said I'm doing the same with the pier, I'm showing Saltscar in all its moods. I explain about the sequence and the depth of field and the calendar aspect - the whole project, right? - and she just says, 'It should be the cliff.''

'She was upset?'

'The thing is, she's right!' Ferdinand closed the toolbox lid, softly as a caress. 'A cliff's more like a mountain than a pier. A pier's man-made. Then it suddenly hit me, and I thought, 'What a fucking idiot I am.' I mean, *idiot*, mate! The Master understood that the mountain, the sacred site, that's the constant around which the ephemeral wheels, all the little things the men do. His focus is the human scene and Fuji just sits in the background, the one constant; unchanging, ancient - all that stuff. Any road -'

'Frank!' Ferdinand gestured. Frank stopped. He settled on the iron stool by the bar counter, undismayed. 'What was she upset about?'

'Does it matter? She was fine at the end. We're going up Moor Cliff when there's good light.' Ferdinand took the box to the shelf under the counter. Frank rolled a cigarette. 'Another thing,' Frank continued. 'She took three pictures. She put 'em on her wall. She put 'em on a diagonal. They looked great. Got me thinking.'

'I hope it wasn't me,' Ferdinand said.

'Look at these straight lines.' Frank gestured to the stringed walls. 'Perhaps we should have a rethink.'

'A re-think?'

'The lass might have some ideas.'

Ferdinand felt something shift beneath him, as when a skiff is hit at an odd angle by a wave, is lifted, pushed, and the shore that seemed so attainable becomes a doubt. 'Dad loved the pier,' he said. 'The pier is Saltscar.'

''Appen. But there's no harm exploring all the possibilities.' Frank took his lighter from the shirt pocket. He knew not to smoke in the cell.

'You came here to tell me that?'

'Nah. Fresh air break.' He lit up. 'Just bouncing ideas.'

'Frank - fag.'

'Aye, no worries. I'm off.' He had a final flourish. He was dark in the doorway. 'The lass has summat to offer. She's got no tits, mind, to speak off. But she 'as a fabulous arse.'

'Dear God, Frank, she's a child! Don't even mention it!'

'Nah. Mr. PC, me. Talk to her.' He showed the back of his hand and went.

Ferdinand brooded. He had given up a career and a woman for this life. He did not understand why he found Lillian so difficult and so unsettling. She had done as he asked, and that was unsettling too. What had he said to upset her? Why did it matter? Was it Fiona? One little barb from a stranger, what was that? The fragility was showing. She needed her familiar things. But she moved him. She darted around their lives with the irregular decisive flight of the swift. She was taking up a much greater space than he had expected, and just as she was unprepared for what was to hit her, so they were unsuitable ushers. But he couldn't give up. She was the little girl who had held his fingers and trusted him, the big boy, his first responsibility.

He left Fiona to her lettering and scampered under the arches where Whistling Joe was practising scales. He acknowledged gestures and nods, but did not stop because he had to catch Lillian Delph. He called in the hall. The Holy Family tumbled before him in answer, so he repeated her name, and was answered.

'What is it?"

She looked down from the landing.

'Can I talk a minute?' he asked. She regarded him warily.

'Frank said I upset you.'

'No. No. I'm sorry, it's me-'

He raised his hand. This seemed to happen a lot to her. 'You mustn't be thin-skinned up here, Lillian. We're sometimes such as stripes may move, not kindness, but underneath … We know this is a terrible time.'

'It'll be sorted soon. Daddy has contacts, you see –'

He held up his palm again. 'I'm sorry if I was insensitive. I'm on your side. One hundred per cent.'

'Really, it's nothing – it's just – why do you all look down on me?'

It was an odd thing to be asked from a head so far above him. He was about to deny it when Frank's door opened. It opened with uncompromising fury. 'Has tha' bin upsetting the lass again?' he asked.

'I'm sorry, what?'

'It's not thee, though, Ferdy. That lanky bitch what thinks she can paint.'

'It's all right, Frank,' Lillian said.

'Sincere, my Yorkshire arse.'

'It's ok, Frank.'

'The lass is a good lass.' Frank pointed at Lillian.

'Thank you, Frank.'

'What? Aye. Right.' Frank nodded in confirmation of whatever point he thought he had made. 'Whatever. If tha' needs owt,' he addressed Lillian,' yer Uncle Frank's at the end of yon corridor.' They listened for his door to close.

The cousins once removed looked at each other, and suddenly giggled. Lillian said. 'I don't know why I had to come here. It's awful! Everyone behaves like I'm lucky!'

'Come join me for tea.'

'The teapot sat between them on the dining-room table; emblem of settled domesticity. 'Let me explain about us,' he starred. 'Do you mind?' Lillian put on her serious face. This was grown up. She was understanding and sensible. 'My father was born in Rebburn, where the poor people live. His family were badly off and embittered. One day, he told me, he walked along the beach to Saltscar. When he got there he noticed how people walked. In Rebburn people either slouched or were hunched. In Saltscar they moved without fear, and that made him realise the clue to success. In a place like Saltscar you didn't waste your energies in suspicion. Anyway, he married an Ellesker. The Elleskers were once big in this area. When he was made redundant, he drove taxis and bought the shop, as I said. The cell - I called it that - was our flag, our coat of arms, it was his love of the town, and he worked at it whenever he wasn't on the road. Then he had the accident. Not his fault. He wasn't too badly hurt, but he got sepsis and died very quickly. Someone at the hospital bungled. I wasn't here when I heard. His family could hardly speak to us at the funeral. I swore then I would stay whatever happened and finish his work. He left us a partly renovated shop and a lump of debt. Of course, it's mum's shop really, but she won't take an interest because it brings her back to dad and she wants to move on. The shop is all me. But you see, Lillian, we have our own battles. You mustn't get upset with us if we're not what you're used to.'

Lillian had not heard anyone give such a long speech in her life unless it was from a teacher.

'I've lost my dad, too,' Ferdinand said. 'I walk the beach every day, musing on my father's wrack.'

'I haven't lost mine!' she retorted.

'No, but it's a shock. What's happened.'

'I just want things to be normal,' she said.

Ferdinand deliberated. 'Let's go for a swim,' he said.

She looked up in surprise. 'Whatever for?'

'It'll do us both good.'

She shook her head. 'It'll be cold,' she said.

'It's the North Sea. Why on earth should it be cold?'

Lillian was no expert on irony. 'Are you sure? I'm not a good swimmer.'

'I taught you once before,' Ferdinand said. 'I can do it again.'

Lillian wanted to curl up, and to think of nice things, and to be left alone. 'I get paid for the café work in a few days. I'll have to buy a swim-suit.'

'I can buy you a swim-suit,' Ferdinand said. 'Pay me back when you can.'

She did not like the idea of a man buying her swimming-gear. She did not like it when Edward glanced at girls in bikinis when one floated into his view. She squinted at Ferdinand and considered; does he want to oggle my bum? He was a man in his twenties who lived with his mum, which was weird enough, and he had his head stuck in the clouds, but he didn't exactly seem pervy. If he was interested in that side of her, he had disguised it so far exceedingly well. She was after all, at the seaside, and the sea was a boon.

'Can we go tomorrow then? I'm tired now.'

'I have a delivery at ten. We'll go down at eleven.'

Lillian was not entirely happy about this, but she would have a phone soon and she might have something that looked positive to send on Instagram. What was the harm? Also, it might rain, and that would let her off the hook anyway.

It did not rain. She chose a modest one-piece at the surf shop, a yellow that matched the beach and her hair. She was as slim as a frond of kelp. Ferdinand, however, with his trunks beneath his baggy shorts, was round like a seal and white below the neck. He saw Lillian glance at his belly.

'I know I'm fat,' he said.

'You're stout, that's all.'

She watched him breaststroke, the sea around her waist. He was more elegant in the water. The dogs stood up to their shanks in the breakers and barked at them. Ferdinand surfaced and gestured them to lie down. Unaccountably, Mary and Joseph obeyed. Jesus trotted along the margin until distracted by a smell.

'Let me watch you,' he said.

She was not well co-ordinated and craned her neck upwards. 'I get a bit panicky when my head goes under,' she admitted.

'The sea is a moody old god,' he said. 'His size helps us. He does not care about flotsam things bobbing in his margins. You have to meld.'

'You mean, put my head under?'

'Think of it as returning. Pull your legs up as your arms make the downstroke: the kick then propels you, and then you bring your arms forward and breathe out with your face down. You glide. That glide takes you back through evolution, down to our ancient origins...'

Lillian clapped her hands over her ears. 'Just tell me what to do!'

'Crouch down. Then kick off. Keep your body as straight as possible, then stand up.'

Lillian did this five times. On the fifth came a solid calm.

'Keep your body as straight as you can,' Ferdinand advised again. 'If your legs bend it'll force your head down.'

On the sixth, Lillian kept her legs high and was at ease in the isolation of soundless water. She grinned at her half-cousin. 'I've got it!' she said.

When they swam alongside Jesus went frantic. He plunged towards them, and tried to jump up, barking, which was not an elegant sight, and in his excitement, he paddled a circle. They swam together for twenty stokes, Jesus barking behind them. They stood to let him catch up. Instead, he turned to shore and, as soon as his paws touched sand, he bounced onto the beach, shook, then raced in a wide arc around the spots of people.

'We'd better join the pack before he jumps on someone,' Ferdinand said.

Mary and Joseph acknowledged them with wagging tails. Ferdinand called Jesus and sat with a towel over his shoulders. Lillian lay back and closed her eyes. She heard Jesus pad next to her, his pants a counterpoint to the slow shush and plop of the sea, then felt his breath on her forehead. She pressed her eyes shut in anticipation of his tongue, but received instead a rasping long lick on her ear, and then she heard him drop on the sand and a great soft calm welled inside her. The calm was like love, and she breathed long in anticipation of a rare sexual thought, but instead, struck with a new image, she turned on her side and looked along the beach to the pier

'Gus?' she whispered.

It was not Gus. As soon as she lay back, eyes closed, a whole childhood summer woke inside her and she saw a woman standing on the beach with folded arms smiling at her, and Aunt Jenny's voice sounded: 'Ferdy's very good with her,' and the woman with folded arms said in response, 'Oh, dear. She's happy here.'

She knew it all. She knew the pier, the café with the round metal tables, the ice creams, the handsome guys with surfboards, the burgundy and cream funicular, its wheeze as it set off, the smell of fried fish and the seagulls' cries, and the old craggy arm of Mount Cliff that told her the beach was held firm and was real and forever.

She sat up. 'I've been here before,' she told Ferdinand, and Ferdinand, who was looking out to sea, said, 'Of course you have.'

She had indeed. She was playing giddy-up on the back of the big boy. She kicked her little heels into his ribs, and he whinnied for her. Her Auntie Jenny handed her an ice-cream and a slender, serious woman, blonde like herself, walked towards them, and she asked why the lady was sad. She was in bed, listening to voices downstairs, and she heard footsteps and pattering paws on the stairs. She was crying on the landing. The door opened and in the crack of light a woman's frame bent towards her, and the woman said, 'Can't you sleep?' 'You're talking downstairs,' she answered. 'We have something serious to talk about.' She was held in a man's arm, briefly, and then she saw little Ferdinand sitting at her bedside so things would be alright. She was in a hole in the sand and digging. 'The tide's coming,' she screamed. Ferdinand was digging as well. They were making a wall. 'The tide's coming!' The water seeped round the sand wall, and she dug. A wave breached the defence and she screamed again, in fear and delight, as the water rose round her waist.

Ferdinand was staring out to sea. 'It will become more familiar in time,' he told her.

Lillian had not been up this early since the Duke of Edinburgh's trip to the Brecon Beacons. That was the one when she'd waited outside the tent hoping it would not rain while Chloe had sex with the guy from Bradfield. There was no hint of rain today. The sun belted light from over Moor Cliff along the bay, brushing the undertips of clouds and running the bay from a rich tumeric around Lillian's ankles to a pale straw where the industrial buildings glinted. The spindly legs of the pier cast long shadows, crisp as toast, along the littoral. Wetness glassed the sand. Clouds sailed in the glass.

'Under the pier,' Frank said.

Lillian did as she was told, but protested, 'The light's behind me.'

'Let me worry about that,' Frank answered.

Lillian jumped up and down and skipped before the camera. She flung out her arms and flicked her hair. Frank gazed over the lens in confusion.

'What the fuck's tha' doing?'

'Don't swear. It's not clever. I'm looking happy for Instagram.'

'Looking happy?' Frank seemed to think this the height of unreason. 'Never mind about happy. Just walk.'

'Just walk?'

'Aye. From theer to theer. It's not 'ard. You put one leg -'

'I know how to walk,' Lillian pouted.

Lillian walked. Frank clicked. A seagull watched.

'Champion,' Frank said. 'Now stand and face me. Proper portrait. I'll call it The View of Delph.' Lillian had no idea why Frank found this funny. He unclasped the camera from the tripod and walked to the sunward side. 'Close up,' he said. He clicked around her face. It was intrusive.

'Right then. Now for the hard bit. Up Moor Cliff.'

'Can I see?' Lillian reached for the camera.

'Tha's a reet proper narcissist, ain'tcha?'

Lillian thought she was normal. 'That's rude,' she said.

'When we get back then. Now fer the cliff.'

Lillian had the camera bags and the water and snacks in her haversack. Frank carried the tripods over one shoulder and a holder with a cushion and the little folding steps in the other. His was bulkier but hers was heavier. He smiled a wrinkled malicious smile at the base of Cat Knoll.

'It's harder than it looks,' he said. 'Take it steady.'

Cat Knoll had a clear broad trail, broken by steps that curled behind the slope. It was the precursor to The Dragon's Back, which was precursor to The Neck of the Dragon, which, Frank had already assured her, was the final climb. 'The Neck's the killer. The Back's more gentle.' The A-road hummed behind them.

'You might regret only having a t-shirt,' Frank said. 'It can get parky even in summer, and if a sea-fret comes, well...'

'I don't know what parky means. And I won't.'

'As yer like. Off you go.'

The breeze was welcome. She ascended on light steps. Soon she looked down on the people and dogs walking the stretch along the stream in the Valley Garden. They disappeared as the path curled, and she was surrounded by tough grass, gorse with its swarm of vivid yellow dots and packed brambles. After the steps cut between the grass, the path levelled towards the hump of The Dragon's Back. She started to trot.

'Pace yoursen!' Frank shouted.

There were more brambles, and flowers in clumps, the names of which she did not know, but they were pretty, as was the single cloud with silver fringes from the west. Its shadow trailed behind the crown of Saltscar, darkened the valley, then swallowed Lillian and billowed over the sea. The path gave out to stubby grass and rocks with moss on them. She would soon be bored, so she set her face, and lengthened her stride. Down one depression, up again: there was farmland to her right, a white farmhouse, the searing yellow rapeseed, then burnished yellow stubble, and in front the sudden rise of the Neck. She slowed because the haversack was bumping. Faint, high-pitched, like the thin cry of a bird, Frank's voice sounded far behind.

'Fucking pace yourself!'

At the top, broad steps were cut into the bump that was known as The Neck of the Dragon. There was more bright gorse to her left: its clumps of flowers were bright as children's sweets. She'd heard it smelt of vanilla so stopped to sniff. It was true. It smelled of vanilla. The farmland remained to her right, but ahead of her, beyond it, she spotted the dark blue-green of the moor. She straightened the straps over her shoulders and took the last steps looking at her feet so the view would be a surprise, and when she hit the last one she looked up and saw a deer.

It was an actual deer. It had little antlers, delicate feet, a short tail with a white bob at the end, and it was so unexpected and cute it might have come from a story book or a film. Then it turned its head from the shrub it was eating and looked at her. She noted the twitching nose, the slanted eyes, the tuft of hair between the antlers and, as the sun burst over it, she had her breath stolen by the hues of its flanks and thighs. She suddenly heard the breeze through the gorse and the grass with the far shush of the sea beneath it. The deer looked at her and she looked at the deer, the one in caution and the other in wonder, until the deer turned with a disdainful rise of its head and tumbled away. It checked, looking over its shoulder to see if she followed. She was still. She noted the weight of the thighs on the skeletal legs and the varnish of antlers in sunlight,

'Fucking' 'ell.'

Frank was scrambling into view. His bag dragged after him. He stopped when he saw her, breathing heavily. The deer crashed away. She watched it disappear over the rise and stared into the space that was empty of deer.

She sat to wait for him. He dropped his bag beside her and plopped down into splayed legs.

'What the fuck?' he asked.

'There was a deer,' she said.

'Let me get my breath.'

'A literal deer. With antlers and everything.'

'I'm glad about that,' he answered. 'I can't stand them metaphorical ones.'

'Where did it come from?'

'How did you do that?"

'What?'

'You're not even puffing.'

These northerners were feeble. 'I'm young,' she said. 'You didn't see it?'

'I once saw five or six does over yon, moseying around, all flighty, like they were looking for a buck.'

'That's disgusting. And sexist.'

Frank frowned, then understood. 'A buck!' he said. 'A boy deer. With a 'b'.'

'Oh.'

'They come down from the moors in summer. One fell off t' cliff last year.'

'That's awful.'

'Aye, well, they're none too bright. Here we are then. The Neck of the Dragon.'

Lillian looked around. She had no idea what he wanted to photograph.

'We're staying here?'

'No. We go about a mile along the cliff. There's a right turn to a disused shaft.'

'Come on then,' she said brightly, and set off. 'I've seen a deer!' she shouted back.

The path scoured the edge of the cliff, the steepest on the east coast, below which the sea was blue as in a bad painting and the rocks crinkled at the base, like raisings scattered over crust. She repeated, 'Morning,' to a middle-aged couple with double walking sticks, and stepped aside for a younger party of four women with no make-up who walked past with an air of wholesome endeavour. Lillian took the Armani sunglasses from one pocket. She stood a step from the edge and raised her arm and told Frank to photograph her.

'Watch yoursen,' Frank warned. 'We don't want an Incident.'

She led on for ten minutes when they passed an iron ring with metal shapes attached to the inside like old teeth which she assumed was a sculpture. 'Charm Bracelet,' said Frank. It didn't seem to her a good use of money, though perhaps it was ancient. They had such in parks, where at least there were people to see them. Its shards suggested toughness, but, if that was the idea, it didn't pass muster because it was playful, and made the cliff walk actually less wild. The track might be more severe further on, but as she stretched out Frank called her.

'Along here,' he said.

They mounted over a stile and went on a rise away from the cliff over a field and through a gate and rose to a concrete structure near the top. Lillian climbed over a metal gate and trotted the last rise and stood by the crumbling tower and felt pleased with herself. It was a charmless concrete block, weathered and roofless, with a blackness where an entrance had been, taped off in wasp yellow and black with a warning sign. She waited on Frank who trudged past her to the top.

'Come over here.'

Lillian obediently went over there. They looked back where the ridge of Moor Cliff edged into the sky. It was soft green and gentle. The morning winked on Saltscar, perched like a crown on the buff, a gold glint, and laid before them the long bland stretch of the bay, a dropped tan ribbon. She could make out the needles of the wind farm, and the smudge of spent industry at the estuary that had dismayed her on the train.

Frank was assembling the tripod.

'Is this it?' she asked.

'Look the other way.' He pointed away from Moor Cliff, along the path they had taken. There was a cove further on, with the glint of roofs, a gleam of sand and sea, beyond which the cliff rose again to the moors.

'It's very pretty,' she admitted.

'It is from up here. It's desolate as 'ell when you get there.'

'What do we do now?'

'We wait.'

'What for?'

'For the moment.'

This made no sense, but she didn't care. It was sunny, and soon she'd be home and might never return. She sat and ate yoghurt with a plastic spoon and drank the Pellegrino. The grass was moist and cool, and she didn't care about that either. She quite liked it. It was pretty up here, and if Frank was rude she could ignore him and return back to town. She dropped raspberries into her yoghurt. They were tart. She handed Frank his pasty. He took it without thanking her and kept his eye on the camera. It was pointing over the bay.

He dropped the paper bag. 'You shouldn't do that,' she said.

'What?'

'Litter.'

'Aye, 'appen.' He picked it up indifferently and stuffed it in his pocket.

'Why do you talk like that?'

'Like what?'

''Appen' and 'mesen' and 'thee' and ... and...'

'Si'thee.'

'Yes.

'And 'si'thee yon'.

'Why do you do it?'

Frank looked through the lens again. 'I never thought I'd be criticised fer speaking me own language.'

'Aunt Jenny doesn't.'

That got his attention. 'Yer what?"

'Why do you speak like that if your sister doesn't.'

Frank looked over the camera at the glinting sea. 'It's an identity thing. Yer Aunt Jenny's comfortable in her own skin. She talks like everyone around her. I'm a loner, me. I carry me roots around inside. Not like yer mother.'

Lillian stared at him with the spoon to her lips. 'You don't know my mother,' she said at length.

'Appen not.'

She frowned at him. 'You don't. She's spent most of her life in Australia.'

'Appen.'

'What do you mean, 'appen'? She has!'

'You know best.'

'Yes, I do. She went with a man called Jeremy. Aunt Jenny said she was in Scotland, but if that's so, it's recent.'

'Right. She went with a man called Jeremy.'

Lillian finished the yoghurt and filled the cup with tissue and replaced it in the haversack. She felt patronised again. Frank changed the subject. 'People don't get landscape photography,' he started. 'They think it's nice views and composition, and perhaps light, whereas composition is the least interesting part of the visual arts.' (Oh, God, here we go again, thought Lillian. Ideas.) 'It's all about the moment, just as much as photo-journalism. There's a little cloud o'er yon. There's five ships in a queue fer the port. When the shadow of that little cloud is ovver them ships, then, click! Tonal variety. That's what you get with the sea.'

Lillian lay down and thought of Harrods.

'Ferdy don't understand it, you know,' Frank droned on. 'He thinks the coast is stories; history, people, hardships, and shipwrecks, and smuggling and all that bollocks. It's not. It's about transcendence. Think of that whole sweep of sea and sky as a giant Barnet Newman. It's the infinite revealed, or glimpsed any road. Aye. It overwhelms us because its beginnings and its ends lack definition. Even the light -'

Lillian clasped her ear. 'Please!' she shouted. 'I'm not interested.'

Frank grimaced. 'Please yoursen,' he finished and waited for his cloud. After a minute, however, he started again. 'Course, the Sublime elements and the abstraction would seem to run counter to the narrative thrust of *The 36 Views* -'

'No!' Lillian shouted. 'Shut up!'

Frank was aggrieved. 'That's no way to talk to your elders. I'm jus' -'

'Whatever.'

Frank laughed. It was not a mocking laugh. It was the laugh boys make when someone in their number bumps into a post, comfortable with disorder. He then whistled something badly. Then he was silent. He looked through the lens. Lillian noted successive clicks.

'Bingo,' Frank said.

'Have we finished?'

'I want to mosey o'er yon. See if I can do summat with the mineshaft. Then I'll do one of thee - if that's acceptable, miss.'

'Yes. Whatever.'

She lay back and let her head fill with the good times gone, the stuff she would buy when this was over, of her father's bad temper, and, unusual for her, a sexual thought, and then the deer. A wild deer. Whose was it? Where had it come from? Where was it going? A Swiss girl at school had been mad about animals, and could tell you how dormice slept, and Lillian liked looking at large mammals on You Tube, but it had never registered until now that wild ones really were allowed to wander, that they had blood, and eyes, and a brain that registered fears and hopes. She wondered how much anyone on the Instagram feed would be impressed that she had met a genuine wild deer.

Frank's stride sounded soft over the grass. She shielded her eyes to look up.

'Any good?' she asked.

'Appen. I'm whacked.' He plopped down. 'Nice sleep?'

'I wasn't sleeping.'

'There's nowt wrong with sleeping.'

'I was thinking.'

'Oh, aye. So it were the grass that were snoring. Right.'

Lillian was offended. She rose. 'Shall we go back?'

'I'll tek one of thee looking out to sea.'

Lillian thought it rather rude to photograph her back, and rather feared he was perving her bottom, but she had no make-up on, and when he was finished they could return. They took the gentler and longer slope through the farmland. Frank cast glances into the verges like a forager, and occasionally photographed something that had to Lillian's nothing of interest at all. They curled round and joined the steps at the bottom of The Dragon's Back. Frank complained as they dropped down that this was bad for his knees, but Lillian, happy at having done something her hosts must approve, ignored him. When they got to Saltscar, already lively with the mid-morning visitors, Frank insisted they took the funicular as he wouldn't lug the equipment up the steps after all that effort. The funicular was fun in a quaint old-fashioned way if you could forget the London Eye: it had fitted pine benches and painted images and fish and mermaids on the glass. The little children, a boy and a girl, stood on parents' knees to watch the sea appear as the machinery rose. Lillian remembered that attention, so quickly born, so quickly gone, like a pause in gusting winds. At the top Frank ran his fingers through his hair and blew out his cheeks as though his efforts had made the cabin rise.

'That was a morning's work,' he said. 'I'm ready fer a bite. Fancy cake?'

'I'm going for a run,' Lillian answered.

He regarded her with amazement. 'Bloody 'ell. We should enter you fer the Saltscar Scramble.'

'Of course,' she said. 'If I'm here.'

It was the evening of Lillian's first pay.

Ferdinand burst into the clatter of chairs being turned upside down on tables. Lillian was doing the clattering. Anne-Marie, perched over a lap-top at the counter watched her with interest: a look of reappraisal perhaps. Marian - Maid Marion of the Many Tattoos – stepped from the back room and yawned, a good-natured yawn of animal pleasure.

'Ai, I'm fair whacked,' she announced.

The two slim women did not acknowledge this, nor Ferdinand. Lillian swung the last chair, and spun it, and with swift grace placed it on the table. Ferdinand raised his waxed hat.

'Here I am,' he said, 'Ferd of the North.'

'Hello, Fuckwit,' his sister acknowledged him. Marian tittered. 'Come look at this.'

'Hello, Ferdinand,' said Lillian, happy with action.

'Good evening, Lillian. Out of doubt, you were born in a merry hour.' He joined his sister at the screen. Lillian picked up a used cardboard mug from under the last table, screwed it up and took it to the bin outside.

Brother stood beside sister and both regarded the screen. 'That's an estimate for stock based on a few calls and the prices you've given me so far,' Anne-Marie said. 'This is an estimated weekly running cost, not adjusted for inflation.'

'Seems a bit steep.'

'That's without staff.'

He pointed to a detail. 'What's that?'

'Tax. Business rates are higher than residential.'

He was grave. 'Difficult,' he said. He threw out his arms. 'But not impossible.'

'Daddy says', Lillian chimed in, returning, 'that one man's debt is another man's income.'

'Apart from the gender privilege,' Anne-Marie responded, 'Daddy is right Not that it's worked out for him exactly, has it?'

'Marie!' Ferdinand whispered.

'Just stating facts,' Anne-Marie said, but she saw Lillian's face. 'Sorry, Lillian, it's just an example. I'm not making a judgement.'

'I didn't imagine you were.' Lillian flushed. 'I've finished here. I'll get my coat.

'You are harsh, sister,' Ferdinand said when Lillian had gone.

'I'm the only one actually helping her,' she said. 'And I have good reason to be harsh. All right, I'll make it up to her. We'll take her to Barby Blackstone. She got her first pay today. We'll do girly things in the charity shop.'

'I'll do something manly in Costa.'

'Mum wants to take her to Scotland.'

Ferdinand glanced at the door behind which Lillian was retrieving her coat and bag. 'She's said nothing to me.'

'It blurted out. You know mum.

'When she thinks she must speak.'

'I'll forbid it.'

He pondered. 'Be gentle, sister. O wonder!' he exclaimed as Lillian returned. 'How many goodly creatures are there here! We're going to Barby Blackstone, Lillian.'

'What's that?'

'A place where the people are beautiful and the buildings are white. Yorkshire through and through. If you haven't seen Barby Blackstone, you haven't seen Yorkshire. Without acquaintance with Barby Blackstone, your idea of Yorkshire would be seriously squew-whiff.'

'Is it rough?' Lillian asked.

'Not as rough as Brixton on a bad day,' he reassured her. 'It is not the Isle of Dogs. And it has Costa.'

Lillian felt like a child taken on a trip to the countryside. She sometimes considered the family was ushering her into a lair. It was a lair scented with wildflowers and Aunt Jenny's excellent food – praise where it was due - an island of amiable though often incomprehensible sounds, and which had lost some of its power to hurt since her trip on the cliffs with Frank. Nevertheless, she was resistant. Aunt Jenny had once again suggested a trip to the Ellesker home, the farmhouse, where the monstrous Dorothy awaited. She pronounced the surname, her mother's maiden name, as though it had a special significance to them both, though as far as Lillian was concerned the Elleskers were a long-forgotten clan, or a people from story books who had nothing to do with her. Ferdinand asked her about the shop as though she cared, and it was a strain to be polite without London insincerity. Even Anne-Marie on the way from work had said she was sorry that it was below her skill level.

'That's the north,' she said. 'We work below our abilities. South of Oxford it's the other way round.'

And what would you know about the south? Lillian thought, but did not say. All this time her father was in difficulty and she was not there to help.

Ferdinand twisted round. 'I forgot the ask about your father,' he said.

'Yes, he's out.'

'Ah! You must be relieved.'

'Of course.' They didn't care about Daddy.

'You're holding up wonderfully well,' he said.

'Thank you.'

'Shortly you'll be out of the land of the Elleskers and in the lotus land of Barby Blackstone.'

Yes, this was once her mother's land; her mother, who had gone to Australia with Jeremy and was now in Scotland, where Lillian had never been. This is what her mother had taken from her when she had walked out of her life, with the exception of a week or so one summer, but that was no great loss. They passed nondescript fields and circled a roundabout and then rose between hedges over a wooded hill, no more interesting than the flatness around the A303 to Devon and Cornwall. Why had her mother gone, anyway? Why had these people only appeared when she and her daddy had difficulties? It would have made more sense to burst upon them when, in the first triumphs of his career, he had bought the house in Kensington. They had a lot to offer then. Perhaps they were taking advantage for the day when they bounced back.

'What do you think of it so far?' Ferdy asked.

'Standard countryside,' she said.

'Ah, but wait till you see Barby Blackstone.'

He was being sarcastic, surely. She expected it would be dull. Then the car came down the hill, entered another roundabout with a car park to one side, and, after the car park, an avenue of limes.

The avenue opened to a broad main road. There were houses with bent bays in pale sandstone. A classical town-hall faced a row of Georgian terraces, some with geraniums on the bottom sills. A stream burbled beside the road and flowed under a quaint stone bridge before the green. Lillian stood, a slender flower, on the market street of Barby Blackstone and noted that almost all the parked cars were 4x4s.

'It's quaint,' she said.

'Mum's car lowers the tone,' Ferdinand remarked. 'It's a good job it's not Sunday.'

'Why?' the sister asked.

'This is the new Conservative Heartland. All cheese here is artisanal. Black pudding is eaten raw. No whippets. On Sunday no car is allowed below an Audi. The sumptuary laws state tweed skirts for the ladies and cravats for the men-'

'Really?'

'Lillian,' said Anne-Marie, 'get real.'

'Oh.'

Lillian looked around. There were shops, but none with inviting light in the windows. She had made ninety pounds. That was more than she usually had to spend. On the other hand, her father was no longer buying her Stuff: it was the things that were bought one that counted. Her old London friends were at the age when they were given their first second-hand car. That was well beyond her horizon now. It was September; the Autumn collection would have been out for weeks, but for her there was not even a Christmas outfit. Barby Blackstone was like a film set for a period drama, but apart from that, what was the point of it?

'What have you noticed?' Ferdinand asked.

'Sorry?'

'You seem transfixed.'

'Oh, nothing. Why are we here?'

'So you can help me choose a new scarf,' said Anne-Marie. 'This way.'

'Can't I come?' Ferdinand asked.

'Girl stuff, Ferdy.'

'I wouldn't mind him coming,' said Lillian.

Anne-Marie leaned over to her. 'I want to talk to you,' she said. Lillian knew something bad was about to happen. She wasn't reassured when she looked back and saw Ferdinand looking after them.

'I'll see you in Costa,' he shouted.

Anne-Marie led onto the cobbles that fringed the tarmac, remains of the old street on which the market stalls of yore had stood. It was a solid village of pale stone along a wide main street, with a lawned square at one end around which houses with rounded bays gleamed in the six-o'clock September light. Some of the shops had bays as well, with little windows set in frames, that made it even more like a set in a costume drama. One of them had a Barbour sign. There was a lot of Barbour up here. That was the outdoor thing. There was a cheese shop next to it, with lists written in chalk on a blackboard outside. Lillian guessed they were trying to impress her.

'It's a lovely village,' she said.

'If you like country living. In here.'

'It's a charity shop!'

'You don't do charity shops, I take it.'

'Oh, yes,' said Lillian. 'I take all my old clothes to the Octavia Foundation off Holland Park.'

'I bet you do. Whatever that is. Come on.'

Anne-Marie knew her mind, but her mind did not always know what was best. She was drawn to sky colours – bright blues, white, and yellows - when she was obviously an earth person, with auburn hair and almond eyes and olive skin. Lillian, in contrast, was sky.

'This one goes with your hair,' Lillian said.

'Edinburgh Woollen Mill.' Anne-Marie held it up. 'It's a bit dull.'

'It looks quite rich against your pullover.'

Anne-Marie gazed at Lillian's suggestion in one hand and her pale blue cashmere selection in the other. 'Oh, bugger it,' she said. 'When in doubt get the cheapest. It's only a scarf.'

Anne-Marie was superficial.

The 'word' seemed forgotten, but when they came out – which took a minute because there was a problem with the card machine and the elderly lady volunteer was clueless – Anne-Marie gave her a rare smile and thanked her, then suddenly said, 'You seem to get on with Ferdinand.'

'Oh, yes. He's been very nice.'

Anne-Marie pondered. 'Yes, he is. What do you think of the shop?'

'It's very impressive.'

169

'I think he suggested you help him.'

'It wasn't put very strongly. I'd love to, but you see there's the job at the café and I can't commit because –'

'Don't even think it,' Anne-Marie said.

That pulled Lillian up short. Anne-Marie tugged her arm to move for a man behind. The man touched the peak of his cap as he passed in thanks.

'This is the point,' Anne-Marie went on. 'I love my brother, but he's hopeless. If you make any promises about it, you'll be here forever. He'll never get it started. His life is a series of failures, and one day he'll use up all the money we have. He'll be forced to leave Saltscar. I've explained this to him and to mum, but they're deaf to it all. Mum stays out of it on principle because it's about Ferdinand and dad and it helps keeps Frank on the straight and narrow. I've promised to help, and I will, but I resent it.'

'Oh dear.'

'It's a charity, Lillian!' she said. 'It isn't a business at all. Mum owns it as a charity for her son and her brother. Ferdy runs it as a charity for Saltscar. If that's what you want, fine.' They stopped at the crossing lights. 'It annoys me that Ferdy effectively gets dad's money to lose and I get nothing. That's what happens to the older sister. When he was little dad took him to rugby and I stood on the touchlines until he'd finished being bad at it. Nothing's changed, bless him. I'd like to be shut of it, but, you know - family. But you, why do you stay?'

The street that had moments ago had appeared solid and quaint and settled, now seemed too wide, the people dwarfed. 'At the moment, I don't have much choice,' she said.

'Of course you do! You're eighteen. You can do what you want.'

'Yes. Oh, yes. But Daddy thinks –'

'Never mind him. He loves you, but what use is that, really? Save every penny from the café and then get a job. Share with a friend if need be. Sell something. That watch must be worth a fortune in itself.'

'It was a present,' said Lillian.

'Oh, well.' Anne-Marie, the false friend, tucked Lillian's arm into hers and marched them across the street. 'There's another thing. Your mother. She's family too. I've no idea what you think or feel about her, but there's always the chance she'll turn up one day. Unless you're absolutely happy with that, you ought to have an escape route. Save every penny you can.'

'I was led to believe,' Lillian said, 'that my mother's in Australia.'

'From whom?'

'Daddy.'

'Mm.' Lillian did not like mm.' 'Mm' was reflective. 'Mm,' did not consent. Anne-Marie was looking to cross the road. 'She left Australia years ago,' she said.

'But she did go?'

'I believe so.'

'Is she in Scotland?'

'Highlands. Mum sometimes meets her in Edinburgh, though not often because of the expense.'

'In Edinburgh?'

Anne-Marie stared at her. She continued to stare even though pedestrians had to walk round them. 'Yes, Edinburgh. The capitol of Scotland.'

'Aunt Jenny suggested I went with her one day.'

'Mum's as big a fool as Ferdinand. He likes you a lot, by the way.'

'You're lucky to have such a brother.'

'No, I'm not. And don't imagine you can take my place. He'll break your heart. Come on.'

Anne-Marie swept over the road with Lillian in her wake. Lillian blew out her cheeks in outrage. Who did this woman think she was, or what Lillian herself was, for that matter? Anne-Marie did not hold the door when she went into Costa, but smiled back, put her finger to her lips, and sailed in to where Ferdinand sat reading in the gloom by the far wall. He closed the book as she sat.

'You have to congratulate Lillian,' she said.

'Well done, Lillian,' Ferdinand said and held out his hand. 'What for?' he asked his sister, sitting.

'She went into a shop and didn't buy anything even though she's been paid.' Anne-Marie smiled the thin smile of a shared secret.

'There wasn't much there,' Lillian said.

'You didn't look hard.'

Ferdinand sat back and held imaginary lapels. 'It's a truth universally acknowledged that a single woman in possession of her first pay-check has to look after her brass.'

'Thank you, Mr Darcy,' said Anne-Marie. 'What do you want, Lillian? Was it Mr Darcy? Colin Firth?'

'Near enough. What do you want, Lillian?'

'No, please.,' Lillian said. She wavered, but finished, for she would not save every penny whatever Anne-Marie said. 'I'll get them.'

'I'll have another Harrogate Spring Water,' said Ferdinand. 'Five pounds fifty.'

'How much?' Lillian was shocked.

The siblings laughed. Lillian was abashed to be so foolish twice in an hour. 'We'll make a Yorkshire girl of you yet,' Ferdinand said.

She regarded them from the counter. Anne-Marie flapped the back of her hand in remonstrance at Ferdinand's arm and Ferdinand held it in mock-agony. Anne-Marie was smiling at something he'd said. She was buttering him up in case he realised her part in Lillian's departure. They were lucky, nevertheless. Lillian had never missed a sibling, but if she'd had a younger brother, even only a year younger, she would have loved him like a mother. She would have been the best sister in the world.

She heard a murmur beside her. She was blocking the queue.

'Sorry,' she said and stepped aside for an old couple.

The man held the tray. 'You carry on, love,' he said.

'What do you think of Barby Blackstone?' Ferdinand asked when she set the tray on the table.

Lillian didn't just want to make a conventional remark. She was a serious woman, but when she pictured the street outside, she realised what had made it a little unreal. 'It's very white,' she said, 'ethnically.' She checked herself; that might sound judgemental, or, worse, an approval. 'It's very nice. It reminds me of the Cotswolds,' she added as a palliative.

'Without the undesirables; ex-Prime Ministers, newspaper magnates, television presenters, Russian mafia.'

'You're such a snob, Ferdy,' Anne-Marie said.

Ferdy's not a snob, Lillian thought. He's just misguided.

At breakfast the next morning, Aunt Jenny was in a flap. The seriousness of an Aunt Jenny flap was not easy to gauge as flapping was sort of her thing anyway. She was talking into her phone as she brushed her hair before the hall mirror. Her gabble clarified as Lillian came down the stairs.

'The tall one's in hospital. Yes, you'd think so, wouldn't you, but there it is. The trouble with a cancellation is that we might have to refund and that's … exactly. I need you to look at the terms of our insurance, and I'll ring round and see what we can do. At least it isn't the holiday season now. Yes, thank you, Nigel. I might be a little late back,' she told Lillian. 'The Shore Singers are one down. I'll need to resolve that today. Do you like folk music? You must try the porridge. It's Jumbo Oats and I add caramelised apple.'

'I don't think I've heard any.'

'It's not in fashion. And modal scales aren't for everyone.' She plumped her bag on the dining room table and went through it. 'Ferdy likes it, of course, but Ferdy likes anything to do with the sea. And there's blackberries. Mrs Simpson gave me a bowlful from the hedge at the top of the bank, Rebburn way. Are you at the café today?'

'Only the lunch shift. Aunt Jenny?'

'Yes?'

Aunt Jenny was the only person Lillian knew who calmed down when a new issue arose in a crisis. 'Why does Anne-Marie run the café?' she asked.

'Where -? What an idiot. I left it on the hall table. To tidy her over. She insists on her contribution. '

'But she won't do it forever?'

'Good heavens, no!' Aunt Jenny laughed. 'Anne-Marie is like you. She's destined for greatness. I never worry about Anne-Marie. She's waiting for the right job. She's turned down two already. One was in Milton Keynes – I can understand she wouldn't want to go there – and the other was in Leeds. That's better than Milton Keynes, but still …. But mainly it's Dave. An odd relationship, curiously passionless, but they share the same values.'

'Ah!'

'Exactly. Is that Frank?'

Frank's tread was heavy on the stairs. Aunt Jenny rose to catch him. 'Frank. I might be late today, so you'll have to sort yourself out. Rummage through the freezer, Frank.'

Frank gave a thumbs up. 'Morning, lass,' he said.

'Morning, Frank,' Lillian shouted from the kitchen. She was spooning Aunt Jenny's porridge into a bowl.

'Wish us luck. We're starting the 'ang.'

'Oh, Frank! How wonderful!' Aunt Jenny announced.

'Pop in, Lillian, love. Yer've got the Eye.'

'He's been a man transformed since he had a purpose,' Aunt Jenny remarked when the door closed. 'That's down to Ferdinand. And you, of course, a little bit.'

'It's a very exciting project.' Lillian sat opposite. 'But, Aunt Jenny, why doesn't Anne-Marie run it until she leaves?'

'That's a whole Issue in itself.' Aunt Jenny stood. 'How do you find the porridge?'

'It's delicious.'

'Oatmilk,' Aunt Jenny exclaimed. 'Since oatmilk came into the supermarkets my porridge has gone to a whole new level. No, Anne-Marie doesn't need the shop. Frank does. Ferdy does. Look at the time. Lillian, you're very bad keeping me here. You will be all right by yourself?'

'I've got lots I can do.'

Aunt Jenny sighed with satisfaction. 'You know,' she said, 'It really might all work out!'

Lillian ate the porridge. She reflected as she ate that she liked Ferdinand in small doses and knew that Frank liked her. Aunt Jenny was kindness itself, which she dolloped out in carless portions to any passing waif. Saltscar people recognised her: they greeted her, and Curly and Jean asked how she was: when she'd bumped into her on Top Prom Jean had asked her how much she missed the buzz of London life, which Lillian had considered a sensible question. She liked the Holy Family. The Holy Family liked her. But it was getting complicated. Lillian did not like complications. She felt the expectations of a community squeezing and moulding her for the first time in her life, and she was wary of it. As she fastened the pink trainers – salt-stained beyond recovery, but still the indomitable pink trainers – Anne-Marie's advice seemed the grown-up option.

In ten seconds she stepped into the new day with a fixed expression and her Rolex on her wrist and after the run marched into the jewellers despite her sweat. The woman behind the counter did not at first understand its value. She squinted at it and then at Lillian, and asked, 'Where did you get this?' and Lillian told the truth.

'From my father. It was my eighteenth birthday present.'

'I see.' She tapped on the keyboard, checking a serial number at the back of the watch. She looked from the screen with a serious expression, then turned to a door behind her.

'Pamela,' she said.

An older woman appeared.

'The young lady wants to sell this watch,' the younger said. The old lady appraised Lillian with a glance, then checked the screen. 'She says it's a birthday present,' the younger explained.

'Do you have a receipt?' Pamela asked.

'Why?'

'For a watch like this we need to establish the provenance.'

'The provenance. You mean where it was bought? Boodles in Bond Street. I can show you the box.' Lillian spoke in the clearest RP. It almost scratched the glass of the cabinets. The shopkeepers hesitated. 'It would sell in the York branch,' the younger finally suggested. The older handed the watch back.

'Could you give us a contact number?' she asked. 'We'll get back to you later today.'

Lillian was serving a pot of Yorkshire Tea to a couple with faces like potatoes when the call came through. She answered before arranging the service on the table. She was appalled. 'But it cost six thousand!' she protested. The woman – it was Pamela – explained the position. 'I can't accept less than three thousand,' Lillian said. The potato-faced couple studied the teapot with deep attention. 'Two-eight is my final offer.' Lillian sighed. This was her daddy's craziest present. Even The Trophy had smiled at her delight when she cradled it in her fingers and then kissed him. 'Yes? I can come in this afternoon,' she said. She thrust the phone in her trouser pocket and attended to the table. 'I'm so sorry,' she said to the two open mouths and the wide eyes that stared up at her. 'Let me take the tray.'

Lillian had kept few secrets in her life. There had been no need. But she told herself that when and why she returned to London wasn't really any of the Goodman's business. What she needed was to get Daddy to insist, then she could tell the Goodman's she was leaving as though she was sorry to go and that would leave no-one offended. It was Friday: he'd been out of hospital a week. She would go on Monday. She and her father would resolve the arrangements over the weekend and the result would be that she had to leave for London on Monday.

That was her conclusion when she returned from the café, her hand on the black wooden gate, and heard her name. Frank was walking with almost a swagger up the street.

'Ey up, lass. Tha's not seen the 'anging yet.'

'Hello, Frank. How are you?'

'Champion.' He squidged the vanquished roll-up with his sole. 'Solid day's work. We've got a couple of thee on the walls.

'Lovely.'

'Tha'll be round tomorrer then?'

'Sometime.'

'I'm that chuffed,' he said as the dogs circled round their legs in the hall. 'Why not nip down and 'ave a gander thi'sen?'

'I've got to speak to my father. I've had some mis-calls when I was at work. I think it's important.'

'Oh, aye, in that case,' Frank said and looked solemn.

Daddy was not answering so she lay on the bed and thought of the things she could do in London. She'd get a job: she knew she could handle that now, and with three thousand pounds she could find a flat-share and still have enough once she was earning. It would be hard, but it would not be for long. Daddy was out of hospital, and he could be back at work in a matter of weeks, days even. She'd knock around with Maria, and she'd even call on the crew, just to show she was tougher now, undaunted, and strong and didn't take shit, and that stuff about her father was rubbish. Then he answered.

'Hello, Randa, I've got some encouraging news.'

'Oh, Daddy, it's so exciting.'

'Mr Shevchenko has a place for me.'

'That's brilliant. Listen, Daddy –'

'It won't be for a while, of course. There's a lot to get through before it happens, but it's a light at the end of the tunnel.'

'Daddy, I'm coming home!'

'What?' His voice sounded like a bullet shot.

'I can come home now!'

'You can? What's happened?'

'I've made a decision.'

'Have they upset you?'

'No. Not especially. I just want to get back.'

'Randa, Sweetie, hang on.' He was speaking to someone. There was more than one voice in the background, so she called to him again, and heard the downstairs door open and Aunt Jenny called her name.

'Just a minute, Aunt Jenny.'

Why would he have to speak to someone? Who? When he returned he was composed, as though he had taken the pause to collect himself, and his voice was a closed door.

'Sweetheart, I won't be here for a while.'

'You have to be. Look, this is what we need to do-'

'It's unavoidable, Lillian. It's business. Then there's this police thing – that's an inconvenience, nothing more, but it won't go away for a while.'

'It's nothing to do with up here.'

'Are you sure you're all right, Lillian?' Aunt Jenny called.

'Fine. Yes.' She answered back with impatience in her voice. She hated being angry with Aunt Jenny. But Daddy wasn't helping. 'If there *is* something wrong up there-' he said.

'Nothing's happened!' she shouted at him.

She felt Aunt Jenny staring up the stairs. She heard Frank's tread towards her and the scamper of paws. 'It's more to the point to know what's happened down there!' she said.

'Randa, my love, it's just too complicated.' Edward sounded unhappy. Did he not want her? Was it really impossible? Was he being controlled? 'Look, this is what we'll do. We'll have a few days together when I get back from this visit. We'll go to a nice place. The two of us.'

'I don't want to go to a nice place,' she objected. 'I want to go to London!' This was the end of the conspiracy. 'You don't tell me anything. You're hopeless.' She switched off, then stared at the phone in amazement at what she had done. Aunt Jenny came to the door of the sitting room and Lillian stomped past her, the angry teen, until she came to the kitchen where, having run out of elsewhere to stomp, she turned and plumped on a chair in the dining-room. Aunt Jenny stood in the doorway. She waited. The dogs, leads trailing the floor, brushed past her, wagged tails at her and turned back to Frank who had joined his sister. Lillian retrieved her hands from her cheeks.

'I hate my dad!' she said.

'Oh, Lillian,' Aunt Jenny breathed back.

'He doesn't love me.'

'Oh no, Lillian! That's not true at all.'

'He's told me not to go to London!'

Aunt Jenny was about to say something, decided against it, and in the pause Frank stepped forth. 'Tha's speaking rubbish, lass, but I know how tha' feels.' He sat opposite her. Aunt Jenny, torn, answered Jesus's yap with a pat. 'The adults are talking, Jesus.' Jesus replied with a stifled whine. It was unclear if this was a whine of consent.

'If yer want to see yer dad, go see him,' Frank said.

'He's going away.'

'Get him before he goes.'

'Shall I speak to him, Lillian?' Aunt Jenny suggested. 'This situation, you know, it won't be forever.'

Frank kept his face on Lillian. 'Follow yer 'art, lass,' he said. 'Don't take shit, even from tha' father.' He pronounced it with a flat 'a' which made the injunction even firmer.

'But if he doesn't want –' she faltered.

'Then you will 'ave demonstrated the urgency of the case.'

Lillian returned his stare. She saw the unkempt hair, the collar twisted on one side, the underside of the eyes cracked with drink and sorrow, the thin mouth softened with care. He was a good person really.

'What about the 'ang?' she asked.

'The 'ang'll be here when you get back.'

'I don't want to make him angry,' she said.

Frank glanced up at Jenny. An understanding, swift as a bird's wing, passed between them. 'You must be sure, Lillian,' Aunt Jenny said. 'It isn't easy just now for either of you.'

'I'm so sorry, Aunt Jenny,' she said. 'I want to go home. I have to see just how he is.'

Chapter 5

S he felt guilty at leaving the holy family in a crowd by the door. It was not entirely untrue that she would return, for she fully expected the visit one day. When she did, she would not wear her most expensive clothes. She would be modest and friendly, and she would laugh with Aunt Jenny about the naïve kid who had turned up that summer ten years ago. Anne-Marie had nodded at her, the nod of fellow conspirators, which had rather annoyed her. Aunt Jenny's innocent assumption she'd be back and feeling better in two or three days, however, had made her feel mean. But she was jocund as she strode early to the white fence. She had survived the north. That was something to tell what remained of her friends. She had also shared Frank's portraits and got numerous likes, though by people not in her immediate set. This time she did not cower on Darlington Station. She settled in the single seat in second class and smiled at her face in the window.

Her self-esteem rose on King's Cross piazza. People moved more quickly here. She sucked in like perfume the lines of travellers going in different directions, the ethnic stalls, the purposeful traffic. At Charing Cross she noticed without qualm the excessive competitiveness of her fellow commuters at the barriers, and that no-one spoke, and marked the contrast between tourists standing beside bags on the concourse and her fellow Londoners who had somewhere to get to and strode meaningfully on. When she crossed the Strand to the restaurant and told herself that her father was in there. waiting for her, however, the ridiculousness of herself as a visitor struck her. Not only that, but, to be honest, she had neither a plan nor a return ticket. A little of her gaiety escaped, like steam from a coffee-machine.

'Miss Delph.' The stylish lady looked through her book. This was the first restaurant she remembered, and which had hardly changed. It had no Michelin stars. It did not attract celebrities, but it was hers and daddy's, reliable and elegant, to which only the most reliable friends were invited. 'They're waiting for you.'

In her eagerness she did not register the plural until she saw the other man. Both stood. Daddy was the same old daddy, with the cheek bones and that familiar and reassuring air of absent-minded authority, but something had changed. He called her name, but his smile came from a distance, as though summoned, and the sight of the stranger next to him knocked away her impulse to hold onto him, to hug him to concentration. The stranger was Mr Harris. Mr Harris was in business suit. Daddy was more casual. It was the grey jacket with the rumpled sheen.

'Lillian,' he said, as though she were an old friend, someone once familiar but now an infrequent guest. It was he who broke off the hug. 'You really shouldn't have come, you sweet, silly girl. You remember Mr Harris?'

Lillian and Mr Harris shook hands.

'I hope I can set your mind at rest,' Mr Harris said, sitting down.

'It isn't disturbed,' Lillian answered. 'Not now I can see you so well, Daddy.'

'You look really well, yourself, Randa. The sea-air suits!'

'Did you have a good trip?' Mr Harris asked.

'What?' asked Lillian.

'The Edinburgh-King's Cross is an excellent service,' Mr Harris continued. 'It can get rather crowded, no?'

'I suppose.'

'I heard Virgin are in trouble with it,' Edward commented. He held the menu.

'There's much nonsense spoken about British trains,' Mr Harris ploughed on. 'They're actually up to scratch in competition with the continent and as for America ... well.'

'The train's not an option in America,' Edward agreed.

Lillian looked at her father with enquiry. He was studying the menu.

'We're apt to forget America's a continent.' Mr Harris showed a staggering inability to gauge the situation. 'New York and San Fransisco are wonderful cities, but there's nowhere like London, is there, Lillian?'

'There certainly isn't. That's why I've come back.'

Mr Harris smiled as though he had made a misjudgement. 'Absolutely,' he agreed.

Edward raised his face from the meu. 'Has anyone decided? he asked.

'I haven't looked,' said Lillian. 'Have you been to the house yet?'

'Not as such.'

'What does that mean?'

The two men snatched a mutual glance, and Mr Harris arranged a face of professional sympathy. 'Your father has been back on business, not as a resident.' He said, 'Let me explain as the family lawyer.' Lillian's eyes widened. Edward looked at her with a serious face and let Mr Harris continue. 'The bankruptcy and administration terms mark the house as collateral, you see, and for the creditors a quick sale appears best. In these cases, of course, the administration makes the decision, not the debtor. In fact, a very good offer came in, above the administrators' level – it was essentially an auction.'

'You remember Mr Shevchenko?' Daddy asked. 'You met him at the hospital.'

'Was he the man who offered me a hundred pounds?'

'Did he? I didn't know that.'

'Mr Shevchenko is a big player in the London property market,' Mr Harris said.

'You live in one of his flats?'

'No, no, that was only a few days.'

'So what about my stuff?'

'Your stuff?' Daddy looked at Mr Harris who looked at his cutlery. Then he opened his mouth and closed it again.

'My clothes! My jewellery. My pink panther. My ... mementoes.'

'Actually, that is a point,' Edward conceded to Mr Harris. 'What did we do about the portable property?'

'Oh, dear,' Mr Harris responded. 'This is all very painful.'

'I don't have the money, Daddy, to buy a new outfit.'

'She must have some clothes, Simon.'

'Indeed. The personal effects were part of the sale, I believe. I'm sure some arrangement –'

'You mean Mr Shevchenko has my pink panther?' Lillian was outraged.

As for the pink panther itself –'

'Oh, *Daddy!*'

'Lillian, Sweetheart, listen.'

He was interrupted by the waitress who arrived with predictable bad timing. 'I'll have the lobster,' he said. 'Mr Harris is paying as a business-meeting, sweetie, which, in a sense, this is. That way it's set off against tax. What are you having, Randa?"

'Can I have the pigeon breasts as a main?'

'I'm sure you can,' the waitress assured her.

Lillian was miffed. She was not sentimental about stuff. Stuff was, in the normal course, replaceable, but this was not a normal time. And where was she to stay in the next few weeks. Where was Daddy, come to that? Edward rested his chin on his fingers and leaned at her. 'Sweetie, listen, please. I know you're upset about the stuff. That's understandable. But you must give me time. There's bigger things to worry about now.'

'I'm sure, Lillian, you'll have far more stuff in the future,' Mr Harris added.

'I certainly will,' Lillian said. 'One day.' She rose. 'Will you excuse me, Mr Harris?'

She did not see if they watched her, but when she was ensconced in the loo she brushed her hair for comfort and sent a text.

Get rid of him daddy.

She gazed in the mirror. It was odd. She looked like a little girl and a woman at the same time.

The square tables with the white napkins, the high ceiling, the clean lighting in place of windows - the air of unassailable comfort and modest elegance – was so familiar it seemed ridiculous she would not be able to visit when she wanted. She sat as food was served; the ensuing silence gave her the chance to ask, 'So where are you staying, daddy?'

'At your grandparents.'

'Really? But you stopped speaking to them.'

'We still don't in any meaningful sense. It's bloody. We're exiles in different courts, Randa.'

'So where will I stay now?'

'Stay?'

'Yes, Daddy. Where will I sleep?'

'Sleep? That's a point.'

'You haven't thought?"

'I rather assumed you'd be staying with friends. Lillian has many friends,' he pointed out to Mr Harris.

'Not anymore,' she retorted.

'The current account is active,' Mr Harris said.

Edward grimaced. 'How long were you thinking of staying, Randa?'

'Forever?'

'I mean, now.'

'So do I.'

'But we don't have the resources just now, Sweetie. Do we, Simon?'

Mr Harris took his cue. 'The current account is active, as I said. I've managed to filter some money into it, but there's no other income as yet. If grandparents are really out of the question ...' Both Edward and Lillian shook grave heads. 'There's hotels, but, of course, it won't last forever.'

'I can't stay in a hotel for very long.'

'It wouldn't be wise, Edward,' Mr Harris said. 'Court fees coming up.'

'This is terrible,' Edward said.

'I've got the Rolex money,' Lillian said. 'Would that see us out until it's sorted?'

'What Rolex money?' Edward asked.

'I sold it to come here.'

Edward lay down his cutlery. His shoulders sank. Mr Harris studied his fish. 'Oh, Sweetie! It was a present.' Lillian did not contradict this. Edward slumped and looked for an answer in the ceiling.

'You make me very unhappy about myself,' he ventured.

'It's very upsetting.'

'Yes, Randa, but it *is* temporary. Believe me.'

'I'm not very happy about all this, Daddy.'

Edward looked at Mr Harris and Mr Harris nodded, and Edward said, 'Simon, could you give me a minute with my daughter – once we've eaten?'

'Of course. I have some calls to make.'

'Finish your fish first, Simon.'

He smiled at his daughter as though he'd settled something. He took up his knife and fork. 'I do love lobster,' he said. 'I hope the food up north isn't too awful.'

'Aunt Jenny is a massive foodie,' Lillian replied, temporarily appeased. The men looked very interested in Aunt Jenny's foodiness. 'Her lemon chicken is wonderful. There's a quaint little deli called Grubby's, though it's not, not at all. It has a server who sings. There seem to be a lot of vegans. Also, of course, fish and chips. You can smell them all along Low Prom, but I don't take them as I'm in training. I run, Mr Harris. They're a rather eccentric family.'

'I don't care so long as they're nice to you, Randa.'

'They're very nice,' she said. 'They mean very well.'

'I'm sure they do.'

'And there's wild deer.'

'Wild deer? Really?' Mr Harris was intrigued. 'On the banks of the Tyne?'

'On the moors and the cliffs,' said Lillian.

'Isn't it the Tees?' Edward asked.

'Is it? Oh, yes. One mixes up these northern places. They're all close together on one's psychological map.'

Mr Harris was an idiot. 'I got very close to one,' Lillian said.

'Lillian loves animals,' said Daddy.

'Wild deer. That's very Balmoral.'

'It's quite old-fashioned. And very white, though not completely. And everything goes slowly. Even the local train.'

'This is why leaving London is not a viable option,' Edward told Mr Harris. 'Dynamism. Only the failures leave.'

'And only the failures stay up there,' Mr Harris added.

'Yes,' said Lillian, and thought with regret of Ferdinand.

Mr Harris patted his stomach when the fillet was gone to signify that he was now more than happy to make his calls. Edward and Lillian gazed at each other frankly. He had regained more assurance.

'It's really not too bad, then, Randa?"

'Daddy, I really had hoped to stay for a while.'

'Listen, Randa - how was the pigeon, by the way?'

'I don't care about the pigeon, Daddy.'

'No, and that's what I want to tell you. It isn't about the little things. I'm going to talk to you as an adult, which, in fact, you are. This is it, Randa. You're right, I could get something mediocre pretty soon, but that's not the Delph's way, now is it? If we're really going to bounce back, we need to be patient. We must make sacrifices now for the sake of the future. That's deferred gratification. You're good at it. It's the foundation for success, science tells us. Firstly,

I've got my health back. That's part of the bounce, you see. I could have said, 'Oh, I'll just be feeble and demand my daughter helps me through,' but, no, that's not our way. We take the rough. We get the smooth. Then there's this investigation thing. We're making real progress on that. And then there's the working of contacts. If I went for a short-term solution that would limit my chances of the real thing later. It really would. I need to reserve all my efforts for this struggle. You see, you deserve everything, in terms of lifestyle and of *attention*. I couldn't concentrate on you and do the things I need to do, and you deserve concentration. It's for you, Sweetie.'

'Yes, Daddy, but you should have warned me ages ago.'

'And worry you in your examination year?'

'We could have cut back.'

'And take you out of private school? What sort of parent does that?'

'I suppose.'

'I trimmed Madelaine's sails. She wanted me to trim yours too, but I'm so proud that I didn't.'

'I thought I might get a job here.'

'Oh, Lillian, you're so good. Do you have any idea of rents? Students who work do it from home. God, Lillian, you'd be living like an immigrant. Those people in the north may be dull, but they're very convenient, and remember, the more we put up with things now, the better in the future. You're strong, Lillian, aren't you?'

'Yes, Daddy, I'm strong.'

'You're still my girl?'

'I'm still your girl.'

'There you are then.'

How silly Anne-Marie's words seemed now. The world was not as easy a place as she'd thought. Lillian sighed out her disappointment.

'This is really quite upsetting,' she said.

'It's utter rubbish at present, but it's temporary. I do it for you.'

Daddy still loved her. He was a silly daddy, but a determined one, and they would win in the end.

'I'll save the money I make in the café.'

'That's the spirit. And we can at least have a nice lunch together. What about pudding?'

'I don't care about pudding.'

Mr Harris was making his way between tables.

'Later we can meet at one of our favourite places.'

'I don't care about favourite places either. Not really.'

Mr Harris stood over them. 'A call,' he said. 'We can't put it off, I'm afraid.'

'What?'

'Half an hour.'

'No! It's as though they're testing me.'

'I really wonder if that isn't the case.'

Edward threw hopeless eyes on his daughter. 'You see? It's like this right now. This is why we must delay. My life's not my own.'

'What is it, Daddy?'

'I'll be about an hour – two hours. Two and a half?' He looked amazed at Mr Harris who confirmed the latter with a look. 'These bloody bureaucrats! Sweetie, can you do your own thing until around five?'

'I'm meeting Maria.'

'Good, Where'd you like to go afterwards?

'But if I'm going back today, the last train leaves at six.'

'No!' Edward was shocked. 'That's *so* disappointing. Randa, darling, I'm so sorry.'

'It doesn't matter, Daddy. It is what it is.'

'It is what it is, Randa.'

'I'm afraid that's the case,' Mr Harris agreed.

Father and daughter rose as in mourning. 'We'll bounce back, Randa,' Edward insisted again as Mr Harris waded away to settle. The dinner had passed like a flit. 'It will be gumdrops by Christmas.'

'I don't care about Christmas.'

'Then you'll be lighting up Paris.'

'I don't care –' but she stopped. That was taking stoicism a step too far.

They hugged outside. It was reconciliation. It was the embrace of families parted by war. 'God knows when we'll meet again, Daddy.'

'Don't you worry, my girl. Listen.' He held her by the shoulders. 'Gumdrops is coming. We'll be up roses more than a garden in June. You've a whole life ahead of you and this will seem, well, like a little dream.'

'That's poetical,' Mr Harris said. He was ignored.

'Just one of those blips.'

'Yes, Daddy, but you shouldn't have got us in this situation in the first place.'

'You're right,' he said. 'I've been unlucky.'

Strolling up the Strand, she brooded on her father's betrayal. She did not doubt his love: her earliest memories were of her daddy chasing her round a park, of him reading to her, of being silly to make her laugh, of combing her hair. How unusual was that? He had never missed a parents' meeting or forgotten a present. He had never left her at school all weekend when working away, but had got her home among friends. When they went to Paris he had sent his girlfriend shopping while he took Lillian to Euro-Disney. He had addressed the great crises of her life – puberty, examination stress, petty injustice – with a tender humour, as though life were a sport, not a war, a battleground without casualties. She was always the first to be hugged when he got home. He had filled her days with an airy optimism, and she had always believed that, in the end, whatever the problem, the Delphs came up roses. She had never known the barrier-breaking intimacy of a mother's care, but she had always felt the protection of a father's love, as when, crossing a series of puddles he had wrapped an arm round her waist and lifted her on his hip and ran across while she screamed and laughed, and shouted, 'Daddy!' People on the pavement had laughed as well. At the corner of Drury Lane, however, she realised the weakness of her position. She was being sent back from the city she'd always called home.

'It's just not fair,' she told Maria in Nero over espresso and skinny muffin. Lillian loved Café Bertaux, but this was not a day for their prices and chaos. Her world was shrinking. 'It's like I'm being punished for what someone else has done.'

Maria agreed. 'It's like when you've done something you don't want your parents to know about, but the other way round.'

'I'm tempted to stay for a couple of days anyway.'

'I'm working,' Maria warned. 'And I've a family thing on Sunday.'

'I could work,' said Lillian.

'Then you'd have council tax and energy bills and all that stuff. Mind you, it must be bloody boring up there.'

Lillian wasn't sure what council tax was, but it was clearly not a good thing.

'It's just not practical, is it?'

'Not really.'

'How humiliating! Don't tell the crew.'

Lillian watched the staff behind the counter with their urgent, brisk moves and wondered how they managed to do it. That was another mystery about London: no-one could afford to live there, but millions did, who knew how? To live in London, as a Londoner, as native born, you needed a room of your own and twenty thousand a year, minimum.

'Lillian?'

'Sorry. What?'

'Chloe.'

'What?'

'You know she does coke?'

'She didn't when I was with her.'

'It's the boyfriend. You were a good influence, Lilly. Now she's all over the place.'

'Good.'

They looked at each other and laughed. 'Do you know when you'll be back?' Maria asked.

'No idea.'

Maria was thoughtful. 'It's all very mysterious.' She was twisting the little milk jug with thumb and finger and offered a meditative pout. 'What is it?' Lillian asked. Maria sprang back and shook her head. 'I had a silly thought. You know how it is. Something jumps up in your head and it grabs you a minute and then you realise you're being stupid. I had a that kind of silly thought.' Lillian was waiting for her. Maria shrugged. 'Nothing.' Lillian still waited. 'The silly thought was, perhaps he's thinking of this criminal business and he doesn't want you to know, but then I knew that was stupid, because you couldn't hide it. I sort of lowered myself for a moment. Forget it. Sorry.'

'If it was anything drastic, I'd know,' said Lillian.

The girls drifted among the stalls in the market. There was a street act in the square, as usual, and a violinist under the roof. London buskers were a higher standard than everywhere else, and the ones outside the Royal Opera House were the best in London, though Lillian herself was no great lover of the solo violin. The market was fake, and lively, and had style: but the girls were desultory because it wasn't Maria's thing, and Lillian was distracted. She had the Rolex money, but what was the point? If she couldn't get something from Fortnum's or Harvey Nicks – and she hadn't – Covent Garden was hardly able to satisfy. There was no occasion speeding towards her that required an accessory. She touched Maria's arm. 'I think I'm going,' she said.

'Already?'

'I messaged Aunt Jenny I'd get the 6.30, but I might as well get back.'

'I wish you could stay,' Maria said. 'If my parents leave the flat at all – you'll be the first to get the invite.'

'That's so nice.'

Lillian stood on the King's Cross concourse with joyless patience. Her anger was turned to a desolate cold no hug could penetrate. The journey north was long. All that time in a seat on a crowded carriage! At the end; Aunt Jenny's smothering concern, Anne-Marie's hostile glances, Ferdinand's nonsense, a single bed in a room too small for stuff. Autumn was on them: the days would draw in, she would serve tea and cheap sausage sandwiches to people with the complexion of potato skins until, one day, her father sounded the trumpet call of return. Paris seemed a long time away. When she saw the line of eyes on the noticeboard waiting for the platform number to light up she saw herself in a crowded second-class carriage all the way to the north, and her dismay soaked her as though dumped in a cold sea. There was at least something she could do about that. She went to the ticket office and returned with a first-class ticket just as the platform was announced.

She snuck onto a single seat and dumped her bag on the opposite one to discourage any intrusive man-spreader. She put her ticket on the table because she knew what look the inspector would give her. She did the same with her ID when the trolley came round and ordered white wine.

'White wine for the lady,' the attendant said.

She smiled back and thought, Fuck off. He did not say it the second time. The third time she had to go to the booth. She was asked for her ID. She flourished it. The attendant looked at it briefly and handed it back. She smiled again. When she sat down a man in a grey suit, who had been talking business for an hour, glanced at her. He was thinking who she was, what she was doing. Lillian put on her headphones, listened to Ariadne, and then watched You Tube dolphins and elephants with babies, and dozed a little, then she was at York. A man took the opposite seat. She pretended to doze, her bag on her lap, but under her lids, in the dark, she felt unsure, almost panicky, so she went onto Swimming with Dolphins, and decided one final drink. The battery went minutes before Darlington so she could not tell Aunt Jenny she would be early, but Aunt Jenny wouldn't mind. She wouldn't notice.

The cool evening air on the platform made her giddy. She was just a tiny bit drunk. She corrected her stagger. She had not made a spectacle of herself, but it was not a good look. She sat on a bench at the forgotten end of the platform where the local trains stopped. It chugged in like a decrepit butler who was not in the least surprised his master had returned early.

Saltscar on a Saturday at the hour of nine was more like everywhere else than at any other time in the week, for then tiny bands of revellers poured in to get drunk and still feel safe. Lillian walked behind one such, calling to another such: without the background of traffic and music and neon the acid laughter was raw. She crept along the white fence and into Devon Street resigned to conceding defeat, though Aunt Jenny's fuss was better than gloating.

She realised at the door she had not taken her key. To ring the bell was to announce she'd been unsuccessful, but what choice did she have?

Aunt Jenny was flustered. 'You're not meant to be here!' she said. Jesus was barking. His parents followed his lead with low woofs. 'I mean, you're early. Dear me – well, it's done – it might even be the best –'

'It's all right, Aunt Jenny.' Lillian stepped past her. 'It didn't work out as – oh.'

There was another woman in the corridor. She was standing with hands folded in front of her. She looked at Lillian with a bent head, but Lillian saw the woman's eyes fixed upon her. She had seen that face in a photograph.

'Oh, my god.'

'I was just leaving,' the woman said.

'Lillian.' Aunt Jenny's arms wheeled in all directions. 'Lillian, this is your mother.'

Lillian looked at Aunt Jenny, then at the woman. Her mouth was open to speak, but no words came. She ignored Jesus's paws at her hips and dashed upstairs as the walls wheeled around her. 'Sorry, sorry,' she said. 'I've had something to drink.'

She plunged into the toilet and was sick in the bowl.

Chapter 6

Blue: a gleam into which you seemed able to sail beckoned in the broad gap between the curtains, but Lillian had no escape. She was besieged.

When Aunt Jenny peered around the door, she pretended to be asleep. She thought the house was empty, and showered, then Anne-Marie shouted up, 'Lillian? Do you want coffee?' Anne-Marie made it sound like a command.

'I don't feel very well,' Lillian said.

'That wasn't what I asked.'

'Yes, thank you. But I need to go back to bed.'

'As you like.' Anne-Marie had a heart like a winter sea.

She shoved on her pyjamas and a pullover and crept under the duvet. Anne-Marie's coffee was not as good as Aunt Jenny's, but it was not as bad as Frank's. Lillian looked around, mug in hand.

'I've nowhere to put it,' she said.

In reply, Anne-Marie whisked the curtain further open and looked out. 'Heavenly day,' she said. 'You could almost love Saltscar on a day like this. All right, come on, you can have my room.'

Anne-Marie's bed was a good one. It had an oak frame and a soft mattress. But the room had no carpet, no pictures, and a grey blind instead of curtains. The wardrobe was a dark brown hulk in the alcove next to the defunct chimneybreast. There wasn't even a lamp, but there was a bedside table at least. The only concession to design was a duvet as coldly blue as its owner's heart with a gilt moon on its centre.

'Don't get used to it,' Anne-Marie said. 'I'll reclaim it when I'm back. So what happened? You wimped out?'

'Daddy wasn't encouraging.'

Anne-Marie did not pursue the enquiry. 'No plans to go back, I take it?'

'I don't know.'

Anne-Marie ripped up the blind and let the insulting light in. 'You didn't find anything out?'

'Not really.'

'So, no immediate plans.'

Lillian willed her to leave, but she stood at the end of the bed like a doctor assessing a patient. She was remorseless. 'If you're staying you ought to offer mum board.'

'Of course.'

'Don't move my things.'

'Board.' That was an old-fashioned expression, as Aunt Jenny would say. It didn't bring Paris closer. The second instruction was easy. There was nothing to move.

She had slept, partly from boredom, for an indefinable time, for the light was unchanged, when the second steps sounded. She recognised the tread and its accompaniment of paws, and she relaxed. Ferdinand knocked. 'I'm awake,' she said.

'Dogs, ahoy!' His head appeared round the edge. 'A little canine comfort?' he asked.

Lillian sat up and Jesus jumped up. He put his nose in Lillian's ear, made two circles and plopped down. Joseph followed. He sniffed his son to check it really was him, then settled by the footboard. Mary crouched, caught between Ferdy and the bed. Ferdy patted. She rose softly, silently, and rested her back against Lillian's hip and slept. Lillian accepted their attentions.

'Does it hurt physically?'

Lillian shook her head.

'Do you wish to talk?'

Lillian shook her head again, but asked, 'Why has my mother come?'

Ferdinand threw out his arms. 'A cousin can visit a cousin, I think. And her cousin's son. They thought you wouldn't be here. They had good reason to think so. I felt a little sorry for Emily, as a matter of fact. She sees her daughter for the first time since the daughter was a baby and the daughter's response is to be sick upstairs. Are you sure you're not ill?'

'I was in shock. Was she actually upset?'

'*Actually*, we can ask her,' he replied and before she'd even realised what he'd said, her defences down, he was at the door and shouting her mother's name. She hadn't combed her hair, not properly. She hadn't cleared this with her father and had only returned his call with a text that said she had a cold xxx. She had no words prepared and the duvet clashed with her pink pyjamas. It was awful. The dogs shuffled in response when Emily appeared and stared at her with interest. though Joseph only raised his neck to look round and dropped it again. Lillian straightened herself as best she could and very softly did the breathing.

'Hello,' she said. She didn't know the correct address. 'Emily,' she decided.

'Lillian.'

Pause. There had been more effusive versions of this well-established archetype: a child returned, a mother found. Lillian focussed on what she saw; a robust looking woman, with thick wavy blond hair, and no make-up, who stood, feet apart, in old jeans and a baggy jumper. She was not tall, but she looked like a woman prepared for action, aggressive if necessary, and was dressed for it. Her face was older than her body, with tiny creases under her eyes and above her top lip; it was a well-worn face, an outdoor face. Lillian gazed for seconds at this older and rougher version of herself because she could still think of nothing to say, but she wondered if she'd look so in twenty years' time. With a burn in her stomach she realised that actually, yes, she probably would. Emily waited. Her gaze was unwavering. Lillian felt that stare absorb her. Ferdinand awaited both.

Finally, Emily took the initiative. 'You look lithe,' she told Lillian. 'Do you climb?'

Lillian hadn't expected that. Perhaps her mother was on the spectrum. What could she say? 'Yes,' was untrue. 'No,' sounded like rejection, so she said, 'Not yet.' Emily only offered a wistful smile, but no words. Lillian glanced at Ferdinand to intervene, but he was looking out of the window.

'Did you have a good journey?' she asked.

Her mother was silent. Her mother was thinking. Lillian felt her own inadequacy, but then Emily retorted, pleasantly enough, 'Same as ever. What about you?'

'Oh, yes. Very smooth. Thank you.'

Ferdinand stifled a giggle.

'Good.'

'Are you staying long?'

'I'm at Dorothy's.'

'Oh.'

'Shall I leave?' Ferdy suddenly asked.

'No, I am,' said Emily. 'I make you awkward, Lillian. That's understandable. I've no right to impose, but if you want to talk to me, let me know.' She leaned forward: Lillian thought with alarm she was going to kiss her, but she only said, 'Your choice,' and then turned away. She hesitated on her way out, however. 'I hear you run,' she said.

'Yes. Yes, I do.'

'So do I.'

'Running ... running is good.'

'Running is very good. Perhaps we'll do it together one time?'

'Oh, yes, quite possibly.'

Emily nodded. She avoided Lillian's face. 'My lost girl,' she said, more to herself than the world. 'Your call,' she finished and went.

Lillian breathed in, held it, then blew out through puffed cheeks with such force Jesus aimed cocked dears at her. Ferdinand in contrast seemed pleased with himself.

'That wasn't too hard, was it?' he said when Emily was out of earshot. He raised a finger: the door closed downstairs. Jesus woofed its tap to conclusion. 'Feel better?'

Lillian had her hand on her chest. She closed her eyes. She settled her palms on the duvet. 'Why didn't you warn me?'

'About what?'

'She should have asked! That was my mother!'

'You asked if she was upset – she was below. My intuition told me –'

'She didn't seem upset!'

'She's not a woman of many words. High Frank-factor.'

'She's one of you,' she said. 'She didn't like me.'

'Bollocks.' It was a shock to hear Ferdinand swear. 'She invited you to meet her. Will you?'

Lillian was trapped. It was not fair that she was trapped. She feared many dangers. What would daddy think for one thing? But it was clear that a flat refusal would displease her hosts, and she had no motive to upset them. She wavered. 'Do you want me to?' she asked.

Ferdinand was incredulous. 'Do *we* want you to? It's about you, Lillian.' He cocked his head, rather as Jesus did when you spoke to him. 'You're not as London as you think, lassie.'

'I've no idea what you mean. It's exhausting, all this.'

'You'll cope. But it might be an idea not to let mum know. She might see it as a breach of the gates and come crashing through.'

She hid for two more days. In the absence of a practical plan it seemed the only thing to do. She did not spend the entire time in bed, for she had to eat, and she gave herself dog-walking duties, leading them across the beach away from the town where she was less likely to be addressed by someone who knew her. She told Aunt Jenny not to fuss please, and no, she hadn't come down with depression, though when she stood in the little supermarket and saw the intimidating rows of cartons and bottles and jars and stacked plastic packets she wondered if this was how depressed people felt; overwhelmed by choice. Anne-Marie was in Newcastle: Frank was in the Lake District, whatever that was, Ferdinand and Aunt Jenny were at work, so Lillian and the dogs slept, and stretched, and yawned through the day, though Lillian had the advantage of You Tube, headphones and a tablet. The sounds of neighbours and the town intruded through the windows. Lillian told her father she was doing just fine, and hoped he'd soon have some good news for a change. The beach was a comfort. The days were sun and wind and bullied clouds. Ferdinand insisted you could not count the blues of the sea, but Lillian made a go of it anyway: she got seven before she gave up, and surrendered to the big, brilliant sky and the sea's inarticulate whisper and the silvered sand. It was all right to be alone on the beach.

Ferdinand left the shop to check on her. He was a kind man. Only he could have summoned her mother up without it seeming a direct attack. 'You're ruining those dogs,' he said.

Lillian fluffed up her pillows with sudden vigour and sat up. 'You can take Mary and Joseph, but I need Jesus,' she said.

Lillian ventured down to Aunt Jenny who was eating a bowl of Tuscan soup and watching a Netflix drama. Aunt Jenny did not hear her under the sound of the television, until Lillian addressed her.

'I am under instruction,' Aunt Jenny replied to Lillian's greeting. 'I am not to badger you. Soup?'

Lillian sank with relief onto a chair. She had feared mother-talk and had prepared a defence: ('It's too soon now, Aunt Jenny, and there's my father to consider. I'll talk to my mother when things are more settled.') That was such a sensible reply she could imagine no objection. Aunt Jenny, however, following a series, was not intrusive. She was pulled to the drama. 'That child really is evil!' she pronounced. 'She's vulnerable as well, they've brought that out. Mind you, other vulnerable children don't become killers.'

'Aunt Jenny?'

'That's bad procedure. They'd have no trouble getting a warrant.'

'Aunt Jenny!'

'Yes, my dear?'

'It's quite loud.'

Aunt Jenny went for pause. It took a few goes, but she got there. 'Sorry?'

'I was thinking – I ought to go back to the café, but transport's a problem now.'

'It's a wonderful idea! You could do with the routine. And the cash. Of course, you don't want to push yourself. Transport, though? I might have an idea. Give me a few days.' She contemplated. 'You have all the time you need, Lillian. We can wait as long as it takes.'

Lillian did not ask what they were all waiting for. 'Should I pay board?'

'Pay board? That *is* an old-fashioned expression. You absolutely shall not, Lillian.'

'Anne-Marie thought I should.'

'Anne-Marie!' Aunt Jenny exclaimed. 'Anne-Marie is loyal and loving and she's very responsible, but she's not very spiritual. She's on the science side. She gets notions. I know! Pay just a little board. A peppercorn rent. A lovely expression. Then we can please Anne-Marie and tell the truth, and still be happy ourselves.'

'I ought to do something.'

Aunt Jenny paused the detectives in their grim work and appraised her guest. 'You can just be you,' she said. Lillian had no idea what this meant. 'Yes. Until we know when you're able to leave, we should find you a role.'

'I just need something to pass the time,' Lillian said.

'We really must go to the old house!' She softened her voice. 'Your mother's gone now, so all in due time. You could give a bit of a tidy tomorrow, if you wish. You're not really bothered about Crime, are you?' Aunt Jenny pointed the remote at the screen.

'Crime? Oh, television. I don't like the violence.'

'Such a noble soul. Is there anything you would like to watch?'

'I can listen to something on my tablet.'

'Excellent. But you can always join us, Lillian. You live with us now.'

Lillian lay on the bed, breathed a long relaxing sigh, and rubbed her cheeks. You live with us now. Well, yes, but largely because she was too annoyed at Daddy and Daddy was too embattled for any alternative. The austerity of Anne-Marie's room made it like a cell, and her little room was worse, yet she was expected to be grateful. Her life was waiting. She hated it.

Tomorrow she would tidy. She would tidy in a way they had never seen. She would tidy to astonish the world. Then she'd focus on the Saltscar Scramble. When she'd left her mark, she would seek out her father, ready or not.

'Lillian!' Aunt Jenny shouted up the stairs. 'Lillian, are you awake?'

'She's here, mum.' Ferdinand pointed to the kitchen door where Lillian appeared.

'Perfect. It's lovely to see you about, Lillian, my love - my word, this is different.'

'I hope you don't mind,' Lillian said.

'Mind! You've done a cracking job.'

'They say 'banging', mum. That's the expression they use.'

''Banging'?' Aunt Jenny let the word resonate in her head. 'This is as banging as banging gets. Look at the little utensils she's hung there!'

'I've done some rearranging of the shelves. I thought – if you really don't mind – I had this idea – you see, it might be a good thing –'

'The bow is bent and drawn, Lillian,' Ferdinand said as he forced the stalks of beetroot into the vegetable drawer. 'Make from the shaft.'

'I thought we might de-clutter.'

'De-clutter?' Aunt Jenny asked.

'Well, we could tidy up so we knew where things were, and get rid of the things we don't want, and perhaps free up the junk room. We could even hang Frank's pictures and give him room in his office.'

'Get rid of things?'

'Only those we don't want.'

'It sounds great in practice,' Ferdinand said. 'But how's it work in theory?'

'Oh, the theory is sound,' Lillian answered innocently. 'It's in Marie Kondo.'

Aunt Jenny was disturbed. 'I wouldn't want to throw out the children's toys just because Ferdy and Anne-Marie don't use them,' she said.

'Or dad's,' Ferdinand added.

'Oh, of course!' Lillian agreed. 'This is your house.'

Jennifer Goodman softened. 'No, Lillian. This is your home too so long as you need it, and if you want to de-clutter, we shall de-clutter. It will be banging,' she concluded.

'It's good to see you active,' Ferdinand said.

The first stage was straightforward. The obvious clutter was sent on three trips to re-cycling. The things to be kept were stacked in the junk room. Then came the borderline stuff; old books, crockery long lost in cupboards, worn cushions, a litter of half-spent candles, the lining of old curtains, musty and beige, a cracked wooden doorstop, over-chewed soft toys, a toolbox of rusting secateurs and nails and screws, packets of creased paper napkins, ancient clothes. Out went the fading sunflowers, and two of the fading yellow cushions, and in came upright aliums with tight round heads of tiny flowers like the deep sky in frozen droplets, lilies clean as virginity, and a table centrepiece of cornflowers – a condensation of summer in impossible blue. By the middle of the second day Ferdinand and Lillian could manoeuvre the room more easily. Mother and son noticed the obsessive focus of their charge. She searched the recesses of cupboards and the dim corners of wardrobes and cabinets, and lumped boxes of jumble with a cold fury they felt they could not touch.

'She's very thorough,' Aunt Jenny said. 'More is less, so it's said. Personally, I never actually understood that.'

'Less is more, mum. Lillian needs this. It's better than moping in bed.'

The holy family, at first anxious, then curious, then baffled, sniffed the news piles, followed the carriers with heads cocked, and finally retired to their bed and awaited the outcome with resignation. When Aunt Jenny returned on the third day, she found Lillian with her hands on her hips staring at the overflowing plastic containers on the dining-room table. Lillian was thinking.

'Dear me,' Aunt Jenny said. 'It goes on.'

'We'll finish tomorrow, Aunt Jenny.'

'You won't be too severe, will you?'

Lillian checked Jenny's expression. She was not cross, but she was unsure.

'We won't throw anything out you want,' Lillian said.

'I'm sure you won't, no, of course not. I'm thinking of the fen shui. Do you know that term? It's rather eighties. Chinese. Jean has a very good sense of fen shui, but, of course, she doesn't always hear.'

'But if you like it more ... crowded, Aunt Jenny, you can start again.'

'Why, yes. I can, can't I? I don't have to live up to it entirely, do I?'

'We need to make some decisions,' Lillian said to Ferdinand the next morning. She was drinking coffee, Goodman style, from a bowl at the dining room table.

'We certainly must.'

'We mustn't make a mistake.'

'Our indiscretion sometimes serves us well.'

'Sorry?'

'When our deep plots do pall,' he explained.

'I hope Aunt Jenny doesn't mind.'

'Aunt Jenny is on board. We were at the Hall with Dotty and Deaf Jean. We considered all sides.'

'And?' Lillian asked out of politeness.

'Mum said things were essentially emotions. They were little symbols of the life that had been - a Proustian emblem - which was why she kept so many of dad's things. Symbols are not to be tossed away lightly. But Dorothy countered that it was a better meditation to live in the present: the relics might diminish or at least distort your memories. Jean then piped up to mention Freud. Mum and Dorothy thought she was off-piste because deafness so they shouted that they were talking of de-cluttering, but Jean explained that you don't need triggers to remember the good things, only the bad – hence, Freud. We all agreed this was unassailable. Then Dorothy pointed out that repressed Victorians had packed their houses with decorative horrors, whereas the looser moderns had trimmed things back. Dorothy is not one for repression. Also, a sparser house was more eco. Besides, the mess had always annoyed Anne-Marie: a more orderly house might entice her home more often, so by the time they'd finished the chips with mayonnaise mum was, for the present, a confirmed minimalist.'

'That's good.'

'Let's start before she returns to her original position.'

Truly, Ferdy remarked, organisation was an intellectual thing. How to measure to value of a book you knew would never be read again, but which had once given pleasure, against a snatch of magazines you might flick through that were ugly on the shelves and even uglier in a pile on the floor? (Cut out the articles you want, Lillian said. Duh). Would the old camp-bed really be useful again, when the sofa might suffice for a teeming house, or should it stack under the stairs in place of the boxes of forgotten glassware and board-games? And clothes! Perhaps Ferdinand really would lose weight, and so find use again for those trousers with pockets in the legs he had so loved. And if they went, what incentive had he? And of the six vases, which three were the best?

'This is where Anne-Marie would produce one of her algorithms,' Aunt Jenny said. 'You haven't touched your dad's things, have you?"

'No, mum.'

'Perhaps we should ask Anne-Marie.'

'She'll love it,' Ferdinand said. 'I told you. She's always complained about the mess.'

Lillian went to the local hardware store and bought a rail with butchers' blocks, a gimlet and screw hooks and even raw plugs and brackets. She knew about this because she'd done set design in drama. She solved the book problem by organising high shelves in the dog's room, shushing Jesus who sat on the bed and barked. Unsuccessful, she ordered him into back yard and completed the job.

Ferdinand had brought the spirit-level from the cell. 'We call this the goldfish fart,' he said. Lillian did not comment. 'Spot on,' he confirmed.

Under Aunt Jenny's bed Lillian found a box with a photograph album in which were more photographs of her mother. She left it.

She had not quite finished. In the cupboards above the fitted wardrobe in Aunt Jenny's room she found some old lamps. She bought bulbs and rewired the two that were dead. She laid out Frank's photographs along the hall and landing, and rearranged them, but they all felt they should wait for Frank's return from Cumbria before they hung his pictures.

'But this is quite radical!' Aunt Jenny said.

'That's oxymoronic,' Ferdinand answered on his knees over a canvas. 'You can't 'quite' radicalise.'

'I'll oxymoron you if you throw out my Elizabeth David first edition.'

'You've got room to put the cookery books together,' he said.

'I have, haven't I?'

Lillian did not understand what this had cost Aunt Jenny until she saw her wandering dazed from the sitting-room with a pile of books stacked on her forearms. 'Where do I put these?' she asked.

'I can do it, Aunt Jenny. Are you all right?'

'I'll put them on the coffee table for now.' Lillian followed her back into the room. Aunt Jenny dropped them and let them slither. 'I'm being silly,' she said. 'I just looked around and thought, 'This is no longer my house,' but of course it is! We must adapt to you as you to us. And, of course, it's really very much better.'

'I hope it is.'

'I'll just have to try and live up to it. It will be a very good change in my habits,' she said without conviction.

Lillian had never considered that some people actually liked mess. 'It will make it easier to find things,' she said.

'Of course! And we've got a new room!'

'Frank could use it for his office,' Lillian said. 'Then he wouldn't have his clothes in a pile by the bed.'

'That wouldn't stop him. No,' Aunt Jenny insisted. 'That should be your room, Lillian.'

And Lillian, who had not expected that, and was touched because she saw what she had done was a judgement on Aunt Jenny herself, opened her mouth to object, but closed it immediately because she deserved it, and it would feel less like being a prisoner if she came into a dedicated room instead of her bedroom. Even kidnapped girls had a bed, but they never had a room of their own where they could organise their stuff.

'Oh, Aunt Jenny. That's so kind.'

'Yes, dear. You are the one with Needs, after all. Let's hug.'

The hug was a good hug.

Her room had a comfortable chair and an old writing desk with drawers and a beaten leather top, the whole in serious need of restoration, and she added a side table she had bought for fifteen pounds from the second-hand furniture shop. It was her own space; nevertheless, when she left Aunt Jenny to the television and sat there alone for the first time, she still felt a little naughty, for she had the box under Aunt Jenny's bed on her lap. The television sounded. Ferdinand was out with the dogs. She opened the box.

It was lined with a delicate blue paper and filled with forgotten things; an old pincushion, an old school exercise book, and photographs in an envelope. They were on glossy paper of different sizes. They were not crisp: some were faded. But they were clear enough. She placed them on an open book. If Aunt Jenny's door opened, she would put it in the bookcase and pretend to be browsing.

What did she think her mother would be? The encounter had dented her vague imagination of a woman in The Trophy mould who had naughtily run off to Australia with Jeremy. She was wary, however. Who knew what awkwardness, what assaults, what battering at her past, her mother could unleash upon her? She gazed at pictures from the pre-digital age like a spy uncovering maps of the enemy's lines. Here was her mother on the side of a rock, in full climbing gear, giving a thumbs up to the photographer; her mother with aboriginal children – that was the Australian connection – apparently at work;

her mother laughing with friends at the seaside on a blustery day – oh, it was Saltscar – her collar turned up; her mother in the background at a house with a huge window, a family gathering, because there was Aunt Jenny and a slimmer Ferdinand, and Dorothy. There were three of her walking away on a path between hills with mountains in the distance. Lillian did not find a picture of her mother with Jeremy. There was her mother and Aunt Jenny; Aunt Jenny grinning, all open-hearted cheer, her mother with a cautious smile. Over the page was her mother crouching by a tent by a river, younger, staring without favour at the camera, and another woman behind, waving.

There were no men with her mother in these photographs. That was a puzzle.

Lillian put the book on the shelf. She took up *The 36 Views of Mount Fuji.*

She looked at a snow dredged village in the lower slopes of Mount Fuji and thought of her mother. It was odd to consider this other life, the life that had started hers, going on however it chose unrelated to her own. She did not care, but she was fascinated. She could ask Aunt Jenny: but could she trust Aunt Jenny to enlighten her? Aunt Jenny was artless and kind, but it was odd how she had appeared so soon at the start of her father's distress. Had they plotted that? She turned a page. This poor villager was carrying wood on his back up the snows of Mount Fuji. And then, her father, who still kept the truth from her, what did he know, or not know, about Emily? Whom could she trust? Frank: Frank was solid, but limited. She had little hope in Frank. The only person she could trust, without qualm, was Ferdinand Goodman, and Ferdy wasn't good on facts.

'Oh well, I don't suppose it changes anything one way or the other,' she mused.

The television cut out: Aunt Jenny opened the door, then closed it, and knocked, but opened it again before Lillian replied. 'I've been thinking,' she said. Lillian waited. 'I looked round the house. It's a triumph, Lillian. Those days in the V&A were not wasted.'

'Thank you.'

'Thank you, my dear. You must be pleased.'

'Yes, very. I know you think I'm shallow and selfish-'

'I beg your pardon?'

'Not all the time, of course. But –'

'Lillian!' Aunt Jenny was outraged. 'We love you! Don't be stupid. You've done wonders for Frank, for a start, and that's no small task.'

Lillian considered. 'I have, haven't I?'

'You mustn't misread our northern ways. We're the children of manufacturing and farming, you see. And Methodism. And Quakerism too.' Aunt Jenny pondered of what else they were the children. 'And decline,' she finished. 'It makes us seem unpolished, but we take things seriously. Of course, we also have fun. Don't underestimate our sense of fun. I only wish you could have more. You must miss young people.'

'Not as much as I thought I would. Aunt Jenny?'

'Yes, my dear.'

'Did you explain to my mother I couldn't see her because I wasn't well. I wasn't deliberately rude.'

'Emily's very self-contained. Self-reliant. Always rather stubborn –.' Aunt Jenny dropped her voice. She spoke as one naughty girl to another. 'If ever you do wish to meet her, you have only to say.'

'I'm keeping my options open.'

'That's very pragmatic. You'll understand more at your mother's old house.'

'I don't think I'm quite ready for that just yet. You see … this is all very strange to me.'

'Naturally.'

'I don't want to rush …'

'Exactly!'

'But I am grateful.'

'There's no need for that, Lillian. It's been so long.'

Lillian toured the house to admire her handiwork before bed. It was well done. It had cleansed her. She had value. She did not need to go begging for the truth from anyone. Her father needed her as much as she needed him, and she'd lived without Emily as well as Emily had lived without her, and she was doing ok, so if they wanted to hide something, they could hide it, and, if they wanted to speak, they could all bloody well come to her. She sat in Anne-Marie's bed with *The Thirty Six Views*. She rather liked them.

Money had once been a river; a trickle during a draught, but never dry. As she slowed from her morning run, however - hood up, headphones on, the sea wrinkling between grey and blue and silver - she noted the little shop that Ferdy had marked out as Very North Yorkshire and remembered quaint Bronby Blackstone. She looked through the window and saw some very smart leather bags, expensive outdoor boots, and Barbour dresses. There was indeed a lot of Barbour. Barbour seemed a northern thing. Guys never understood that the fun of shopping was the hunt, more than the purchase, so the glimpse of things worth buying in such a small space gave her a pang. Oh, to be at Liberty's or even on the Oxford Road with two thousand pounds! But there was no financial stream at present. Once the Rolex bonus had vanished, what then?

Nevertheless....

Aunt Jenny was at work. Ferdy was at the shop. The dogs slept. She ventured out; anonymous, invisible, safe. She told the over-friendly assistant she was fine, she was only browsing, but came out to the far shrill of Whistling Joe with a pair of soft leather shoes, a cashmere shawl in cream with a gold trim that matched her colour and a hairbrush with a hazelwood backing. To hold the weighted plastic bag made her feel normal for the first time since leaving London. Aunt Jenny sent a text to call in for milk at the supermarket.

She was on the way to the till when she stepped past a woman in electric blue leggings that gleamed like neon, a tall woman whose limbs sprawled down the aisle, a basket like a child's toy on her arm, cursing among the toiletries.

'This fucking shop,' she said to a friend. The friend was shorter; more hunched, standing. 'They're always out of what you want. It's the worse fucking shop in England.'

'Not quite the worst, Char.'

'Second worst then,' said Char. The woman rubbed her cheeks in confusion. 'And where's the mouthwash?' she asked.

'I know where that is,' Lillian said.

She pointed out the bottom shelf at the end of the aisle.

'Brill,' the woman said. 'What a silly bitch!' She crouched, sticking her bottom in her tight pants in the air instead of bending at the knees like a lady.

'You're the running girl, aren't you?' the shorter woman asked.

'I do run regularly,' Lillian answered with caution.

'Char,' she addressed her companion. 'It's Lillian.'

It was Chardonnay and Shelly whom she'd met at the Mindfulness Centre.

Char sprang up and dropped the pale blue liquid in her tray. 'You're lightning,' she said with finality. 'You're the Goodman girl, aren't you?'

'My name's Delph.' Lillian edged away.

'Really?' Char squinted.

'Father's name,' Shelley said.

'Right. You're Emily Ellesker's daughter, yeah?' It was the nonchalance that threw Lillian. She looked as though she'd never heard the name. 'Jenny Goodman's cousin. Lives in Scotland.'

'Massive Scrambler,' said Shelley.

'Yes. I believe so.' Lillian glanced away.

'Is she in Saltscar now?'

'Not at the moment.' This was getting worse.

'So what is a beautiful girl from London doing in Saltscar?' Shelley asked.

'I've seen you with Ferdy in the shop,' Chardonnay said.

'Yes, I'm helping.'

'Is it open soon?' Shelley asked.

'We hope so.'

'I love Ferdy,' Chardonnay added. 'He's a dear.'

'He certainly is,' said Lillian, who smiled, waved and moved off.

Lillian took Green and Black's dark chocolate for Aunt Jenny. It was not on the list, but Aunt Jenny liked it, and liked to be considered. Suddenly, Chardonnay was behind her. 'Me again,' she said. 'Are you really doing the Scramble?'

'I haven't entered.'

'You run like you should,' Chardonnay said. Shelley joined them. 'We're doing it,' Chardonnay continued. 'Aren't we, Shells?' Shells nodded. 'Come and run with us later.'

'I'm not sure I can this week,' Lillian said.

'I work,' Shelley said.

'Are you as fast as your mum?' Chardonnay asked.

'I don't know.'

'I'm a mum,' Shelley said.

'Where do you drink? I haven't seen you. And how's Ferdy? He hasn't done me granny for over a fortnight.'

'Sorry?'

'She pays him to tidy up the garden.'

'He's been busy with the shop,' Lillian explained.

'We're running after work tomorrow,' Shelley insisted.

Lillian did not want to seem rude. 'I'd like to,' she said, 'but I'm going back to London very soon.'

'After the Scramble, though?' Shelley asked.

Chardonnay may have finally picked up on Lillian's shyness. 'Don't badger her, Shells,' she said. 'We're running for charity. So much for each position off last.'

'I see.'

'Child Hunger,' Shelley added. 'What's to object?'

'You could improve us. We'd be first, second and third.'

'A bit lower than that, Char. To be honest.'

'We'll be in touch. Come on, Shells.'

Lillian idled, but she caught them nevertheless at the tills waiting for an assistant to clear a bottle of vodka. Chardonnay, seeing Lillian, rolled her eyes again. 'This fucking shop,' she mouthed. Lillian smiled despite herself. It was true that such bumbling inefficiency would not be tolerated off the King's Road. 'How's Anne-Marie?' Chardonnay shouted across. 'I went to school with her.'

'Fine. She's in Newcastle.'

'She was clever,' Shelley said.

'Newcastle's cool,' Chardonnay said.

Lillian moved from the tills as the women bantered with the attendant. She was almost at the exit, and safe, when Deaf Jean lumbered up as out of a magician's box before her. 'Hello, Lillian,' she said in her low voice. 'This is timely.'

'Oh, yes, hello. It's –'

'Jean. It's ok. My hearing aids are on. Are you shopping?'

This was such a ridiculous question Lillian was stuck in stupefaction. While she was stuck the younger women strode up. 'This has to be the most half-arsed fucking supermarket in the whole of fucking England,' Chardonnay said. 'Hi, Jean.'

'Hi, girls.' Jean said.

'Actually, I have to dash,' said Lillian.

'I wanted to ask,' Jean ploughed on in her quiet relentless way, 'Would you and Ferdy like to take drinks at the Hall one afternoon next week? My American friends come Toosday.'

'We're trying to get her to run with us,' Shelley said. 'She goes alone.'

'She's quick,' said Chardonnay.

'You should absolutely do that,' Jean told her.

'Of course. Sorry, I'm –.'

'Brill,' said Chardonnay. 'Give me your number.'

Lillian was reminded of her first meeting with Aunt Jenny in the V&A. She told them she'd forgotten her phone, at which Jean said they could get her number from Jenny.

'And when we've done running,' Shelley said, 'we can go down Smuggler's.'

'It's nice of you to ask me,' Lillian said, and settled her bag on her arm in a must-go way.

'You could help us,' Shelley said.

Instead of turning through the arches into Station Road with its hint of escape as the street rose to the brow, she turned seawards and walked to the shop. The sea itself glanced at the end of the rows, like a painted window, a blue from story books, a freedom not enjoyed. She had never thought the name Prosper-oh more silly. But it was closed. Typical. Ferdy was a nice man, but he was elusive as a wind. She clattered into the house and shouted a greeting. He was lying on the sofa with the holy family piled around him, an open book at his side. He raised a lazy arm.

'What are you doing?'

'Thinking,' he said.

She would never get used to this family. 'I met Jean,' she said. 'She wants us to meet her American friends.'

'They may be hard to avoid.'

'Why would Americans come here?'

Ferdy squinted at her. 'To west coast Americans, we are quaint.'

'Chardonnay and Shelley want me to do the Scramble with them.'

Ferdy was in his weird state. 'Don't do it,' he said.

'Is it rough?'

'You'd probably win.'

'Why shouldn't I win?'

'It's not Saltscar. When Rebburn thrashed us at football a PE teacher wrote to Town Talk to say Saltscar needed to start a proper football team. Anonymous wrote back to say that losing at sport was a Saltscar tradition. It's part of our identity. There's something insensitive about that narrow kind of success. We reserve our energies for the battles that matter.'

Lillian looked at him in repose, covered with dogs. 'I suppose you're reserving your energies now.'

'I'm grieving.'

'Didn't your father die three years ago? I'm sorry – I didn't mean it's not hard.'

Ferdinand sat up with a general shuffle of dogs. 'For the world,' he said.

'That's just stupid! I'm going to do it, anyway. I'm going to win the Saltscar Scramble.'

'Watch out for Jane Brown.'

'Who? Oh, it doesn't matter."

Lillian cleared the dishwasher. The kitchen was in a better state that when she came, much better, but standards were already beginning to slide. She rinsed the sink. Ferdinand was at the door.

'You're being very forceful, Lillian. That's not a criticism.'

She did not care if she was forceful or not. 'Were you Anonymous? I bet you were, weren't you?'

'I was thinking about the shop,' he said. 'I was being uncommonly practical. Dave is closer to a move to London.'

'So?'

'It has – implications.' He smiled at this trim little creature that looked so frail and punched so hard. 'Let's go for a swim again,' he said. 'A proper one.'

'It's too hot.'

'Which is to say, Too cold for hot chocolate, Too wet for a duck, Too big for ambition and Too small to carry,' he said. He stepped over and kissed her on top of the head. 'Come on, cousin. It will be like old times.'

She was reluctant to swim because he was better than her, but at least she was better than last time, and both were better than Jesus, who was also distracted by seagulls, and explosively distracted by another dog's ball. When Ferdinand said he would stay with the holy family for a while to ensure discipline, she decided to continue. The rhythm of her strokes and the underlying growl of the sea melted the world away. The screams and laughter of the teenagers who were splashing each other was a whisper from another land. She plunged along the bounce of the swell, and spat out salt water, and blinked in the glare when her head rose, and noted the unearthly blue across the horizon, and was happy enough not to notice she was content. She turned direction and swam towards the pier, which was crisp in the sun, and towards Moor Cliff whose burnished clay had turned a weathered pink, like flaking paint on a dried door. Her legs were fine. Her thighs had bulked just so with her running, but her under-exercised arms had started to ache, just a little, so she floated on her back to rest, and then she heard Ferdy screaming at her.

She had drifted out to sea. He ran in and plunged. She swam towards him. She sputtered a few times when the falling crests pulled her head deeper than her intention, but she could see no reason for his panic. He joined her just as her feet were able to touch bottom.

'You were drifting out,' he said.

'Not very far.'

'You didn't seem to be aware of it. There are currents.'

A wave slapped her on the back. She took a step forward.

'I'm sorry if I alarmed you,' she said, and laughed.

Jesus was barking at them in the shallows. Mary stood beside him with her ears cocked, her tail waving like an arm, while Joseph paced in herding mode to and fro behind them. She let Jesus jump up at her when they drove out of the wet and hugged all three when she sat on her towel.

'I'll make a good swimmer with practice!' she announced.

'It's not about being good, exactly.'

'What is it about then?'

'Hearing the voice of the sea.'

'Oh, I heard that!' Lillian said, drying her hair. 'It doesn't say very much.'

'Then you didn't hear it.'

'Let's have an ice-cream!' she said.

She dried herself and changed in the brick building marked Public Conveniences and brushed her hair with the hazelwood brush. When she arrived at the chrome tables of the Surfer's Café, Ferdinand had placed a serving of raspberry gelato at her seat. The dogs were slumped under the table. Lillian settled into the post-exercise rest.

She ate in miniature scoops with the plastic spoon. 'I've done this before,' she said.

'We were all little once.'

'No – I mean, here.'

She moved her seat to let a fat man with two children squeeze by.

'That wouldn't be surprising.'

'I spilt tomato ketchup on my front at the fish restaurant.'

'I don't remember that.'

'I do. It was traumatic. You used to carry me over the pools because I didn't like the slimy bits.'

'That's likely.'

'I don't think I was very nice in those days.'

'Are you saying you're nice now?'

She looked at him with a spoonful held before her mouth. 'That's so rude!'

'Pardon my northern manner,' he said.

'My mother was here with me.'

'Yes, she was.'

'She was born here.'

'That is also true.'

Lillian jabbed her spoon into the remaining ice-cream. It stuck up like a miniature flag. 'That's awful,' she said. 'Aunt Jenny's right. I'm half-northern.' She gave up on the spoon and bit. She used the paper towel to wipe her lips. 'And I *am* going to do this Scramble, and I shall do whatever I need to come first.' She crunched into the cone.

'Then you will be the jewel of the north.'

'The Lilly of the north,' she corrected. 'With two 'l's.'

'No. One.'

'Look at the sea-mist.'

It had already devoured the horizon. Its fingers were probing soundlessly along the brow of Moor Cliff. The white horses, far apart, skittered over the grey, but over the deeper bed, a flat velvety violet-blue lay prostrate before the advance. Suddenly, despite the sun on the pier, the t-shirts and the shorts, they felt a September chill.

'Curly's right,' said Ronnie. 'These are the crepuscular shores. But that poem will never be good.'

'This day hasn't gone as I expected,' said Lillian.

'Jordan's,' Aunt Jenny said. It was by repute the best steak pie in the north.

This was also an ambush. Lillian looked from the album through the window. The western rooftops were dark against the open blue behind them: it made her feel shut-in, but in a good way, a solid way. The pleasure in Jenny's voice meant, We'll eat the same thing at the same time. In this house, of course, that might not mean in the same place. Lillian closed the album pages. Aunt Jenny waited in the doorway.

'Lovely,' Aunt Jenny, she said, stretching.

Lillian was ready. She laid the table deftly as a mouse while Jennifer in an untied apron heated gravy and steamed the vegetables and warmed the pie and hummed a tune from her favourite band, *Dire Straits*. Lillian had become accustomed to Aunt Jenny's mixed signals. She went to a cupboard for salt.

'Almost there,' Aunt Jenny said.' We'll have mash. I'm boiling them in their skins, and then I'll blitz them with the blender. More fibre. Very smooth. Earthy. What's that?' she asked.

'I thought we could eat at the table,' Lillian said. 'Daddy and I used to.'

Aunt Jenny was taken aback. 'It's rather unusual,' she said. 'But it might be nice for a change.'

It took Aunt Jenny a few minutes to accustom herself to the new arrangement, but once Lillian had tried the pie she sighed and said, 'I've been looking through that album

- the dark blue one.' Aunt Jenny paused the cutting of her broccoli. 'It has photographs of my mother.'

Aunt Jenny put down her cutlery. 'Rather out of date now!'

'I wonder why didn't she never got in touch with me?'

'That's a very big question.' Aunt Jenny was uncharacteristically cautious. 'She's my cousin. We're close though we're different. Perhaps I'm not the best person – though if you're *comfortable* with talking about her... '

'Was it my father?'

'She never said so.'

'So, then?'

'Anne-Marie says it's not our place to interfere. She's very strict about that.'

'But if I want to know?'

'And when I mentioned her, when you came here, you looked very fierce and I thought, and Anne-Marie thought as well, that we can let sleeping dogs lie for a while.'

'She should have tried harder.'

'To be honest, I've never quite understood Anne-Marie's position. I have to say, Jordan's, considering they make so many, albeit in store, is really very good, though personally I'd go for a bit more pepper and a little less salt, but Anne-Marie always says I trust my intuition too much, but that's really Ferdy's weakness; mind you, the has a powerful intellect, really, he does. Anne-Marie's disapproval is a fearsome thing, but she knows I'd never ever do anything to hurt you. We mustn't bring you out before you're ready. It's about triggers! We didn't have triggers when I was at college, but now they're everywhere.'

'Something must have happened.'

'I rather think it did.'

'What?' Lillian forked Jordan's. She chewed to the border of vulgarity, to show she was undaunted. Aunt Jenny put a hand to her mouth with her elbow on the table to show she was thinking. Lillian waited.

'What I do know, with all my heart and hope to die as we said when we were little, is that Emily never actually chose to leave you. She lost you, more like. Oh.' She stared in dismay at the questing snout that had appeared in the doorway. 'Jesus! He only does this when it's Jordan's. I think he recognises the word.'

'How can you lose someone?' said Lillian.

'We're about to lose Jesus. Go on, Jesus. You'll get yours later.' Jesus departed with his head turned back. Aunt Jenny shut the door upon him. Lillian was not deflected.

'How?'

'The thing is, your mother, when she was young - I mean, your age – she was impulsive. She was brave. That's the Ellesker thing. To a fault.'

'She went to Australia with Jeremy.'

'Jeremy? I don't recall a Jeremy.'

'I told Frank that and he didn't seem to agree, and then he clammed up.'

'You told Frank?'

'Everyone clams up when I mention her.'

'The thing is – and this is not a judgement – how do you find the mash?'

'Delicious.'

'I'm so glad!

'So what is it?'

'It's not such a big thing, not to me, not in itself, but, as I said, Emily is brave and she got into scrapes, and through a scrape she ended up in Australia, and when she looked to find you again she got into another one. The scrapes are history. There's only one person you should hear it from.'

'My mother herself?'

Aunt Jenny toyed with her food. She nodded. Then she said, 'Excuse me just a minute, my dear. I want to check something.'

She left the door open. Jesus sneaked in and sat begging by Lillian's seat. 'No, Jesus,' she said. 'You'll get me into trouble.' Jesus yapped. It brought in Mary and Joseph. The parents observed her. Jesus looked down, perhaps in shame, and crawled under the table. Mary and Joseph sat on either side of her chair. 'If Jenny finds you lot here when she comes back, she'll only shush you out,' Lillian said. Jesus looked up from the floor. He was watching her. Mary and Joseph gazed upon her without expression. They were not there for food. They were there for her.

They were extraordinary dogs.

Aunt Jenny came back with a bottle of wine. 'Don't tell Frank,' she said. 'I hid this. It's very naughty, but it's very good, and I think this conversation needs it.' Lillian was patient as Aunt Jenny rattled in the kitchen for the corkscrew. She returned in triumph with the bottle and two glasses.

'Did you phone my mother?' Lillian asked.

'I was looking for an old letter, but didn't find it.'

'Oh.' Lillian took this in. 'What did it say?'

'It was a post card. All it said was, as I remember, 'Coming home, and ready for Lillian.' She poured, she sat, she sipped and sighed in pleasure. 'Delicious. Shall we have a toast?'

'No, Aunt Jenny. Not yet. So why did she go to Australia in the first place?'

'We don't know,' she said. 'She ran away when she was very young, and disappeared, and then she was married and then she was not, and then, like a genie, she came back. We don't ask.' She met Lillian's gaze.

'That's as maybe. What does she actually do?'

'She runs a camp.'

'She's in tourism?'

'No, goodness me, no. Well, yes, in a way. Climbing mountains, racing down fells, swimming rapids, hiking, canoeing over waterfalls; healthy outdoor things. She drives young delinquents over moors. She's a tomboy. A tom-man. Tom-woman? I'm not sure of the expression. Also, sometimes she goes to a monastery. Very Zen.'

'For a woman who loves me, she hasn't tried very hard.'

'Well, you know, there are different ways of trying.'

'I don't understand that.'

'Lillian, my dear, you know you can meet her.'

'Yes,' Lilian said. 'If she asks.'

'Of course!' Aunt Jenny beamed. 'We can certainly toast that!' She held out the glass, but Lillian was cold.

'If Daddy agrees.' Aunt Jenny was left with the glass aloft. 'He brought me up. He never left me. He saw me

235

through school. He was there for my first period! Where was my mother then?' She cut a portion of Jordan's with cruel precision. 'Those who do the work deserve the love. It's a rule.'

Aunt Jenny lowered the glass and stared at the fierce face before her with awe. Lillian saw the anguish and softened. 'You're very good to me, Auntie. I love you, really. But if my mother wants me she can bloody well earn it! You see?'

Aunt Jenny held her glass again. 'I'll toast to that,' she said. 'You don't have to join me.' She raised it to Lillian. 'To you, my dear.' She sipped. 'It's easy to forget, but you're an Ellesker too.'

'Maybe I am.' Lillian dropped her cutlery. 'I really can't eat any more,' she said. 'If I'm hungry later I'll have a banana. I'll clear up.'

A doggy whine, sharp as a reprimand, sounded under the table. 'Jesus only wants us to be happy and loving,' said Aunt Jenny. 'He knows when things get difficult. He wants Jordan's as well, but he can sing for that.' She left Lillian to clear the kitchen and process what had been said, but Lillian was glad when she returned from the dining room to see Aunt Jenny emerge from the television, and she accepted the hug.

It was her first plod round the course of the Saltscar Scramble.

She looked across the valley to the ring of stone apartments on High Prom, the crown, as a place to conquer. She reckoned the point at which to increase her speed was the south entrance to the Valley Gardens where she would overtake the fading opposition on the descent to the shore road before her final sprint along Low Prom. She could hear the cheers already.

'Thank fuck we walk to the top and then go down,' said Chardonnay.

Lilly had agreed to try the route with the two women because it was only a trial, and it didn't matter if they held her back.

'Save your puff for the bank. It's a bitch,' Shelley said.

It was advice more honoured in the breach, for the ladies were accustomed to chat. Lillian tripped ahead down the rough path along The Neck of the Dragon. The path curled round the hill like the slide on a helter-skelter, then dropped off onto the walkway along the A-road that led to the car park by The Smugglers before it curled back up the buff to the town on the other side of the valley. They had to walk at the bottom to avoid bumping into the careless children and old people with dogs, which pleased Shelley and Char, and irritated Lillian. Then came the climb. They fell silent as they jogged up to the town except for a groaning 'Fucking hell,' from Chardonnay. Shelley was the stoutest and clung to the pole at the lights while they waited to enter High Prom.

Their language and their dress were terrible, but it didn't matter up here.

'Lillian isn't even panting,' Chardonnay said.

'She's a star,' said Shelley.

'She runs like her mother.'

'I don't know my mother.'

Question marks rose from her heads of her companions.

'She left when I was a baby.'

'Oh, darling!' Chardonnay exclaimed.

'It's not an issue,' Lillian said to their shock. 'It's complicated,' and she sped off without regard for their pace. At Hazel Grove she stopped: Chardonnay waved and smiled as they approached, and Lillian ran at her lowest pace for them for fifteen minutes past the allotments that lined the railway tracks out of town. They turned under a railway bridge, red brick with tendrils and branches grasping at it, and onto the unlovely road with modern houses and a little garage that led back into town, where Shelley stopped them because she met someone from work. Lillian turned off the stopwatch and was patient. They resumed past the cricket club and Mindfulness Centre where Aunt Jenny was at that moment working, crossed the top of Devon Street itself into the very heart of the town, on Station Road, and cut right and south on the wide street where grand Victorian houses and the Hall fronted the top of the Gardens. Lillian led past the War Memorial and the bandstand and after a quarter of a mile turned left at the southern entrance to the Garden itself. Chardonnay gave a jubilant 'Wheeee' as they skimmed downwards between the thick secondary wood and, when they finally hit the flat again after the Italian Garden and the steps and the quaint wooden bridge over the stream, they all waved to the children on the miniature railway. Shelley suggested with good sense that she finish along the beach instead of Low Prom, which was crowded.

Lillian sprinted over the sands on which she had once made castles.

'Fuck me, Lillian, darling, you're a pro,' said Chardonnay. And they followed up behind her.

Lillian was looking at her wrist. 'It's just over seven kilometers,' she said. 'Apart from the bank it's flat or downhill. My heart didn't get above 180. The bank is the clue.'

'How do you know that?' Shelley asked.

'It's on the app.'

They crowded round the watch. Lillian explained.

'The appliance of science!' said Chardonnay. 'I want one of those.'

Shelley made a circle with thumb and finger. 'Pro,' she said.

Lillian showed them her stretches on the beach. Chardonnay fell over and screamed. Shelley laughed with her. The elderly on Low Prom turned their heads, but made no comment. They reminded Lillian of the Lower Sixth when they'd arrived at a hotel on a school trip and couldn't get over their excitement.

'Pub?' asked Shelley.

'But you'll undo the good work of the exercise,' Lillian pointed out.

'No, Lillian,' Chardonnay answered. She put her hand on Lillian's arm. 'The exercise undoes the bad work of the drinking. Come on, Lillian. I'll show you photographs of my baby girl. She's beautiful!'

They were both quite silly, but Lillian accepted their parting hug and agreed that next time she join them for a swift one in the Smuggler's. She felt grown-up: she had running partners older than herself, but as she turned into Devon Street, she knew she needed Ferdinand.

Anne-Marie and Aunt Jenny regarded her with serious faces as she entered the sitting room. 'It's all right, I'm going for a shower. Running', she said, but when she crossed to her room and heard Anne-Marie below she paused, hands on the banister. 'I know what I promised,' Anne-Marie was saying, as she walked out of the room, 'but the situation's changed.' Lillian waited until Anne-Marie returned from the kitchen, in case Aunt Jenny followed, and spoke about her. Instead, Annie-Marie came back and said, entering, 'It's pointless, mum!' The voices returned to a low burble. Lillian was still. Then Anne-Marie said through the open door, 'It's not fair on Dave, mum.' Lillian darted into the bathroom as Anne-Marie came up the stairs.

Lillian snook into Anne-Marie's room and took a coat from the wardrobe. She waited. The toilet flushed. Anne-Marie went back. On her way downstairs, she remembered Anne-Marie's conspiratorial glance in Costa while joshing with Ferdy at Barby Blackstone and thought, What is your problem? She walked out without speaking to them. Anne-Marie watched her through the window as she turned down the street. They think I'm being rude, she said, but she didn't care.

Ferdinand was not at his best. He was standing over a fallen rack. Cards and envelopes were scattered over the floor, and a few had fluttered onto the sill. He raised his head to Lillian with the tragic air of a man over the corpse of a beloved, and said, 'I stepped backwards.'

'Ferdy, you're so clumsy! Why did you do that?'

'I was looking at the walls.'

Lillian saw why when he gestured at them. Frank's photographs were finally displayed. 'Oh,' she said. 'It's the 'ang!' They were good. She'd thought they were good in their nascent state when he'd showed her prints and she'd put three on her wall, but these were different. Most surprising of all was the fully three-foot-wide picture of herself, a black and white Lillian Miranda Delph, turning to look across the edge of the cliff to a distant black-and-white Saltscar upon which the sky pressed in colour. Her image gazed as in surprise to see the blues of the sea and sky, the washed and thick greens of field and shrub and the yellow globules of gorse. At the end wall she saw her black and white face raise her desert brown eyes to the viewer. It was a challenging stare, almost scary. Moor Cliff behind her, thick and black as wet slate, gave no comfort. Lillian Cordelia Delph as a witch! Frank had made her a wild thing of the shore.

'Impressive,' she said.

'More upstairs. You're not in all of them.'

'Let me help,' she said.

They had almost re-stacked the up-righted stand when he asked her if she'd seen a black ring-binder around. It must be here somewhere, but it's not where he thought, though it would turn up.

'Is it important?'

'It is rather.'

'Ferdy, you're hopeless!'

'So my sister keeps persuading me.'

'She and Jenny were in a serious conversation.' Lillian slipped in the last card and squinted at the rack.

'Telling mum to persuade me to give it all up.'

'What?'

This fitted exactly what Lillian already knew, but it sounded harsh put so plainly. '"This battles fares like to the morning's war, when dying clouds contend with growing light,"' he said. 'It looks like I'm on my own.'

'Then you've got to stop knocking over the stock and losing files.'

He confronted her with a stare. 'It is rather crucial, isn't it? Do you think I can do it?'

'I'm sure you can,' she lied. 'A least, with a bit of help.'

'Would you be interested?' he asked.

She had always pictured herself with a shop. A shop was a name. When her friends in school-plays saw their names in lights, on the credits of a film or heard them chanted from the stadium seats or credited above a stall of wondrous garments, she had rather thought of hers above the lintel of a high street shop. Delph's. It was not in the least discouraging that no-one knew the faces of Marx and Spencer, or of Mr Boodle, or that Fortnum and Mason were long dead. And she had a name to remember: Delph, an English version of somewhere in The Netherlands. A shop gave you a presence in a place, and the presence was physical. But here? Ferdinand's? Now? There was no way.

'I'm too young yet,' she said. 'Anyway, I'll probably have to leave soon.'

'True.' he mused. Then, as if she had heard her thoughts aloud, he said, 'Goodman. Ellesker? What's in a name? Surely, it's the local habitation that needs a name.'

'My mother keeps cropping up,' she said.

'Where?'

'In conversation.'

'Is that a problem?'

'I don't know. Is it? Is she?'

'Let's go for a walk.'

'But your work!'

'It can wait.'

He was incorrigible. They did not speak until they had rounded the wide sweep of High Prom and dropped down through the dense banked wood of Hazel Grove that marked the natural western boundary of Saltscar, just as the Valley Gardens did the east. They crossed the end of Low Prom to the beach and glanced together at Moor Cliff which was hazed in a faint blue mist, on the top of which the treeless fields rolled away to a clear sky, as to freedom.

'It's lovely,' said Lillian.

'Let's leave the madding crowd.'

The receding tide was at the three-quarter mark so they walked freshly wet sand that gave a little to their tread and made meditative their steps. They thought their separate thoughts. Ferdinand could not entirely dispel the gloom in his mind, despite Lillian. The seas shuck and plop muttered it, the wind that lifted their hair whispered it and a protesting seagull announced it: the heavy doom of exile. What was there in Saltscar if the shop failed? He could not live with his mum and weed her old acquaintances' gardens for ever. And this place, that drew to its bent shore the ones who hurt in order to be healed, the artists to inspire, the world's wanderers to be calmed: this place alone in the world he could call Home. Lillian was thoughtful too. Stand on high prom on a blustery day when the beach was trailed by only a few, or on Cat Knoll, or even the pier, and watch the steps of the solitary ones or the couples: they had the poise of people looking inward, or away from the human shores to the wilder creatures of the sea. This was a vision he knew well.

'I'll miss the beach when I'm gone,' Lillian said.

He led her down to the edge of the waves, and she continued, so wrapped up in her thoughts that she walked in a straight line without regard to the long clutch of the water so her feet were sodden, and she exclaimed, 'Not these as well! My trainers are already white with salt,' then shrugged and walked on.

'You're preoccupied,' he said.

'Yes.'

'What was the serious conversation – between Anne-Marie and mum?'

'It wasn't my business.'

'I guess it,' he said. 'She wants to go with Dave. It's fair. I might manage. I've only got to make enough to stay here.'

'I think the idea of a business is to make money and then to expand,' she opined.

'Not all businesses,' he said.

'I was thinking – if I had a shop here, apart from the online sales, I'd do You Tube videos, and I'd set up a Vlog and I'd make all this -' gesturing to the sea '- like a stage. Do a profile on Frank.'

'Wouldn't that rather put people off?'

'I'd sort him out. You create your clientele. You don't just find them. That what Pheobe Darlington's mum says, and she's got shops in London *and* Bath. It would be a project.'

'So it does interest you?'

He stared out over the grey slither of water with its crashing foam and out to where a tanker with a white top was stuck like a toy on the blue iridescence, and she looked out too.

'We have a different philosophy,' she said.

He glanced at her: 'In what way?'

'I'm happy when I try very hard and I need other people to try hard as well so I try harder, whereas you like to be still and to think about things.'

'Lillian Miranda – you are right.'

'It doesn't mean we can't respect each other.'

'We love each other,' he said simply. 'It's a magical thing – as though we were little children again.'

'I sort of remember that. It's more like a dream than a memory. I think you looked after me.'

'Yes. Your mother was here. I think she'd just come back. It was a turbulent summer.'

'My mother again.'

'It's natural you resent her.'

'No, I don't. But if I got to know her it would change my relationship with my father, and that's not fair on him.'

It was his turn to reflect. 'You're very wise, Lillian,' he said. 'You disguise it, but you are.'

'I'm not stupid, that's all.'

'That's a lot. Of course, your mother might improve your relationship with your father. Have you thought of that?'

'I don't see how.'

He touched her on the arm and moved off. 'Come on, I'll show you something.'

He led up the grass banks above which in modest grandeur stood the remains of the church. 'Cut through here,' he said. 'Up there lies the spirit of my father and a portion of his ash.'

'I can't imagine life without my father,' she said, following.

It was a spire on top of a tower, and nothing else. Gravestones, and an unromantic housing estate over the road, a bench against the stone wall, and sea and sky, and that was it. She noted his face as they looked over the wall, but he was calm. 'It's halfway between the Salscar he inhabited and the Rebburn of his birth,' he said. 'The shop was his idea. He was a true handyman. I want his legacy to be a shop you could *only* get here. Local artists, local performers, local taste. That doesn't mean insularity. By no means. We steal and make anew. Do you see?'

'Not really. Just the local market?'

'Absolutely not! A local shop selling local things for non-local people!'

'Souvenirs?'

'Of a particularly spiritual kind.'

'Good luck then,' Lillian said. 'I'm not sure what Daddy would say to such a business plan.'

Ferdinand looked to his feet, to hide his thought. Then he said, 'But it hasn't worked for him, has it? The rational materialist drive?'

She liked being with him on this walk, so she quelled the offence. 'His troubles are temporary,' she said. 'It's a feast and famine existence. He has contacts. He's very employable.'

He considered this. 'Lillian,' he said, 'You don't think perhaps your father's just a little bit controlling?'

'What?'

'In a loving way. You call him 'Daddy'.'

'He *is* my daddy.'

'Now I've offended you again. Ferdinand Goodman is having a below par day. On this the people agree. I don't doubt he does everything for you, but no father is perfect, not even mine.'

Controlling. The idea! Anyway, Lillian liked control; the authority and security of it, the world's plenitude made orderly and so available, the regularity of the beating heart. They were having a nice time together, she and Ferdy, each with their problems in tow, so she only said, so as not to spoil it, 'Oh, my father's far from perfect. He can be very silly. But he's never stopped me doing what I want – within reason.'

'Good,' he said, but without conviction. 'Let's go back along the top. There are some more things I want to show you.'

He led along the edge of the housing estate to the path back between the railway track and the allotments, so familiar to him but new to Lillian – she had not noticed them on the run - though it was Ferdinand who told the names of the plants that grew there, and who greeted the elderly who pottered among the sparse early Autumn beds. In one there flew a flag in red and yellow stripes with the European Union emblem in a corner. He waved to the man, a trim and middle-aged gentleman weeding under the flag's supple flapping, and shouted, 'Viva Catalonia!'

'Viva Syndicalista,' the man shouted back.

'Any news?' Ferdinand asked.

'Cuixart and Sànchez have made a new statement. Indissolubility of the union, my arse. Fascism dies a slow death. Who's your friend? We've not been introduced.'

'This is kin, Herbert. Lillian Delph. Lillian – Herbert.'

'Hello.'

Herbert nodded.

'Lillian is negotiating identities. She's from London. The squash is in flower. Impressive.

'Dry summer. It's all been a bit shrivelled this year.'

'His great uncle fought in the Spanish Civil War. For the anarcho-syndicalists,' Ferdinand explained as they moved away. 'He flies the flag in all senses.'

'I don't know what that is. No, I don't want to.'

He led her unspeaking for a quarter of a mile, perhaps a bit less, then stopped and gestured through a wire mesh over blue corrugated fencing to a particularly scruffy patch. Lillian was blank. He saw her blankness. 'See it through my eyes,' he said. Lillian looked again. 'Nothing there to eat,' he prompted, smiling, and she understood. She thought she understood.

It was a mess of flowers. In the far corner a ramshackle fence in faded blue was shrouded by the remnants of sweet peas on crossed bamboo sticks. There was an outsize water butt against them; actual bamboo, untrimmed, spread gangling along the side fence, mixed with Michaelmas daisies and black-eyed-susans. There was a visible patch of dirt in the centre with a cloche of blue netting, crowded by hollyhocks and greying aliums, around which rivers of more black-eyed-susans wound between grasses and spent shrubs to the far fence where they made a yellow mist. Borage, still flecked blue, had been allowed to roam along the corrugated fence and to thrust its leaves through the wire mesh. The remaining borders were dense with shrubs through which brambles thrust their arms. Honeysuckle hung fronds like the arms of exhausted refugees over the mesh in the corner and, to announce the end of summer and the first fires of chill autumn, a clump of orange dahlias offered their vulgarity to the evening light. On the corner, over fence and hedge a plethora of nasturtiums heralded in bright orange the end of the blues and greens of summer and the coming of the burnt hues of autumn.

'You like it because it's natural,' she said.

'I like it,' he answered, 'because it's pointless! You take things away from allotments. Normally, you eat them, or you sell them, or you give them away. This is rambling profusion for its own sake. Like the nasturtiums handing around over there, sprawling and floppy, and all over the place, and rather lovely like ... like a Virginia Woolf paragraph.'

'It's in a children's story.'

'It is. It's a little bit of magic in a practical world. Perhaps it would be better to grow onions and give them to a food bank, but there has to be a place for eccentricity, for an overflow of joy, like this. The lady who runs it is from South-East Asia. I've never spoken to her, but I guess she find seasons exotic. I imagine her slogging away at the weeding and watering, at turning the soil and then just sitting and listening to the bees or whatever. It comforts me to think someone in the world is doing that.'

'You'll never leave, will you?'

'Unless the shop fails. Then I may have to.'

'Well then,' she said primly, 'you must make sure it doesn't.'   They walked beside the railway tracks and past another housing estate, a small one, a modest one, and a modern church and were once again at the top of Hazel Grove. Lillian suddenly realised this was the route of the Saltscar Scramble in reverse. They followed the curve of High Prom and he threw an arm to the shore below.

'When you grow up with that great gap of sea and sky on one side, everywhere else seems enclosed.'

'I can see that.'

Her nose twitched at the smell of evening fish and chips from Low Prom. The mist was gone: the September sun wrapped a warm arm round the curl of the land north. He stepped into the little formal garden to better appraise the sweep of the bay, as though to demonstrate in his stance the truth of his words. The pub in the town's white stone was beginning to twitch into its evening life. The chatter of the strollers, and the cries of children in the tiny park on High Prom, bounced off the faint whisper and collapse of the waves. She looked at him: his beard was thrust to the horizon, and she felt his imagination bobble along the ruffled water, a warm glow in the west and a cold silvery blue around Moor Cliff. She saw, though she could not entirely share, his love of the place. She realised something. 'I should have stayed there,' she said.

'London?'

'I came here in a panic. I should have stayed and faced it all.'

'I'm glad you did come,' he told her.

'So am I, but I was a wuss.'

He was surprised at the expression. It did not seem very Lillian. 'You're not at all a wuss, Lillian,' he said. 'You're breaking out.'

On impulse, she slipped her arm into his. 'Whatever that means.'

'My cousin once-removed.' He kissed her head.

'You're sort of my brother now,' she answered.

'That's genetically inaccurate. I'll take it as metaphor. Help me look for this file?'

'I'm hungry. It's the fish and chips. I will tomorrow if you don't find it.'

She walked alone under the railway bridge and along the white fence to Devon Street. She gave a great exhalation, a long relieving sigh, as though blowing out tension. Aunt Jenny was right. Ferdinand loved her, and the best thing about it was that there wasn't even the faintest whisper of sexual tension.

As she passed the front window she noticed Anne-Marie rise. She'd been waiting. Lillian announced herself with a shout and dashed to the kitchen and spooned a serious portion of chicken casserole onto a plate and took it to the dining table, and was not surprised to see Anne-Marie at the door.

'Well done,' she said. 'Great de-cluttering.'

'It's better, isn't it?'

'You've made the place quite your own. And you've got a room of your own!'

Lillian was not pleased that Anne-Marie sat opposite her. 'It's not like other people can't come in,' she said.

'I'm sorry Ferdy thrust your mother onto you. He shouldn't have done that, especially when you were so shocked to see her the night before. Mum says you're taking up the job at the café: no timescale on your father yet?'

'It's still a fluid situation.'

'It's difficult, isn't it?' Lillian doubted the sincerity of this sentiment. Her face remained neutral. 'Do you fancy a trip to York? Dave and I are going when he's next down. You might as well make the best of where you are. You could visit us in Newcastle if you wanted. Saltscar's not got much to offer young people, after all.'

'That would make a change,' said Lillian. It was not clear to her why Anne-Marie was being so understanding. She needed to hold her ground, so she said, 'I don't think Ferdy meant any harm when he called my mother. I think … he made it more normal. It was a good thing.'

Anne-Marie nodded. 'You're getting quite close to him, aren't you?' she asked in a low voice.

'Your brother's a very nice man,' she answered.

'He has a dangerous charm. He's easy to love.'

'But you're right,' Lillian suddenly announced. 'He's useless at the shop. He hasn't even considered his online strategy.'

Anne-Marie nodded her agreement. 'And yet he loves it,' she said.

'He loves it,' Lilly echoed.

'There's the problem. It has given Frank a needed boost. Mum was right on that.' Anne-Marie glanced in the direction of the door, less to indicate she thought her mother was coming through than to suggest she ought not to hear if she did. 'It's partly to do with dad. And the fact that Ferdinand's failed at pretty well everything – his engagement, his Ph.D – he dropped out of that – his book. The trouble is, mum doesn't get that it's better he stop now than when he's used up the resources. That's the classic Ellesker fault. Stubborn. We'd run at a wall with our heads if it stood in the way.'

'It's a very difficult situation.'

'It is. Men and mums are a dysfunctional combination in the world of practical affairs.' Anne-Marie giggled. Perhaps she was high.

'Perhaps I could help him.'

'He'd love that. I ought to be jealous. I could easily be jealous. You're halfway to being the sister he actually wants. But, hey, life's short and I'm doing fine. Of course, you have your own battles.' Anne-Marie stood. The discussion was not quite finished, however. 'If you want my room, carry on. I can sleep in the little bed.'

'Are you sure?'

'I'm only here a few days. You might as well.'

Lillian had one last question before Anne-Marie left. 'If he doesn't do the shop, what will he do?'

'What all the failures do. Teach. Like mum used to. He's brilliant with children. They love him. In the evenings he can think about Shakespeare.'

Lillian returned her clothes from the small room to what was now officially her own. She had much to reflect on. Anne-Marie was right: it was best to cut your losses than to throw good money after bad, but Ferdy had a dream, and a dream was a thing, after all.

It took three attempts to get her father. She was brisk with him. 'Sweetie, at last. I've so missed speaking to you. Listen, I'm back from some meetings and they went well. It's just a case of seeing it through. It won't be easy, but –'

'Good, Daddy, but I don't want to talk about you now. I want your advice. Can you tell me about running a shop?'

'A shop? Where's that come from all of a sudden?'

'It's important.'

'Why do you want to know about that?'

'Preparation for Paris. I'm going to make a success of it. I want to know everything. Can you prepare a dossier for me, and I'll collect it when I see you?'

'You're sounding very grown up. Yes, of course, I'll do my best, though it's not my speciality.'

'What about a meeting with someone who knows then?'

'What? Really? Yes, yes, I think so. You've rather taken me by surprise.'

'I'll check that you do it.'

'Randa, I'd be delighted. It's good to see the Delph spirit coming through.'

'How's your Delph spirit, Daddy? Is it high on the gumdrops scale?'

She paid more attention to the tone than to the content of his answer. When she spoke to him, she pictured him in the old home, often in his study, but sometimes stirring milk into his coffee at the island or with his feet on the coffee table in the reception. Now, however, she looked around the bedroom and decided to turn it more to her taste. She promised her father to ring back every day from now on and sat on the bed with her hands behind her head, her back propped on the pillows. She heard Jesus woof, and his paws clatter in the hall, and, seconds later, noted Ferdy's heavy tread outside. She had made no commitment either way, but it was always good to keep a spread of options.

She had acquired recognition. She was no longer Aunt's Jenny's niece or Ferdinand's cousin once-removed. Perhaps she'd shed her little-girl-lost look, or maybe the defiance of her running, that arrow course through Saltscar frivolity, had softened. The singing waitress at Grubby's thanked her by her name. Whistling Joe, under the arches, nodded to her, whistling. Curly took off his hat and waved it at her from the other side of the road. She was stopped by Jean and her Americans in the street: the Americans did not wear baseball hats, but were dressed like normal people in loose trousers and jackets, and grinned at her as though she was enriching their England experience. Chardonnay and Shelley listened to her as they started their second assault of the Saltscar Scramble.

They were at the bottom of the Dragon's Back. 'To do it properly, 'Lillian explained, 'you need a really good heart-monitor so you can measure your recovery time. If you have a trainer, she'll work out what your heart should get up to at points in the race. There's no time for that now, so we can just use the wrist monitors and work it out roughly. We need to push it so our bodies get to deal with the lactic acid.' The ladies shared a look and a nod, in conformation of an agreement about Lillian, and Chardonnay gave a double thumbs up. 'I'll probably race ahead. Do you mind?'

'Go for it, Lilly,' said Shelley.

'Wait for us at the end,' Chardonnay demanded. 'Smuggler's. No refusal.'

Lillian knew the dangers and the chances. She needed a sprint at the start so she didn't get jammed behind on the track down the slope. Then she would trust to her balance and keep a high step and let gravity do its work. It was on the bank where she had to be cautious. She looked at the time on her wrist when she turned into the climb. She was better on flat than on hills so she shouldn't worry about the lead at this stage. It was the next part that was crucial, the long broad sweep of High Prom. She would have preferred to keep the acceleration for the passage between the first railway and the allotments, but it was too narrow there for safety, so she stretched out past the high apartments and found herself well breathed at the entrance to Hazel Grove. She kept her heart around 190 as she left the Catholic Church and the town behind her. The 2.17 to Bishop Auckland rattled beside her and faded with a lowering groan. She was at 180 and comfortable as she went left under the brick bridge and back to the main road, along which she kept up her pace despite the annoyance of dancing round walkers. Then came the right turn away from the station entrance up the broad street to the head of the Valley Gardens. This was where she would need to assess her position and ensure she had enough left for the final sprint. She pushed herself on the tarmac path between the tall trees. A labrador got excited when she flew past and chased at her, barking. She ignored him. He was distracted by a smell, some canine's delectable defecation, and answered the owner's call. Over the stream: her tread sounded resonant on the wooden planks, and then she cruised the flat track between the the miniature railway and the water and thought, Here I must be close to the leader, or ahead, but not closed in: but after a hundred yards the field spread, there was no trouble there. She pushed to 190 again on the straight flat to the road where the sea suddenly appeared, a wrinkled grey-blue, cold and heaving, and she sped over the road with a wave without a glance to the slowing bus and turned left onto the final; Low Prom. It was busy. She veered past the queue for the fish and chips, turning heads, and held back a little by the café and the surf shop, but saw a clear line beside the crazy golf and the beach huts and went for it. The end would be where the railings stopped at the entrance to the beach and the spread of the ground at the bottom of the track down Hazel Grove, and there she slowed too abruptly so she could check her time and came to a stop after a circle. An old man with braces under his waistcoat and a flat cap and sagging stomach watched her.

'Scramble?' he asked.

She nodded, wheezing.

'Thought I'd enter meself til I saw you,' he said.

'I'm nine seconds behind the record!' she answered.

The man thought about this. 'Nine seconds is a long time in professional sport,' he observed.

She had finished her stretches and bought water by the time the ladies joined her. Shelley put her hands on her hips, heaving, and acknowledged Lillian with a wave. Chardonnay, though taller and slimmer, came in after her and leant over the railings.

'My tits are too big for this lark,' she said.

'You don't run with your tits, though, Char,' Shelley gasped.

257

The Smuggler's looked as a pub called The Smuggler's would; dark wooden walls and trestle tables, a hearth, and patterned carpet and pictures of ships. Its little latticed windows gleamed with almost unnatural brightness against the dim walls, little portals that secrecy conceded to action. George, the barman, nodded a nod of old recognition. 'Working up a thirst?' he asked.

'We're in training for the Scramble,' Chardonnay announced, with a victory pose. 'This is Lillian. She's from London. She's going to win.'

'So I've heard.' Lillian's ears pricked. 'The guys at the Surf have been watching you. They're impressed. Sin' you myself. Like an arrer.'

'Get in there, Lillian,' Shelley whispered to her.

'Chardonnay, Chardonnay?' asked George.

'Named after it. Drink it,' said Chardonnay.

'Half Worthington,' said Shelley. The barman raised his eyes to Lillian who asked for sparking water. The ladies groaned.

'Come on, Lillian,' implored Chardonnay. 'Half a fucking lager. Initiation. One won't hurt. Not after that slog.'

'Just a half then.'

She had to admit it slipped down, cool and savoury, without a murmur and made a fine accompaniment to the photographs of Chardonnay's baby girl. ('Fucking lovely, isn't she?' She was indeed). It was a new experience to be a teacher, not a pupil, and particularly to two women older than her, one a mother, and both with jobs, though she had no idea what work they did. Their jobs did not seem to dominate their minds. That was the Saltscar, or the north, in them. She settled into the snug dark old-fashioned space and said, 'I suppose they smuggled here,'

'Ay,' George confirmed. 'All along the coast to the south. Big business in them days. The only tax was custom's tax. It were a grand tax avoidance scheme. This row was the only houses here. Everybody were in on it.'

'That's how it got its name,' said Chardonnay.

'Not then, though, Char,' said Shelley.

'Not a good business plan,' George agreed. 'Not the best place to hide contraband in a place with a name like that.'

'Do you have a boyfriend, Lillian?' Chardonnay asked.

'No. I had, but we decided it wasn't working, and now I'm only here for a while. I mean, I'm not looking.'

'You've got to have a bit of fun, though,' said Chardonnay. 'You're so young. And the buns on some of those surfers!'

'What do you do for fun?' Shelley asked. 'There's a cocktail bar open on Milton Street on Saturday. You'd meet plenty of young people there.'

'I'm afraid fun has been rather off the agenda, lately,' Lillian said. 'Family difficulties. I mean in London, not at the Goodman's.'

The women looked grave. 'Aw, hun,' said Shelley. 'You must miss London. I know I would.'

Now they mentioned it. Yes.

'You're fucking amazing,' said Chardonnay. 'I was fucking useless at your age.'

'No need to swear, Char,' said Shelley. 'Lillian doesn't.'

'Who's swearing? I'm not swearing.'

'You are a bit, Char.'

'Saying my baby's 'fucking lovely' isn't swearing. Calling Lillian 'fucking amazing' isn't swearing. It would be swearing if I said my baby was 'fucking ugly' or that Lillian was a cunt, which she obviously isn't. No fucking way. Anyway, swearing can be good. Therapy. You should try it, Lillian.'

'It's not always good, Char,' said Shelley.

'I don't always swear. You're very grown up,' said Chardonnay. 'Isn't she, Shells?'

Shells nodded.

It was odd to Lillian – it had never occurred to her previously – that since the thing with her daddy fun had been off her agenda. That wasn't normal in a person her age. There was, of course, plenty of time to catch up, but the thought crossed her mind that she was turning into one of those people who must grow up very quickly because there's no-one to look after them, 'I have lots of fun in London,' she answered, but her phone excused her. She stood to take it.

It was Anne-Marie. 'Police?' Lillian said too loudly. The ladies exchanged a glance and were silent. George, noting this, looked over the handles where he was draining a barrel. 'Right, yes, I'm coming. I'm sorry,' she said to the gaping couple, 'something's happened, something – I have to get back.'

'Fucking hell. Finish your drink,' said Chardonnay. 'No, sit down. Calm yourself. Do the breathing thing. What about police?'

She had enough presence of mind to limit the chances of gossip. 'It's my father. Witness, or something.' She downed the rest of her half in one go and sighed in satisfaction to show she was calm. Shelley stood. She picked Lillian's phone off the table. 'Don't forget this. And the door is always open to you, isn't it, Shells?'

'It certainly is, Char.'

They were nice women.

'And don't think bad of yourself,' said Chardonnay. 'My dad did time and I've turned out fine.'

'Better than fine, Char,' said Shelley.

'I'm sure it's nothing,' Lillian answered and dashed, but the women came with her. They marched as though under orders by her side. Chardonnay opened the front door of a VW polo for her. 'Get in and don't fuss. Devon Street, Shells.' They said nothing all the way until Lillian opened the door and Chardonnay leaned across and said, 'Go on, fucking swear. Good therapy.'

Lillian smiled. She waved as the car growled away. She straightened at the door. Fuck, she thought. The words were like sandpaper against her head, but then Anne-Marie opened the door before she had chance to grip the handle and she was into the action. 'Come on. Mum's here. We can't get Ferdy.' She gave an acknowledging wave to the disappearing Polo.

'Has something happened to Daddy?'

She skittered through to the dining-room where man and a policewoman sat with Aunt Jenny at the table. The man rose when he saw her.

'Lillian Delph?' the man said. He showed a badge. 'Chief Inspected Hodge, Fraud Department, Scotland yard.' He pointed to the woman. 'This is Constable Sally Jones. Don't be alarmed, miss.'

Lillian sat with unnerving composure. This was to be the most serious moment of her life: more serious than the first examination, more serious even than with fluttering stomach she and William had finally done it, and more serious than when the debit cards failed, for now she was to witness the event unfold. With this knowledge, her trepidation dissipated: she needed to focus now, so she sat with legs crossed and hands in her lap as still as patience while Aunt Jenny caressed the knuckles of one hand with the other and Anne-Marie gazed balefully at her feet.

Lillian did not need the kind expression into which Sally Jones had arranged her face, and she did not respond when Sally Jones said. 'This gentleman just wants to ask you some questions.'

Inspector Hodge put a photograph on the table. 'Have you met this man?' he asked.

'It's Mr. Shevchenko,' Lillian said.

'That's right,' the inspector said. 'Do you remember when you first met him?'

'I'm confused,' Anne-Marie interrupted.

'Sorry, miss?' Inspector Hodge offered the smile of someone who had been told to be pleasant.

'You've come all the way from London on the off-chance Lillian is in to show her a photograph that you could have sent to her phone? Why?'

'There are good policing reasons,' the inspector answered. 'If you could just answer my question, miss,' he returned to Lillian.

'Lillian.'

'Sorry, miss?"

'You don't have to call me 'miss.'

'As you like – Lillian. So, when did you see this man?'

'Just before I came up here.'

'And that was -?'

'Sorry,' said Anne-Marie, 'but it does seem a waste of taxpayers' money. You could at least have warned her you were coming.'

The Inspector smiled. It was a knowing smile. 'I'm not casting any aspersions,' he said. 'But we don't work that way.'

'That's right!' Aunt Jenny announced from the kitchen. 'It's in *Line of Duty*. They like to surprise the witness because, if they don't, she gets in touch with the suspect who spins them a line. I think that's the right phrase. Inspector, I'll put your milk in to save time but do say if it's too much or too little. Of course, there's no question of such collaboration with Lillian.' She put two mugs before the inspector and the constable and sat at the opposite end of the table.

'Thank you. Perfect.'

'It still strikes me as crazy,' said Anne-Marie. 'You could simply ask a a local detective to study the brief and report back.'

'We could have skyped,' Lillian said.

'I'm local,' said Constable Sally Jones.

The first irritation troubled Inspector Hodge, though he still forced a smile. 'I come by train. I return by train. I work on the train. It costs the taxpayer £130. This is a necessary part of an investigation involving financial crime into millions, and might even ... might clear up some other important things ... Please, let me ask Marion here-'

'Lillian,' said Lillian.

'Sorry? Yes, of course, sorry – Lillian.' Anne-Marie rolled her eyes. Lillian suppressed a giggle. 'Let me ask my questions and we're through!'

Anne-Marie gave a tiny shrug. The inspector lay four male faces in front of her. Lillian gazed upon them with mild disdain. 'Have you ever seen any of these men?' he asked.

'No. Mr Shevchenko was at the hospital.'

'Sorry?'

'Your previous question. When did I see Mr Shevchenko? He was at the hospital the day my father went in. He left us alone. Then he offered me a hundred pounds, which I thought rather rude, so I didn't take it. But then I did. I can give it back.'

'He offered you money?' Lillian did not deign to confirm. She looked at Inspector Hodge with the tolerant calm of a president's wife during speeches at a village fête. 'Any stipulations?' the inspector tried. 'Why would he do that?'

'Because I didn't have any?'

Now Anne-Marie had to suppress a smile.

The inspector returned the photographs to his file. 'So, tell me about Mr Shevchenko.'

Lillian considered. 'His favourite flower is the lily, if that helps. '

'So you know must know him quite well – to know his taste in flowers.'

'No. He mentioned it because it's my name.'

'Diminutive of Lillian,' Aunt Jenny explained.

'I understood that. And do you remember any mention any of these people?' The inspector took a list and slid it along the table. Lillian didn't look at it.

'They didn't mention anyone. He left and I talked with my father.'

'Ok.' Inspector Hodge seemed to have finished with Mr Shevchenko. 'You've seen your father only once since you came up here, yes?

'How did you know that?' Anne-Marie asked.

'He told us. Were you alone with him?'

'No.'

'Was he with Mr Shevchenko?'

'It was Mr Harris.'

'Ah, yes. Isn't that a little odd? You're staying up here with your relations while your father goes through this ordeal, and on the one occasion you get to see him you have a chaperon in the figure of the family solicitor. Would you – did you get the impression your father wasn't entirely free to talk?'

'You don't need to answer, Lillian,' Anne-Marie said.

'Actually, miss, she does.'

'That's right, I'm afraid,' Constable Sally Jones said.

'Lillian's the victim, Inspector,' Anne-Marie insisted.

'You talked about me with my father?' Lillian asked.

'But not now, surely, Inspector.' Aunt Jenny leaned towards them with urgent eyes. 'Lillian is in a vulnerable position, Inspector, and she's been doing so well we don't want her further upset. She was in bed for three days when she got back!'

'Really?' Inspector Hodge turned his head from Aunt Jenny to Lillian with deliberation. 'Do you feel vulnerable, Lillian? You don't look vulnerable. If our questions upset you, please say. So – you saw your father a week last Saturday. How did that go? Did it go well?'

'Not really.' Lillian's voice was faint.

'Sorry?' Inspector Hodge fixed her with his eyes. He was like a housemaster. Lillian was a particularly honest girl, but she had spent her teenage years with the mistresses and masters of deceit: Annabel Hamilton-Smith had talked herself out of trouble when John Whitson was found in her room one night after her room-mate was spotted sleeping on a mattress in the corridor with a brilliant story about a family trauma on John's part and an argument about the need to learn to give emotional support. Lillian had no doubt she could deal with Hodge.

'Sorry?' Inspector Hodge repeated.

'It was Daddy.'

'Yes?'

'He didn't want me to stay with him.'

'And why was that, do you think?'

'Because he has no money.'

'I see,' he said, biding time.

Anne-Marie looked up and scrutinised Lillian and Aunt Jenny breathed a tragic, 'Oh.' Constable Sally Jenkins offered a wan smile.

'Inspector, please take this the right way,' Aunt Jenny chimed in, 'but perhaps you need to show a little more empathy. You ought to listen to Woman's Hour then you'd know about these things. Have you seen *The Killing*? I mean, Series 1 –'

Constable Sally Jones showed unexpected resolve as she took over. It was something to stop Aunt Jenny in the flow. 'Lillian, it will help your father if you tell us everything you know.' She glanced at the inspector who gave her the nod, though it wasn't clear if this was because he respected Sally Jones, or took on board what Aunt Jenny had said, or was just sulking. 'The more he tells the police the less he need fear. You see, we know there are people leaning on him, and Mr. Shevchenko is probably one of them. They're dangerous people, Lillian, but you might be able to help us make them a lot less dangerous. Do you see?'

'Mr Shevchenko is dangerous?' Lillian asked, alarmed.

'Constable Sally Jones has put it well. Very well put,' Inspector Hodge said, still gazing at Lillian. 'We want you to help your father. You see, we think he's protecting these people. Perhaps they're bribing him. They may even have threatened him. You might just be able to help us free him from them. Then you can be together again.'

'He might be, or he is?' Lillian asked.

'That's what we need to establish.'

'We know it's hard for you,' Constable Sally Jones admitted.

'Has your father, for example, ever given you a large sum of money to keep?'

'No.'

'Or any information to store?'

'No.'

'I must ask you -' Inspector Hodge resumed, but Lillian cut him short.

'What has he done?'

'Your father?'

'Obviously.'

It was the turn of the police to hesitate. 'You don't need to know all the details, Lillian,' Constable Hodge reassured her. 'But if you just answer the questions as well as you can ...'

'Why don't you arrest him?'

'The evidence against your father –"

'I mean, Mr Shevchenko. If he's bad, put him in prison.'

'It's not so simple. We have suspicions about Shevchenko, but no hard evidence. Look, we know you've done nothing wrong,' the inspector added.

'I can't answer your questions if I don't know why you're asking them,' Lillian insisted.

'We only wish you to confirm or deny a few things.'

'No, you don't. Mrs Jones asked me to tell you everything I know. That's not the same.'

'She's right,' Anne-Marie said.

'Perhaps you'd like a little time to think about it,' Aunt Jenny suggested.

'I've a right to know,' Lillian said.

Inspector Hodge looked into her face. Lillian offered two shining eyes, and two fine cheekbones, and a set mouth, a heart apparently as cold and adamant as a coroner's knife. He put his file neatly in front of him to signify the end of little things and leaned his elbows on it and said, 'I'll explain it as simply as I can, Lillian. Then you'll see how important this is. Firstly, it is still possible your father is innocent, and telling us all that he knows. He may, however, be guilty. He also may also be innocent, but still not telling us everything. This is the case. There is an import/export company on the outskirts of Moscow that we believe is a front. It's fake. We call them Shell companies because there's nothing inside. The Russian authorities won't do anything about this fake company because their standards are not like ours. Frankly, it's as corrupt as hell. This company takes in money from criminal activities and sends it to one of the companies your father worked for as payment for rendered services. The Russian firm, if it is legitimate, is very generous because it pays way above the market price for these services – mainly auditing. It also seems to offer a lot of unusual gifts. School fees for instance. Now, and this is important, Lillian, it's part of your father's job to point out to the company anything suspicious about their finances. He is obliged to ensure everything is legal. Do you see? However, it appears that he hasn't done this. He did rather well from it. So, our question is: what does your father know about this company and these men who are part of it? We have a very good idea, but we need some hard facts.'

Lillian was silent. She thought for a long time. It was so tense even the motes of dust in the stream of light from the window seemed still. Was Daddy a prisoner of evil men? Was he one of them? Constable Sally Jenkins seemed to guess her thoughts.

'Your father isn't the person Inspector Hodge cares about most,' she said.

'There are some very bad men around him, Lillian,' Inspector Hodge said. 'Any little thing could help free him from them.'

'And endanger Lillian?' Anne-Marie asked.

'What do they do? These very bad men?' Lillian asked.

'The money from the Russian firm is certainly criminal. Drugs. Sex trafficking. Probably people smuggling.' Inspector Hodge did not say, 'the usual stuff', but his tone implied it. Anne-Marie leant forward and put her hands on her face. Aunt Jenny looked at Lillian with her mouth open, appalled. Constable Sally Jones looked sympathetic, and Inspector Hodge looked serious. Lillian alone kept her composure.

'My father is a silly man,' she said. 'That's why he loves me more than anyone, and why his girlfriends leave him. I don't think he's a bad man. He'd never let me know about this stuff. What do you want me to do?'

The inspector and Constable Sally Jones looked at each other, and the inspector shook his head. He gave Lillian a card. 'Keep that safe,' he instructed. 'If you hear anything that might help us you'll let me know. When will you see your father?'

'I don't know.'

'This is the thing, Lillian.' Inspector Hodge put his hands together on the table and leaned forward again. 'Your father wants to protect you, but he's going about it the wrong way. He thinks that if he trusts this Mr. Shevchenko and his associates, they will look after him. We believe that's a mistake. If he told us everything he knew, we could free him from them, so if you hear him say anything at all about his business friends, including Mr. Shevchenko, it just might help us bring this to an end.'

Lillian looked down. She knew all eyes were upon her. She had built her life on the idea that if she were obedient the good people who guarded her would remain loyal. But what was the truth? Like the tread of a giant on tiptoe, the scale of her father's misfortune crept towards her.

'You're not suggesting she's wired?' Aunt Jenny gasped.

'Daddy thinks he will be proved innocent,' Lillian said. 'Is that likely?'

Inspector Hodge heard the courage in her voice. He stared her honestly in the face. 'I can't say, Lillian. He may not be deeply implicated, however, and he may have been pressured. Let's say, he has been foolish and got in out of his depth.'

Lillian recognized that as a likely account of her father.

'Thank you,' she said. 'It's serious, isn't it?'

'It is, I'm afraid,' Inspector Hodge admitted.

'You're very brave, Lillian,' Constable Sally Jones told her. Lillian ignored that.

'I really don't know who those people are,' she said. 'And I don't believe my daddy is hiding anything from you. Or me.'

Inspector Hodge rose. The interview was over. He thanked Lillian and addressed Anne-Marie. 'Don't worry about Lillian or the taxpayer.' he said. 'The reason I came here unannounced and used Constable Jones was deliberate. Only we know this conversation happened, and we can keep it that way. We don't think Lillian's in danger, but let's not take any chance. If there's gossip, we were

271

here about a car accident. Lillian, if you hear anything, you have my card.'

The three women were silent at the table as the police left. 'Thank you,' Lillian said to Anne-Marie when the door closed.

'They're not very bright, are they?' she said.

'They're brighter than they pretend,' said Lillian.

Lillian and the Goodman's then did what people usually do after awesome news: they returned to their usual habits, but with a muted attention, as though filling time until the end of all things. Lillian watched the television to prove her composure, but her head returned to the same thought. Daddy had not been level with her. She felt desperate for him: but she was angry as well. The Trophy had been right to warn all along. If Daddy had only listened to her! This was a thought as humiliating as strange and awoke in her a fierce cold anger so that when Ferdinand stood in the doorway she only shook her head and looked away. That night she hugged Jesus, and gave Mary and Joseph a supportive pat, and met Anne-Marie on the landing.

'Do you need to talk?'

Lillian shook her head. 'Only to my father,' she answered. 'Whatever he did, he did it for me. He's got to know it's not necessary any longer.'

Anne-Marie regarded her with fresh regard. 'You've had me fooled again,' she said. 'I thought you were a snowflake, but you're a tough little bastard, aren't you?'

'Heads will roll,' Lillian breathed, but added, 'I will *very* unhappy if he's into organised crime,' and went to her room. Yes, she was angry. She did not know at whom she was angry: her father, of course, and this Shevchenko, and all the vague and nefarious forces that had somehow turned her funny and clever and affectionate daddy into a villain. She lay on her bed and fumed at the ceiling, and heard the footsteps of the women below, and knew they were discussing her, so she did the breathing. The grown-up thing to do was to walk the Holy Family down the Valley Gardens and work out her plan and to let Ferdinand know she was on top of it all. She was Lillian Miranda Delph.

Chapter 6

Lillian returned to the V&A with a new outfit; cream trousers and long cream jacket with the pale tan blouse that matched her hair and set off the leather bag she'd bought in Saltscar. Her shoes had platform heels, which made her taller and older without impeding her gait. She felt sophisticated, Parisian even; a month ago she would have wished she could meet one of her old set so they would double-take and say her name with surprise, and she could smile back and ask very calmly how they did, and walk away. She caught sight of herself in the window of the Piccadilly Waterstones: her appearance made art seem artless, and that was good style, which she needed now against the world.

And the V&A had changed. She used to see it as a great store, a giant Harrods and speculated on where to put an exhibit in her house should it become hers but, gazing at the The Bed of Ware, she realized that the people who made all this stuff were no more, and the things they knew and took for granted were no more either. These grand works of hand and mind were not at home. The British Museum or the V&A was their orphanage, and the world was waiting to understand their stories. She considered this in the quieter rooms of Dutch porcelain. That Delft vase would do well on the little table by her seat in Devon Street, but it could never quite belong to her as it had the original owners. She expected that Ferdinand or even Frank had an opinion on all this, and on the The Bed of Ware, though she couldn't imagine what it was. But then, she reflected, moving on to the silverware, that didn't matter because she didn't have an opinion on the Bed of Ware herself, although she wouldn't mind trying it out for a while if she ever had a house big enough.

She returned to the foyer where only a few weeks earlier, though it seemed a year, she had been called by Aunt Jenny, and now saw Maria waiting for her, dressed down in jeans and a long t-shirt and a canvas bag like a student. She called. Maria turned and hugged and said she loved her hair in the brisk, grown-up way she had. Yes! Thought Lillian, and said, 'Coffee?'

They marched through the great hall as though it were a street, and Lillian insisted she sat in the gallery and not the Morris room, just as she had with Aunt Jenny and for the same reason. Maria passed on scraps of gossip then sat back on the wall sofa and said airily, 'Chloe had a bust up with her mum and dad. Did you hear?'

'I hear nothing from any of them.'

'She wants to move in with Dave. They're not happy.'

'Still doing the coke?'

'Still *bragging* about it. Rich girls' drug of choice.'

Lillian shrugged. 'It all seems so childish now.'

'Chloe is immature. You can't dislike her because she's fun, but she's an arse.'

'She's fun,' Lillian agreed. 'But she betrayed me.'

Maria nodded. 'It's typical they haven't been in touch with you. Now you're interesting, they've sort of given up. I don't mean,' she hastily corrected herself, 'you weren't interesting before, but, you know – in your circumstances.'

'They never liked me,' Lillian said.

'That's going a bit far!'

'They thought I was boring.'

'They should speak!'

Lillian laughed. She was surprised to laugh. 'Don't let's talk about them,' she said. 'I've got my dad to deal with.'

'Will he really be in trouble?' Maria spoke softly.

'That's what I want to know.' She did not tell the whole story: her father had lost his job and was interesting the police, though as witness or criminal was unclear. 'These really bad people, they're trying to put stuff onto him, but we'll see.' Her new relations were on her side, of course, but they could only give emotional support. It was a Big Thing.

'God, Lilly, what will you do?'

'No idea. When I dwell on it, I get angry, so I don't think about it. I've always been good that way.'

Maria nodded. 'But sometimes, Lillian, it's good to talk about things.'

'Yes, but you can talk too much.'

'I guess.'

'There's at most three people in the world who really love me,' Lillian sighed. 'One of them's a dog, and the other two I'm not sure about.'

'I love you, Lillian,' Maria said simply.

'No, you don't,' Lillian told her. 'You like the fact I'm on your side against those others.'

'Harsh,' said Maria. 'You're the only one of the crew I can take seriously now. I wish you could come back to London.'

'I wish I could too.'

'Really not possible?'

'If I could find somewhere to live.'

'I'll have a think how it can be done. King's Cross then?'

'My ticket's for the six o'clock, King's Cross to Edinburgh. Five thirty on the concourse. We have phones. Meanwhile, have you seen The Bed of Ware?'

'The Bed of Ware?'

'It's in Shakespeare. I'd like to know what you think of it. Come on, we've got twenty minutes.' Lillian rose and expected Maria to follow her.

She was dismayed, but not surprised, to find Edward was not alone. The hotel had a doorman and a revolving door, so at least the appearance of privilege remained, but however much the décor could restore Lillian's sense of social power, it could do nothing for the deflation of seeing her father on a sofa next to a man, and listening with his head down and so missing her entrance. It got worse. She recognised Mr. Shevchenko. Daddy and the dubious Shevchenko! She had imagined an apologetic father holding her hand and explaining all that had happened, followed by a Solid Plan and a Big Hug, and reassurance that the police were way out of line. That wouldn't happen with Shevchenko sat like a toad by his side. She drove back through the revolving door. She did a breath: a gusty exhalation, like a snorting horse, straightened, and pushed back. The doorman raised an eyebrow as she passed.

Edward registered her new hair with a look, and sprung up, at which Mr. Shevchenko rose with dignity. His hug was strong. It was between a hug and a cling.

'Look at you!' he said with admiration.

'I'm different, Daddy.'

'My little girl is a woman!'

'Actually, yes.'

Mr. Shevchenko offered his hand, which she took smartly and sat on the sofa opposite Daddy. She had to cross behind Mr. Shevchenko to do so, so said to excuse her as she squeezed past.

'Watch your back,' Edward said with a smile.

'Lillian would never stab the goose that lays the golden eggs in the back,' Mr. Shevchenko said, smiling also, 'if you'll forgive a mixed metaphor.'

'Is that a Russian expression?'

'I'm Ukrainian. Of Russian extraction. The child of two tragic histories. Can I get you a drink, Lillian?' he asked as she sat.

'Yes, please. Something expensive.'

'You seem to be bearing up very well, Sweetheart.'

'Gumdrops,' Lillian answered. 'Not quite goody, but gumdrops.'

Mr. Shevchenko caught the attention of the waiter at the bar with a delicate lift of his hand and a finger. He was a man who believed he could achieve large effects with minimum fuss.

'I've missed you so much, Sweetie. How is it up there? Is it awful?'

'Yes, but it's temporary. Actually, no …. it doesn't matter about up there … When can I come back?'

'We're working on that. And guess what? The current account has a significantly increased income!'

'Is it all legal, Daddy?'

Mr. Shevchenko turned his face to her. Edward stared with his mouth open. 'Lillian!' he said at last.

Mr. Shevchenko stood to meet the waiter and murmured an order.

'I'm only asking.'

'It's a service our legal team were happy to help with,' Mr. Shevchenko answered in syllables clipped sharp like scissors.

Her father looked grave. 'Lillian, Sweetheart, you really don't need to worry.'

'What about university?'

'What about it?'

'Somehow, I've got to pay my way through, and now we've no money I'll be like those poor students who end up with debts and a job at MacDonald's.'

'When your father's affairs are settled -' Mr. Shevchenko started.

'You'll be fine, Sweetie,' Edward told her.

He looked at her with the look teachers give to pupils to point out that what they've done is serious; a carved stillness, unblinking eyes, and no sign what will come next.

'Really?'

Mr. Shevchenko sought to lighten the tone. 'I wouldn't be ordering you Cloudy Bay in a hotel like this if we were broke, Lillian.'

We? It was true, the hotel was smart, but it wasn't the Dorchester. The seats were not the best leather, and though there was a grand piano the grasses and ferns around them were probably artificial. They had tasteful lamps and wall lights, and a huge rug over the boards, but the circular mirror in the gilded frame over the fake marble mantelpiece was too big and she hated the gilded chandeliers. Also, the black bar counter was all wrong with the mustard walls and the brown seating. It was exactly the kind of hotel gangsters would think classy. It was like drinking in a wasp's nest.

'The police paid a visit, Daddy.' She rolled her eyes to Mr. Shevchenko to warn him or at least to indicate who was the main subject of that conversation, but Edward was not dismayed. He sat back as though he now understood everything.

'Bloody cheek!' he exclaimed. 'You see, Ivan? They hunt every corner and they've still found nothing. That shows they're desperate.'

'I hope not, Daddy.'

'Lillian! You can't possibly think I'd do anything that might harm us.'

'I suppose not. But, you know, they're taking an interest and Mr Shevchenko is Ukrainian. I've seen the box-sets.'

'Lillian! Please. Don't stereotype. I'm surprised.'

'Sorry, but I'm not comfortable with the idea that everything I had might be dodgy.'

Her father was taken aback. Mr Shevchenko indicated an increased interest by sitting forward, hands together between his knees. 'Lilly!' her father exclaimed. 'What's got into you? Is it those people you're with?'

They're not Those People Lillian thought. 'No, Daddy,' she said.

Edward threw a petulant a toss of his head. He was unsettled. 'I may have made a mistake,' he countered, 'it's nothing unusual for people in my profession.'

'Were the police polite?' Mr Shevchenko asked. 'I hope they didn't upset you.'

'I don't care about their manner. I just want to know where I stand.' .

'That's perfectly fair, Edward,' Mr Shevchenko said. She was chilled and flattered by the care with which he regarded her from the side of his eyes as he sat forward and folded his hands. His smile was faint, a ghost-smile, an echo-smile, which she'd seen years ago flicking between the faces of adults when she'd said something precocious or innocent, but this one was focused solely on her. 'Would you listen to me for a minute? I can advocate for your father perhaps better than he can. You both have a lot to gain or to lose, after all.'

'Where did you learn that old-fashioned English?'

'I've lived here for twenty-three years. My first wife was from Kilmarnock. My sixth-form education was at Harrow, and I attended the Massachusetts Institute of Technology - it doesn't matter about that. Would you allow me?'

Lilly sat back and folded her arms. Her father avoided her stare. She hardened herself against the obvious pain in his face. Mr. Shevchenko waited for the waiter to put her wine on the table. Lillian drank deep. It was a very large glass.

'Edward faces some charges of fraud. He will plead Not Guilty. *Not*. We will win. There's not enough evidence. He may lose some credibility, but he won't lose all his colleagues. There is a position available in a few months' time, which will be perfect -'

'Never mind that. What are you supposed to have done, Daddy?' The wine really was very good.

Edward was still offended. 'I've worked very hard and taken great risks to get us a future. I'm the victim here. The police are bloody idiots.'

Mr Shevchenko pondered. This was for gravitas. He knew full well what he wanted to say. 'He's done nothing wrong or unusual. Think of it like this. We must all make a living, and that means in a free market we get the better of others as they try and get the better of us. We weigh risk and consequence. That's all. Let's say that lovely jacket you're wearing was made in sweatshops in Pakistan. How terrible! Does the maker care? Only if public opinion risks their market share. Companies obey the rules because it suits them. When it doesn't, they do everything they can to change them. Consider global warming. It may destroy your generation's future. Yet the President of the United States of America says it does not exist. Really? Thousands of scientists have data from millions of instruments gleaned over decades, data that is collated, and checked, and counter-checked by thousands of experts, all looking for flaws in every hypothesis. They have the temperatures from the stratosphere to the deep oceans, they measure the meltwater of the poles, the rain that falls, the speed of currents - and can count the total of the world's carbon emissions with staggering accuracy. They do controlled experiments to test every conclusion. But President Trump thinks it's a Chinese conspiracy! What an arse, he is, Lillian, to be sure. Why? Because the oil and coal companies make it worthwhile for him. And it's all legal, perfectly so. Your father has none nothing like that - the real criminals are those who corrupt government for profit.'

'What has he done then?'

Lillian drank.

'He trusted people. They told him everything was above board. He believed them. The point is, Lillian, your father has ambition.' Edward caught Lillian's eye, and gave a smile like a shrug, as to say he wouldn't deny it. 'He's prepared to take the necessary risks,' Mr. Shevchenko went on. 'You can't win without risks.'

'But he lost.'

'That's temporary,' Mr. Shevchenko insisted.

'That's right.' Her father was cheered by Mr. Shevchenko's triumph of reason. 'It's the companies I worked for - the people who ran them.'

'Look at Sir Henry Broughton: he was found guilty but released on appeal, and quite right. I always admired his charity work.'

'I don't care about Sir Henry. Who is he anyway?'

'He could be useful to me in future, Lillian,' her father said softly. Lillian drank again. 'My mistake was a simple accountancy error,' he explained. 'Really, Sweetie, the news today is good news.'

It was less the matter than the manner of these explanations that annoyed her. This was not the time to call her Sweetie. She was a child no longer. 'This tells me nothing,' she said. Edward looked at her in confusion.

'Please, Lillian, let me-' Mr. Shevchenko said.

'No, actually.' She shone her eyes on her father. 'I'm sorry, but you keep me in the dark.'

'What don't you understand, Lillian?'

'What happens to me if you go to prison.'

'Randa! Don't be silly!'

'Don't call me silly.'

'You needn't worry, Sweetheart,' Edward said, but she was not convinced.

'Of course I worry,' she said. 'A detective from Scotland Yard of all places to question me for nothing!'

'What! The Yard?'

'When was this?' Mr Shevchenko asked.

'It doesn't matter when. His ticket cost the taxpayer a hundred and thirty pounds.'

'Bastards!' Edward exclaimed.

'You don't waste taxpayers' money for nothing.'

'You don't know the public services, Sweetie. Wasting money is what they do.'

She looked at her father with sad eyes. 'It's money laundering, isn't it?'

'Lillian!'

'That's a very general term, Lillian,' Mr Shevchenko said.

'Not me, Lillian – the firm!' Edward protested.

'Madelaine was right. You hide things from me.'

'Lillian, you're young. You don't know how these things work. I'm simply trying to protect you.'

'Lillian, may I-?'

'You may not, Mr Shevchenko. My mother's in Scotland, Daddy. How about that?'

'Your mother? What on earth –?'

'It's drugs, and sex, and -' the phrase 'rock and roll' came to mind, but she knew that wasn't right, 'and other bad things,' she concluded.

'Lillian, please. You're upset. The police have been their usual insensitive selves. No respect. They didn't even tell me. Can you believe that, Ivan?'

'I'm afraid I can.'

'I'm getting nowhere,' Lillian said. She hoisted her bag over her shoulder. 'I'm going to look at some shops. Call me when you've got somewhere for me to stay.' She rose.

'Sit down, Lillian!' Edward commanded.

It was a public space. She could not make a scene. Her father could not splutter what it was he wanted to reply, so he splayed out his arms in bewilderment.

'You haven't finished your wine.' Mr Shevchenko gestured her to sit with a hand.

'That's one true thing,' she said.

She drained it down and smacked the glass on the table. 'Delicious!' she smiled and squeezed past Mr. Shevchenko again. Edward stood: he raised his arms, imploring. She turned her head from him. She could feel her tread on the carpet, she could even note the heads turned to her as she walked past and could hear the faint hum of the air-conditioner, but it was like floating through a dream until her father caught her at the door when it turned into a film and not a very good one. She saw the shock in his face.

'Lillian, Lillian,' he said. He put his hands on her shoulders. 'You're not going to leave me! Not you!'

It was impossible to give an answer. The question was not binary. 'No, Daddy,' she said, 'but you've let me down.'

'No, no, no...' His mouth opened and closed. In any other person at any other time Lillian would have found it comic. Mr. Shevchenko was watching. He rose too.

'I can't trust you,' she said.

Edward held her shoulders. He was gentle for it was a public place and he smiled. 'Yes, you can!' he whispered with urgency. 'I'll show that you can!'

'Why didn't you tell me my mother had left Australia?'

'Don't talk about your mother,' he said.

'You see!'

Despite their propriety, it was a scene. A few shoulders twisted in their direction and turned back. Edward went for the hug of reconciliation, but Lillian resisted.

'Your mother? What in god's name...? That was years ago, Randa.'

'We don't even meet together,' she said. 'Get rid of *him* and then we can see. I – I delapidate you.' She spun away. She did not care now if anyone was looking. She stamped into the revolving door, but she followed it round and shouted, 'Repudiate!' in correction at her father's bewildered form and continued until she stood gasping on the forecourt.

She had bolted down the wine on an empty stomach.

'Taxi, ma'am?' the doorman asked, imperturbable.

'Too expensive,' she answered. 'I can take the tube.' Her father approached the door. 'No, fuck it, why not?'

She felt surprisingly buoyant as the car nosed along Holborn where the wankers, dickheads, fuckwits and arseholes who still lived in the innocent world trundled along the pavements.

'You here for a holiday, like?' the cabman asked.

'No. I'm here to destroy my past,' she answered.

'Sounds a bit drastic.'

'Yes, well, needs must,' she concluded and got the giggles. But when she got out of the cab into a familiar street, she was angry again. It was Mr Shevchenko. Daddy didn't see her alone. He thought it was all business when it was about *her*.

When the door opened, she was able to offer her most winning smile. That both parents stood before her showed Chloe had passed on the full message. *I can't get to the bottom of it, and I don't know where to turn.*

'Hello, mother-fuckers,' she thought, but said. 'May I come in?' and stepped forward.

Lillian unsettled Mrs. Tengu-Watakins's poise, but she took only a second to recover. 'Yes, of course. Can I take your jacket?'

'I'm fine, thanks.' Lillian marched through.

There was a new objet d'art on the glass coffee table over which Lillian and Frank faced each other. It was a glass sculpture. Lillian thought it rather good, though it was hardly Delftware, but she knew it was expensive.

'Lovely sculpture, Mrs. Tangu-Watkins,' she said.

'Call me Lucy. We're very pleased with it,' Mrs Tangu-Watkins replied in her considered way. Chloe's mum and dad were the opposite of their daughter. Whereas Chloe was loose and impulsive they wrapped up their self-esteem in deliberated gestures, as though they had practiced. Frank sat at the end of the sofa while Lucy used the chair, so Lilly had to sit next to Frank. 'It's by a young Nigerian woman with a studio in Clapham.'

'Excellent. My father -' Lillian started.

'I'm not working on his case,' Frank told her. 'And even if I were, I couldn't say anything. It would be illegal.'

'Lillian, before you start,' Lucy butted in, 'can I get you anything?'

'No, thank you. Actually, can I have a glass of wine?'

'It's early. But, yes, of course.'

'A large one, please.'

'You've become a drinker?' Frank asked. 'You didn't used to be.'

'I am one today.'

'Let's have the Dr Loosen. It's light,' he suggested.

'What can you tell me?' Lillian asked.

'How do you feel, Lillian? How are you?'

Lillian shook her head. 'It doesn't matter how I feel,' she said. 'I just want the truth.'

'First, can I ask, why do you want to know?'

'He's my dad!'

'Exactly. Your father was always affectionate with you. Hasn't he confided in you?'

'Not really. I can never get him alone. He's always got some guy with him.'

'Some guy?'

Stop playing games with me, Lillian thought. 'Yes,' she confirmed. 'Mr. Bloody Shevchenko. Though last time it was Mr Harris.'

'You've met Shevchenko?' He was interested now.

'I can't get rid of the fucker!'

'Lilly!' Lucy protested lightly as she brought in the bottle and glasses on a tray. 'When did you start swearing like that?'

'About an hour ago. Good therapy.'

Lucy poured and handed the glass over. The Tengu-Watkins only had little drinks themselves, but it was the middle of the afternoon, so that wasn't surprising. Lillian took a robust swig of hers and sighed.

'Wow, that's good as well,' she said. 'So, Frank, Mr. Tengu-Watkins, on a scale of 1 to 10 where 10 is Hitler and 1 – oh, I don't know, say, Jesus, you like Jesus - where does he rank?'

'I'm sorry, Lillian.' It was impossible to know if Frank's gravity was a response to mention of Mr. Shevchenko, who clearly had a reputation, or just his general way of dealing with her. 'Your father's been working for some very bad people. Shevchenko certainly knows some of them, though I don't believe there's anything on him himself. I've deliberately not enquired too closely. It might be he did something borderline, and these bad people then sucked him in. I do know it's been going on for a long time.'

'Jesus!'

'It doesn't mean he's guilty, or, if guilty, found so.'

'Fuck fuck fuckety bastard fuck.'

'Lilly, you can swear as much as you like, but not if you want me to answer your questions.'

'Sorry. I'm making up for lost time. My future's screwed, isn't it?'

'That's rather dramatic.'

Chloe had never once said her father was angry with her. In front of him, she had been pleasant, almost flirtatious, bouncing her gaiety off his dignity like a ball against a wall. She had tended to be a little scornful of her mother, but to see them together at parents' meetings was to see a charming child indulged by parents who knew she would come good in the end, whose authority was so settled they could indulge her whims. This was a little group who could never be buffeted.

'It's awful for you, Lillian' Frank went on, 'but I've seen so many worse cases; children taken into care, ditched off on relations who don't like them, even young people who have to leave where they live. A policeman sees a demoralising quantity of misery. Whatever the outcome, a judge will take your interests into account when it comes to sentencing. And you do have a lot going for you.'

'So he's guilty?'

'I didn't say that. That he hasn't yet been charged does suggest the opposite.'

'But what has he *done*?' Lillian insisted.

'I honestly don't know. Can I be frank? You might not like it.'

Lillian took another swig. It worked. With the help of the previous Cloudy Bay she felt a surge of courage.

'Carry on,' she said.

'Edward's not a strong man. He's easily pressured. He takes risks, as you have to in business, but that can come from desperation as much as courage. You see, when a man like Shevchenko introduces himself as a businessman there are four possibilities. He may be what he says. He may even be a spy for the Kremlin – for Putin, the president.' Lillian knew what the Kremlin was, actually. 'He may be a member of an international mafia. Or, and this is the typically Russian part, he may be any combination of those things. You have leverage with your father, Lillian. He loves you. You came for advice. My advice is to make it clear to your father that the harder and honest path is better than tricking your way out of trouble, especially with the Shevchenkos of this world.'

'Are you saying this because you're a policeman?' she asked.

'Lillian,' Lucy said, 'we're saying it for you.'

Lillian was suspicious of the unctuous tone. Now she understood why Chloe had never felt so warmly to her mother. She was not a sincere person. She was too much in love with her beauty. Lillian looked at Frank and saw a different kind of assurance in his face: the assurance of knowledge. She realised it may not have been wise to barge into the home of the fraud-squad while tipsy. Frank saw her doubt. 'I've interviewed hundreds of suspects,' he continued. 'They make the same mistakes, and the most common is to believe that their accomplices can protect them better than the courts.'

'So why did you stop Chloe from speaking to me?'

That at least got Lucy to shift in her chair. Frank raised his eyes. Pleased, Lillian swigged the last of her wine in one, and replaced the glass defiantly. That glass sculpture was too big for its place. It should be tucked away in a modest corner to be discovered with wonder, like a secret or whispered wisdom.

'I mean,' Lillian explained. 'I might have said something she could use against my father. Were you protecting me?'

'You think I'd use Chloe as a spy?' Frank smiled. 'It's the opposite. If it goes to trial you could be called as a witness, if only to show Edward was a good parent – which in everything but this, he certainly is. The prosecution would try to demolish that, and if you'd said anything to Chloe that would not go down well. You should never withhold criminal evidence, but that doesn't mean you should expose the dependents.'

'Ah, so you've grilled her.'

'We want to protect her. And you. All parents would,' Lucy said.

'It wasn't for me then. Some people say,' she tried, 'that all companies would break the law if they thought they'd get away with it.'

'That's crass,' Frank answered promptly. He was offended, as though answering an argument with which he had had to deal too often. 'The banks sail close to the line, but that's nothing compared to the world of money-laundering on which sex trafficking and serious drugs depends. Lilly, you haven't processed this yet, and if you ever want to talk, you're welcome. Really you are. But whatever happens you must face the truth and tell it. I'm sorry.'

Lily was contemplative.

'You have somewhere to stay?' Lucy asked.

'Why, are you offering? I'm catching the six o'clock King's Cross to the north.' She exhaled a great sigh and stroked her hands through her bob upon which they had not made a comment. 'I'm returning to Jesus. He loves me, at least.'

'That's marvellous, Lilly.' Lucy smiled. 'You know I was brought up as a Christian among Muslims. My faith was not always easy, but-'

'Jesus is a dog,' Lillian stopped her. 'An actual dog, with paws and fur and stuff.' She rose abruptly. There was something satisfying about standing as they sat. She was making a habit of it. 'I've a lot to think about,' she said. 'I'd hoped you could simply tell me that he was innocent – or not. Never mind. I'll see myself out. Thank you.'

Now they rose too. That image of family unity prompted Lillian to have the last word. 'About facing the truth,' she said thoughtfully. 'You know Chloe does coke? She was always a bit partial, but it seems it's now a habit. You might search her room. Also, glass on glass doesn't work.' Frank and Mrs. Stevens regarded her with appropriate shock. 'I'm sorry.'

She could not run in her platform heels, but she could still walk at a zip. She was starting a mile west of Notting Hill, but she was at Shepherd's Bush before she'd cleared her head. She was not sure if she was going home as a habit, or to look upon her old house for the last time, but she stopped outside the tube and bowed her head and exhaled with sudden exhaustion. What was the point? She stepped into the station, leaned against the wall. As she gazed at the commuters coming from and going into the tunnel like ants on their urgent and mysterious purposes, she felt herself adrift in the world, almost an orphan, exiled from her powerful friends, a part of no grand movement, who had ripped up her past or had her past ripped up. No-one who wanted to be a friend of Chloe could now be a friend of hers, and Chloe, cheating, monstrous Chloe, was still the centre of her old crew. Maria was loyal, but Maria was one.

She went into a pub. She was the youngest person there. She had a shot and came out. She walked on.

Piccadilly was doing fine without her, too fine. She wanted to be a famous person and to barge through the crowds with bodyguards on each side. She sat on a bench in Old Bond Street. She was a teeny bit tipsy. She read out the names on the shops opposite; David Morris, Mikimoto, Boodles, Carlier. Oh, those lovely lovely names! Tiffany's was a little further down the street and Ralph Lauren was behind her. Like Chloe's mum and dad they were secure in their own worth and had no need to regard the anxieties of the less established things of the world. She was at ease with them, but had an impulse nevertheless to find a brick and hurl it at a window. She sat with hunched shoulders and saw herself in front a smashed window at the centre of a commotion, bundled into a police car and finally a cell. The cell was next to her father's cell, and they communicated by taps on the wall between them.

It was goodbye to Boodles, but, when all is said, who cares? Well, she did. She was born to this. She was born for it. This was the environment to which, like a creature in a nature documentary, she was perfectly adapted.

She called in at a pub in King's Cross and had another shot. Maria sent a text to say she was on her way, so she had another at the champagne bar in St Pancras. She saw a man in his thirties in an expensive jacket eyeing her, so she crossed her legs on the stool, but as she wasn't wearing a dress it didn't have much effect. Nevertheless, he eyed her again, and she smiled and raised her glass. He drained his and left his stool, but she slipped away, and giggled. What possibilities this London held for a girl like her, and yet she was to leave, and all the nerds and the bragging fat men and the floosies would flourish there, whatever a floosie was. She bounded onto the concourse where the comforting figure of Maria turned and saw her.

They hugged again. It was the hug of people who have got through something, like at the end of a performance of a school play. 'How was it?' Maria asked with concern.

Kings Cross at five-fifteen made you anonymous. It was loud and serious, with faces fixed on the announcements and people at tables with luggage and coffee or beer, and sudden surges to the barriers and single people engaged in humourless fingering of goods in shops.

'Let's have a drink and I'll tell you,' she said.

She ordered another large wine. Maria went for a latte because she was out with her boyfriend later. Lillian did not say she had spilled the beans on Chloe's drugs. She made it clear, however, there was to be no reconciliation. 'Basically, her dad told me tell the police anything that I knew, which isn't anything, and he would say that anyway.'

'You're really brave,' Maria said.

'What choice do I have?'

'It's the way you get on with things. I sort of envy you.' Lillian looked doubtful. 'The reason our old friends don't want to talk to you about it is that it's too big for them. I can't see Steph coming from a photo-shoot and dealing with the Russian mafia, can you?'

'The reason they don't want to see me,' Lillian countered, 'is because I can't afford to go to the places they like any more.'

'I'm really glad you've confided in me,' Maria said. 'Perhaps I'll come and see you in – what is it?'

'Saltscar. The Jewel of the North.'

'What's it like? Is it rough?'

Lillian swilled. 'Not in the least. The poor people live at the end of the bay. It's got a good beach and a lift thing you go up and down on, and there's a cliff where you can commit suicide, and everyone talks rubbish about art and life, and they stop you and talk in the street whether you want them to or not, oh, and I saw a deer.' She belched softly and giggled. 'And the men are not ever so attractive.'

'Lilly, you're drunk.'

'Just a little. Come if you want. There'll be room when Anne-Marie goes back. I'll ask Aunt Jenny. Woah, here we go.' She had a text from Chloe. She offered Maria the screen.

You fucking bitch. Whatre you doing.

'She could have put a question mark at least,' Maria said. 'There's another.' She turned the screen to Lillian who took the phone and read it.

'I thought we were friends

Lillian shrugged. 'Yes, come to Saltscar. There is a bar there but I've never been.'

'Will your auntie mind?'

'I don't think so. I mean, if I'm there, it's got to be a bit on my terms as well. I'm family, after all.'

'I was thinking – there might be a way you could stay in London?'

'Really?'

Maria nodded. 'You'd have to work. I mean, really work, but I think it's doable.'

'Tell me.'

'I think your train's called.'

'I've got to go to the loo. Tell me on the way then I have to catch my train.'

She wobbled when she stood. Maria noticed. She gulped down the wine, nevertheless, if only to defy her condition, and concentrated on the way to the toilets so she didn't knock anyone over. There was no queue. Lillian leant against a cubicle door. Maria, concerned, stood before her.

'What was that about London?' Lillian asked.

'Are you all right?"

'Perfect.' Then her eyes bulged, and she barged through the door and was sick.

Maria thumped on the door. 'Lillian, are you ok?'

'Fine, fine, no problem,' Lillian said, barged out, and drank heavily from the tap and splashed her face.

'Does this happen often?' Maria asked as she emerged. Lillian gave out a cleansing breath. Her head was clearer, and her legs obeyed her.

'I'm not used to drinking, that's all.'

'You'd better hurry.'

She was glad to have a reserved seat first class. She was young and crumpled and drew a suspicious look from a lady with a husband and necklace, so she looked forward to showing her ticket to the inspector. She would do it with a flourish. He had to wake her, however, and she felt eyes upon her as she looked through her bag. She smiled up at him when she lay the ticket on the table, and then brushed her hair with the hazelwood brush as though she was in her own room. The train skimmed to the north, as though it couldn't wait to get there, and she watched meercats and then dolphins on You Tube, which was nice, and blocked Chloe, and had water and the hunter's chicken, then asked for crisps three times. She had a little sleep and woke to find the train was about to enter Darlington so she scrambled off, relieved she had not woken up in Edinburgh.

That was close, she thought, and went for a coffee in Pumpkin, sober as a stone.

Maria was a good egg, she thought, and would be a good London companion: she was confident, focussed, relentless, but she could not understand her new life. She hoisted herself out of the café and slouched to Platform 2 where the two-carriage groaner awaited. It's fumbling departure into the unlovely urban night, ferrying locals to or from their unglamorous revels, marked the diminution of her life. She did not doubt her father's love: but she knew him unwise, unreliable, weak. He was little use to her now. She dropped her head against the carriage wall and glanced at five people her age, three girls and two boys, who were engaged in raw banter; they seemed so silly. No, it was not an absence of people who could love her that shrivelled her. It was the absence of people she herself loved. There was only one person in the world right now to whom she felt properly close, whom she trusted. It was fitting to the bitter season of her life that Ferdinand Goodman was such a failure.

The failure awaited her return.

He hung more pictures. He filed invoices – the ones he could find. He surfed the web for galleries to see how he compared. At low tide he walked over the seaweed-lathered rocks almost to the edge of Moor Cliff and saw the darts of the kitty-wakes in agitated swoop and dips, and felt the sea at play with itself, and lifted his mind to the thin cloud that was blown, that made no decisions, and died inland, and he felt better. He hung the last of Frank's pictures. He was closing up when he heard the helicopter. It swung loud and low through the dying light, invisible, in the direction of the cliffs. He listened for the sound of its hover, but its thrum continued to lower and fade, and he was reassured. He pushed home through the gathering Saturday crowd, but saw the train wheezing and whining into the platform so he waited, just in case and, sure enough, Lillian Miranda Delph stepped gleaming forth in her cream suit. He called her and she waved.

'How was it?' he asked.

'Terrible. I need to ask you something – as a philosopher.'

Lillian was turning into Anne-Marie. It was a scary thought.

'You've had a long day.'

'Do you fancy a drink?'

'Now?'

'They serve cocktails round the corner,' she said. 'I had one at an opening once.'

Saltscar on Friday and Saturday night was not the Saltscar of Moor Cliff, the sweeping bay, the children excited in the funicular, or The Smugglers Arms hunched against the rock. The drinkers from the residential estate, from Rebburn and from the villages along the line of the cliff poured in for noise and laughter. The Asian fusion restaurant was clattering behind its plate glass with its string of lights. A man was disputing change in the fume of hot fat at the Station Pizza, and in the square kids stood on bicycle pedals and turned circles. Voices loud with drink competed around them.

'You want to join the crowd?' he queried.

'Don't be a snob, Ferdy. Where shall we go?'

'If you really want to talk, we could get something from Sainsbury's and go to the cell.'

'My running friends drink vodka.'

'That's a little too Old Frank for me. I'll get some wine.'

He took a screw top and they sat under the ceiling light at the counter in the cell like two old salts in a snug talking contraband. 'It's red,' he said, and she shrugged. He took two glass tumblers and they clinked.

'Chin chin,' she said.

'So how was it?' he asked.

'Daddy still says he's innocent. He might be. I think he is. He seems to be in the grip of this Shevchenko guy. I'm thinking he's the baddie.'

'How do you feel about it?'

'Confused. Angry. This is very nice wine. Are you sure you can afford it?'

'As a regular tipple – no.'

Lillian swigged: it made her more tired than brave. 'How has this happened? I've always done what I was asked; sometimes more. It's not fair.'

Ferdinand folded in his fingers on the counter like a sea-urchin its tentacles. He thought. He waited.

'What am I meant to do? I don't have anyone else.'

'I'm sorry,' he said.

'What about my future? It's in ruins.'

'But you think he's innocent?'

'Why doesn't he tell Shevchenko to fuck off and let me in on everything? He doesn't *want* me to understand.'

'Ok.' Ferdinand, the philosopher, had reached conclusion. 'I need to ask you a question. Hold steady on the wine. What most worries you? Take this hypothetical situation. Let's imagine your father is guilty, that he's done something horrible, but only you know that. In that case – hypothetical, but plausible - would you testify against him? In other words, what most distresses you – the shame that he's done a criminal act or simply that you're losing his protection?'

It took Lillian a few seconds to understand this. Then she did. 'Oh,' she said. It took a few more seconds to formulate an answer. 'It's both,' she said.

'I think it might help you to clarify your feelings. Imagine he is acquitted, but you know he got away with something – or is starting something new. He gets a good job. He buys you things. Do you accept the gifts, knowing where they came from?'

'Oh.' It was a whimper.

'You're gulping down the wine.'

'I've drunk more today than in the rest of my life just about.'

'That's how Frank started.'

'I don't want to know about Frank just now.'

'You need a proper talk with your dad.'

'I can never get him alone! There's always bloody Shevchenko. Or Mr Harris. And – he just gets upset!'

Ferdinand saw her quail. 'Lillian, you father loves you?'

'Yes!'

'I'm sure he does. Imagine you have the strength to live without his protection. He then needs you more than you need him. You call the shots.'

Lillian considered this. She glared into her wine as though some baleful poison lurked within it. 'It's not fair. I'm not meant to teach my father.'

'No, it's not fair. It really isn't. And he's probably innocent.'

'Oh, god! I miss London! I miss my old life! That doesn't mean I don't love you all,' she added in correction.

'Let's go to the beach.'

'The beach? But it's dark.'

'The sea at night is a beautiful thing. It clears the mind. It will do you good.'

'Does it have shops?'

'No.'

'Can we take the wine?'

'No.'

'All right then.'

He gave her his coat. It was absurdly long. She swung the limp ends of the sleeves and laughed. The streetlamps on low pier glowed a fierce white, and on High Prom the orange lamps reflected grotesquely on the roofs of cars, while the band in The Marina belted out old rock into the gabble of summer drinkers. It was ugly. But Ferdinand was looking at a flashing blue light at the base of the cliff. White lights blinked, playing peekaboo around the spar. The cliff itself, dark against the rich blue of the eastern night, like a stone tsunami, paid no heed to anything. Lillian followed his stare.

'What is it?' she asked.

'It seems like an Incident. I heard a helicopter earlier.'

'A suicide?'

'Or someone caught by the tide. It's an odd time to be out, if so. The cliffs are more dangerous than they seem. They tempt the desperate to jump. They erode and drop stones that can crack skulls. They trap whelkers. Thalassa: she gives and she takes away.'

'This is cheerful,' said Lillian.

'Come on.'

He led down the steps and strode west to the end of the prom away from the pier, and over the shingle and on towards the winking red lights on the wind turbines by the estuary. Ferdinand shone a torch and Lillian held up her lit mobile phone, and strode away from the Saturday night noise. The road lights out of town glowered orange behind the banks.

'Half tide,' he said. 'It's coming in.'

They stood on the fringe. On cue the streetlights went out and the half-moon flung a sash of silver across the waves which was scattered by the surf before it reached their feet. They turned off the torches and looked out. The two white lights at the cliff base were still and the blue flashing had ceased. 'The Incident seems reaching resolution. I love the sea, but I would fain die a dry death.'

'Why do you like it so much?' Lillian asked.

'It's ancient,' he answered promptly. 'It's alien, and yet it's where we belong. Most of humanity's long history has been spent by the sea or by rivers. And we are an island people. There is salt in our veins. The stories of the sea are of danger, but we are drawn to the beast as we are to high ground.'

They were still and quiet and breathed as though in meditation. 'I like it because when you're hot you can float in it to cool down,' Lillian said.

'There's that too.'

'And it's empty and big.'

'Also a boon. Although -'

'I'd like a canoe.'

'Dangerous.'

'Don't be so northern.'

He hesitated. 'You know, that decision about your father. It isn't urgent. You may not have to make it.'

'Whatever happens, it won't be the same. He went bankrupt. We're poor, actually.'

'The readiness is all. This is your existential moment.'

Lillian breathed deeply of the moist salt-air, and exhaled with relish, and thought she would never forget the moon's banner flickering on water. 'What the fuck,' she asked, 'is an existential moment?'

'You make a decision that is yours alone. It will define you.'

'Wow.'

'Exactly.'

'Follow me then,' she said.

The lights on Low Prom and the pier went out. The white lights had disappeared. Moor Cliff hid itself in the thickening night. Two green pricks on the end of night anglers' rods wobbled against its blackness. Once they had rounded the closed amusement shed, she made him stop. 'I've just thought of something.'

'Go on.'

'It's a thing – hypothetical but plausible – for you to decide. Imagine daddy is guilty but acquitted and I let him pay for Paris and everything. Would you still love me?'

She heard his smooth intake of breath. 'That's a question,' he answered.

'It is, isn't it?' She was suddenly pleased with herself. 'Well?'

'The quick answer is, yes. I'll always love you, Lillian. We'll always love each other. We have a spiritual bond, unbreakable. That doesn't mean, of course, you wouldn't break my heart.'

She thought she knew what he meant. 'It would affect your view of me?'

'Of course it would.'

'It's all suddenly difficult,' she said.

The sea sounded relentless. It did not care. The shush and plunge and suck was not regular, but it was unceasing. It was lovely and it was bleak, and she suddenly wanted to finish the wine and curl up warm and to wake in a day where all was resolved.

'I know it's hard,' he said

'Oh well, I'll survive. Whatever. If others can, I can!' she answered as they turned off the pier. 'You do give me confidence, brother.'

'Likewise, cousin. It's the sea. It whispers to our unconscious and, bleak or cheerful, it rarely leaves us weaker.'

'Yes. As well as that we can finish the wine. Come on.'

She rolled up the sleeves of the ridiculous coat and led first up the one hundred and sixty-seven steps.

Chapter 7

The rising sun made crimson the top bricks on the wall outside the dining room. Lillian Miranda Delph, hangover recovering, spooned her banana, raspberry and yoghurt and told herself if that back yard was ever hers, she'd sort out the crumbling wall and paint it white, and tidy up those bins and clear out those rusting chairs and that bent metal table and put down decking and even consider a glass roof and, whoosh, a stylish room. She was preoccupied, stirring, and found she'd turned breakfast into a pink mush. Then her father rang.

'Lillian! Oh, thank goodness. Are you alone? Are you calm?'

'Of course.'

'Which?'

'Both.'

'Good. I don't know what happened to you yesterday.'

'I was cross, Daddy.'

'You've never been like that before. What I couldn't say – you wouldn't let me explain – is that I'm close to a new position.'

'Like, not bankrupt?'

'It was a tactical administration, Randa. It isn't as great as the previous one, and –'

'Daddy!'

The exclamation drew a supportive bark from Jesus in the lounge. She heard a double thump of a dog descending from a chair, but it was Joseph who appeared at the door. He listened with his eyes fixed on her ankles, as though in grave concentration.

'What?'

'It's the wrong way round,' she said.

'Lillian, I know you're upset. You want to come home. I get that. But you've got to help, just for a few more weeks. Listen to me. This is important. I need to know what the police said to you. What did you tell them?'

'I didn't tell them anything. I don't know anything!'

'Yes, Lillian. But –'

'No. You don't understand! It isn't about money, or even coming up here. I don't actually think you're a criminal.'

'That's a relief. Thank you, daughter. And I'm not! What is it then?'

'I can't explain it,' she said. Now Mary padded through, and Jesus jostled at her side.

'If you can't say what's wrong, how am I expected to answer?'

'I'm tired of all this.'

'You're not yourself, Randa. Those people – they've been bad-mouthing me.'

'Not once, Daddy.'

'Then what's got to you? Is it the police? I was bringing good news.'

'What it is, Daddy –' What it was, she now realised, was that her daddy annoyed her. There was something in his tone, as well as his circumstance, to which she objected. 'I just think ... You need to be a bit more humble.'

'More humble? *Humble*. That's how losers think, Randa.'

'Possibly.'

'Yes. Come on, I'm sorting it, Lillian.'

'With Mr Shevchenko?'

'A good man, Lillian, really.'

'Goody gumdrops, then, Daddy. Goody gumdrops for you.'

She rang off.

The quiet that followed was a drowning depth. It swallowed in a gulp a decade of chatter, like a singing bird pulled under waves. She sank to the floor, back to the wall, hands on hair. Joseph sniffed at her ear and curled beside her. Jesus trotted to take up guard by her other side while Mary, dutiful, sniffed at the tableau and, happy that the boys had the situation covered, padded to her bowl in the kitchen. Lillian did not know how long she stayed thus. Ten minutes? Two? An adolescence? The telephone rang ten rings and stopped. When she rose, she stood over the smoking wreckage of her past. She was not upset. She was not even angry. The question was whether to leave it or to try and repair what was not lost beyond recall.

In the low-contrast light along the shore Moor Cliff settled into itself. The beach reflected neither blue nor cloud, but lay dull and at ease, a damp stage between dramas. Lillian Miranda sped to Low Prom in faded pink trainers, hood up, pumping her arms and stretching out past crazy golf, the beach huts, and Surfer's Shop to the red and white shed where Amusements still blinked and hooted behind the glass doors and from which the pier stretched out, grey over grey, a lonely sentry in an empty land.

The run had cleared her mind, as her running was wont to do, as it was meant to do, and she knew she had a problem with her father. She waved at the Thai waitress in the café and walked with her hands on her hips and head down along the tarmac track into the Valley. With each step she understood a little better: she had to consider the possibility that she would never go back. She would finish college and perhaps go abroad, or take a self-sufficient job in London, or marry someone and be a mother and do baking. She hadn't left home. Home had left her. Once she had formulated this she trotted with short steps and with arms barely moving. The trees on the valley sides had lost their sheen, but had not yet turned, so she looked upon them with a notion for the first time that this place was now a shelter to her just when it appeared least interesting.

When she reached the wooden bridge over the burn, she was stared at by an old fat woman with an old fat beagle who stood at the facing entrance. Lillian smiled into the stare and carried onto the bridge with her eyes on her feet, but the old woman called her name. Lillian did not share Saltscar's admiration for its Valley Garden, particularly today: it was not a patch on any of the main London parks. This section, however, from the platform to the miniature railway, over the bridge with a view of the Greek Temple scraped by branches on the west valley side, and up into the Italian Garden, and then through the stepped flower borders and onto the sweep of the broad avenue to the band stand and the war memorial – that section did have charm, she would concede. It was taken from a child's storybook, like *The Railway Children*, or *The Wind in the Willows*, or even Harry Potter. When Lillian found herself addressed on the bridge by the fat woman with the fat dog, therefore, she was taken aback. It was as though a real witch had appeared in your bedroom when you were reading about one.

'I was hoping for Ferdinand,' the woman said.

'Sorry - are you speaking to me?'

'This is Marjorie. You're living with the Goodman family, no? Could you tell them that Monty is dead.'

'Could I say what?'

'Monty is dead,' the old fat woman repeated.

'Of course. Certainly,' said Lillian.

'Ferdinand will want to know.'

'I'll tell him. Marjorie, yes?'

She stepped aside, but was addressed again.

'You have a story to tell.'

'I beg your pardon?'

'Your story: of exile, of loss. It is a great archetype.'

'I'm sorry, I've no idea what you mean.'

311

'Ferdinand hasn't told you about The Club?'

'No. Sorry.' She edged away.

The woman noticed Lillian's reticence and pulled back her shoulders in surprise and offence, as though the girl was walking away from an oracle. 'Ah, well, yes, I see,' she said. 'That's surprising. It would be so interesting to hear your perspective.'

'I'm afraid I'm rather out of perspective just now,' Lillian answered, 'but I'll remember your message. Monty is dead.'

She was away. Sometimes it was necessary to pretend to be stupid. Saltscarians didn't get that.

The house was still empty of all but dog. Jesus lumped next to her on the sofa, and she lay her hand his back, for solidarity. Mary and Joseph looked round the door, waddled over for a pat, and retired, assured that all was in order. 'Monty is dead,' she told Jesus, though whom Monty was she neither knew nor cared. The phrase had a gloomy ring that she liked. The landline sounded again. She ignored it.

She did not expect to find Anne-Marie at the shop. She and Ferdinand did not express surprise at her intrusion onto what was clearly a serious discussion, but she felt herself an outsider as they looked at her.

'I can come back,' she said.

'I'm just going,' said Anne-Marie. 'I'm only here for the day.'

'Has something happened?'

'I hear you've had a show-down with your father.'

'Two show-downs, actually.'

'It's hard,' said Anne-Marie who was being particularly gentle. She picked up her knap-sack, thrust her arms through with accustomed speed. She was the kind of person to have a knap-sack even after school years. 'You know you're always welcome here,' she said and lay a hand on Lillian's shoulder. Then she and Ferdy embraced. This was not usual. Something had happened.

'I didn't think Anne-Marie was here.'

'Family stuff. How are you, this morning?'

'Monty is dead,' Lillian said.

'Monty?'

'He's dead.'

'Ah, yes! Monty. Poor Marjorie. You saw her ...?'

'Is it her husband?'

'No. It's one of her dogs.'

'Oh, is that all!'

'Lillian,' he remonstrated gently. 'How would you feel if Jesus suddenly died?'

'Jesus? Jesus can't die. I couldn't bear it. Jesus must live for ever.'

'Exactly.'

She looked down at the street through the window as though checking for a spy or an assassin. 'I thought she was rude. Marjorie. How would she know me?'

'Saltscar is a small town.'

'It's better in the city where no-one knows you. Who is she anyway?'

'She's a retired lecturer looking to relive her greatest lectures. She has a blog. She ran an open house like a salon for the *intelligensia* of Saltscar back in the day. My friend, Dave, and I used to go pre-college – it seemed sophisticated and wonderful, like we were the greatest intellectuals the world had seen. Then we grew up. He did, anyway, and became an item with Anne-Marie. Marjorie has a part in the story. What should I do with these pictures of Frank's? There's too many for the walls.'

Lillian was thrown by the silliness of the question. 'Put them in a rack in the centre,' she said. 'Get easels and put them on those, like they're paintings. They don't have to go on the walls. It's not a rule.' She returned her semi-malevolent gaze to the street, while Ferdinand scratched his head.

'Why did that not occur to me, and come to you so quickly?'

'Because you haven't done enough shopping. Shopping is serious. It's hard work, like art. You're very quiet. Are you sad? Is it Anne-Marie?'

'Dave has finally got a job down south. She's going with him.'

'Oh. Is that sad? You'll miss her?'

'It leaves me on my own with the shop. Inevitable, but it's sooner than I expected.'

'You knew that would happen.'

'There's a sub-text. She wants my permission, my blessing. Ah, well, I'll have to man up.'

'You gave it, your blessing?'

'Of course. I hate emotional blackmail. It's cancer.'

'What about Aunt Jenny? She a good organiser.'

'She's happy with her job, with the people there. I'll manage, Lillian.'

He retired, subdued, to the back of the shop, through the gap into what he called the tiring house where his bench was. She regarded him with ruler and plane, the firm soft stroke of his hands on a card, the stillness of his head as he cut with a Stanley knife and she thought, He's good at that sort of thing. She looked onto the street again which was reviving under thinner cloud, with a couple coming from the print shop opposite and a mother and child going into the sweet shop next to it, and a man passing the window, whistling – not Whistling Joe - and she said, 'I'm thinking – perhaps *I* should help you in the shop. I mean, full time.'

'I'd love that,' he said.

'Would you!'

'You'd be perfect. Can you do figures?'

'That's what my father does. He'd show me.'

'You'd make a lot of people happy with that decision.'

'It could be my way to pay board.'

'You'd share in the profits. It might take a bit of time.'

'To do it properly would mean giving up London, more or less, and possibly even Paris. That's a lot to give up.'

'Specifically?'

It was difficult to define. It wasn't just things. It was speed; Londoners walked more quickly, talked more quickly, *thought* more quickly. They *knew* about things. They answered phones and crossed bridges – often at the same time – at a speed that would blur the eyes of a Marjorie. Marjorie: what kind of a name was that? If something big was to happen, it would happen in London, the greatest city in the world.

'Potential,' she said.

'You'd be free to go at any time.'

She nodded. 'I don't know, though, Ferdy. It's all – up in the air.'

'It's worth considering.' There was a hint of tension in his voice. She did not like that there was tension. But still – it would be a thing to tell people! *I'm co-manager of a shop. No, I mean, I make the decisions, oh, on layout, stock, forward planning* … It's in a seaside town, she'd explain, very lovely, great beach. Not a bad thing to have on your CV. *And what's it called, your shop? Actually, it's called* …

'I don't like the name,' she announced. 'What does it mean?'

'To the shop? It's a pun. It's from a character in Shakespeare.'

'Is that the person you keep quoting?'

'Yes.'

'Why?'

He threw out his arms. 'It cheers me up,' he said.

She thought about this. 'It's not very grown up,' she answered.

'It's jokes, Lillian,' he defended himself.

'You call it 'the cell'. That's not very positive.'

'Another family joke.'

'We should call it *Delph's. Goodman and Delph*. It trips off the tongue. They're names to remember.'

Delph's. Goodman and Delph. That was a new notion. He was not sure what he thought about that. Mum, of course, would have it Elleskers. *Prosper-oh* was a place of small harmonies and little perfections, a magic backwater that could not exist except by the Saltscar shore. But with Lillian Delph at the centre, it's triumphs would be its end; if the world discovered and ransacked it, took its magic elsewhere, it would make its own demands, fashion its character, negotiate terms, until the original had dissolved and left not a rack behind. He could see it with Lillian, the child-woman, sharpened by the crispness she brought to places and times and to things, holding its own on Milton Street. He wanted a salon. A gallery, and more than a gallery. A happening place; a quirky and a creative place. He hoped Lillian Miranda Delph would appreciate that. 'We can consider it,' he said. 'It *is* a local shop,' he pointed out. 'It is to be the essence of the place.'

'Oh, it can be that,' she said. 'That's your bit. I'd make it look nice. And stop you from losing things.' Suddenly, she sighed. 'My stupid father!' she said. She was about to say more, but they were interrupted by a call. They were hailed. A body looked in, hand still on the outside handle.

'Hi. *Towntalk*,' the body said.

'Good lord, yes! Simon, isn't it?' Ferdinand stepped forward to greet him.

'Yes. Ferdinand Goodman? I know you.'

Simon, encouraged, stepped into the shop. He had floppy golden hair, and swaying shoulders, a manner something between swagger and apology. Lillian knew the local magazine: it appeared in take-aways and the surgeries and some of the cafés. She'd flicked through it: local news, feel good; how the work on the funicular was

317

going, the rich avian shore life, Saltscar takes 3rd place in the Coast Towns In Bloom competition – that sort of thing. She did not feel the lanky frame and appeasing smile of Simon would produce genius, but if he was to write about the shop it could do no harm, so she was fast on the heels of her cousin-once-removed and offering her hand.

'Lillian Delph,' she said.

'Yes. Absolutely. Brilliant,' Simon said.

'It's Ferdinand's shop. I'm only helping.' You always started modestly. You sucked people in and let drop the achievements and the ambitions as though they were things that had simply happened to you.

'It's you I'm after actually.'

'Oh.'

'It's human interest. Do you mind?"

'Lillian is the Exotic Other that pulls us together,' Ferdy said.

'It's about the Scramble,' Simon explained.

'Not about the shop?' Lillian asked.

'It's more, like, about you.'

'Me?' said Lillian. 'I'm doing the Women's Scramble. I'm eligible, and I'll do my best to win. What more is there to say?'

'Yes. Right. But you're Emily Ellesker's daughter.'

'Ah!' Ferdinand gasped his understanding.

Simon saw the question on Lillian's face. 'We thought it would be interesting to local people, you know - the great Saltscar Scrambler reconciled to her daughter after blah blah years, doing the Scramble together. A real heart-warming story. I've seen you run. You're very fast.'

Lillian was dumbfounded. Ferdinand stepped in. 'Emily is a Saltscar local and has always come back for the Scramble. I believe she often won it in the past?' He addressed this to Simon, and then returned to Lillian. 'It is a good story, when you think about it, but perhaps you'd rather speak to Emily first? Lillian's only been in Saltscar a few weeks.'

'Yes. Yes.' Simon was nodding vigorously. 'Absolutely.'

'My mother's running *against* me?'

'So we understand. Or together,' Simon said.

'I've never heard of such a thing!'

'In Saltscar, all is possible,' said Ferdinand.

'Families run together on the London Marathon, but they stick together.'

'We thought perhaps – but, of course, you're both serious runners, like ...'

'I'm running to win,' said Lillian. 'For me. For the shop.'

'We sort of thought, perhaps you'd do a little interview together. But I see you've not actually spoken. Perhaps in a couple of days...'

'God, but that's so *weird*. Who is she anyway?'

Simon was discomposed. He brushed his hand through his hair. 'I'm sorry. I may have been misinformed. I can come back. I mean, it doesn't go to press for another two weeks, and it's only – you know – a local rag.'

'Do you still live on Moon Street?' Ferdy asked.

'Yes. Same old place.'

'With Jerry, isn't it? How is he?'

'Oh, Jerry's fine, fine.'

'It's Chardonnay and Shelley, isn't it?' Lillian asked. 'They told you.'

'I'm afraid I don't know. I mean, I just do these interview features.'

'They meant well, I'm sure. But they should have asked me first. Oh, well, sorry, I've got nothing to say. Not at present.'

'I understand perfectly. I'm ever so sorry for intruding like that.'

'You should do a feature on the shop sometime,' Ferdinand said. Simon looked relieved.

'That would be brilliant. Yes. I'll mention that to Mark. Absolutely.' He stood with his hand on the door and glanced at the rain and waved at them.

Ferdy lent him a *The Scream* umbrella in full blood-sky colour and smiled him into the rainy day. Lillian doubted it would ever return. Suddenly Ferdinand thought of something. 'Simon! The Incident. Any news?' She watched the two men with serious faces through the window and saw Ferdinand's expression and realised with a faint shock, like an unexpected and unwelcome kiss on a dance floor, he might know the person involved. The two men shook hands, a firm single shake, and Ferdinand bustled back. 'I don't think Simon will make a tabloid journalist,' he said. 'He's not exactly forceful.'

'What about the Incident?' she asked.

'The worse,' he said. 'A jumper. I sometimes think those cliffs encourage it.'

'Do you know who?'

'One of the surfers. A Gavin. Only by sight. He had a blond ponytail, very distinctive.'

'Oh my god, I've seen him,' said Lillian.

'You won't be seeing him again,' he answered. 'There's a ceremony on the beach later this week.'

'Will you go?'

'Of course.' He settled again to the business of framing. 'I'm sorry you learned about your mother like that.'

'It's not your fault and I suppose …. Compared to death …' Her thought trailed into nothing. 'But how could she enter for the Scramble and not ask me? Shouldn't Aunt Jenny have said? It isn't just me, is it? It is actually a bit strange.'

'That depends.'

'On what?'

He put down the ruler and pursed his lips. He turned his head gently from side to side. He looked at the ceiling, troubled. 'What?' Lillian prompted.

'Don't take this the wrong way,' he said. 'I think originally when she heard you were doing it, she pulled out in case you found it awkward, but then you had the chance to talk to her and you didn't, so she changed her mind – it's not malicious, but, well, if you're not interested in her it might not make sense to change her habits. She sort of *is* the Saltscar Scramble. But I can get mum to talk to her if it really upsets you.'

'Oh.' Lillian had not considered her own behaviour. She remained troubled, nevertheless. 'I can't stop her,' she said. 'But you don't think she can beat me, do you?'

Ferdy laughed. 'No, Lillian,' he said. 'That would be unlikely. Unless you fall over, or bump into a tree. At her peak, she probably would, but not now. She's thirty-nine. She might even be forty.'

'That's something anyway.' Lillian plopped onto the stairs and dropped her hands over her thighs. 'This is proving a difficult day.'

'Do you want to walk? Have a coffee? They have a new cake at Grubby's.'

'No. You need to work. What's to be done?'

'To be done? In the shop? Well, I'm finishing off this picture, and there's a repair to a window sill, and I've got to pick up some stuff in the van –'

Lillian stood. She straightened to an exclamation mark. 'We ought to make a list,' she said.

His gaze was clear and definite as the east wind. 'Don't just jump in, Lillian. Choose. You've no obligation.'

'Never mind about all that. Shall we start?'

Aunt Jenny was agitated. 'This rain! But we needed it. Lillian? Ah, there you are. Yes, yes, Jesus, I know. Dear dear dear! Have you seen Ferdy, Lillian?'

'We were in the shop together.'

'On your bed, Jesus. Yes, good boy, off you go. Oh, that's good. Thank you, Lillian. How was he? Of course, he's not your responsibility. Good lord, you're eating toast. That's not like you.'   Lillian shrugged. 'It won't do any harm just the once.'

'It's a small concern in the grand scheme. Anne-Marie is going off with Dave. That makes it sound like a romantic elopement, which, of course, it's not. It was inevitable really, though it's rather sudden. I ought to be glad for her, and I am, no mother wants her daughter to pine, and I won't stand in her way, but it's a shame for Ferdy who's got to battle on alone with the shop and all the stress, though of course if he really wanted she'd keep her word and stay because family loyalty is a very big thing. But it works both ways. And what of her career? Ferdy won't insist. She wants her freedom. Frank should be here now as well. And I haven't had time to ask about London. Ferdy said - he was very tactful - you had Issues?'

'I got cross with Daddy.'

'Oh, dear.' Aunt Jenny sat down. 'And there was an Incident.'

'He has an undesirable friend.'

Aunt Jenny sighed. It sounded like an organ bellows left to empty itself. Her shoulders sagged. 'That's very difficult for you. But, believe me, Lillian, it really isn't the end of the world. You will bounce back. You are a bouncer and people do, and a criminal parent, if that's what he is, though he almost certainly isn't, and won't be, well, you're hardly the first – oh.'

It was now that Frank returned. He burst through the front door with a cheery, 'Da Dah,' and set off a clatter of dog paws and barks. 'Now then, mutts,' he greeted them and stepped down the corridor to where the women sat in suspenseful silence, and he held out his arms and announced, 'Frank Ellesker returns in triumph.'

'Sorry, Frank,' Jenny said, 'we're talking.'

'Morning, Lillian,' he said.

'Afternoon, I think, but, yes, hello,' she answered.

'You are looking at -' he started, but his sister stopped him.

'Frank! Serious here.'

Frank looked quizzical, 'Let me not interrupt. No, ma'am.' He turned to the mirror in the hall. 'Now then, Frank,' he addressed himself, 'how's thee got on? Has ter? Paid in full? By, that meks a change. Tha' must be chuffed to bits. I 'ear tha got some well-acclaimed shots of hikers in't sunset o'er a mountain. Good on yer, Frank, and welcome 'ome.'

'Frank, don't be such a narcissist. Lillian has a crisis, and Anne-Marie is going south.'

'Ay, well, latter's no surprise.' He joined them, unabashed. 'May an 'umble commoner mek himself a coffee while the great deliberate?' he asked and ploughed through to the kitchen.

Aunt Jenny mouthed 'issues' at Lillian. Lillian was direct with him. 'My daddy's best friend is a member of the Russian mafia,' she said. 'Allegedly.'

'Fucking 'ell!' He turned to her and she saw the bravado drain from his features. 'What'll thee do, lass?'

Lillian shrugged.

'Staying 'ere then.'

'That's as maybe,' she said. 'And how was your trip, Frank?'

Frank offered his palms to Lillian and looked at his sister. 'There, you see? Breeding. This shows all that money on a private education didn't go to waste, even if it were tainted.'

'Tainted?' Lillian asked.

'Frank!' Jenny remonstrated.

'I see what you mean. Oh, yes.'

'It's not your fault, lass. Jenny and me, we come from a long line of rogues and criminals and look at us. Innocent as lambs.'

'I'm sure there's nothing tainted in your past, Lillian. This is a new thing.'

'And if it isn't, join the clan,' Frank shouted from the kitchen.

'I'm not sure,' Aunt Jenny cried back, 'you are the sort of role model Lillian needs.'

'Bollocks. Middle aged, recovering alcoholic, penniless, lives with his sister – what could be happier?'

'I might be wrong. It might still be all above board.'

'There y'are then,' said Frank.

Aunt Jenny shook her head to signify the end of this discourse. 'I'll call off work this afternoon, if you like,' Aunt Jenny told Lillian. 'I've only got a few bits and bobs to finish off – that expression really shows my age. We can have a nice walk and if you want to discuss –'

'That doesn't matter, auntie,' said Lillian. 'I'm going to the café soon. But I'll stop working there now. I have some Rolex money left. While I'm here I'll concentrate on the shop.'

'I must say, you're being wonderfully calm about it.'

Lillian shrugged again. 'It's too big to go all dramatic. You know, it might be a good idea to finally visit Dorothy's.'

'The family seat!' Aunt Jenny exclaimed. Lillian had a vision of a grand carved chair dominating a room with timber beams and stained glass, a Goodman version of The Bed of Ware. 'Where your mother grew up.' Lillian looked doubtful. 'And believe me, darling, Dorothy's a tonic. And she has horses. And a rescue deer.'

'A deer?' Lillian asked, surprised.

Aunt Jenny settled her hands on the table. 'Lillian, I'd very much like you to see our old family home. Dorothy rescued it.'

'The home or the deer?'

'Both, I suppose. She'd be delighted to receive you, if only for your mother's sake.'

'And they have a deer?'

'It's a little nervous, but on a good day you can cuddle it.'

'Oh.' Lillian bravely crunched the last of the toast. 'I'd like that,' she said. 'I've never cuddled a deer before. But not today, Aunt Jenny. I need a few days to find out what I think.'

'Of course, Lillian. And we ought to give Dorothy due warning. Take as long as you like.'

Lillian chomped the last of her toast. Aunt Jenny was very understanding, but she noted, though she wasn't sure how, she'd got her own way.

Moor Cliff, guilty or not, was a sullen presence at the ceremony. The sun no longer set over the grassy links and the smudge of browns that was Rebburn: it had shifted north over the grey shape of land that faded towards the next county, and so warmed the west water of the bay with a yellow gleam, a fragile banner, a sullen pink line between the clouds above it. Striations of grainy sea-coal reminded

Lillian of charred toast. To the east, however, the water was a cold grey, and the cliff a featureless lump, as though hiding from the line of surfers who awaited Black Board. They had the informal deflation of travellers waiting a long-delayed train. One, that Lillian recognised, had his arm around the shoulders of a pony-tailed woman whose head was bowed. Lillian's group on Low Prom, respectful behind the railing, seemed to her more sombre because larger and just as quiet, and actually more still. A gull protested once, and was ignored.

'We should have had music,' Curly murmured to Ferdinand. Ferdinand shook his head.

'Think what they'd have chosen. And who'd play it?'

'We're having music at the shop,' Curly noted.

But now Black Board appeared. It was carried from Surf Shop by the most venerable of surfers round the back of the respecters on Low Prom and down the steps at the side of the pier onto the stony fringe of the beach. Ferdinand thought: thus, during long centuries in such forgotten places, the left-behind, together and alone, have banded in lines on the burnt sliver of sand to commemorate a gap in their lives as the price of the sea and the rocks. Lillian thought that if she'd fallen off a cliff, she'd have wanted something grander than this, though she knew it wasn't the actual funeral with hymns and stuff. But now the clapping began. It followed the process of Black Board to the group on the beach, and faded, hesitantly.

Without a word the surfers waded into the sea, Black Board tied to the waist of the carrier. They paddled in a line to where a small boat bobbed beyond the breakers. Some on Low Prom now dispersed talking quietly or not at all. Lillian's phone beeped. Ferdinand and Curly continued to stare out to sea.

'Cide,' Curley said. 'It's a syllable I detest. Greek: kill, destroy. Latin: *caedere*. It sounds like the hiss of a snake or the tear of knife. It's a rum sound.'

Ferdinand nodded. 'These inkhorn terms are euphemistic. But none of the parties involved care about that. '

'Someone should have done something,' Lillian joined in. 'He was ill.' Her phone beeped again. She took it out. It was her father.

'I accept the reprimand,' Curley said, smiling.

Lillian squinted at him. Then she understood. 'Oh, no,' she protested. 'I was just thinking aloud.'

The surfers had reached the boat. They sat on their boards as Black Board was handed over. The boats chug sounded like an embarrassed cough. Then it growled away eastwards towards the village down the coast where the surfer's family lived. There was a notable relief among the respecters, an assumed sigh; job done, all correct, and people moved away in small groups and spoke normally, as though it was unnecessary to be cowed by a tragedy all too common in this neck of the woods.

Lillian was reflective for other reasons. She let Curly and Ferdinand step ahead and stood behind to talk to her father outside the shop. The small group inside were taking wine and talking with post-funeral ease. Lillian waved through the window at Aunt Jenny, but no one remarked her: the shop light was warm: the street was in gloom. This had to be done.

Her father's voice came with the shock of presence: his crisp consonants and brassy announcement drove into the softly sinking day.

'Randa! I was beginning to wonder!'

This was the third call since the argument. The first had established they had a problem. The second had cluttered the minutes with apologies, protestations of honest intent, for she must understand, he was the victim here

'You weren't answering,' he explained.

'Sorry. We were at a ceremony.'

'Okay, fine. Listen, I've got great news – at a what?

'A ceremony. A surfer died. We were on the beach.'

A what? A surfer? You mean, someone who surfs? Not someone you knew? '

'Only by sight .'

'That's alright then. Listen, we have a breakthrough! Things are looking suddenly much better. A witness has pulled out. You don't need the details, but the legal thing is just about done.'

'That's marvellous.' Lillian acknowledged deaf Jean with a nod. Deaf Jean rolled her fingers in greeting, smiled, and went into the chatter.

'You don't seem overjoyed.'

'Everything's so confusing, Daddy.'

'You don't need to know, Randa. It's amazing news!'

'Wonderful, yes.'

'And listen: I've accepted a new job - with Mr Shevchenko. Randa, Sweetie, we're bouncing back!'

'Oh.'

'Haven't I said all along I'll get through this? We're turning it round! Trust me, Lillian, we'll be coming up roses.'

'It's gumdrops?'

'Not quite goody yet, but it's getting there.' Lillian was less pleased than she should have been. 'I reckon you'll be home in less than a month.'

'That's – wonderful.'

'It isn't quite packing bags time yet, Randa, but it's nearly roses time! I said I'd come through for you. I think you got a little panicked.'

'I suppose I did.'

'You poor thing. I do feel bad about that.'

'Yes, Daddy.'

'We're on the right track. And what about you? Are they still nice to you? Is it bearable up there?'

'Everyone's fine.' Her father knew nothing of her Saltscar life. She did not elaborate therefore on the neutral observation, except to add, 'I'm helping with the shop.'

'Really? For nothing? That's good of you, Randa, but don't let them take advantage. You're too good-natured.'

'I can look after myself, you know.'

He laughed. It was the first time since hospital. 'I'm sure you can. And, of course, those people have been useful to us.'

When Lillian saw Aunt Jenny watching her through the window, she understood the gulf between herself and her father. Aunt Jenny smiled: she was wondering what was happening: she knew it was her father on the phone. 'Yes,' said Lillian, 'very much so. Daddy, I'll telephone in the morning.'

Ferdinand was with Curly and a man with hair too long for his age and a woman with black lipstick too young for hers. They were serious. 'It's discouraging,' the man was saying. 'Young, but through the teenage years, you know? It's about as healthy a life as you can get in a place that's known for calm and satisfaction. Then, wham!'

'Aye, the blue space,' Curly said. 'That's the psychological term. Shore and sky. Calm and creativity.'

'And for a surfer to find no help for his disorder,' the man said.

Lillian looked around. They shouldn't be talking like this. They should be noticing the shop and she should have been introduced. They should remark the industrial feel of the exposed brick against the floor lights with the white pillar shades, a tough look for serious retail. They should see how the large table in the inner space was lit by the curving lamp, a focus on the precise matter of framing, and how the display of frames and the arrangement of tools said, Work. They should note the grouping of the photographs so as to avoid crowding or dominance by the brickwork, and the artful placing of the two best sculptures on the upper story. They should read the chalk announcements on the oversized blackboard – casual but bold – and be grouping around the screen in which the video of Frank talking about The Sublime and stuff showed it was a shop that was more than a frivolity, but a statement

'It's not so strange,' Ferdinand joined in. 'There are no guarantees. The shore also attracts the wounded, the outcasts, the melancholy hermits and the extrovert-unhappy alike. It's worked for my uncle. But to come to heal and find no relief on the magic island is cruel indeed.'

'Like Christmas,' Lillian said. All regarded her. 'Lots of suicides at Christmas because it's worse to be lonely and unhappy when everyone else is having fun.'

'Exactly,' said Ferdinand.

'She's hit the nail on the head. It's Lillian from London, isn't it?' It was the woman who had told her to use her London insincerity. 'I love what you've done with the shop.'

'Oh, thank you.'

'The picture-framing thing is genius. It brings everything together. You come for a frame and then you get drawn into the pictures and the items and buy the stationary, and it's good to walk into a shop where someone is doing something and not hanging around waiting for you. More *artisanal*.'

'That's the idea.'

'Yes,' Jake agreed. 'You come into so many shops, and it's a dead space.'

'Thank you.'

'Lillian is also one of the favourites for the Scramble. She's making her mark,' Ferdinand added.

'Will you stay?' the man suddenly asked.

'Oh, I don't know. It's all up in the air.' Lillian looked around and caught Aunt Jenny's glance. 'I've got college next year, and a position in Paris in January.'

'That sounds promising,' Jake said.

'You must come to my studio and meet some new people if you do,' the woman said. 'You know Shelley Perkins?'

'Shelley – the Shelley I run with?'

The lady nodded. 'She's doing a textile course. She has an eye. Ferdy has my number, if you want.'

'Right, yes, if I stay, of course.'

'Shall I get you a drink, Lillian?' Jake offered.

'I think Aunt Jenny wants me. She's making faces. Thank you, though.'

Aunt Jenny put down her glass on the counter to hug. 'So good of you to come,' she said, 'though I'd expect no less. This is Sally. Sally runs courses at the Centre. She is virtually a Yogi.'

Sally held a wine glass by the stem, letting it rest between her fingers, and turned her body like a bent exclamation mark. She smiled a refined smile. 'This is Lillian then?' she said.

Lillian said hello and turned to Aunt Jenny. 'This is a wonderful gesture,' she said, 'and it's real champagne, but, Aunt Jenny, is it from shop funds?'

Aunt Jenny reassured Lillian with a hand on her shoulder. 'Curly,' she said.

'Oh.'

Sally's face registered, yes, it would be, wouldn't it, so that was understood by all parties.

'Lillian is very business-orientated,' Aunt Jenny told Sally. 'This is her first Incident.'

'How many do you have?' Lillian asked, surprised.

'Last year we had four,' Aunt Jenny answered. 'We do attract the hurt and the wounded.'

'I'm not hurt and wounded,' said Lillian.

'I'm not sure we actually attracted you, but here you are!'

'The famous Lillian Delph!' Sally said.

'I'm not famous yet,' Lillian answered. 'Not even here.'

'Ah, but the word is out. The youngest Ellesker is back and she's making her mark. Can Saltscar cope?' Sally turned her smile onto Aunt Jenny as though sharing a common joke. Lillian thought it rich that she herself had been accused of insincerity when Saltscar had people like Sally.

'Lillian is one of the favourites for the Scramble!' Aunt Jenny said.

'Not Jane Brown? You see, Lillian, Jenny is always bigging you up.'

'Get on with you! What an expression.'

'It's a thing,' Sally said. 'Jenny has a heart of gold, but she doesn't praise lightly!'

It was impossible to respond to this, but Lillian didn't have to, because Ferdinand was clinking a glass for silence, which fell. He checked all were ready. There was a shout from the restaurant down the road, an answering call, a few sentences, unintelligible, which he let disappear. He looked very grown-up, Lillian thought, very composed and at home, and she was suddenly proud of him, which was not an emotion she would have expected a month ago.

'Curly,' Ferdinand said.

'Felicity,' Curly answered.

The waitress from Grubby's stepped forward. A busker Lillian recognised with a guitar was beside her and a man with a mandolin was poised with head down on her other side.

'The person, not the concept,' Curly added. 'On happier days she inhabits the concept. Aye. This is a song for those who know the sorrows of life by the sea.'

Felicity sang, and the guitar rolled chords and the mandolin picked out a counter melody. The tune was dreary as hymns, but Lillian's thoughts were elsewhere anyway.

'Oh, my love has built a bonny ship

And he set her on the sea ...'

Her father's news had not lifted her heart as it should have done: how little he knew her. She had kept some things from him; she had assumed he'd guessed she'd had sex with William, and there was an agreement he would not enquire about the details of the girls' nights out. She had kept Chloe's antics from him, and when she was found in the wrong place with the wrong people at the wrong time at school, she had said she had a rehearsal for a play, when in fact it was detention. That was normal. But her father knew nothing about Ferdinand, the shop, Moor Cliff, Frank's accent and his photographs, the Saltscar Scramble, about Curly and the crepuscular shores, or the Ellesker family home. He had never been particularly curious about her life ever. He had protected her: until this summer he had done that exceedingly well. He had made her laugh, and she had made him smile. He was always glad to see her. She was always glad to see him. But of what trembled under her ribs, of what touched her better nature like a stroke on her cheek, to whom she confided, for whom she feared, with whom she laughed and by whose side she learned and alongside whom she walked in understanding, he had no grasp. But, then, why should he? He was only her father. Did fathers generally know those things?

'*But the weary wind began to blow, the sea began to rout...*'

The room began to hum along, a drowsy sound, a sad sound, like bees in summer. And everyone was so still!

'*My lover and his bonny ship turned widdershins about.*'

No-on looked around. Most turned their eyes down. The hum swelled as though it was made in the air, dropped among them, to mend without hurt, a sweet medicine.

'*There'll neither quiff come on my head nor comb come to my hair,*

And neither coal nor candlelight shine in my bower mair.'

Lillian realised she was humming too.

'*And neither will I marry more until the day I dee*

For I never loved a love but one and he is drowned in the sea.'

It's because they all know each other, Lillian concluded. It's a bit like boarding school, only different ages. There was an inner sigh, inaudible but tangible on the final chord, and during the clapping Lillian caught Ferdinand's face and rolled her eyes to the door.

'Has something happened?' he asked.

'Can we walk round the block?'

He looked through the window. 'Why not? They don't need us. So long as we're back before everyone leaves. What is it?'

'My father's just told me he's not going to be charged. He's off the hook.'

'Isn't that a good thing?'

'Of course!'

'You didn't say it as though it was.'

'Let's go down Sapphire Street. I want to hear the sea.'

He zipped his jacket against the wind. Lillian defied it. 'I don't think he'd lie about it, because it will all come out, and he says he's got a job.' She decided on instinct not to say it was with Mr. Shevchenko. She had said bad things about Mr. Shevchenko. 'If all this is true, he'll want me to go back. I'm going to do the things I said though, Ferdy.' She slipped her arm through his. It seemed the natural thing to do. 'I'll help with the shop, and do the Scramble, and I'll go to Dorothy's, and, of course, even if I'm back in London I'll come up a lot to see you.'

'Ah.'

'What does that mean?'

'You've decided to go?'

'The thing is … how can I say …? It would be very hard to get him to understand why I'd chosen Saltscar if he gets somewhere for us in London. It would feel like I'd rejected him, and if he's innocent, really innocent, I mean – he's the only parent I've actually had.'

Ferdinand nodded. He waited.

'I can't just walk away. And there are London things I miss. It's my home. Look at all the lights on the sea! It's win-win, isn't it? I get back to where I was, but I've got you and Aunt Jenny and all the others as well.' She looked up for a response. He drew her over the road to look out and down on the pier.

'You must do what's right for you,' he said at last. 'Only –'

'Only what?' She jerked his arm. 'Only *what*, Ferdy?' she insisted.

'I'd miss you terribly. That's selfish, I know. It's not that.'

'What then?'

'You won't like it.'

'Ferdy!'

'You won't like me.'

'I'll like you not at all if you clamp up!'

'All right, then. I've never met your father, but I think he's bad for you.'

Her eyes were wide. 'That's rather rude,' she said.

'I only mean – the you that identifies with him is less attractive to me than the you that doesn't.'

'I see.'

'You may hit me, if you wish.'

'I don't want to hit you. But you don't know what you're talking about.'

'I dare say you're right.'

'Let's not argue now. The sea's quiet with this wind.'

'It's the street sounds that interrupt it. Listen.'

She listened. Yes, it was its usual unrelenting self. She looked out at the lights that curled round the waves' edge, those of Rebburn and the towns beyond, and the line of red lights behind them, and asked what they were.

'I think it's along the A19. Going north beyond the north.'

'How very far away we are,' she said.

They were groping for the ease they'd had with each other half an hour ago.

'Ferdinand,' she resumed after a pause. 'If I want my London identity, I shall have it.'

'Of course.'

'I see now – Aunt Jenny has been trying to rid me of it.'

'No, mum's not -'

'She doesn't realise she's doing it, but she is. I'm still the insincere southerner. Well, so be it. What you lot don't understand is that I intend to have it all – London and Saltscar and a future, a father and a mother and a past.'

'Oh, my dear girl! Whatever you do will be right.'

'I wouldn't bank on that!'

They were just in time as the guests were spilling onto the street, and among them was Aunt jenny who noticed her son and his cousin once-removed approaching arm in arm, like an old couple. She beamed, ignoring Sally who was fussing in her bag. Lillian saw that her face was joy and touch with love.

'Hello, Aunt Jenny,' she said. 'We wanted some air. When are we going to Dorothy's?'

He left with the dogs when the women were settling for bed and Frank was in his screen-lit cave. He had turned them up the street to the main road and they had pulled forward, for this was the way to the Valley Gardens and they wished to get there before he changed his mind. But he did not change his mind. It was silent and dark. He flashed his torch along the broad path downwards; there was a scattering in the undergrowth, and dead leaves glistened silver in the beam.

'No, bacons. Follow,' he commanded. The pack turned with regret from the scratches of small creatures between the trees. She will leave, he told himself, as he dropped down towards the wooden bridge. First dad, and then Anne-Marie, and now Lillian Delph: she will leave. The shop will seem a deserted court, and there will be no-one to correct my mistakes. Unless, of course, it fills with the visitors and becomes what I dreamed.

'Jesus!' he called.

Jesus scrambled out of the beck.

'You're filthy, you muck-pup!' he scolded.

She will leave and my heart will break. She loved us, but she will go back, at first out of duty, but then her old life will rise over her. She will swim in its currents, turn in its eddies, drop down to its depths, and forget us, for those are the waters that made her, the tides that she knows. He put the hounds on lead as he came onto the broad green on either bank that led to the road and the beach. The lights that scoured Low Prom blackened the sea beyond, and though the Smugglers' windows gleamed a cosy amber, it was an unromantic glare on the picturesque set. But he took in Moor Cliff to his right. There was a haze in the sky; the moon diffused through cloud, a mist-light that fell upon the deserted roll of the cliff top: the drop was as black as death. The waters licked its base. He rarely went up there. To jump: to know the irreversible plummet to oblivion.

The terror of that second! It was a step he dared not tempt, and yet Frank tramped around the top as though it were a meadow in May. He loved it.

'There's no accounting for temperament, Jesus,' he said. Jesus had no opinion, but Mary suddenly brushed against him as though to remind him of they were present and that dogs had needs as well.

'We'll go back through the woods,' he told them. 'We'll smell the cold and melancholy Autumn together.'

He let them off the lead, for indulgence. Let them at least explore their native land with never a thought of exile.

You can be exiled from a metropolis too, he told himself. It was only right to remember that.

'This is our East End,' Aunt Jenny said as they climbed into a village of generally unkempt stone. 'Social Issues.' Lillian looked out for the homeless, the drifting hoodies, the violent graffiti you could stumble upon not too far from Liverpool Street Station, but saw instead a village of comfortable scruffy houses, a Spar supermarket, a little square and a dark church, and considered that northerners really had an odd sense of extremes. Ferdinand had said that he did not need much to be happy; live close to hardship and you are grateful for a modest success, which Lillian did not think showed sufficient ambition. 'It was wealthy once,' Aunt Jenny continued. 'Tin. Steel. Now it's welfare and drugs. No work. Depopulation.'

'Saltscar isn't like that,' she said.

'Saltscar has tourists,' Aunt Jenny said. 'We're very lucky. And, of course, we're North Yorkshire.'

They drove through fields, through another village slightly scruffier than the first, then another scruffier still, and out into broad fields with glimpses of the sea to their left, and on the risen horizon before them the ochre autumn moor. A white farmhouse gleamed a mile along the side. 'There!' Aunt Jenny exclaimed. 'This is real Ellesker country. The fertile strip between the sea and the wild. That farmhouse is where you stayed the summer you were with us.'

'That's Dorothy's?'

'It is. Your mother came back at the very same time after years away. She hadn't anywhere else to go, to be honest. Your father brought you because it gave you a holiday at the sea-side while he was away.'

'Did he know my mother was here?'

'No. We'd arranged a holiday with you, and then, out of the blue, Emily appeared. It was a quandary, but we thought, well, Emily Ellesker – then Delph, of course, but she changed back to the family name - has a right to come home, and you have a right to the seaside, and if they happen to be at the same place and at the same time, that's nobody's fault. It was a bittersweet summer. Dorothy's husband had bought the house and that was important. It drove Uncle Sebastian crazy, but that's a story for another day.'

They were twelve minutes out of Saltscar. Lillian had checked.

'Why didn't my mother stay with her parents?'

'Disputes. It was your great grandfather Jim Ellesker, who made the mistakes. A problem with rationing during the war. He fell foul of the authorities, which was not too bad around here – smuggling country, you see – and then Emily's father, your grandfather, my Uncle Sebastian, got into difficulties rather as your father has, and he lost the house to Dorothy. When Emily stayed there he was furious. He remained so until his death, which is why she didn't inherit anything. Look, we're there.'

'It's a lot to take in,' Lillian said.

This tangle had something to do with Lillian. Rather, Lillian had something to do with this, though she couldn't think what. There was a history on her father's side: Grandma and Grandad Delph, and an argument, a rupture, and her father very cross about it, and behind Grandma and Grandad there was the original Delph who had a shop in Mayfair and a house in Wimbledon, and there was also a family called Wilson in Bristol on grandma's side. That was that, and nothing much to care about. This new family line was like finding a door in your garden that led to another garden behind. It did not seem a tidy garden. It sounded as though it had been abandoned or lost, had had bad things buried in it, old treasure hidden there, but nothing entirely relinquished or forgotten, and she was part of the unfinished business.

The farmhouse stood by the seaside, a faded white gleam, on the rise to the moor, overlooking a tawny field, the cliff line and the blue itself. Aunt Jenny drove up the lane to the side yard in the eight-teen year old golf and stopped with a scrape of the gear. Cats flopped off the wall and scurried under the hedge and round the twisted wooden shed. A great ginger cat challenged them on the doorstep. Its fur was flame and its eyes pure malice.

'Shoo,' said Aunt Jenny. The cat licked its paw. 'Ratters,' Aunt Jenny explained. 'Farm cats. Feral. You can't touch them. Perhaps we'll call Dorothy.'

Lillian strode to a metal bin and thumped it three times. The ginger cat, bemused, or offended, sauntered away.

'You really are a wonder, Lillian. And a boon to our community.'

Dorothy answered the door almost before it had ended the ring. She was wearing black trousers, a white blouse that hung over her waist, a black velvet bow tie with long straps and her usual bright lipstick. It was vampire red. 'We're feeling very Bloomsbury today,' she announced. 'Come and meet the zoo, Lillian,' she said.

A man in a wheelchair was in the kitchen next to a tall man in blue trousers and sandals and a long shirt that dropped over his thighs like a smock. The kitchen was a country kitchen with an aga as well as an oven, and a long table in the middle and wooden cabinets instead of fitted cupboards. Lillian had never actually seen the like before. The man in the wheelchair had curled his fingers round a mug while the taller man buttered scones. He put down the knife and offered Lillian his hand. It was rough and firm, like his stare, and he said, 'I'm very pleased to meet you, Miss Delph,' in a resonant voice. 'I'm Charlie, Dorothy's brother.' The wheelchair man nodded at her. 'This is Mike,' Charlie introduced him. 'It's Emily Ellesker's child, Mike.' Mike nodded again and gave a twisted smile and a thumbs up.

'We'll leave you to it,' Dorothy said. 'Come look at the house, Lillian.'

It was a big house. Lillian had rarely seen bigger. A long corridor had four doors at either side and one at the end, but Dorothy led them up a winding stair onto a landing and along a corridor with more rooms on each side, and another stairway climbing steeply at the end. They followed through central double doors into a light that made her blink. An enormous bay with French windows and draped curtains led onto a balcony. Light burst off the sea that sparkled beyond. Dorothy perched on the edge of a chaise-longue at the side of it and Aunt Jenny sighed in satisfaction as she settled into the adjacent sofa.

'It always surprises me,' she said. 'And yet, it shouldn't. Sit next to me, Lillian,' she said.

'I'll spare you the rest of the house until next time,' Dorothy said.

'It's lovely,' said Lillian and obediently sat. The sea winked at her in the distance.

'It's ridiculously big,' said Dorothy. 'If it was up to me, I'd sell and live in Saltscar, but Mike won't hear of it. He can't give up the view.'

The room was feminine and rather grand; sage-green swags above the window, pulled with a deep red tie, a huge antique dresser against the far wall with ormolu trim, the chaise longue of burnished gold and brown upholstery with rust-red cushions, a bookcase with glass windows and a chintzy sofa. But the furnishings had no patina while the carpet was faded, and the walls the colour of a turning leaf were a little too rich for Lillian's taste. Nevertheless, it had potential.

'This is where your mother was born,' Dorothy said, as though she knew what Lillian was thinking.

'I sort of know it,' Lillian said.

'You stayed here when you came as a little one – when was that?'

'I think it's all of twelve years now,' Aunt Jenny said. 'She may have stayed in Devon Street, but she came here.'

'Is the deer around?' Lillian asked.

'Charlie will show you the deer when he's finished with Mike,' Dorothy replied. 'How would you like a day shopping in York?' she asked Lillian. 'Take your mind off things.'

'I believe York's lovely,' Lillian said.

Dorothy leaned towards her. She was too pleased with herself, a bit of a show-off, but she was grave when she said, 'This house is always open to you, as it is to Jenny. Jenny is my special friend.'

'Get on with you,' Aunt Jenny butted in.

'You're doing the Scramble, I hear?'

'That's right. It gives me a purpose.'

'We're rooting for you.'

'My mother's running as well, which is quite strange.'

'It's family tradition, though I'm not sure she's decided. Has she decided, Jen?'

'Not when I last spoke to her.'

'Oh,' said Lillian.

There was a roll and regular bump of the wheelchair on the stairs. Charlie was hauling Mike up backwards. Dorothy went to hold the door open, and Aunt Jenny put her arm on Lillian's and said in a whisper, 'This is the most life-loving house that I know. The tragedies that Dorothy has dealt with!'

Charlie wheeled Mike to the opposite side of the window to Dorothy and pulled up a wicker chair, while Aunt Jenny asked him how he was in a loud voice, and Dorothy said to get his baseball cap for the glare, but Mike waved his hand in dismissal.

'This is Emily Ellesker's daughter,' Charlie repeated to Mike. Mike gave Lillian another twisted smile and put his hands together, Asian style, then pointed to the window.

'He wants to lose himself in the view,' Dorothy said. 'The sea and the sky is his theatre.' She went over and kissed him on the head.

'Can I see the deer before I go?' Lillian asked.

'You can see her now,' Charlie said and rose. 'We'll give her a feed.'

He pressed Mike's shoulder for farewell and invited Lillian through the door.

He collected carrots and apples from the kitchen and a bucket of yeasty grain from the shed. Lillian took the vegetables in the orange Sainsbury bag and followed him, scattering cats, to a field fenced with barbed wire in which two horses in the far corner showed them their backsides. He whistled. The horses turned and strode with aristocratic calm towards them. 'They've seen the bag,' Charlie said. 'There's Maisie.' He pointed to a brown smudge and rattled the bucket. The smudge moved, ungainly and hesitant, in their direction. Charlie took the bucket. 'She'll come,' he said.

'Do the horses think she's the same as them?' Lillian asked.

'She more likely thinks the horses are deer. You do Derby and Joan. It's mare and foal.'

Lillian fed the carrots and apples to the snorting pair. She did as Charlie said: laid the food on a flat palm and let them rake it up. She had not known horses had such comically large teeth, or that their lips would be so dry. The deer limped close. Her outsize ears were turned to her. They had bristles on the ends. 'Give her a minute,' Charlie said. Sure enough, she edged forward. It was her front right leg that was lame. She put her head in the bucket, but her swivel eyes were on Lillian.

'Her poor leg,' Lillian said.

'That was a big job. It was broken in two places, but I still had the vet's practice then. She must have stumbled and broken it on the moors and the mother given her up. It was a wonder a fox didn't get her. She healed surprisingly quickly.'

Lillian felt a flood of sorrow for this nervous creature, alone and frightened and in pain, and now adopted into a strange and diminished herd, a half-citizen, a hobbling misfit, uprooted and dependent. Charlie saw her face.

'You all right?' he asked.

Ferdinand called her name. The horses pricked their ears at him. Maisie pushed her snout towards the voice. Lillian emptied the last of the carrots into the field and faced her half-cousin. Charlie retrieved the bucket and Maisie, surprised, ears flicking, nose-twitching, edged backwards and trembled her tail.

'I'll leave you to it,' Charlie said and nodded to Ferdinand and walked in his firm stride back to the house.

'I brought the van,' Ferdinand said.

Lillian folded the bag very neatly and slotted it into her pocket. 'I suppose you've come to fuss,' she said.

'Only if you want it. The ladies have been clucking, I take it?'

'They're very nice,' Lillian answered, 'and Dorothy's even weirder than you – though she's very nice, as well, almost. like, fake with it.'

'My eccentricities are of the place and my history,' he said, 'Dorothy's are a form of self-admiration. Of course, she has good reason to admire herself. And she's been very good to us. Beneath the pose, she's as loyal as the wind to the clouds.'

'The arrangement with Charlie and Mike is very alternative.'

'No more so than Frank living with us.'

'Oh, yes. She has a lovely house.'

'She has a *big* house. The loveliness is more moot.'

Lillian giggled. 'It is a little bit vulgar,' she said. 'But such potential! My mother was born here,' she said. 'Allegedly.'

'There's nothing alleged about it. Look around you.'

He gestured to the woods on the rise above them, the moors behind, and down the winding road, and then to the sea. 'This is the landscape your mother and mine knew as littluns. Mum was actually born in Saltscar, but it was then a close family.' He rested his back and elbows on the fence. 'It's yours to explore.'

'You're all so keen that I should like it.'

'We want you to like us, I guess.'

'What's the agenda?'

Ferdinand laughed: a bark. 'That's so London! Why did Charlie rescue the deer?'

'Is it for my mother?'

Ferdinand saw she was serious. 'Not in my case,' he said.

'The summer I was here, with her, do you remember it?'

'In vivid and random patches.'

'Why wasn't I told who she was? Was there something terrible about her?'

'I was twelve. I didn't understand those things. From what I remember, she was tender with you. Emily's not easy, but she's on the side of the angels.'

'She nice?'

'She's not *nice*, exactly. She's a force of nature. She walks the cliffs twenty-nine miles to Whitby then sits to breakfast and says, I *must get some exercise, I'm growing lazy*."

'I suppose she has a family of her own?'

'I don't think so. I believe she's bi-polar.'

'Oh.'

'She helps run an outdoor centre. She takes troubled children and drags them up mountains and tumbles them over waterfalls to improve their self-esteem.'

'That sounds fun.' She did not smile, however. She had no animation in her face. 'I ought to be angry about her,' she said, 'but I'm not. Only, I might become angry if I spent time with her.'

He nodded. 'I understand your caution,' he said. 'One step before the next. Let's get back.'

The mare behind them whinnied. She shook her mane and cantered, foal following, over the field. The deer, alone, glanced up at them from a lowered head, twitched, and spun away. They watched her ungainly run

'The deer doesn't like me,' Lillian said.

He faked bemusement. 'Why should she?' he asked. 'We don't either.'

She hit him on the shoulder, and they went in together.

There was an air of interrupted discussion in the room; Dorothy reclining against the back of the chaise-longue and observing them while Aunt Jenny twisted round and said, 'Here they are.' He plodded next to Dorothy and Charlie. Lillian perched on the edge of the sofa. Jim turned and gave another twisted smile.

'We were just saying, Lillian, it's a shame you haven't any young people to be with,' Aunt Jenny said. 'You must miss their company. Dorothy's nieces will be here soon so you might want to meet them, and they can introduce you to her friends. Would you like that?'

'A lot of people have said that. I don't mind.'

'You're doing the Scramble,' Dorothy said. 'You know, we'll have a soirée in your honour. I know this wonderful violinist who busks in York.'

'You haven't had one for ages, Dorothy,' Aunt Jenny said.

'Perhaps you'd like to stay here for a few days,' Dorothy suggested. 'You'd be completely safe here, my love, and it's easy to get into Saltscar. There's the bus.'

'The house is at your disposal,' Charlie added.

'That's very nice,' Lillian said.

'Shall I show you round?' Dorothy asked.

'Don't pressure her,' Ferdinand said. 'She has enough on her plate.'

'Lillian's very loyal,' Aunt Jenny said.

'I must be getting to the shop,' Ferdinand said. 'Could you help me, Lillian?' he asked.

'I'm thinking,' Charlie started, 'I could do with a hand around the place. Perhaps two days a week, till Mike's back on his feet. Perhaps Lillian would like a bit of animal husbandry for ready cash?'

'But she has the shop, Charlie,' Dorothy said.

'Aye, well, it's only a thought.'

'I will consider it,' Lillian said. 'Thank you.'

'Lillian's very gracious,' Aunt Jenny remarked.

'I'm going.' Ferdinand spoke with uncharacteristic decisiveness. 'Coming, Lillian? Or staying?'

'See, they were buttering me up,' Lillian said as he pulled out onto the road.

He nodded. 'They're offering you full membership.'

'They want me to know my mother.'

'It's why I came.'

'What?'

'You don't need the pressure.'

They were silent for the five minutes until the car wound onto the road down to Cat's Knoll. 'It wouldn't be a bad life, though, would it?' he asked. 'Taking charge of the shop. Perhaps netting a handsome surfer lad, one of the posh ones. Getting to know your mother a little. Jesus, and mum, and the beach and the cliff and the sea?'

'No. It wouldn't be bad,' she admitted.

'There is a 'but' in your tone.

'I do miss London.'

'I notice you haven't announced your father is free,' he said.

'I'm a coward.'

'That's the last thing you are.'

They curled down to Cat's Knoll. 'You must meet your mother, though,' he said. 'For balance. To be sure.'

It was high tide, and a wind. Sunlight crashed through a break in the clouds onto the wave-lashed Low Prom. 'Thalassa,' she said.

'Thalassa,' he repeated.

It was the morning of the Saltscar Scramble and Lillian was hanging herself with a chain in the shop as the customer left. 'You're an idiot, Ferdy!' she said.

'She'll come back.'

'She will if you don't charge her!'

'It's symbolic. The first ever.'

She blew out in happy exasperation and squinted at the frame. She was not sure about this as a promotional strategy, not from simple modesty but because it might appear narcissistic to prospective buyers when they saw her behind the till. Also, her mother was coming. Also, she ought to be getting into the right mental zone for the Scramble.

Her nose was a foot from the back of the canvas. 'Is that straight?' she asked.

'Down a fraction on the left,' Ferdinand replied from his den.

She had her hands on the frame when her mother walked in.

Aunt Jenny and Dorothy and Jean strolled in behind, gabbling, and jolly, and gave a choric approval to what they saw and all four faced Lillian on her perch.

'Oh,' Lillian said.

'This is *good*,' Dorothy said.

'Ferdinand's handiwork and Lillian's vision,' said Aunt Jenny. 'It's industrial chic.'

'But is it *straight*?' Lillian insisted.

'What do you think, ladies?' Ferdinand displayed himself at his table in the alcove.

'These are Frank's pictures?' asked Jean, pointing.

'They certainly are.'

'They look well!' Jean said as though surprised.

'Jan,' said Dorothy, 'you've saved your brother!'

'Oh, nonsense!' said Jenny, delighted. 'We did what any family would.'

'Lillian looks *sensational*,' said Jean gazing at her images.

'Are you going to stay up there all day?' her mother asked.

In Lillian's head the previous night Emily had been apologetic; 'You never knew how I longed for you,' she'd said with a wistful look over the bleak waves from High Prom. Or she'd been sharp, for she had thought her father would try to reconcile her with her only child, but she'd received only silence, and Lillian had blushed and run away. But in both cases, she had been impressed by Lillian's polish, her *suavité*, her self-definition. But Emily the woman in the room stood like wood and made no judgement. Was she on the spectrum? Lillian stepped down, appraised the hanging frame as though checking it, and then readjusted the children's picture books on the table below the picture.

'Let me show you upstairs,' Ferdinand said. He was buoyant.

They clattered on, then Emily murmured behind her, 'Leave that. Let's have a coffee.'

'Oh! Yes. Well, fine, but what about – I'll have to get my wallet. I think Ferdy –'i

'Guys!' Emily shouted up. 'We're for coffee.'

'Where?' Aunt Jenny asked.

Emily tapped her pocket. 'Phone.' she said.

'I wasn't expecting –' Lillian started.

'I won't eat you. Come on, we can't spend all day pretending.'

The five-piece brass band were playing old favourites in the square, their black trousers and red tops too formal for the grey day, although a few café customers sat outside to attend the old favourites. Emily turned down a jewel street, the oompah's ¾ time following them like a forlorn and discarded friend. At the end of the road on High Prom, a few young men were jogging in preparation for the Main Event, or just to attract attention. Moor Cliff showed a dull ochre, more vivid at least than the beige beach, and on the horizon the moors showed a thin rusty line, a wavering grasp at drama in the lonely scene. Lillian kept in step with her mother's muscular stride, and thought to start the conversation, as it seemed she might get away with pleasantries, but at the end of the road her mother suddenly turned and said with grim force, 'Understand this. I won't make excuses. I'll die for you, if need be, but I won't wheedle at you.'

Lillian had no idea how to respond, so she followed like an obedient dog. 'In here.' Emily continued to the ugly red-brick pub from the upper rooms of which on a Saturday night you heard bad music. 'You're having a difficult time,' Emily added as they stepped between the outside tables. 'You'll get through it. Almost all of us do. Running – running is good. In here,' she finished and went through.

'This is my first pub in Saltscar,' Lillian said. She didn't know why she said that.

'It serves coffee,' Emily answered. 'I love it. It's so common.'

Dark wood; a grubby carpet, a smell of beer despite the morning hour, and cubicles separated by high backs against which crimson plush sofas had been solidly fitted. The walls had pictures of burning sunsets over the seas, or of heroic sailing ships, and one showed villagers gazing in horror at a shipwreck. There was a group of elderly people under the wide window at the sea end, with two whippets that watched them come in. It was designed for a different age, in which cheery local working folk sang popular songs to the old Jemimah before the beer kicked in and fights broke out.

They sat in a small booth, the farthest from the window, the most private, but a Scottish voice spoke from behind the bar.

'Emily Ellesker! Now what can possibly bring you of all people on this day of all possible days into Saltscar?'

'Hello, Stuart,' said Emily. 'This is my daughter. Lillian.'

'Is it now? It's a privilege and an honour, Lillian. How's the auld country?' he asked.

'Wet,' Emily answered.

'Ay. If you can see the mountain it's going to rain. If you can't see the mountain, it's raining. And how are you, Emily? That's the point.'

'Stuart – I'm doing fine!'

'Still fighting the crags?'

'Fighting crags, Stuart! And you?'

'Not as fit as you, Emily, but doing fine. Your mother and I go way back, Lillian. You might say she brought me here.'

'I think you brought me!'

'And it worked out just fine! What do I get you?'

'Coffee and sparkling water for me.'

'Ach – running then. Well, fancy that!'

'I met Stuart at a bar in London,' Emily started when he attended their business. 'He looked after me once when I got very drunk. You don't need to know all the details. So: what do you want to know?'

Lillian did not know if this sudden swerve was a tactic, or just how Emily was. She was ready. 'Nothing. I mean, what do you want to tell me? Don't you want to ask *me* anything?'

'My information was you were doing just fine. I made it clear when I left, I only needed to be called upon. But I've never intended to break up a good thing. That's not my way.'

'So why did you go? Originally. Was it Jeremy?'

'Jeremy? Who's Jeremy?'

'I thought – I'm not sure where it came from - you went to Australia with Jeremy.'

'I went to Australia. I've no idea where a Jeremy comes into it. There was a Geoffrey who helped me organise it. Stuart helped me again when I got back. Perhaps you mean him. I was too ill to do it myself.'

'I'm sorry. Geoffrey was...?'

'Hell, Lillian, a guy. Someone. An acquaintance. A nice man. Let's clear this up. If you're going to spend a lot of time around the Goodman's you're going to be spending time around me, so we should get things straight. First, I didn't run off with anyone. I'm bi-polar – not so bad now. It gets worse during pregnancy. I was a danger to myself and possibly to you and I was kept in hospital once you were born. You were with me. I breast-fed. You were happy. Look, I won't speak against your dad. He was young too, and I was borderline psychotic, and he was very attractive and there were plenty of women ready to take you on – and he had solicitors and a well-paying job, and contacts, and probably a partner lined up. I had a mental illness. Yours was the second home I ran away from.'

'I see.'

'Do you? Do you really?'

Lillian was not to be intimidated. 'But if you were ill – I mean, really ill – you should have sought help here. Unless...' She was struck by a new and awful thought. 'Daddy didn't throw you out, did he?'

'No. Thanks, Stuart.' Stuart served with dignity. He would not intrude on what was clearly a serious business, but when he'd finished, he said, 'I'm in the tap room, Emily. If you need me, ring the bell, aye.'

'You're a great man, Stuart. Look, I went to London when I was sixteen. I was a bi-sexual tom-girl from a respectable family on a farm who longed for the bright lights. I had my first girlfriend when I was fourteen and my first boy six months later. I ran off to London like the girl in The Beatles' song and I married before I was twenty. Your dad was twenty-five. I thought he was a hero and that marriage was part of the adventure, but he wanted success, money, all that stuff and marriage turned out to be about matching the curtains to the carpet and a baby meant it went on forever. I have to say, he was brilliant with you. He was a proper dad, but I was climbing all over the walls. My parents wouldn't take me – a failed mother, a runaway who'd lived a life of sin in the big bad city – but this Australian farmer, a vague relation, wanted someone to keep house and help on the farm so off I went. He was shocked when he found out I was married and a mum, but I worked hard. It was *outdoors*. I need outdoors.'

'But you came back.'

'Yes. Why didn't I get in touch? That's what you're after.'

'I want to know if you're a friend or an enemy,' Lillian answered.

Emily considered. 'Wow,' she said. She regarded her daughter with new respect. She considered for some seconds, then smiled, like a chess player who appreciates an opponent's move because she has realised his strategy.

'Wow,' she said again. 'That was right off the cliff.'

'Like – what – mad?'

'No. This is Cleve-Land - the land of cliffs. 'Off the cliff' means 'of the area'. Direct. Fearless. Dangerous. Confrontational, perhaps.'

'I don't think the people here are fearless at all. Do you see me as a friend then?'

'No. You're the crying wee thing that came out of my body, which I left to your father and fate.'

'Oh, right. I see. Actually –'

'You don't see. Don't you hate that expression, 'I'm there for you?' You can only say that if you don't know what 'being there' means. This is the truth. Listen up. I wanted to make contact, but things went wrong. Jean and I – Deaf Jean, you know – made our way back from Australia to Europe. We each got a boyfriend for protection and for transport and for sex, to be honest, and we hitched and sailed and bussed across the world. They were glorious days. We worked where we could. Most of the work was legal. Then we got to Europe, Jean took a proper job and I came home to see what had happened to my little girl. But some of the drug guys persuaded me to take a last punt and that was that.'

'Sorry, what?'

'What do you think?' Emily laughed. It was not clear what she found amusing. 'Customs got me with cannabis in my bags. That screwed the reconciliation.'

'Did Daddy refuse to let you come?'

'He didn't need to. They banged me up, Lillian. I did six months in prison.'

'Oh.'

Emily shrugged: 'That was over,' the shrug said. It also said; 'Don't look so shocked.' Or, perhaps, 'It wasn't such a big deal.' But what made Lillian gape and look around the room without seeing it was the knowledge that both her parents at some point in their lives had run foul of the law, though neither seemed particularly bad people. But if Emily was disbarred from her presence because she had been a convict, what did that mean in terms of her father's difficulties? It was bad enough to have a father with dodgy partners, but to have a mother with parallel history was beyond unfair. What were the chances?

She looked into the espresso stain at the bottom of the cup. 'Fucking *hell*!' she whispered.

'Don't be so tragic,' her mother said. 'I survived. You can look back. You can look forward. Jenny looks back. I don't. Prison happened. It won't happen again. Lesson learned. I heard over the years you were doing well, so why barge in? I had enough guilt from running away without adding to it by running back.'

Stuart had returned to pour Guinness. He looked at the pint, and rolled his eyes, and smiled in complicity. '

'Guess who stood by me when I got out?' Emily asked.

'Aunt Jenny.'

'Actually, yes. But –' Emily nodded her head at the barman who finished pulling the pint with gravity. 'He brought me up here to Jen, where her friend Dorothy had bought the family home. She did it partly for me. My parents never forgave her.' She laughed briefly. 'Stuart liked it here and stayed. Stuart?'

'Aye, Emily?'

'How long have you been here? In Saltscar?'

Stuart looked upwards to think. He blew out his cheeks. He frowned as he cleared the pipes to the Guinness. 'Fifteen. Why?'

'You remember the summer I came back?'

'Aye. What of it?'

'Do you remember a little girl. Blonde. Skinny. Lively. Who hung around?'

'Only very vaguely. Was it your wee lass here?'

'It was. Was I in a state?'

He flung the poured black sludge down the sluice with satisfaction. 'You had things to deal with, aye.'

'These people saved my life,' Emily told Lillian.

'I think you're putting it a wee bit strongly there,' Stuart protested. 'I thought to bring you back. It worked out.' He was gone through a door to the tap room.

'He got me in touch with people at an outward-bound centre back home – in Scotland. That's what got me stable. Jenny calls it 'the healing process.' I've never made much money, but at least I'm active and I'm *outdoors*.' She stood. 'And that's enough confession for one day.'

Lillian was shocked at the abruptness. 'But don't you want to know about me?'

Emily leaned to put her hands on the table rim. 'Yes,' she said. 'But not now. I've said I won't speak against your father, and I won't, except for this. When he was winning, he pretended I didn't exist. Now he's down and, hey presto, my little girl's back! It's my turn now to be off the cliff: I'm not sure I'm the one who needs to earn the trust. Now, my child, let's go out and win the Saltscar Scramble.'

Emily led into the hallway, but disappeared through the opposite door to find Stuart in the taproom. Relieved for a moment from her mother's physical presence, Lillian breathed in deeply, sighed out, and told herself that considering what her parents were, or had been, it was a wonder she wasn't in prison herself.

It was a lot to take in.

Now the barriers were up and the road was closed. A pair of high-vis jackets were discussing the exit of the mobile homes from their slots on High Prom. Lillian noted this with faint pride, but Emily shouldered up Ruby Street towards the town centre with her remorseless square stride that would not move for anyone or anything; if a tree got in its way, it would be the tree that suffered. Lillian was stirred and humiliated in equal measure. Emily could be a little more aware of her, she thought, as they strode together into town, could acknowledge her more, but there was something heroic about her. She had assumed all her life her mother had sinned a conventional sin. She had seen at parents' meetings how two became one, a situation so common no-one thought to comment on it. This was different. Her mother had battled. She had been brave. She had made sacrifices, though it was annoying that Lillian herself was one of the things she had sacrificed.

'Do you want a lift to the car park before the walk up Cat's?' Emily asked.

'I'm meeting my friends. I'll walk with them.'

'Good for you. I'll see you at the start. And don't get upset if I beat you.'

Lillian stood outside *Prosper-oh* and watched her mother slip past the band on her way to Devon Street as though it didn't exist. Beat me? No way, she thought. No fucking way.

She wore the iconic pink trainers. They were faded, and sported white patches, and the shape had gone a little from one side, and one of the tongues had a stain that wouldn't clear off, but the pink trainers were history: she would win the Saltscar Scramble in nothing else.

The chatter on the march along The Dragon's Back gave the competition a feel of festival. Lillian's mother, walking behind, was one of the quiet ones. Chardonnay's ambition was modest. 'As long as I don't come last,' she said. 'Gavin'll take the piss for a month if I come last.'

'You won't come last,' Shelley reassured her. 'I'll come last. Trust me.'

'None of us will come last,' Lillian said. 'We've done the data.'

Thirty six competitors were encouraged along a curved line where Dragon's Back spread out, a grassy rise at the end of the track. There was a lot of glancing along this line, and a few couples had linked arms. A few were clearly there for the occasion rather than position. Emily approached Lillian who was flanked by Chardonnay and Shelley, the ball at the cannon sides. 'Don't hold back at the start,' she said.

'I know,' Lillian said. 'There could be some jostling for the track.'

'Some jostling!' Chardonnay exclaimed. 'This is the scramble bit.' She stuck out her elbows and twisted from side to side.

'You're little,' Emily said. 'Someone will try to bully you. Just sprint.' She acknowledged the officials' call and slipped into the line.

'Countdown begins in five seconds,' the starter announced. 'Remember, no tripping. Health and Safety. *Trippers and pullers will be disqualified.*' Big cheer.

The starter and competitors alike started the countdown from ten. It got louder as zero approached. Lillian had known nothing like it. No-one but her waited for 'Go!' but all set off with a fierce cheer and some laughter on 'one'.

The eighty yards to the narrow track was the reason they called it a scramble. Bumping was normal. Pushing with forearms was not uncommon. A few shirts were illegally and stealthily grabbed from behind. A collision saw one of the party suddenly veer down the steep slope on the left to a general cheer. Lillian, a step behind, was a moment confounded, but in a sudden fury belted through a gap, swung safely up the rise on the right and powered down, seeking the front for the track. This was all wrong. This was not The Plan. She heard a yelp as someone fell. There was some laughter and applause. She stretched out, one of the first three for the track, but noticed with alarm her mother was one of the three. The last thing she noticed, however, before she claimed her space in front of the favourite, Jane Brown, was her mother's arm raised across the chest of a bulky woman bearing down on her, and the woman running off the Dragon's Back through raked lines of autumn gorse with a yelp and a curse, to the trumpet cheer of those behind. Lillian was in front. She ought not to be in front. She ought to be just behind the leading group and pacing herself until the final stretches through the Valley Gardens. Jane Brown's tread was close. Would she trip her? There were no officials to check. In this crazy race you could not rule it out. Lillian was resolute in the centre of the track and belted without regard to the plan, taking the steps recklessly, two at a time, towards the safety of the A-road.

The cheer of the spectators on the Saltscar Bank lifted her chest. She knew she was pushing too hard, but it was a shame to disappoint the applause by dropping behind the smooth Jane Brown on her shoulder and whomever else was twenty yards behind them. Her thighs burned at the top: but she ran it off as she surfed the applause along High Prom all the way to the top of Hazel Grove. She turned along the path parallel to the railway tracks still in first place, but she was happy to cede this along the allotments. The Catalonian flag still flew. Calmer now, she let Jane Brown take the lead, but she was sure she could cope. There was still a solid distance between her and the chasers. The stately figure of Jane Brown, her ponytail swishing, her shoulders back, her stride even and high, kept up its challenging pace. But they arrived at the road. There were no spectators until the top of Station Way, which burst into a cascade of approval as they swung round onto the broad street south to the far entrance of the Valley Gardens. Lillian did the breathing. She pumped the arms. Jane Brown remained twenty yards ahead. But it was in the Valley Gardens, on the descent, where lightness and good lungs and youthful balance were key, that Lillian had planned her attack. As she entered, taking the sharp left with a swing of her hips, she glanced back and saw to her dismay that a runner had separated from the pack behind, and that the runner was her mother.

The path weaved round the stepped borders and cut down away from the Italian Garden to the bridge where a few days earlier Marjorie had slumped like a toad to say that Monty was dead. Lillian lengthened her stride and forced herself onto Jane Brown's shoulder. Jane Brown ran faster as well. They saw the bridge. Spectators had lined the grass along the tracks, behind whom dogs sniffed and chased balls and each other as though nothing was new, but, seeing the challenge of the front-runners, the people let out calls, and clapped, and sent whistles into the air. This was Lillian's moment. But as she thumped over the bridge, the sound of their feet raising a staccato drum, she knew something was wrong. She was not doing the breathing. The breathing was doing her. She was sucking at air. They had pulled away from the chasers, but Jane Brown remained smooth as water, and did not look back. Lillian's legs did not ache. She was not finished. She clung on, waiting for weakness to show in the faintest of wobbles of Jane Brown's hips, the merest hint of a shortening stride. It was two hundred yards flat to the road and the turn onto the sprint finish at Low Prom.

The spectators lined along the beach, looking up, crammed the barriers on the bankside of the Low Prom, and looked down from the railings near the funicular. As Jane Brown and Lillian Delph rose past the bus stop and crossed the bottom of Saltscar Bank they hit a furious applause, and rent a spontaneous though ragged cheer, touched with surprise at the ferocity of the competition. At the cheer, as though buoyed by it, or waiting for it, Jane Brown accelerated, and Lillian knew the race was lost.

She came in second, faltering, fending off the challenge from behind by a matter of a few yards.

Her mother came behind the group fighting for third. Lillian took Jane Brown's handshake but neither woman spoke. She rested against the railings as other runners came through, not sure what to think. She did some perfunctory stretches. Then her mother approached.

'You didn't win?'

'Second.'

'That's fine. You'll win it one year if you want to.'

'It was horrible. I thought I had her and then my legs went wobbly. Everyone saw.'

'I was eighth. My lowest. This is my last. You'll have to stay for the awards. The rest should be here soon.'

'Eighth is good.'

'No, it isn't. It's eighth.'

Lillian wandered along the curve towards Hazel Grove. The applause was in part for her, but the eyes were more on Jane Brown. Her toe hurt. It was the little toe of her left foot. In fact, the tops of her toes on the right foot hurt as well. That was not right. She sat on the wall and took off her shoe. Her toes had rubbed. She had not noticed until she had stopped. That was the adrenalin. She closed her eyes. Second! But she'd done all right. She had carried the Goodman – or was it the Ellesker torch – with distinction.

Jane Brown approached. 'You gave me a fright,' she said. They shook hands again, though Lillian did not rise.

She knew all along she was going to win, Lillian thought.

She heard a familiar whoop of delight. Chardonnay was pumping air. She saw Lillian and waved, and Lillian waved back.

'I didn't come last!' Chardonnay was happy. 'Fuck! Did you win?'

'Second. Look - Shelley!'

Chardonnay danced across and hugged her sagging friend. The two of them, laughing and cursing, staggered to the low concrete wall and sat, innocent, good-natured, proud and exhausted.

Lillian could not feel the same happy pride. She wandered onto the beach, nodding to those spectators who acknowledged her, drawn to the indifferent shush of the sea. She stood her toes in it for the salt, which tingled them, and then she sat on the sand, and breathed heavily once, and waited for the endomorphs to swill in their calm. She tied the trainers together, the old pink trainers which had let her down. She was sad for them, like a child for a favourite soft toy, battered by use and worried by pets. The pink trainers were the best of her teenage years; stylish, fresh, clean, the flag of her focussed future. Now they were salt-stained, and the tongue had a browning, aged look that would not clean, and they were attacking her feet. The pink trainers needed to make room for their replacement. The cheers and claps for the stragglers, as warm as for any competitor, had given in to the mixed voices of small groups greeting each other. Here, she thought, I could be a big fish in a very small pond. What a summer it had been. She looked to Moor Cliff. It was a dull lump in the grey October afternoon, but it seemed a quiet and familiar friend.

She heard her name called.

Her family, Dorothy and Jean among them, were gesticulating her back to Low Prom; the awards! Frank was waving with a camera in his hand. Her mother had pulled on a tracksuit. Ferdy was to one side: she couldn't say if he was gazing at her or at the sea. The group was joined by Shelley and Chardonnay; it broke up to swallow them. She waved. She jogged back. She should do the warm down and stretches before the awards, but they were waiting for her, and this was no longer an afternoon for the strictest professionalism. She slung the trainers over her neck.

It ended with the soirée they said was in her honour. She wore the sash: Saltscar Scramble second place, *magna cum laude*. She stepped out of Ferdy's rattling van into the twilight when the house had turned to charcoal and the moor was russet, a dying coal under a smoke sky. It was very lovely, Lillian said, though it must be terrible in winter.

The fiddler was in the house. They heard him as soon as the door was opened. He was playing a tripping jazz jig in the upstairs salon where Lillian recognised Curly who looked unusually normal in a loose grey suit. Aunt Jenny was already there: they hugged: then Chardonnay and Shelley arrived in what Lillian would have said were cocktail dresses. They hugged also and Chardonnay's man, Gavin, a hefty smiling chap, snapped the three of them for Facebook; Lillian with sash prominent.

'We did it,' Chardonnay told Lillian. 'We fucking did it, girl!' But she kept her voice low, because of swearing. Then she turned to the room, raising her glass. 'Ladies and Gents!' She raised Lillian's arm. 'Lillian Delph, the future of the Saltscar Scramble.' Lillian blushed at the applause.

'She'd have me to beat next year,' Chardonnay bragged.

'Bit ambitious that, Char,' Shelley warned.

Bubbly was handed on trays by two girls Lillian's age or a little older, and Lillian took one, and raised it to Deaf Jean who was standing with her mother.

'You are a kind of celebrity here,' Ferdinand said from behind her. She hit his arm in denial.

Her mother came across and gave her a cursory embrace as though they had known each other all their lives. 'Jenny is pestering for us to be photographed together,' she said. 'She's such a sentimentalist. She knows I only do Facebook for work. I hate all that stuff.'

'Thank you for the Scramble,' said Lillian.

'What?"

'You protected me from that woman. She was looking to barge me.'

'That was personal. She got me last year. But yes, that as well.'

There were sundry others on the acceptable side of middle age whom Lillian did not know. They identified her by the sash. They wanted to know what she thought of, how long she intended, had she seen the, where exactly she, had she done the, and didn't she think people were nicer in the north? Lillian could do that stuff. The party was an old-fashioned party in the countryside, but she was touched that they had insisted she wore the sash so people knew she was guest of honour.

The fiddler finished. There was a request for the piano, and it was Emily who obliged, playing a 'light classical piece' on the upright, cursing softly when she corrected herself. Only Lillian was surprised by this. She had a mother who climbed mountains and played the piano, how amazing was that? The serving girls were friends of Dorothy's niece who was around somewhere. They wanted to know if she knew anyone famous in London. Lillian did not. She took another glass of bubbly. Then Aunt Jenny joined her with Dorothy in dark suit and white blouse and red bow tie and her mischievous smile, and said they were proud of her. Dorothy beckoned Emily over.

'No speeches,' Dorothy said. 'Just a toast. To our Scramblers. Lillian and Emily, 2nd and ... 6th? ... 7th? ... well, nearly second then – Emily and Lillian.'

'Emily and Lillian!' the party agreed.

'Where did you find that fiddler, Dot?' Aunt Jenny asked.

'Isn't he divine? He was busking in York. I hired him.'

'I'm so glad you still play, Emily,' Aunt Jenny continued.

'I hardly practice. I don't need it.'

'Emily, cousin, that's such a terrible waste! When there are so many who never had the chance. Of course, it's not a duty –'

'Leave it, Jen,' Emily answered. 'No-one's got cross with anyone today. It's because Lillian's here.'

'Do you know,' Dorothy chimed in, 'I think you're right! Lillian has made us forget out old squabbles.'

'She's lifted the Ellesker curse,' Aunt Jenny announced.

'Don't be dramatic, Jen.'

Mike wanted to see her. A stranger announced it with a delicate touch on her wrist - two fingers, so respectful - so she went downstairs to where Mike, freshly groomed, was in his wheelchair with the ever-attendant Charlie. He held both her hands and smiled and spluttered something. Charlie translated: 'He says well done. Everybody is proud.'

'Thank you for having me,' she said.

It *was* rather like being famous, and without paparazzi, but then Anne-Marie appeared from the kitchen with four bottles as soon as Lillian left the room. Lillian wondered if she'd been waiting for her.

'They got you then,' Anne-Marie said.

'Sorry?'

'You're helping Ferdy with the shop.'

'Yes. No. It depends upon my father - I know you think it doesn't make business-sense-'

Anne-Marie shook her head and interrupted. 'No, it shouldn't, but you've given it a chance. I was wrong about you, wasn't I? I thought you'd be here and be miserable forever. This is hard to say, but I couldn't have done what you've done at your age.'

'Thank you.'

'My brother is happy. I should be jealous. I am jealous, but I'm leaving so I don't care.' Anne-Marie scanned the room as they stepped in. She saw Dave and called him. 'Open these for me,' she said and handed over the bottles. 'No, those are screw cap. Where *is* my stupid brother?'

'I left him in the book room discussing alliteration with Curly,' said Dave.

'Now that would be fascinating.' Anne-Marie laughed. 'He should spend more time with Lillian though.'

'I'm fine, really.'

'Now go away, Dave.' Anne-Marie turned to Lillian. 'I'll say one more thing. Ferdy's like he is because we protect him. Don't get me wrong. I'd scratch the eyes out of anyone who tried to hurt him, but he's indulged. You're a big girl now, and you don't owe us.'

'It's all for my mother, isn't it?' Lillian asked. 'Aunt Jenny took me in for my mother's sake, not mine.'

'Mainly your mother, yes. But for you as well. And, of course, for the Ellesker name. Those fucking Elleskers! Sorry, you're one of them, but you'll learn. Dave's having a little sulk, I'd best go.' She smiled. It was triumphant. 'I've finally got my freedom. From now on, I'll live as merry as I please! You're a good person, Lillian, and you should only do what's right for you.'

Anne-Marie turned, but Lillian stopped her with, 'Is my mother a good person?'

'Course she is! She's like you! Peas in a pod.'

Lillian put the bottles on the table and turned to seek out Ferdinand, but her mother was looking at her. She steadied herself and went over to re-join her with Aunt Jenny and Jean.

'This is in your honour,' Emily said. 'I never got that.'

'You've taken off your sash,' Jean said.

'I didn't want to overdo it.'

'Lillian is very modest,' Aunt Jenny said. 'And she has high standards.'

'I didn't win though.'

'That's what I mean,' said Aunt Jenny.

'You were second, 'Emily said. 'That's very good.'

'No, it isn't. It's second,' Lillian answered, and Emily laughed.

'You beat *me*,' she said.

'It isn't about the position though, is it?' said Jean.

'Yes,' said Emily and Lillian together.

'This is where we have a difference in outlook,' said Aunt Jenny. 'You might call it a difference in values. But I think they rather complement each other, don't they?'

'You play the piano,' said Lillian to Emily.

'Grade 8. Don't practice, like I said.'

'I still think -' Jean persisted.

'The lessons probably broke my mental health,' said Emily. 'You're hearing well, Jean.'

'I find the conversation interesting.'

Anne-Marie had approached. She held her mother's arm. 'Ferdy's being anti-social,' she said. 'No-one knows where he is. He's probably outside. Should we check on him?'

'I'll go,' said Lillian. She turned back. 'What am I checking for?'

'Once in a while he gets the glooms,' said Aunt Jenny. 'I've seen no warning signs.'

'I know glooms,' said Emily. 'Let's go together, Lillian.'

Why did this seem so natural? She was not alarmed when Emily said on the way down the stairs. 'Why not come and see me in Scotland? Stay for a while.'

'If I can. I'd like to. I think I'd like to.'

'The season's over. There's still some canoeing on the loch. Guided climbs until the clocks go back. There's a rehabilitation programme for young offenders: you might be interested in helping. We ride throughout the year. The bridle paths need to be in good nick. It's weather dependent.'

'I'd have to think about that.'

'Yes. Your father. His view. It would do you good though.'

'There's a lot going on.'

'You're going back, aren't you?'

Lillian looked up at her mother. 'I guess.'

Emily nodded. 'For your dad. I'd think less of you if you just left him. You haven't told them, have you?'

'Ferdy's guessed.'

'Difficult conversation, after all this.' Her mother rubbed her on the back. Lillian's stomach burned at the touch. 'Leave it with me. Jenny listens to me.'

'Oh, that's –' Lillian started, but Charlie came from Mike's room and Emily asked, 'Seen Ferdinand?' to which Charlie answered, Outside, and Emily told Lillian to go on, she'd check on Mike a minute, so Lillian went out by herself into the cool night, and shivered, and called out, squinting, and heard Ferdinand call back.

He was sitting on the dry-stone wall. She recognised the oval of his back in the window light. He was looking at the stars. He would be. There was a party in her honour, and he was looking at the sky. He turned his head at the crunch of her steps, and squinted, but turned back as he recognised her tread. 'I suppose you're going to get all poetic about the stars now,' she said, and giggled. She jumped onto the wall, facing the opposite direction.

'Don't get your pants dirty,' he said.

'Emily has invited me to stay with her in Scotland.'

'What? Forever?'

'No! Just a visit.' She re-considered. 'I think that's what she meant. Why are you out here?'

'I had a talk with Dave,' he said. 'He made a new suggestion. I rent the shop out. That would free you as well as Anne-Marie.'

'You've left the party to think about that?'

'To *feel* about it. The stars help. If the shop doesn't make money quickly, the rent would give us a little income and I might even be able to stay here. And it would give Anne-Marie a hand up. It'd be the end of dad's dream of course. So that's my preoccupation, and something less poetical is hard to imagine. Have you had lots of compliments?'

'Billions. But Ferdy, it's your dream as well. The shop.'

'How will I run it without you? Don't let's be maudlin. The summer was epic, in the old sense.'

The door opened, a great swab of warm light dropping on the uneven path and making pocked shadows of the stones. 'All right, you two?' Emily called.

'We're having a good chat,' Lillian replied.

'Join us,' Ferdy said.

Emily walked over.

'But no-one else's dream,' Ferdinand said. He turned round, a little clumsily, as Emily approached. She stood with her back to the wall. No-one spoke, which was strange, because it was a little chilly and the noise of the party wafted through the partly opened windows, so why just stay in the dark? But no-one moved either. Then Emily made sense of it.

'We finally found each other.'

Lillian felt Ferdinand's pat on her back, which was comfortable, in the way Jesus was comfortable when he jumped on the sofa beside her. She wanted to say something profound, something they would remember forever, and came up with, 'Yes, all for one and one for all, like in the book.'

'What, the three musketeers?' asked Emily.

'Without the swords and the politics,' Ferdinand said. 'But Lillian's right.'

'Lillian's right,' Emily confirmed. Lillian felt her hand on her upper arm. 'But she has her dad, of course. Don't forget Daddy.'

Ferdinand dropped off the wall, which ended the spell. 'We should go in. But first we must hug. We are not a hugging family, but the time is auspicious.' He threw out his arms. Lillian walked into the hug and Emily followed. Their foreheads touched. It was more of a huddle than a hug, like a team before kick-off, but their breaths mingled and Lillian was content.

'Where's the deer?' she asked.

'Snug in the stables with the horses,' Emily answered.

'Good.'

She stopped drinking when she found herself tipsy. The last thing she wanted to do was to disgrace herself now she was an established boon to the family. The guests separated into groups as they do at parties, and though Lillian knew she spoke to Chardonnay and Shells and agreed the Scramble had gone as well as could be hoped – though it hadn't – and remembered sitting quietly with her mother and eating something from a paper plate and smiled at Dorothy's jokes at some point and refused a dance with a guy she suspected was with his girlfriend and nodded to Anne-Marie across the room as though they understood each other, she could not detail precisely any conversation she had had.

When she settled in the rattling van for the journey back and Ferdinand asked her how it had been for her, she said, 'Satisfactory,' then corrected herself. 'No, nice. Everyone was really nice.'

'Did you say goodbye to Emily?'

'I'll text her. We're chilled. Frank wasn't there.'

'The booze. He still doesn't trust himself.'

'Of course. How did your talk go with Curly?'

'He's finished his poem.'

'Oh, good.'

'It's terrible.'

'Oh, well.'

Lillian saw the pricks of the stars as the van rose and fell along the coast road and she noted a single blinking red light from a ship and recognised immediately the yellow lights of Saltscar and the orange glow of the road lights towards the west. 'Did you know my mother once went to prison?'

'Of course.'

'You should have said. It would have made it easier.'

'I'm not sure how to unpick that, but you mean, I suppose, you'd have a reason to reject her?'

'It means I needn't have felt so apologetic about my father! These Elleskers are worse than him!'

'You needn't sound so delighted.'

'I'm an Ellesker too! I'm the child of two criminal families. How unusual is that?' She turned serious. 'I'm family now, aren't I?'

'You are.'

'Wow.'

'It'll enrich your life, but it won't make it easier.'

The van groaned up Saltscar bank. The engine shuddered in horror at its task, but finally crawled over the ridge and purred onwards to Devon Street where Frank and Mary and Joseph and Jesus were waiting.

'I don't think I do easy,' Lillian said.

The next morning Edward telephoned to say the case was dismissed and he had taken a flat in Penge. He was upbeat. Lillian could come home.

Chapter 8

'It's not as it was, but it will be. We won't let those bastards grind us down, not at all. The case should never have been brought against me, Randa.'

They were at the Brown and Green Café in Penge. Edward had chosen it to show that Penge wasn't all downmarket, that it had many advantages other than price, not least the Crystal Palace, which was perfect for her fitness regimes.

'It's a battle, Randa. I'm fighting for us both.'

'I know. But you won't risk it again, will you?'

'I was too trusting, Randa, if that's what you mean.'

'I suppose I do.'

Edward smiled and waved with delicate fingers at a waitress wiping the next table, who smiled back and asked if everything was all right. 'The people here are friendlier than in South Ken, that's a fact. You know, I thought it would be a year or more before we were fighting again, but look how quickly we've got on track. You'll be fine here, Randa, won't you?'

'Don't worry about me, Daddy.'

'I have to worry, Randa. It was *for you.*'

'I know, but ...' Lillian struggled for the concept. 'I didn't ask you to take these risks.'

'I was losing money, Sweetheart. Bad luck. We have to take risks, and it's the definition of risk is something that can go wrong. No shame. It's the bouncing back that proves your worth.'

'But it isn't about money and stuff.'

'It is a bit, Randa.'

She flopped back. 'I see things differently now. My mother went to prison.'

He was not expecting that. 'I know. Did Jennifer Goodman tell you that?'

'No, she did.'

'I see. Really? When?' He was discomforted. 'You must have had a real heart to heart for her to disclose that. Why would she tell you? It's not the kind of thing that comes up in casual conversation.'

'You're changing the subject. We'll come to my mother.'

He laughed. 'You mentioned her, Randa!'

'We don't mention you. It's like a rule.'

'So you speak a lot? I didn't know she was still such a part of the family.'

'She came back to run in the Scramble. She does every year. We had a coffee and she told me a bit about her life in Australia. That's all.'

'It seems as though you've done a lot of thinking with *someone* up there!'

'That's a good thing.'

'Up to a point.' They were interrupted by a waiter. He ordered Harrogate Spring Sparkling with lemon, but no ice and Lillian had her usual single espresso. The waiter looked disgruntled so she asked for cake as well. 'You have to promise me one thing,' she said.

'Anything I can.'

Edward's phone bleeped an incoming.

'In the future everything will be above board. No borderline criminal activity.'

'I've learned my lesson.'

'Especially with Mr. Shevchenko.'

'Ivan? Ivan is completely legit.'

'Completely? The police didn't seem to think so.'

'Then why don't they charge him? Do you know, almost one third of the world's finances have their origins in crime? There's a lot of hypocrisy out there. Just saying. Hang on.' He read his message. 'Madelaine,' he said. 'We're still in touch.'

'You still see her?'

'Not in that way. She has a job. I think she likes it.'

'Gumdrops for her.'

He laughed. It was the first time he had laughed since she'd returned to London. But it wasn't she who'd made him laugh, or the text from the Trophy. If she moved out of the flat in Penge The Trophy would move in. That was certain. Daddy and the Trophy were nailed on. It made financial sense, and her father had physical needs.

But there was London. She did not know how much she had missed it until she saw Maria waving to her on the steps of Tate Britain. In the white morning the grey stone was clean and defined like an engraving, and the desultory visitors draped over the steps had the look of people who would not dream of being anywhere else. Maria worked in the cloakroom: her next shift was hours away, so the two of them walked up Page Street and onto Horseferry and past the abbey and over to St James's Park. Lillian thought how nice the names were that told you what people once did there and gazed upon Horse Guard's Parade from the lake like a tourist.

'You forget how lovely this is,' Lillian said.

'When you're in London you don't take advantage. That's a thing. Coffee? I know a place,' and she grinned.

It was soon obvious where Maria was taking her. 'No!' said Lillian. 'You're joking me.'

'Angelo's on. He was asking after you. Really.'

He was even more beautiful than she remembered. He registered her presence with a well-timed double-take. 'Now, ladies,' he addressed them in that old fashioned way he'd doubtless learned at drama school, 'what can I do for you?'

The Set had always believed he was being suggestive when he said this, for he must have known they went weak at the thighs when he flashed them his perfect teeth.

'Angelo's leaving, aren't you, Angelo?'

Lillian raised her eyes in question and despair.

'That's right. I'm taking a proper job.'

'But, Angelo, what about the acting?'

Angelo shrugged. 'There's dreams, and there's fantasy. I'd wait tables and temp between auditions if I was going to make a break-through one day, but it ain't happening. I'm cool with it. What can I get you, ladies?'

'That's sad,' Lillian remarked when he'd left. Maria shrugged.

'It's better than wasting his life.'

'This is the year,' said Lillian, 'of facing the truth.'

Any further reflection on Angelo's surrender was washed away when Lillian heard her name called. The voice brought up, as in a breaking wave, her girlhood's little adventures, her small hurts.

'Fuck off,' she said.

'Can I sit down?' Chloe sat down. 'How's things, babe?'

'You knew I was here?'

'We need to talk.'

Maria stood. 'I'm going to have a look at the food. I could take one of their salads. You want anything?'

Chloe put her bag on the floor, which signified staying; she did it like rolling up sleeves. 'You told my dad I was doing coke.'

'Which was true. You told everyone mine was going to prison.'

'Also, true. At the time.'

'I was down and you kicked me!'

'No, that's actually *un*true. I was saying, like, 'Hey, Lills is in trouble, mates, we've got to rally around,' and it was the bitches who went, 'Oh my god, Lill's father's going to prison, they've lost all their money, whoah!' You didn't hang around to find out. I was being *supportive*. But then my dad said not to get involved, let it all settle down, which I would not do, and then we all heard you'd left London, like dissing us, mate. No explanation, nothing. So I thought, Fuck it, I don't need her, but it's been shitter since you left. Then you told my dad we did coke, Dave and me, and he said you were angry and fucked up.' She suddenly grinned. It was the old Chloe, who swung between moods like catching juggling sticks. 'That was some rumpus, that coke thing!'

'Why have you gone gansta?'

'Growing up, mate, innit?'

'Did they find some?'

'I'm not so stupid as to leave a stash in my room. I'm off it now. Dave and me are no longer a unit.'

'He's dumped you?'

'Be direct, mate, why don't you? But, basically, yeah.'

'You shouldn't have spoken to the Set before you spoke to me.'

'Yeah. I was impulsive. I need to reign in my natural disposition.'

'Those are big words.'

'I'm a big girl now. No drugs, a bit of a job, and I'm having a holiday from men. Hi, Angelo, can I have an iced tea? Thanks. So. You're back.'

'For the time being.'

'You should stay, mate. We need each other. You kept me on the straight and narrow – mainly. And without me, you'd have been a nun.'

Maria returned foodless. 'I might have a salad when I've finished my coffee. Are you two friends?'

They regarded each other. 'Provisionally,' said Lillian. 'Let's do the South Bank tomorrow and see how it goes. But if we're going to meet, I want you to do something for me. Can you tell your dad to ring me? I need to ask him something.'

'What is it? I'll ask him.'

'I'll tell you about it when I've spoken to him.'

'She was buttering me up,' Lillian said when they were on the tube. 'All this stuff about gathering support. I don't think I believe that.'

'I don't either, but she *wishes* she'd said it like that, which counts for something.'

They did shops. It was old times. Lillian would not spend more of the Rolex money until she had an allowance, but it was riding a bike, so easy after so long, and when the doorman opened for her at Harvey Nicks she suddenly felt important again. Maria dragged her to Burger and Lobster where a friend of her boyfriend had arranged to hand back the headphones she'd lent him. The friend looked at Lillian with a look Lillian knew, but she did not mind, she would take it as a compliment for it was a long time a man had noticed her as a woman, unless Frank counted, which he didn't, and besides he was rather cute.

'He's rather cute,' she said when they mounted the steps to the bus.

'Get in there,' said Maria.

'Don't be silly.'

'He fancies you. It was obvious.'

'Does he have a girlfriend?'

'Like, you're interested?'

'Only asking.'

'He's actually very nice. Oh, look at this – told you.' She held out her mobile. Lillian read, Your friends hot!

'That's not very grown up,' she said.

'What man is? So, are you staying?'

That was the question. Lillian found it hard to reply, and as she considered Maria said: 'You really should. This flat in Penge isn't what it you're used to, but it's London, Lills. You can work here. I've got two part-time jobs and I'm only eighteen. That's normal now. You get used to it, and you're a natural worker. Think of the new people you'll meet. One of them who works in the cloakroom is from Madagacar. She's got a science degree. She's here to get perfect English. She's brilliant. I've met so many cool people this summer from working. You'd love it. And what's there to do in a seaside town in winter?'

'That's a consideration, certainly. Saltscar would be harsh in winter.'

She had never complained about the nights drawing in. She preferred summer, of course, as everyone did, but she liked the lit shop windows and the anonymity of dark streets. It would be awful to be stuck in the countryside all through the darkness, but the city bubbled, and sparkled, and glowed and gabbled happily to itself over winter. Even the Thames, lined and crossed with lights, was romantic. This was a pleasure as she listened to her father when they ate on the South Bank. It was nearly six: already the windows were gleaming and the clocks did not go back until the weekend.

'The place is really very small, there's no getting round that. There'll be a much smaller allowance. There's no room for stuff. You'll have to work your way.'

'I can do that.'

'You'll have to pay for train tickets out of what you earn.'

'I get it, Daddy!'

'You really ought to get something for that work up there.'

'Daddy! They rescued me!'

'Fair point.' Edward smiled. 'You know, when I said I did all this for you, it was actually true. This is rather cheesy, but I remember the first time you looked at me. You were barely hours old and the midwife at the hospital put you in my arms and you looked up and, well, Sweetie, in that moment I grew up.'

'I'm stronger than you think.'

'I *will* get us back in full throttle. We'll do it. We'll stick together.'

'I ought to go back to tell Ferdy. To say goodbye properly.'

Edward frowned. 'Why? You can phone.'

'I suppose so.'

'It's normal. We're busy now, Sweetie. If they want to visit, they can. Where's your mother?"

'Scotland. Near Loch Lomond. Where is Loch Lomond?'

'Somewhere in the highlands. Can you imagine living there in the winter? Utterly cut off?' Lillian could not imagine. 'They'd lived without a thought of you all their lives,' he finished. 'What has your mother ever done for you, really? You might get a card at Christmas.'

Lillian shrank over her espresso. That might be, she thought, but she did think it a shame that Ferdinand no longer had her alongside him to guide and encourage.

He left the shop early. He gathered up the dogs and set off down Dundas Street and dropped through the Valley Garden and strode, walking boots and flat cap and long stick, up Cat's Knoll. He stopped just where the stubby oaks gave out and the gorse began and looked out over the shrouded bay. He would not take The Neck of the Dragon's Back and beyond because he had a respect touching on fear of Moor Cliff in this haze.

Early winter light: Saltscar a smudge on the buff.

When he'd watched her off Saltscar station he'd seen a girl with all the advantages except future tenderness a millennial could wish. 'Hey ho, canines,' he said. 'There is nothing left remarkable beneath the visiting moon.'

The dogs had no response to this remark, but stared into the blown mist with stoic loyalty. That evening he would cook for mum and tidy the room Lillian style. The house was quiet without Lillian. Mum watched television, and Frank had not spoken a word.

It was a day of hard cold: an east wind was dispersed around the streets of the city in gusts, but it flew up the Thames like an attack from the air. Lillian heard it in bed, and she stretched. Marcus stretched as well. She felt his hand up and down her spine which was not an unpleasant feeling, but she had to get on.

'It's almost eight,' she said. 'Don't start.'

'Aw,' Marcus said.

'Heat up the croissants,' she said.

He ate his croissant in his boxers. He was showing off his torso. She ate hers in her uniform. 'You look sexy in that,' he said.

'I don't want to look sexy. Put your top on.'

Marcus did as told, without enthusiasm or distaste. 'What time do you finish?' he asked.

'I'll text. I might have to stay with my dad tonight.'

'He didn't like me.'

'He's just getting used to it.' She topped up her coffee and then poured him a cup. 'He's had a difficult year.'

'My girlfriend's dad is a wheeler-dealer.'

'Do you find that sexy as well?'

'It is kind of exciting.'

'One day I'll tell you about my mother. And my great-grandfather.'

'What about them?'

'My mother was in prison. Her father ran foul of the law as well.'

'Jeez.'

'I'm the child of a criminal dynasty. Two criminal dynasties, perhaps. You don't mess with Lillian Delph!'

'Epic.'

She was Lillian Three Jobs. Monday was her stint at Tate Britain. The cloakroom work was easy, but dull, while the work in the shop was more hectic, but also more fun. She was good with the customers, but she was happy to work on deliveries which was more complicated and serious that one at first thought. Goods for the shop and the restaurants, for maintenance, and for cleaning were delivered each day, and the organisation of the stores entailed decisions. Today she was cloakroom, but she did not mind because during lunch she was meeting a Mr Cobbeling about a job in real estate which was arranged by Mr Harris. Morning was slack. She found the chance to arrange a brief social with Maria for after work and answer a text from Marcus. All good.

It was amazing how her life had filled in a month: three jobs, Maria, dinner most evenings with Daddy, who was mainly chilled about Marcus, new friends, a truce with The Trophy, and always some new thing cropping up. Last week Marcus took her to Bicester where a friend with a pilot's licence took them up in a small plane. On Saturday afternoon she was with the girls on the Portabella Road, and she had reconnected with the old Crew's hang-out. She was more grown up now. Chloe, well, Chloe was fine, but she didn't understand that Lillian had to work so much: the draw of easy pleasure was still too strong in her for deep friendship to root between them. But it was all fine. When she changed from the cloakroom gear into her interview clothes for the mysterious Mr. Cobbeling, she had an image of Marcus watching her undress, and she saw him naked on his stomach, and she pinked. She had discovered good sex for the first time and was still a little ashamed of it.

She was blithe outside the restaurant. She knew nothing about this job: Mr. Harris had said something had come up with a mutual client and he had thought of her. She liked Mr. Harris after all. He was a methodical man who was never hurried; he put his papers in the file before he'd answer your question. Mr. Harris had had a long interview with her in secret about her father which had been reassuring. You wouldn't go on an adventure with Mr. Harris, but you'd be happy to let him organise your kit.

Her faith in Mr. Harris and her blithe spirit was shaken when she heard her name called in a familiar voice, and on turning saw Mr Shevchenko smiling at her.

'You made it! Well done,' Mr Shevchenko said.

'I'm waiting for someone,' Lillian said.

'Mr. Cobbeling – that's my English name. Shevchenko means 'cobbler's son'. I use the Anglo-Saxon suffix. Shall we go in? The table's booked. I can see you're surprised. I'm sorry. I was going to send an associate, but that would have been dishonest. I would have come under my native name, but then you may have refused even to hear me. This is a compromise.'

'I don't know what to say. Does my father know?'

'Not specifically.'

'I don't believe this!'

'It's all good news, Lillian. Do you know a Frank Tengku-Watkins, by any chance?'

'That's Chloe's dad! Yes.'

'I've never met him personally, but we'll be joined by a friend of his shortly. Only for ten minutes. Please, Lillian. At least you get a free lunch. Don't say there's no such thing.'

'Why do you want me?'

'Integrity,' he said, whatever that meant.

Mr Shevchenko turned to the waitress who had appeared. 'Table for Mr Shevchenko. For two. A colleague will be here shortly, but not to eat, and only for a minute. I explained the situation.'

'Yes, of course. This way, please.' The waitress walked away in complete confidence that the customers would follow. Mr Shevchenko stood aside for Lillian, smiled, and said, 'Hear me out.'

Her heart told her to leave, but her brain moved her feet into the smart tinkling lightness of the Tate Britain restaurant. There were a lot of men in business suits and a few ladies in costly apparel, and Lillian knew how she appeared: trophy to a wealthy man. That wasn't the issue. Everything to do with her father and Mr Shevchenko, and finances, and international deals, all that mysterious working of money and services, seemed like a room with moving mirrors, that glittered and tempted, but in which it was hard to know what was plain surface, what hid or what revealed, where everything was reflected in everything else, but in which the actual thing, the hard core, was impossible to find.

'I only have an hour for my lunch break,' she said.

'Try the cold trout with potato salad and beetroot and horseradish dressing – it's really much better than it sounds. I'll have the smoked salmon quiche. That comes quickly. You're looking very well, Lillian.'

'What's this about?'

'Let's order. Are you happy with the trout?'

'Whatever.'

'And drink?'

'Water. With lemon.'

Lillian sat back, both flattered and appalled. This was the life she had once imagined: discussing business arrangements, surrounded by people who were paid to be polite to her. Mr. Shevchenko ordered: the waiter wrote, flew back from whence he came, was out of mind. Why did it have to be Mr. Shevchenko?

'So, let us cut to the chase.' Mr. Shevchenko stopped being charming. He was precise like Mr. Harris, but faster, and louder, and less reassuring. 'Your father has an accountancy job, all above board. He's a good figures man. His circumstances give me an opportunity. I can take his services while others dither – and I know him, and he knows the score with me. You know, I owe you.'

'What?'

'This is the big reveal.' Mr Shevchenko locked his fingers on the table. He looked to see if Lillian was paying attention. She was. 'When your father did some work for me and I checked him out, I was alarmed at the people for whom he had done business. He really thought the work was a standard tax-avoidance thing – legal, but sharp. It was in fact a clever laundering operation that your father had not spotted. Edward is an odd combination of zest, ambition and silliness – would you agree?'

Lillian nodded.

'Such people need guidance. Where I learned business the lines between legal and criminal were porous. Edward is in many ways an innocent man. This is a secret, and it's the truth: the people who tried to trick him may approach him again, and he still has a few difficulties. I employ him because he has skills, but also to protect him. Ah, the drinks. Thank you. Let me pour. It's hard to find true friends in this cut-throat world, but I like your father very much. I am to introduce him to grand opera. He needs rounding out. But let's talk about you.'

'I'm doing fine, really.'

'You will always do fine, Lillian. But I have a way for you to do better.'

'Mr Shevchenko-'

'Ivan.'

'Ivan, sir, thank you for helping my father, but I'm happy with where I'm at.'

'I'm delighted to hear it. Ha, look. Juliette.' Mr. Shevchenko rose to a lady in blue business suit with a smart black bag. She might be taken for an airhostess, except the bag was too well made and the slim broach was expensive. She shook Lillian's hand with a sharp tremble, as though to be thorough, though in haste, and did the cheek kissing with Mr Shevchenko.

'I'm rushed. Sorry.' She managed to smile while saying that. 'This is Lillian, then.'

'Indeed.'

'Perfect. Has Ivan said anything ....? No. It's very simple. We have several flats in the Southwerk area we use for visiting clients. It's preferable to using hotels, much more flexible, and a sound investment to boot. We want someone to manage them; to take the bookings, to ensure there's no mistakes, check the cleaners, order stock, occasionally to take clients from the airport and show them the local facilities. I believe you're planning on Paris next ...' she looked at her notes, 'end of February ... good.

We will need references, national insurance number, all the usual things, and we'll check your qualifications. I've got details of responsibilities and renumeration on this paper. I'm sure it's well within your range of capabilities, and you look just right.'

'Why me?'

'We'll come to that later,' said Mr Shevchenko.

'Could you meet me at the address on the letterhead in the next few days? You can phone to arrange it.'

'I need to speak to my father.'

'Are you sure you don't want anything, Juliette?' Mr. Shevchenko asked as the waiter appeared. 'I told you it was fast, Lillian.'

'Really, no, Ivan.' Juliette glanced at Mr Shevchenko who nodded once. 'Of course! I believe you know Frank Tengku-Watkins? He's given us some good advice in the past. I like Frank. We're in the same squash club. What do you think of his wife?'

'She's very beautiful.'

'She is. I find her a bit of a killjoy, to be honest. She's basically a chatelaine.'

'A what?'

'She doesn't work. I think she dabbles in buying and selling art.'

'You have a relation in the north who runs a gallery, don't you, Lillian?' Mr Shevchenko asked while working his phone.

'What? Oh, Ferdy. It's a shop. He frames pictures and sells photographs. I think he's giving it up though.'

'That's a shame. Ivan said you helped set it up.'

'A bit, yes. Did Daddy tell you?'

'This one, isn't it?'

Mr Shevchenko showed his phone. Lillian looked at the Cell. She could make out herself hanging in the widow.

'Oh.'

Mr Shevchenko was pleased with himself. 'I had a colleague make a trip. He was impressed with the décor. It was largely your work, I believe?'

'Well, yes, but why-?'

'To confirm your talent. I'm thorough, even with friends. How's the trout?'

'Fine. Good.'

'Ivan, I must dash. I have a meeting with the Oblovskys.'

'I hope their English has improved.'

'I may have to trust my Russian.'

'It will do.' As though to demonstrate the point the two of them spoke Russian for a minute. Lillian, mind whirring, concentrated on the trout. She smiled a goodbye as Juliette left and searched Mr. Shevchenko's face. He gave nothing away.

'It must be good to be to be with your father again, despite the small flat, and Penge.'

'Of course!'

'It's very easy to get used to wealth, but difficult to accept reduced circumstances. You know that from experience. Was the north claustrophobic?'

'I liked it, actually.'

'You're very adaptable. That's excellent. You have a great future, Lillian. You have *focus*.'

'You don't have to flatter me, Ivan.'

Mr Shevchenko sat back and chuckled. 'There's an example of your focus. They've ever so slightly overcooked my pastry, but the flavour is delicious.'

'I get the gist,' Lillian said. 'Tell me this. Did my father do very bad things?'

'No. Your father is not ruthless, Lillian.'

'Are you a bad man?' she suddenly asked.

Mr Shevchenko laughed. He did it without opening his mouth, through a smile. 'Lillian, there's no good and bad in business! This is a good country. A good country is one in which it's more in one's interests to keep the rules than to break them. That's why I prefer it to home.'

'I suppose that's true.'

'Morality is for our loved ones.'

'Daddy says a third of the world's money comes from crime.'

'I don't think the figure's that high,' Mr Shevchenko demurred. 'This is Tate Britain: the money came from Mr. Tate. From sugar. That meant slavery, and the most brutal slave plantations were in the sugar islands of the Bahamas and the Caribbean. We won't even get into the Sackler Wing, as was, at the Royal Academy. It doesn't do to enquire too closely at these things. I believe RBS were fined 500 million because of laundering money. No prosecutions. We're innocents, your father and I.'

'This job – is it full time?'

'It could be.'

'The thing is, I don't just want to leave the other ones.'

Mr Shevchenko thought about this. He finished his quiche and wiped his lips with the napkin.

'I would like you full time,' he said. 'But I'd rather have a little of you than none at all. The hours are flexible.'

'Well – I'm flattered. I'll admit that.'

They shook hands on parting. Mr Shevchenko hitched his coat around his shoulders before the revolving door in anticipation of the cold. 'I have a car coming,' he said. 'Can I give you a lift?'

'I'm working here till three.'

He had not quite finished. 'You know, I can name the day I understood what it meant to be successful. I took some proposals to very wealthy clients in Germany. I was met at the airport and driven to my hotel. We had a social meeting in the afternoon; very elegant. Then we were taken to the opera with dinner. The following morning I made my presentations. It went well. At the end we shook hands: my car arrived and I was driven back to the airport. It was all very smooth, very easy, but at Kiev I dragged my luggage to the exit and felt insulted because there was no-one there to meet me. That's how quickly we adjust to power. It fits us like a glove. One day perhaps I'll be able to hand such gloves over to you. You were born for them, my dear. You will take this job?'

'I'm still not sure why me.'

'It will bind my friend close,' he said. 'I would hate to make a rupture with him.' He was still smiling, but Lillian thought his voice was cold. That was something to think about. 'That's my driver,' he said. 'Brian. I'm very proud of Brian. Since working for me he's off the drugs and has brought his parenting skills to a whole new level.'

'Goodbye, Mr. Shevchenko. That was very illuminating.'

She inspected the letterhead and noted the name: Juliette Sherman. Lillian had not actually received a reply from Frank Tengu-Watkins, so she left him a voicemail before she returned to the comforting dullness of putting bags in lockers and hanging up coats.

It was all a rush. There was a locker confusion at the end until someone pointed out to Monique that she had the dock upside down so 39 was actually 93, which meant Lillian was late for the café, though only by a few minutes and in the general clamour of opening no-one noticed. It was busy in winter because people come in from the cold, but they stay longer so the counter work is no more hectic. But Lillian rather liked it hectic. It pumped you up, like the sprint at the end of a run. At six Marcus came in. That was considerate. He managed chat over the heads of the queue as she wrung the grounds into the machine, and asked what the massive was?

'I'm off for an hour in half an hour. Meeting Maria. Come.'

'Hey, we're going bowling. Guys together.'

'Don't come back drunk,' she warned.

He blew her a kiss at the door, flamboyant and happy, and slipped into the pools of lamplight. She smiled. He was shallow and silly and affectionate, but she knew he was a bridge, not a castle, and was settled in the thought that they would not survive her time in Paris. He was too impatient, for one thing, and she was too eager to keep moving. She was shocked at herself for spending nights with a man with whom she did not hope to spend the rest of her life, but she had never felt the need to experiment in that way so she could say she was making up for lost time, and she was unlikely ever to find the right one because all men were silly, particularly her father, and even Ferdinand, though he was silly in a different way; in his soul, like a poet.

The Round House was packed. It would be. But Maria and Lillian put on their faces, and two men offered them stools which they accepted with effusion. 'We made them feel really good,' said Maria.

'It's going to get manic as Christmas gets near.'

'Can you cope, Three Jobs?'

'At least I've got the Saltscar option.'

'A real drink?'

'Got to get back. It's tips night.'

She finished at the transition time, when the street life is gathered and crammed into its frenzied corners; the clubs, the pubs, the stations, the take-away vendors, and when solitary figures push by puddles instead of through people and can look threatening to a girl alone, just nineteen, with £22.50 of loose tips in her wallet. Raymond from Wrexham and Marta from Rio walked with her, and they complained happily about the crush of work, and Lillian felt she was really proving herself, she was fine, and then she dropped into the tube and was on her way, text-message answered, Daddy delayed until tomorrow, to the Barbican and thence to Therese House and Marcus's arms.

He bounced up and threw off the headphones and switched off the screen as soon as the door turned.

'Fancy a beer?'

'Not really.'

'Fancy me?'

'Not really.'

Marcus laughed. 'Long day, babe.'

'Very. Bowling?'

'Fun, but then Jerry and Fiona had a row. Embarrassing. It's weird you not there. Hey, you look tired. I guess you're too whacked to, like, do anything.'

'I guess you're too drunk.'

'Three beers, mate! Moderation!'

'Make me a toastie. I'm getting into my jams.'

She lay on his lap on the sofa but couldn't say when the programme finished or what she'd watched so she went without a word to do her teeth. Neither were too tired, and it was cosy, though she did feel he could have stayed awake a little longer afterwards, and in the quiet of the night she heard a couple of doors bang, and slow footsteps, and a shout, and the thought that had nagged her all day rose in her solitariness and took shape.

She was Lillian Three Jobs and proud of it, but a bit of free time and to go to bed without being exhausted would be nice.

Lillian admitted her world was askew when Mr Vassily threw the wrapping out of the car window. She was already annoyed that Marcus was still going to a gig with friends in Bristol when she couldn't. Daddy had dismissed her idea that one day he would find a job out of London where Mr Shevchenko could not find him. Also, there were road works, so she had to start early. To be late for a client was the unforgivable sin.

403

Mr Vassily looked at her with controlled surprise. She was used to that look because her business suit did not disguise her youth. He sat in the front of the car, only asking, 'You experienced driver?' and spoke on his phone in Russian. She assumed it was Russian. He was not happy when the tailback started.

'This is shit,' he said as though it were her fault.

'Road works,' she explained.

'How long to apartment?'

'An hour perhaps.'

He took this in silence. Then he took the envelope with the brochure enclosed, opened it, lay the pages on his lap, tore the envelope, opened the window, tossed out the paper without looking, closed the window, and read. It was so gratuitous, so soaked in contempt, that Lillian literally swallowed. This was her country. She knew and obeyed the codes of the roads, and her fellow residents and honourable visitors knew and obeyed them as well. What upset her most was that she lacked the courage to speak out, and when at the flat Mr Vassily said, 'Thank you,' in a tone that meant, 'You are dismissed,' she remained mute. She had to admit it: these successful people were not as nice as everyone else.

She was checking the empty properties – a sliding door tended to stick in 53 – when, distracted, she answered a number unknown with her usual, 'Hello, Lillian Delph,' and the number unknown answered, 'Ey up, Lillian, lass. Tha'll never know wheer I am.'

'Frank!'

'London. 'Ow about that?'

'London! Where?'

'Station. We 'ave to meet.'

She was seriously temped to invite Marcus and some of his friends, and Maria with some of hers, to join them for lunch in Borough Market. It would do them good. They would learn much about her from meeting Frank. She avoided the temptation, however, because after the first shock there would be nothing to say, and awkwardness would dominate, and Frank was not here for anyone but her. It was cold: her coat was suitable, but the trousers of her business suit were not. She was about to suggest they meet inside somewhere when she heard her name called, and there he was.

'Lillian, love!' he shouted. 'By 'ell, this city fair puts the wind in yer sails.'

'Frank. What are you doing here?'

'Meeting thee. It's cost me a week's earnings to make this trip. How much is that in hedge-fund manager's terms?'

'I don't know. Three million?'

'Sounds about right.'

'But – why didn't you warn me? I might have been out of town.'

'Took the risk. Didn't give you chance to run away. I wanted to show the urgency of the case. Parky, innit?'

'You mean cold? Yes. Let's find a warm café. Follow me.'

Frank jinked with his camera among the stalls. 'You see, what Ferdy doesn't get is that it's the city where the real stories are. Subterfuge. Mistaken identity. It's a writhing mass of humanity and it's the writhing I like.' He jigged his camera at an odd angle. 'It were a big day when I realised you can tilt the lens. Get the jumble of the streets. One day I'll have a week in this city. Tha's a bit ovverdressed for a market stall, lass.'

'It's my business clothes.'

'Yep. It would be summat like that.' He was not impressed, but that was Frank.

'How is Ferdy? Really?'

'Bad. This place looks alright.'

'It's not, but there's room and it doesn't matter.'

Frank needed two places; one for himself and the other for his pack and coat and cameras. He flexed his arms and sat back, as though settling for the afternoon. 'As I've spent three million quid getting here, I'll leave thee to get the coffees. Mine's a cappuccino.'

'You're very chirpy,' she said when she returned.

'I want yer to come back, lass.'

'Oh, Frank.'

'It's all gone to pot since you left. Ferdy lost heart. The shop has loads of visitors but nobody buys owt. Ferdy's on the point of renting it, like Dave said, which is a bugger for me. Dave and Anne-Marie are far away. It leaves me on a bit of a limb. Ferdy says nowt, but he feels it 'ard. I don't blame Anne-Marie, but she don't have the attachment to the place so it's easy for her to say, 'Give it up.' Jen is sorry fer Ferdy, but she don't know what to do, as we all have to face it, he's not the kind to run a business, 'owever small.'

'But you could help.'

'I try, but I don't have the *feel* for it somehow. And to be honest, Ferdy doesn't see me as a partner.'

'Oh, dear.' This was glum news. 'He always sounded fine when we spoke.'

'Lying for thee, lass.'

'Why would he – oh.' It was a sacrifice for her sake. What did she do to inspire this?

'Lillian, love, tha's done thi' duty. Follow your 'eart.'

'Frank – I have a boyfriend.'

'Oh, aye.'

'And a job now. One of daddy's connections came good. And then there's Paris. I've set my heart on Paris.'

'You know, Saltscar is magnificent in winter.'

'I'm sure but –' Lillian was triggered. She was in the V&A with Aunt Jenny. Aunt Jenny had her hands on her shoulders, and Lillian heard once again as though it were in the room the complaint of a gull, but this time there was snow on Moor Cliff. She heard the sea, an angry whisper, and saw at the end of the bay the old steel works against the sun, dying because she was not there.

'Oh, Frank. It's just not practical. I've got a job, and Marcus, and there's still my father to think of, and my heart's set on Paris.'

'Paris won't go away.'

'And what would I do there? I mean, now the shop's gone.'

'It 'asn't gone, it's on it's way. I 'ave a plan. We remortgage the building and pay Anne-Maire out! Small risk. Smaller if you're there to run it. And you get a share of the building an' all.' He nodded once in chiselled surety of the infallibility of this plan.

It wasn't fair of Frank to make it sound so easy, for now her reasons for staying in London would seem more selfish than they were, and if Ferdinand knew of this meeting he would be twice rejected. She was doing well. It was amazing how well she and her father were doing, and while she would always be grateful to the Goodman's for saving her to fight again, she was now in the fight, and she was winning.

'I'm sorry, Frank. I'd love to come for a weekend, but people here rely on me as well.'

'Oh, aye?'

'I love Ferdy, really I do. But the trajectories of our lives no longer coincide.'

Frank rolled his eyes in admiration or contempt of the phrasing – it was impossible to say which – then rubbed his chin. 'Trajectories, eh? It's all about trajectories. I've got nowt against trajectories *as such*. Sometimes though, they can be a bit of a bully, like. Your mind's made up, lass, innit?'

'It is, rather.'

'Aye, well, I did me best.' Frank gathered his things. He stood and shouldered his bags as though for an heroic trip into the cold. His face was set and his collar was up.

'So where are you going now?' Lillian asked.

'Station.'

'But you've only just got here!'

'I didn't want to compromise the urgency of my message,' he answered.

'Oh, Frank.' She opened her arms for the goodbye hug. Frank accepted the hug but did not return it. 'At least, let he drive you to the station,' she said. 'There must be other things you can tell me about. Aunt Jenny, and your pictures, and my mother.'

'You 'ave a car? You *are* doing well.'

'Not really. It's a company car.'

'A company car!' Frank's astonishment bounced off the walls. There was a barely perceptible turn of shoulders among the clientele against the exclamation. 'You've got a job with a car thrown in? Impressive, lass. We can't offer that. We can give you love, and Anne-Marie's bedroom, but we can't compete with a company car.' Frank's voice seemed to have lost a lot of Yorkshire. He swung his camera strap over his shoulder. 'So what job, may I ask -?'

'It's not such a big deal, Frank. I collect people from airports. It's from one of my father's associates, a favour, and it won't last long.'

'Your dad's associates? I see. Perhaps I'll not take a lift in one o' them cars.' He made his voice gentle. 'Goodbye, lass. Have a good life.'

'Frank - it's not cool to use emotional blackmail.'

'No blackmail, Lillian. I'm promoting a business, that's all.' He turned from her, and it was clear there was no point calling him back.

Lillian could not at first believe how immature Frank was being. Then she could not credit that Marcus had sent Instagram pictures of himself and his mates in Bristol in which regret for her absence did not figure. They had beer already. Suddenly she resented the fact that she was working from three until seven so by the time she got back and changed it was past the cocktail hour and Maria and crew would be already at the pub. She was always tagging on and catching up and leaving early. She did not greet the visitors at Tate Britain with her usual smile. They paid her peanuts and black wasn't her colour, so she no longer wore the uniform with pride. She could get rid of that job, and she would. She made enough dealing with the flats, if only the people weren't so awful.

She got in touch with Edward during loo break. He was very pleased because he'd done a major shop and had cleared away the kitchen so that was that for a week at least. When Lillian suggested they both have a night in, however, he had to disappoint her.

'I'm meeting Sir Henry tonight. His idea. I think he has something for me workwise. I can't turn him down, Randa.'

'Sir Henry who?'

'Sir Henry Broughton. Very good man.'

That made her think. 'Isn't he the man –?' she started.

'What?'

'It doesn't matter.'

She stood in the after-work dark staring over the Thames at the lights of MI5 and, downriver, the glitter of the South Bank and the London Eye. It was a short walk, in Lillian terms, to her old South Kensington, a brisk circuit of the familiar haunts with that sense of solidity and unending comfort that the west-end offers to the lucky ones. She wondered for the first time if that old life was gone forever and understood the advice she had eventually winkled out of Frank Tengu-Watson.

'As far as we know, Lillian, Shevchenko is legit. But you don't want to be dependent on him. I can't say he'll never ask you to do something you'll later regret.'

It was the other Frank she thought of, however, on the tube. In that limbo between stations, each passengers' thoughts buried deep within the brain, the rumble of the wheels the only voice, a place where you can feel so alone, so private, among a crowd, she saw his disappearing back after a gentle goodbye. He had left her for ever! No. She had two identities, and she had been through too much to let one walk away. Frank, of all people, Frank had rejected her! How ridiculous was that?

If the Goodman's gave her up as a bad lot, the Ellesker's would too. That was certain.

Sir Henry Broughton, Mr. Shevchenko, The Trophy. A grim list. She didn't have much to pack when she got in, but she did it anyway because she needed to leave very early and to arrive unannounced for only thus could she demonstrate the urgency of the case. She texted Maria. And, yes, Chloe got a message as well. And Daddy? She ought to explain it to her father. Mr. Shevchenko would not be pleased, and he had the power to hurt. But Daddy had chosen Sir Henry Broughton, evil Sir Henry, over her, as well as The Trophy and Ivan Shevchenko, and, as her mother would say, you can only look forward and if you make that bed you must lie in it. That didn't make the bed any softer.

It was fine, it was not bad up the A1, the AI(M), the A19 and the A174, fast, and easy and hardly any commercial traffic; and then, coming towards the chemical works, she drove into white.

She had relented on the M1 near Nottingham and sent him a text to say she was on her way, then did the same to Aunt Jenny at Wetherby services because he had not replied. Aunt Jenny telephoned back: she protested she should have let them know; she had no room ready for her. 'But you will drive carefully, won't you? This terrible weather!' Lillian laughed. The weather wasn't so bad. But then she hit the sea-mist.

She stepped out of the car into a Saltscar that was hugging itself under sheets, silent and still. In Aunt Jenny's hug there was need as well as affection. 'Whatever's the matter?' Lillian asked.

'He went for a walk,' she said. 'He's on the cliffs.'

Frank stood at the top of the stairs. He looked at her with scrutiny. She met his eyes, and he nodded, once.

'I shouldn't worry,' Aunt Jenny said. 'He's an experienced walker. But why doesn't he answer the phone? Of course, reception is not always good up here – is it Frank? Lillian, why, I'm so glad to see you. What a surprise!'

'By 'ellers like, now who'd a thort it?' said Frank who came down the stairs.

Jesus barked and did a violent circuit of the sitting room, and Mary and Joseph stuck to her side until she gave them due acknowledgement. Lillian sat on the sofa and was licked.

'Thank you, Jesus, that's enough.' She shoved him off. He scampered in his excitement to his water bowl.

'We expected Ferdinand back already,' Aunt Jenny said. 'This weather. Cliffs. You know what he's like.'

'It's annoying. I came up to see him and I'll have to go soon. I have to return the car for work tomorrow.' Aunt Jenny could not understand this. 'I've been to see an old school-friend in Durham,' Lillian lied. 'I'm on my way down.'

'I must say, I'm rather concerned about Ferdinand. It's misty and it gets dark so soon, and this weather – of course, he's been up there so many times, recently, he knows it like the back of his hand, and I'm sure he knows what he's doing, but he doesn't answer his phone, and it is the cliffs. What do you think, Frank?'

'Give it half an hour and then send Lillian after 'im.'

'Are you serious? Of course not. You are, aren't you?'

'Why on earth did he go out on a day like this?' Lillian exclaimed.

'Because he's a stubborn old bugger,' Frank said.

'Excuse me?'

Aunt Jenny took it up. 'He says he has to contemplate leaving Saltscar. He's exploring every bit of it. You know how his mind works. He's got the glooms again. I'm sure they'll pass. They will. He really mustn't miss you, though, Lillian. He mustn't miss Lillian, Frank, must he?'

Lillian was not at ease. 'Perhaps I should go look?'

'Oh, Lillian, you're not dressed. Have you seen that we're trying to keep the house orderly, as you like it? What have you seen at the V&A? I'd so love to meet you there again.'

'I've really been too busy, Aunt Jenny.'

'Ring Emily,' Frank butted in. 'She'll 'ave the foul weather wrappin's.'

'My mother's here?'

'She's at Dorothy's,' Aunt Jenny confirmed. 'She spends quite a bit of winter here as the centre's closed. Frank, I think that might be wise. She's so practical like that – and with Lillian here...'

413

'I'll do it,' said Lillian.

Her mother did not express surprise to learn Lillian was in Saltscar. Perhaps she was never surprised. She was not even surprised that Ferdinand had gone on the cliffs in winter with a mist coming on without a phone in an unsettled state of mind and a record of impractical wandering, but she was not at ease with the idea either.

'Is his van in the street?' she asked.

Lillian passed the question to Aunt Jenny, who affirmed it.

'Check the phone isn't in the van.'

Lillian passed on the message to Frank. Frank stepped out. He gave the thumbs up to the women at the window.

'That's good news,' said Aunt Jenny. 'It means he isn't answering because he hasn't got it. It is rather irresponsible, but it's difficult to tell him.'

'Should we get in touch with the police?' Lillian asked.

'Oh, dear.' Aunt Jenny could no longer keep the grief from her face. Lillian's phone sounded again. 'Make your way to The Smugglers,' her mother said. 'I'll meet you there. What are your shoes like?'

'Sort of expensive.'

'I'm not asking for the bloody price, Lillian. I want to know if you can walk up Cat's Knoll on a wet day.'

'Yes, I think so, but if there's an alternative -'

'Get down there, I'll bring stuff.'

'Perhaps we should call the helicopter out?' Aunt Jenny asked. 'Declare an Incident.' She looked close to tears again, but pulled herself together. 'But it's terribly expensive, and we don't want to be silly like some people, do we?'

414

'We pay us taxes,' said Frank.

Lillian passed on the message. Emily said no. 'They can't come out if there's mist. We have to go.'

'The dogs?'

'The only one with the sense to look for him is Mary and she's too old.'

Aunt Jenny was now alarmed. She looked to Frank and to Lillian with an open-mouth, empty of sentences, an unusual case, and Frank said, 'Steady on, Jen. It's only a precaution. He's probably snug in a pub in Skinningrove.' Lillian remembered a phrase that months ago had proved useful to her.

'Hold it together, Auntie. You're no use to us if you break up.'

She trotted through the near-deserted streets; three kids moped outside the supermarket from which an elderly couple emerged, squabbling faintly. Saltscar hidden from the world, bleached and lonely. She was cross with Ferdinand, but then she saw Moor Cliff from the top of the bank, an unresponsive lump that felt nothing of the sea's lash or the mist's lick, and which crumbled in its own slow time without care for itself or the life that lived on it, and she realised a world without Ferdy was much diminished.

A white van gurgled to a stop in the little car park by The Smugglers as she approached, and her mother got out almost simultaneously with the stop of the engine. She made no greeting but flung over the van doors.

'Put these on,' she commanded her daughter.

Lillian sat above the rear bumper and wrestled leggings over her pants. Then she wrapped herself into the coat that was too big, but never mind, and then laced up the boots. She stood and stamped.

'Well?'

'A bit big, but they'll do.'

'Good to see you,' her mother told her.

'Thank you.'

'Bloody Ferdinand! I don't have spare gloves. We'll share mine if we have to. Don't under-estimate the cold.' Emily hitched up the straps of her pack. 'Have you peed?' she asked.

'No, actually.'

'I don't suppose you'll find anyone to embarrass you, though it might be a bit cool on the bum. Let's go.'

The occasion and the cold robbed Cats Knoll and The Dragon's Back and the Neck of the Dragon, of all resonance. It was not where she had seen a deer. It was not where Emily had scrambled someone out of Lillian's way. It was an obstacle to their purpose. The gorse was empty of yellow spots. The trees took shape as they approached with skinny bare branches like the arms of arthritic old men, black against the mist, looming from it like spectres. They called, and their voices were soaked in the damp.

'How are those boots?' Emily asked.

'The boots are fine.'

'You don't need to turn round when you speak.'

They called at the circular metal statue, the bracelet, Lillian had considered too quaint, but which now appeared old and spiked and cruel. They listened. The sea foamed in formless whispers below.

'What the hell is he doing?' Emily muttered.

'Are you worried?'

'Yes, but I'm mainly annoyed. He may have got to Skinningrove and be on a bus back.'

'Frank said he was unhappy.'

'Of course he's unhappy. He's lost you and his friend and his sister. He's a man of few and deep attachments. Jenny, of course, is hopeless. She could never face the darkness.'

Lillian felt the cold clutch at her with a needy hand on her arm. 'Oh my god – you don't think he's going to jump?'

'Don't be ridiculous. I think he's careless. Let's get on. The next depression is slippery. Shall I go in front?'

'I'll be fine.'

Lillian took the drop deftly to show she had no fear, though when she climbed out onto the level she was unnerved to see how close to the edge the flimsy fence actually was. She called out and listened. Her mother's voice was close to her ear.

'You have good balance. Would you like to learn rock-climbing?'

'I'd love it.'

'We have a practice wall at the outdoor centre. The next bit's straightforward. Hurry.'

They squelched onwards with purpose. The path broadened and Lillian made fists in her pockets. They called. Then they called together. The path led comfortingly away from the edge, and it seemed to both the mist was lightening, a little at least, and as they stepped past the track that Lillian had taken with Frank the day of the deer

Emily called Ferdinand's name, and they received a reply. It was not a comforting reply. It was a noise; not quite the noise of a stricken animal, but not the voice of a cheerful one either. It was a sea-noise, like a faint horn of a ship, or a whale cry, or wind rasping a funnel. But it was certainly Ferdinand's noise.

He was propped against a fence pole. He waved his arms and nodded his recognition. Lillian tried to give him a hug, but he was slippery, unsteady, and in pain. He held up his left foot.

'Herr Tunkle,' he said.

'Sorry?'

'Pain dangle.'

'Ferdy! What on earth are you doing? What have you done?'

Emily was at work. She already had the flask from the haversack, and the cup filled in seconds and thrust it into his face. 'Drink,' she said. 'Come on!' She held the cup. He gulped. 'More.' He gulped and gasped, and panted. 'Breathe deeply. Deeply, Ferdy. There's some fudge in the bag, Lillian. Get it.'

'Herr Tangle.'

'You've sprained it, you idiot. Drink. Thanks, Lillian. Chew on this. It's Yorkshire fudge. Best quality. Eat. It'll save your life. That's it. Right – Lillian: we need to get him moving. Your hands are raw. Take this glove for your right hand. No, just take it. Get his arm round your shoulder, we're going to hoist him. Good. Ferdy, drink this, warm water. Think of your mother, and Lillian here, and all who love you. Now - more fudge.' Ferdinand chewed, nodding his head, swallowed heavily and glared up at them. 'Are you ready, Lillian?' Emily asked. 'Ferdy, we're taking your shoulders and we're going to get moving, so help us. Can you put any weight on that foot at all? Do your best. The pain won't kill you. Here we go – hup! Fine. Steady. Lillian, are you managing your side?'

'Yes, mum.'

'Hold him. I've got to phone.' Five rings seemed an age. 'Dorothy, thank god. We've found him on the cliff. He has a touch of hypothermia. We're on top of it, but call out the helicopter anyway. Visibility's poor, but it's clearing. Apologise, but tell them he has a sprained ankle and he won't manage the descent. You can tell Jenny were on our way back. Just tell her that, don't – well, you know how to handle Jenny. Make sure the pilot has my number so they can triangulate us. Right, Lillian, off we go.'

They did not make an elegant group, but they hobbled, and swayed, and juddered forwards, always forwards, and when Ferdinand cried out in pain, Emily simply said, 'That's good. It'll keep you awake.' Lilian's mother was a fearsome thing. By the time they came to the slippery depression he was articulate, and calm and terribly sorry. He waved his arm at Lillian, like a mute with something urgent to say. Lillian took his hand, then wasn't sure what to say, so she kissed it, which made her feel silly, but she believed his eyes were moist, though that may simply have been the mist. Emily poured him more hot water, and made Lillian take the rest and he swallowed down most of the fudge and he gave a great sigh. He rested against a fence pole to the field while Emily wedged a dry towel under his shirt, and then she got him to beat his arms, while they beat their own arms, and swayed in an ungainly dance, so when the pilot in the helicopter crossed the line of the cliff from the sea and looked down there was no doubt he had found his clients. Lillian thought it rather exciting and scary as pilot and medic scurried towards them with a stretcher.

'We'll sort him,' the medic said cheerfully. 'Standard procedure.'

Lillian kissed him on the forehead when he was safely trussed.

'Sorry, cousin,' he said.

'You're such an idiot, Ferdy,' she said. She was beginning to sound like her mother already.

They watched him lofted over North Yorkshire, a spectacular sight, then Emily sent a text to Jenny and turned off her phone because Jenny was sure to pester and it was better that she pestered Dorothy, who quite liked the drama. She turned to her daughter.

'You did well,' she said.

Lillian sniffed loudly. She wiped her face and nose with an arm. It was all very emotional, so she hugged her mother who did not resist. Lillian cried. It started as suppressed sobs, then gulps and gasps, and a wet eye, and broke into heaving wails and torrents of tears. She did not know why she was crying exactly. She pushed her forehead hard into her mother's shoulder. Rocks long lodged in her chest crumbled, succumbed to rivers that gushed and sprayed through throat and nose and eyes, that geysered in bumbling groans and fat, wet, blubbering sobs. It had to do with her betrayal; with her silly forsaken father, the mother found, the cousin recovered. She cried at the knowledge that it was not enough to be loved, but to be loved in decency; she cried in relief, for her bumbling and visionary cousin, removed once and never, and in gratitude to those who had given her a haven, for the end of childish things. Her mother gave her a tissue and Lillian wiped her blue nose with fumbling fingers.

'We need to get moving,' Emily said. 'It wouldn't be an amusing irony for us to succumb.'

They jogged down Dragon's Back and Cat's Knoll and tore off their wet clothes to dump in the boot of the car and slumped onto the seats. Lillian dropped her forehead on the dashboard, one tissue to her eyes, one to her nose, and exuded a moist catharsis onto her scarf. Emily draped her hands over the wheel and stared out. Lillian's breathing became regular. 'Will he be all right?' she asked.

'He was a long way away from renal failure. I'm not worried. But we probably saved his life.'

'Why did he do that?'

'He's become careless of himself. It's the first rule of walking: don't go alone if there's the slightest danger. But you can't help loving him, can you?'

The sense of safety enveloped them. Emily was looking at the sea, the winter sea for which Lillian was giving up London and Paris. Lillian remained slumped. After a minute, Emily asked, 'Isn't that your friend, Chardonnay, and her husband?'

Lillian raised her head as from the executioner's block, blinking at the world reprieved. She looked across the carpark to where the sea sprawled in dirty foam that slithered over its wrinkled surface, never quite breaking. The mist had turned to light snow. Collapsed clouds murked the horizon so she could not tell where sea ended and sky began, but it was somewhere out where the long grey finger of the pier was pointing. Yes, there was

Chardonnay and Gavin, hugging her child and battling the wind for the sake of a drink and good company.

'With their little girl. They're going to the pub,' she said. 'She's a good person, actually.'

'There's not many young people here.' Emily left the comment hanging, then turned her head to her daughter. Lillian turned her head too. 'Will you cope?'

'There's enough. I've seen them. I'll be at college in less than a year. Marcus won't be too upset. If he cares, he can take his finger out and come up here.'

Emily nodded thoughtfully. 'What about the car?'

'I take it in the morning and get a train back the next day.'

'Don't make a hasty decision. But I do rather think you'll be happier here.'

'I think so too. I'll save that shop. Ferdy will stay here. He loves it.'

'And he doesn't like anywhere else. His loss.'

They sat in mutual silence at the immensity of what had happened. They did not smile, or kiss, or hug, or even talk, but simply sat and looked at the dirty white walls of The Smuggler's Arms. Then Emily said, 'If this turns to snow, we'll never get up the bank. Let's go. I'll take you home.' She turned on the ignition: the engine buzzed, a normal sound, and she drove up Saltscar Bank.

Milton Keynes UK
Ingram Content Group UK Ltd.
UKHW010610031023
429846UK00004B/98

9 781915 164490